THE
SPANISH
DIPLOMAT'S
SECRET

ALSO BY NEV MARCH

Peril at the Exposition
Murder in Old Bombay

THE
SPANISH
DIPLOMAT'S
SECRET

NEV MARCH

MINOTAUR BOOKS
NEW YORK

First published in the United States by Minotaur Books, an imprint of St. Martin's Publishing Group

www.minotaurbooks.com

Library of Congress Cataloging-in-Publication Data

Names: March, Nev, 1967– author.
Title: The Spanish diplomat's secret / Nev March.
Description: First edition. | New York : Minotaur Books, 2023. |
    Series: Captain Jim and Lady Diana mysteries ; 3 |
Identifiers: LCCN 2023019656 | ISBN 9781250855060 (hardcover) |
    ISBN 9781250855077 (ebook)
Subjects: LCGFT: Detective and mystery fiction. | Novels.
Classification: LCC PS3613.A7328 S63 2023 | DDC 813/.6—
    dc23/eng/20230428
LC record available at https://lccn.loc.gov/2023019656

Our books may be purchased in bulk for promotional, educational, or business use. Please contact your local bookseller or the Macmillan Corporate and Premium Sales Department at 1-800-221-7945, extension 5442, or by email at MacmillanSpecialMarkets@macmillan.com.

First Edition: 2023

1   3   5   7   9   10   8   6   4   2

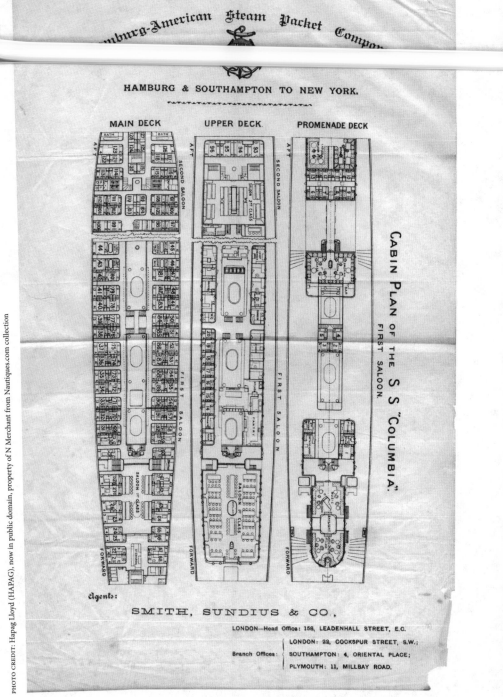

Passenger deck plan for SS *Columbia* (1880–1907), similar to the HMS *Etruria* that features in *The Spanish Diplomat's Secret*. A cargo and passenger steamship, the *Columbia* was the first ship to carry a dynamo to power electric lights instead of oil lamps.

CHAPTER 1

ODDBALLS AND TOFFS

SUMMER 1894
DAY ONE: EVENING

I doubled over the ship's railing and clung for dear life, my head even with my spattered trousers, tossing up the last of a fine meal. The wind whipped around, snatching at my clothes. Around me was wet darkness, the splash and hiss of foam. Waves smashed the hull and sent up a spray that hit my face. More seasoned travelers were enjoying their meals amidships, but I'd known I'd never reach the leeward side and taken my chances at the nearest rail.

The caviar I'd consumed only an hour ago tasted sour coming back up. The HMS *Etruria* rolled until I was suspended high above, like a fly clinging to the top of a Ferris wheel. At the crest it began to dip, nearly upending me. Our hull dropped back into the ocean with a boom. I heaved, but my insides had nothing left to give. Waves roiled, too damn close, as the steamer sliced through vast swells.

Fighting the pull of gravity, I latched on and gasped for breath. Head throbbing, I turned, but the deck chairs seemed far away. Bollocks. My clothes sopping with seawater and puke, I took a step, lurched and clung to the rail, limbs shaking.

"Puis-je vous aider?" asked a deep voice at my shoulder. May I help you?

A white-haired man caught my arm, his head even with my shoulder. I jerked—buffeted on all sides, I'd not noticed his approach. I felt oddly distant, as though gazing at myself from afar and tut-tutting my poor showing.

"I'm all right," I choked. He'd spoken French, yet I could not reply in the same tongue. My French was poor on a good day; at present it was nonexistent.

"Vous êtes un soldat," said the man, getting his arm around me. *Soldat*—soldier. The wind snatched away the rest of his words, but his intent was clear: to ferry me to a deck chair. I took a breath, found myself empty for now, and eased away from the railing on legs of India rubber.

I cursed, as my feet slid—the damned deck seemed soapy, and I'd swapped army boots for leather this evening. Only the older man's steadying grip kept me from slamming onto the boards. He took my weight with a grunt and staggered. Gasping an apology, I made for the safety of the chair.

Once I dropped into it, I panted in relief and gazed around the empty deck. Small electric lanterns glowed every few yards. A jaunty waltz drifted from the music room at the bow. Diana would be twirling around the ballroom . . . I gave thanks that she had not seen me quivering at the railing. Who was she dancing with? The injustice of it pricked me—why was I plagued with this blasted seasickness while other blokes could waltz away the hours?

It scarcely mattered though. Since I didn't know how, I should not mind her dancing with other fellows. And yet . . .

On Diana's birthday two years ago in Bombay, I'd watched her float across the floor, her smile spilling joy into the company, her delighted chuckle rising like bubbles in champagne. I watched from afar because I was on duty, hired by her brother. Afterward though, she'd insisted on a dance with me. A mixed-race man wasn't usually invited to society dos, so I'd never learned to dance. In a dither over how to proceed, I'd

worn feet. I carried

her around the ball now, recalling the thrill of it, my chest compressed with amazement.

The acrid smell of a cigar drew my attention back to my companion.

"Thank you," I said to the gentleman smoking quietly beside me, noting his finely cut coat and the red ribbon on his lapel.

"English," said the man, his tone desultory.

Flicking his cigar ash toward the railing, he said in an unfamiliar sing-song accent, "Stay away from there. It is easy to go over, in thees weather."

We sat in the dim light for a while. Warmed by gratitude, I reached out a hand and said, "James O'Trey. You're right. I was a soldier."

He took my hand with a mild grip, his own bony and papery dry. After a moment, he said, "Me also. Strange to meet here, is it not?"

What was curious was that he hadn't offered his name. Old enough to be my grandfather, he pulled on the cigar, then held it absently over the arm of the chair as he gazed outward without expression.

"Do they return . . . here?" He tapped his forehead with two fingers, the cigar glowing between them. He had a white goatee, but his dark eyes were intent.

Perhaps the dusk fostered confidences, for I would not have answered so in daylight. "The lads I lost? I see them often," I said and drew in the salt air.

The faint waltz gave way to a brisk polka that separated the pair of us from the distant frolic with a chasm as wide as the ocean. Unmoving, my companion squinted into the night. His rigid posture tugged at me, demanding solidarity, even compassion.

I continued, "And the . . . others. I see them too."

He turned his face an inch and stiffened, his shoulders tight. Ahead, the polka continued in painful counterpoint while surf splashed over the rail, misting our faces.

Ramrod straight, the old soldier stood and said in a low voice, "I did my *duty*. It *was* my duty." He gave a sharp nod and walked deftly up the stairway to the promenade deck.

I settled back, puzzling over my unknown companion's parting words. Ignoring the waves smashing at our hull, I contemplated his tone. It held a strange note—stiff pride, and something else I could not name. He'd behaved as though responding to an argument, yet I had given none. What had I missed?

Sometime later Diana approached, peering this way and that as she stepped through patches of light. She spotted me and hurried over in a rustle of silk skirts.

"All right, Jim? You weren't at the table. Thought you might take the air." She glanced at my trousers and made a moue with her mouth as she sat in my companion's chair. "Oh dear. You've had a rough time of it."

We'd been married two years ago, aboard the steamer from Bombay, then emigrated to the United States to make a home in Boston. It still astonished me when I looked at her, so poised and elegant, her arms encased in satin gloves. Her copious curls were piled in a do that looked far too heavy for that delicate neck. Being married was vastly different from anything I'd expected. I glanced at Diana's absorbed face. What was she thinking? I'd believed I knew her every mood, but the open, carefree girl had turned into a brisk young woman whose feelings I could not always read. Recently I'd detected moments of melancholy that unnerved me.

I said, "I had company. Old military chap."

"American? Or English."

"Foreign cove. European, I think."

"Oh." She worried her bottom lip. "Goodness. Not the Spanish grandee!"

"Hmm?"

"You remember, that peculiar . . . occurrence. On the gangway."

I dislike crowds and had kept on alert for pickpockets as we prepared to board. I frowned, trying to recall it. "The woman in the wheelchair who blocked the gangplank—was the Spanish gent upset?"

"Oh, he'd already gone forward. You were speaking with the porter at the time. The Spanish group went up, all dressed in black, the women attendant would̶n̶ ̶.̶.̶.

I said, "I remember that. People tried to push past."

"Yes. The wheelchair must have been stuck. The attendant did nothing. A crewman came to help, but she didn't move. Like she'd gone to sleep on her feet. Bit of an oddball, hmm?"

Oddballs and toffs, I thought, shrugging. The usual companions on a steamship.

Diana's forehead creased in thought. "Jim, I remember it because of that attendant's odd expression. She kept staring up at the deck, like someone in a trance."

"A reluctant traveler? No one came to see them off either."

Most of the transatlantic passengers had been making their animated goodbyes. Friends encircled the well-heeled toffs, offering last-minute gifts and messages. There's something neat and slender about the cut of a well-tailored coat, I'd thought. Though altered to my height, my sack suit hung thickly on me. Diana had bought me other new clothes, insisting I'd need to dress for dinner on the liner. It had been a festive morning, feathers ruffled in the breeze, ladies leaned forward to embrace, gents shaking hands, clutching their hats. Fathers and sons, mothers, sisters and cousins. We had none of these—I'd never known a family and all of Diana's relatives lived in India. Our friends the Abernathys had decided to summer in Scotland and our neighbors the Lins could not leave their bakery to wave goodbye.

Diana said, "That Spanish attendant. Perhaps she dislikes the sea."

I couldn't fault the woman for that. All I wished for that day was a quiet voyage, smooth seas and long sunny days on deck. But there was that other thing, the reason we were going, which I'd taken pains to keep from Diana.

My chair shifted as the deck switched its tilt. My stomach lurched. Eight days, I thought. Could I stand it for eight days?

CHAPTER 2

STRANGE BEDFELLOWS

DAY TWO

The next morning, sliding our trunks back under the beds to make more room, I hoisted a decanter from the set sparkling on a dumbwaiter. Oh, my. Venetian glass? Lifting out the stopper I sniffed the bottle—whiskey, and quite old, with a deep aroma. It likely cost a month's wages.

Our stateroom was a double bed affair done up in cobalt blue and creamy white. In front of a screened dressing area, damask settees curved around a bolted-down table, fitted with a carved railing to protect the crystal. A porthole above a roll-top writing desk overlooked the ocean. But for this, we might have been in the Waldorf, a new New York hotel where Diana's society friends the Abernathys had hosted us last year.

Diana floated in from the washroom, saying, "Thank goodness we have flushing water closets. I'd worried that this was an older ship, but she's just like the *Umbria*."

She wore a new dress this morning, the front patterned in pale green and white, the back made of pink velvet. When I raised eyebrows in admiration, she dimpled. I brushed out my sack suit with a rueful

I'd cleaned my dress old army boots.

It was a fine sunny day as we toured the ship, the rumble of engines vibrating under my feet. Massive twin chimneys towered above us. I noted three masts, fore, main and aft fully rigged. Would we see the sails splayed against the mighty Atlantic breezes this voyage? Fitted with five decks, the promenade and upper decks open to the sky, Her Majesty's Ship *Etruria* was a floating fortress. Brass gleaming, her paint fresh, all five hundred feet of her hummed with anticipation. On the promenade deck, the wind puffed at our faces and snatched at Diana's skirts.

Pointing, she said, "Smoking room—gents only, 'course." She nodded at a thick oak door. "That's probably the ladies' winter garden."

She'd know her way around in no time. Seeing her smile, my spirits lifted. Perhaps it wasn't too late. It would be all right.

A pair of heavyset older men passed us, their wives in great, plumed hats speaking closely as they followed. Fur stoles in this weather? Diana caught my glance and crinkled her eyes in amusement. Heartened that this, at least, had not been lost, our silent language, the way she could guess what I was thinking, I heaved a grateful breath. It was dashed odd, this distance that sometimes came between us.

Something had felt bewildering when I got back from my last assignment. I'd returned to Diana's usual welcome, her relief to see me intact. She'd smiled and said all the right things, but the shadows around her eyes told me she'd not had an easy time of it. Only when I shed my tramping guise and thoroughly cleaned up did she bend. She'd discarded my filthy clothing with the stern look of a quartermaster examining a broken rifle. But that was all right. So why did I hear her stifled crying that night? She'd insisted it was nothing, but I knew there was more. Why had she been so unhappy?

A beanpole of a bloke walked past, his checkered coat bulging. I frowned. What gave his pocket that shape? A book, or . . . a weapon?

"Don't, Jim," Diana said, her voice tight. "Can't we have a pleasant journey without mysteries or anarchists? Just conversation, friendly companions and a bit of dancing?"

"That would be nice," I said, watching the thin fellow. He joined two youths in straw boaters, pulled out a hip flask and leaned on the rail to take a swig.

Diana cast a dark look at me. "Must you weigh them up as though you were going against them in the boxing ring?"

She was right. I arranged my features to modest neutrality. "'Course, my dear. Mustn't frighten the natives."

She shook her head at me. "Ships don't suit you, do they? You were so sick on the *Umbria*."

I'd been laid low for most of our journey to Boston. Recalling it, I shrugged. "Not had much luck with them. I was about fifteen when we were shipped off to Karachi on an army transport. Spent most of that trip with the horses in the hold . . . poor blighters were miserable in the dark. God, the stench! When at last we made land and got out on the pier, I couldn't see—blinded by the sunlight." I'd spent most of my army career on the North-west Frontier and in Rangoon.

"But you must have sailed back to Bombay? Oh." Her voice dropped. "That head wound . . ."

The shot had struck above my ear. I didn't recall that voyage, but someone had been near me . . . who was it? A turbaned man, perhaps, who tended me as if I were a child. I snatched at the memory, trying to hold it, but it dissolved.

Diana bit her lip, sending me a thoughtful glance.

Presently our ship turned, bringing the sun into our eyes. As of one mind, we proceeded into a fine lounge with gilded chairs and velvet draperies.

A raised voice drew our attention to the trio who'd blocked our gangway while boarding. The invalid's ire was directed at both attendants. The younger nurse had come in at a run, her scarf askew, blushing and out of breath.

"I *have* searched, Mrs. Barlow," she panted. "It's not in the valise. But I'm certain I packed it. We'll surely find it in your trunks."

THE SPANISH DIPLOMAT'S SECRET 9

"Then what are you doing here, you ninny? Unpack them!"

"But you said to come back," whispered the harried girl.

"I'll do it, Madam," said the thinner attendant, her hair pulled back in a tight bun.

Her employer snapped, "Nonsense! Dora had it in her hands as we boarded! Wait, Dora! Where are you going? What's the matter with you?"

Dora hurried back, her childlike eyes wide with hurt.

"Oh, for goodness' sake," Diana said under her breath, and went up to the group. Flashing a smile that could charm the keys off a warden, she said, "I am Mrs. O'Trey. Has something been misplaced? Perhaps I can help?"

"Ah, child, knitting is my only comfort," the mollified woman in the bonnet said, and introduced herself. She glowered at Dora's bent head, grumbling. "Tsch! Can't get good help for love or money these days!" She grabbed at the back of her wheelchair. "Where's my blanket? Did you forget my blanket? Alice, you dolt! What are you standing about for? Fetch it!"

As Alice set off, a woman seated across from me whispered to her husband, "Mrs. Barlow's in fine fettle today."

Her husband looked about a hundred pounds heavier than his wife. His eyes met mine. Since we were only feet away, I offered, "Evening. Have you sailed on this ship before?"

Rather than return my greeting, the pair exchanged a startled glance, then moved to a couch farther away where they plunked down with doubtful looks in my direction.

Well now, I thought, amused. Was it my mixed race, or the fact that I'd been a boxer? Without Diana's mitigating presence, I could not expect entry among what she called the ship's "best people."

I recalled the easy camaraderie of Smith and my old cavalry company, blokes who'd ride with you all day and tell stories all night. But that company of dragoons had been disbanded sometime after our debacle in Karachi. Would I meet Smith or the remaining blokes again? Invaliding out of the army, I'd been hired by Diana's brother Adi—the tragic death of his wife and sister gave me my present career. Diana had said goodbye to her close-knit family and sacrificed her inheritance to marry a rough soldier. Despite everything, she'd accepted me, so we left Bombay's social taboos for a life together in the States.

Meanwhile, she had calmed Mrs. Barlow's attendants and was now deep in conversation with the older one.

I picked up a newspaper and glanced at the headline: ASSASSIN EXE-CUTED. The past June, an anarchist, Sante Geronimo Caserio, had assassinated French president M. F. Sadi Carnot. France had just guillotined the fanatic. What drove such a man? President Carnot was the third world leader murdered by European anarchists. I read with concern, because last year we'd had a run-in with just such a group at Chicago's World's Fair.

Diana returned, saying, "Poor Alice! She's all sixes and sevens. And Dora was close to tears." She explained that Mrs. Barlow was returning to Liverpool after a decade in California, where her late husband had owned a vineyard. "She's not as old as I thought, Jim. She had a riding accident twenty years ago. Her nurse has misplaced her knitting basket, so her usual diversion in trying times is not to be had."

I smiled. "And your usual diversion in such times, my dear?"

Diana dimpled. "Watching you alarm fellow travelers, 'course!"

Grinning, I offered my arm with a flourish. I must be mistaken, I thought. Whatever troubled her, it was past.

* * *

We dressed formally at luncheon. One was excused the first day, but now the ship's protocol held sway. I had a nicely cut coat to go with my formal striped trousers, much like the dandies on board. Time to meet the troops. I stamped into my boots and laced them up as Diana picked up her embroidered stole.

Seagulls squealed, hovering out of sight in the fog as we took a turn around the upper deck. Both this and the empty promenade above were open to the sea air. Diana hugged the shawl, running a hand over the trailing bougainvillea pattern. Was she thinking of the wide verandahs and canopied trees in tropical Bombay where she'd grown up?

A raised voice came from above us. A woman's voice, torn with agitation. "I tell you, it is him! Why don't you—"

The woman stood on the companionway beside the glass-fronted bridge. An officer stepped out from the lighted room and protested, his tone insistent. "It's been twenty *years* . . ." The rest was lost in the breeze. The woman replied with a shriek of protest.

Diana's grip tightened on my arm. "That sounds serious, Jim. Should we help?"

I considered interrupting the pair, but in a moment it was unnecessary.

"You know! But you do *nothing*! *Nincompoop*!" With that, the woman stamped down the companionway. She passed us, her face hidden by her bonnet. My tenderhearted wife followed her progress with a worried glance.

A ship is a city in miniature, I thought, with all the conflicts and quarrels of human association. On it, small dramas unfolded, attachments formed or broke, friendships built while others fell apart. The woman's distress echoed in the rigged sails snapping at the wind. Clearly, some expectation had been sorely disappointed.

Long after she had passed, the thickset officer stood looking down, but did not appear to see us below. When he squared his shoulders and disappeared into the bridge, Diana and I made our way to luncheon.

"Wonder what that was about," she said as we entered the dining saloon. "It's strange, isn't it? Like opening a book to the middle and not knowing what came before!"

The saloon was intended to impress, with ceilings of painted angels and clouds, burgundy velvet on chairs and drapes, walls lined with ornate, framed landscapes and pillars gilded like in a maharaja's durbar hall.

At our table we greeted the company. Glad Diana had pressed my second-best suit, I shook hands with a pair of dandies who gave their names as Vernon and Algernon Farley.

In a sober black jacket and crisp, high collar, Algernon bowed over Diana's hand. Vernon, the younger brother, wore his hair curling down to his flounced shirt, his vest unbuttoned à la Oscar Wilde and gazed at Diana doe-eyed.

Both young pups sat up like terriers eager for her attention. Their cabin was on the saloon deck too—going to London to visit an uncle who lived in Pall Mall. I was expected to recognize his long, hyphenated name. When I didn't, their eagerness dampened.

Algernon named others at our table: Mr. and Mrs. Evansworth, taking their brood back to England, and Miss Felicity Rood who completed the company. High-spirited and fair-haired, Miss Rood greeted us with the manner of a vestal virgin receiving homage, then gave Vernon her attention.

As the salads were served, apparently approving of Diana, Mrs. Evansworth spoke about her children, punctuated by her husband's occasional, "Quite so, my dear."

I doubted he had heard her at all. Instead, he continued a conversation with Algernon, the older, stolid brother—a short nod, and the name of a corporation, followed by "Good solid stock," or a disapproving "Oh, I don't know."

Feathered hat quivering as she moved her head, Mrs. Evansworth said, ". . . our older two are Rose and Leonard—we call him Leo. The twins are three, my dear, you never saw such . . ."

Diana glanced at me and dropped her gaze. Although she nodded at Mrs. Evansworth's patter, her face had altered in some undefinable way. She sat upright as always, cutting her ham neatly into pieces. In recent weeks, she seemed to retreat into herself more often, and for no discernible reason. Her distant look gave me an odd, unsettled feeling in the pit of my stomach.

Her frozen little face held a polite smile. I bent and murmured, "Diana?"

In a brittle voice, she asked Vernon, "Would you pass the pepper, please?"

Here it was again. Something was wrong between us, but I didn't know what.

"I say!" Vernon said to me, his flounced cuffs curling. "The chaps are going to lay bets. I think we'll do thirteen knots today. Algy's keen on sixteen, but I don't think she'll do it. Not all at once, you see? Not out the gate, but on a tailwind, don't you think?"

Algernon offered, "She had the blue riband some years ago. Over eighteen knots! Dashed fine weather too, I expect. But sixteen ought to do, today."

When I declined to bet on our ship's speed, his enthusiasm wilted.

I watched his puzzlement and guessed the question in his mind. Why had a dashing fine lady like Diana accepted such a big, plodding fellow as myself? What on earth did she see in me? Sometimes, when that quiet look closed her off, I wondered too.

The younger brother gave Diana a shy grin. "Do you play croquet?"

"Vernon!" cried Miss Rood, adding, in apology, "We'd just made up a foursome. Though if Mr. O'Trey would join us . . . ?"

"Come now, Felicity, 'tisn't like tennis," Vernon protested, then asked Diana, "D'you prefer shuffleboard?"

Despite his fawning manner and the consequent disgust of the debutante, the party got along tolerably well. Breakfast was cleared away, but Diana had not looked at me once.

Vernon glanced around the table. "How 'bout a riddle: Why's the ocean so sad?"

The company exchanged glances and shrugs.

"I love riddles!" cried Miss Rood.

Vernon grinned. "Because it's blue! Here's another. Why did the fish blush?"

"Don't be daft," said his brother.

Smiling and curious, Miss Rood said, "Go on, why?"

"Because he saw the ocean's bottom!"

Miss Rood laughed, then covered her mouth. Glaring, Mrs. Evansworth gasped. "Mr. Farley! You are outrageous!"

The Evansworths got up to leave, their eyes shooting Vernon bullets of disapproval. Others at our table followed suit with less censure. Algernon pressed his lips together, but Vernon tossed his head with a defiant pout.

As we left, Diana murmured to me, "Saying that in mixed company! Too risqué by far. One can't say 'bottom' or 'legs' in public, not even when referring to a piano."

I pulled in a breath. What the dickens had ailed her? Until I knew what caused it, I could not rest easy. Dammit, why wouldn't she tell me? Couldn't she trust me to protect her?

CHAPTER 3

MURDER

The lower deck and the bowling alleys were crowded, so we returned toward the open upper deck. On the stairs, I'd only said, "What's the matter, sweet? You were so quiet at luncheon."

I knew right away I'd headed toward a bog, but a soldier doesn't retreat without good reason. Like a fool, I pushed on. "Diana, what's wrong?"

She tugged at a glove. "Let's go back."

Startled, I said, "Back to Boston?" Surely she didn't mean Bombay?

She glanced up, her face pale and pinched, "'Course not. I meant our stateroom."

In our cabin, she tossed her gloves on the table and fiddled with her hat. She stabbed it with the hat pin and looked at the trunks as though uncertain where to put it.

The mournful silence gouged me. I said, "Something's wrong, Diana. You've been miserable in Boston, and now you go off into some sort of trance. Let's have it. What's the trouble?"

I shouldn't have said trance. Emotion had made me clumsy.

She frowned, her lips tight. "These walls are paper thin. You know that."

I dropped my voice. "Tell me, Diana. Let's not hide from it."

But it was too late. Refusing to be pacified, she huffed, "It's always me, isn't it. You plow ahead blithefully unaware and wonder why I'm upset!"

"What did I say?" I tried to recall where I'd misstepped. "We passed those children, so I only said, 'Someday,' didn't I? You know I won't push you to it?"

"But you'll hint and smirk and raise your eyebrows. It's not funny!" she cried.

I sobered. "Come now. Is that all? Sweetheart, you said you wanted a child. I just wish . . ." I struggled to find a phrase that wouldn't hurt. Meeting her gaze I said, "I wish you'd make up your mind. Or at least tell me when. When d'you think you'd be ready?"

Diana swung around, outrage stiffening every inch of her tiny frame.

We had a blazing row that afternoon, although Diana whispered her accusations, and I retorted through my teeth. It scorched me, and left Diana even more remote. How did it go so wrong? I struggled to understand. Was this why she'd been crying quietly when she thought I was asleep? But she'd let me comfort her then, curling against me in the dark, our fingers intertwined. Damn it all to hell. I'd take enemy fire rather than Diana's distraught disappointment. Worse, it left me unable to defend myself, because any blow that wounded her gutted me.

Retreat was my only option, so I yanked my jacket on, saying, "I'll be in the smoking room if you need me," making it clear by my tone that I thought it unlikely she would. But before I could go, a knock sounded on our door. When I opened it, a young steward handed me a note. "Sorry sir, it arrived while you were out."

Spidery writing crawled across a crisp envelope addressed to "Señor O'Trey."

The note was short. It read: ATTEND ME INMEDIATAMENTE.

It was signed, J. NEPOMUCENO. Wasn't that whom Diana had called a Spanish grandee? His words reeked of urgency—no salutation or formal closing, sincerely, etc. In place of a letterhead, a single crest was embossed on the page.

I asked the anxious steward, "When did it come?"

"Before luncheon. Just started my shift—didn't see it. I'm sorry, sir."

My timepiece showed it was now past two. "What's the number of," I glanced at the note, "Mr. Nepo . . . muceno's cabin?"

His eyes widened. "Don Juan? Stateroom one, sir! Two levels above. Promenade deck, up past the fountain."

"Right." I picked up my hat and took leave of Diana. Passing a marble fountain shaped like a dolphin, I strode up a stairway that might have been designed for a theater and hurried to the promenade level. I'd made a mess of it with Diana. I'd apologize tonight. If only I could find the right words! But just then I was glad that someone had summoned me.

Counting gilded cabin numbers, I went on. Stateroom number one was at the stern. Then footsteps clattered on the open deck below, the unmistakable sound of panic.

A crewman sped across the boards. "Doctor! Come quick!"

I leaned over and called, "What's the matter?"

Perhaps mistaking me for an officer, he said, "It's the don, sir. In the music room. Bigby's getting the captain."

The don? The Spanish gent who'd just summoned me! An accident . . . or foul play?

I had the grim sense of being just moments too late as I clambered down a ladder and joined the crewman and a thin, dyspeptic man carrying a physician's case, hurrying toward the bow. There, a young steward was shooing passengers from a door, saying, "Please, this area is off-limits!"

My pulse sped up as I followed the doctor into a large semicircular room where a bank of windows showed sea and sky. Between them were paintings of barely dressed goddesses, muscular gods and broken pillars. Deep plum-colored carpet covered the floor. Rows of gold-backed chairs filled most of the chamber. Above us, chandeliers moved gently, sending out a faint tinkle.

I cannot tell how I knew there'd been a murder—a smell, some foreboding that hovered in the air, as though the room stood at attention in the presence of unnatural death.

At the front, three people stood to one side. In the center sat a man on a chair. Two officers flanked a distraught young woman—our companion at luncheon, Miss Rood. Hands clasped, she answered questions, but her gasps rendered her words incomprehensible.

I recognized Captain Hawley from his welcome address at our first dinner. Catching sight of us he said, "Witherspoon, thank heaven!" and beckoned him forward.

The man slumped on the chair was dead. I came around and crouched beside him, feeling short of air as I recognized his white curling mustache and goatee. Damn. I had come too late.

White hair awry, hands drooping at his sides, was the Good Samaritan who'd aided me on deck last night. Dressed in daytime formals—dark vest and jacket, his blue lips twisted in a rictus of pain. Yellow stains spattered his beard and shirt. The sour smell of vomit hovered amid the whiff of feces.

A voice behind me said, "Sir?"

An agitated older man in white uniform gazed down at me with a harried expression. I stood and introduced myself, adding, "I work for the Dupree detective agency in Boston."

He bowed. "I'm Johnson, chief steward." His cultured tone should not have surprised me. More than one educated fellow has taken service on the sea. I said nothing about meeting the don before, or his urgent note. Instead, I glanced over the empty hall, seeing debris from an upturned planter. Voices clamored outside. Too many people had been in here already. A young steward was opening windows to let in air.

Johnson whispered to the captain, who turned to me. A thick, well-tended beard covered his jaw, but it was his eyes one noticed. Dark, deep set and penetrating, they demanded an explanation.

I said, "Captain James O'Trey, retired. Heard the commotion. May I help?"

He gazed at me for a long moment. Then in a tight brogue, he demanded, "It's a rum thing, Mr. O'Trey. What d'you make of this?" He gestured to the don's sagging body.

I looked at the old man, recalling the name scrawled so confidently on my note. "The Spanish gent. Don Juan Nepomuceno."

"You know him?"

"Met him last night." The don's head drooped like a pistol broken to reload. The narrow bony fingers that had held his cigar lay crooked and still. Doctor Witherspoon checked his neck for a pulse but there was no need. The don's staring eyes and gaping mouth were clear enough.

The doctor said, "Help me carry him," and took the don's arm, motioning me at the other. The Spaniard was surprisingly light. His head rolled back as we bore him to one side and laid him down, his high collar open and askew. Livid stripes on his throat showed where something had dug into his skin.

Witherspoon examined the don's head for wounds and peered at each hand, his manner coolly systematic. He'd done this before.

"No other injuries," he murmured. The don's shirt and vest were specked with vomit, his face bloated. With careful attention, the doctor lifted his head and moved it from side to side.

Throat tight, I asked, "Strangled?"

Something had fallen near the body. I scooped it up—a black satin tie, stretched and wrinkled. My pulse jerked as I realized what it was.

Witherspoon glanced at the slip of fabric in my fingers. "Garroted. Likely with that tie. Rather inexpertly, I think. I'll have to do an autopsy, but it seems clear."

Multiple red lines marked the don's neck. So . . . it wasn't quick. The killer took his time.

I ran a hand through my hair. The weight in my chest had little to do with fatigue. Last night Don Juan had rendered me aid without making much of it. His quiet company had been a comfort. Yet when he'd sent for me, I'd come too late. Now he lay on the floor, a narrow, crooked body in a well-cut suit and pointed shoes polished to a fine gloss. Johnson brought a tablecloth from an overturned table and laid it over him.

A potted plant lay toppled, soil spilling over the carpet, smeared by multiple shoeprints. Crew members had tracked through, destroying any footmarks that might identify the killer.

I glanced around, puzzled. Something felt unnatural about this chamber. But could one ever be at ease with murder? Perhaps not. So what was it? I turned, taking in the room. Ahead, the remaining palm tree flanked an ornate mirror.

"The glass. His chair was facing it."

Someone had brought the old gent in and sat him before a mirror. He'd struggled. The toppled palm attested to that. But his assailant had yanked off his tie and wound it about his neck, pulling him back, tightening it as he gasped and writhed. Had the killer wanted to see the don's face as he garroted him from behind? Was that why it was done here?

A shiver ran over my skin. Who'd want to torment an old man so?

CHAPTER 4

AN IMPOSSIBLE TASK

While Captain Hawley spoke with the physician, I quizzed Chief Steward Johnson. He answered steadily, though his eyes strayed frequently to the covered body. Miss Rood had summoned him because the door to the music room was stuck. He'd keyed it and had the French windows opened to dispel the smell. He passed a hand over his balding pate, then dabbed at the beads of sweat on his forehead with a kerchief.

As the don's body was carried away, Captain Hawley said, "A moment, Captain O'Trey." His Scots accent curled over the *r* in my name.

He'd remembered my rank. I liked him for that courtesy. "Jim, please."

Hawley ran a hand over his beard. "I'll have to make an announcement soon. News has likely gone round the ship already." His voice turned crisp as he came to a decision. "A nasty business. Imperative we get to the bottom of it right away. Before we reach England. That's crucial."

I stared at him. "Why?"

He held my gaze. "If it isn't sorted out, we'll be held at Liverpool for the inquest. We've nine hundred and forty-five souls aboard, including crew."

I nodded. "It could take a while."

"No one would be allowed to leave. Can't have that. Loads of angry passengers. My employers would be . . . let's just say, unhappy."

"Worse than that, I think," I said. "Could harm Cunard's reputation. A quick crossing, isn't that what people want?"

"A safe crossing. But you're right. The public would not look kindly upon a prolonged delay. You're a detective. You've worked for the agency—how long?"

"Year or so."

"And before that?"

"Bombay police. And the British army."

"Thought so," Hawley said. "Will you investigate?" Though he sounded calm, he was breathing hard and worried creases lined his face.

Solve the case in six days? With almost a thousand suspects? It was a mammoth undertaking, ridiculous, really.

I frowned. "Why not conduct the investigation yourself?"

He blinked. "The deceased. He's not a British citizen. We might be seen as, uh, biased. You're American, a neutral party."

Curious. Why did he need an independent investigation? "I'd report to the court of inquest?"

He nodded, his shoulders easing. "And to me."

His bland face revealed little. Perhaps he didn't think I'd get anywhere. Was that why he was trying to hand it to me? The crew had already tampered with the music room, destroying any trace of footprints. Windows had been opened. By the time we docked, any evidence would be quite lost.

How long would an inquest keep passengers on board? A few days? After that there'd be an uproar and they'd have to let us off. Don Juan's killer could walk off the ship with a bounce in his step.

The deck below my feet seemed to sway. No, Spanish citizen or not, the old man would have justice. I needed one steady thing in this blasted shifting maze of civilian life. Murder could not go unpunished.

"I'd have access to the ship? The decks, bridge, boiler room, the rest?"

The captain hesitated. "My Chief Officer, Mr. Bigby, will accompany you."

I watched him fiddle with his cuffs and said, "Your chief officer—why not entrust the investigation to him?"

His face closed like the doors of a wardrobe clicking together. "I prefer . . . a professional man."

I persisted. "Mr. Bigby. Any reason to doubt him?"

"Eh? No, certainly not. Served with me four years. Excellent officer. Sharp, competent, clean as a whistle. Impossible. Edwin's nothing to do with this."

I hid my surprise. What was it that Shakespeare wrote—My lady doth protest too much, methinks? "But he's to accompany me—?"

Hawley shrugged. "He knows the ship. So you'll do it? Good man," he said without waiting for my reply.

When he put up his cap, I moved to stay him. "If we've only six days, there's little time to lose. Toward the end of dinner, ask that anyone who saw Don Juan today stay in the room. Insist. Make a point of it, moral duty, that sort of thing. And we need to take statements from all those who leave, record their whereabouts."

"Those who leave? You mean those who stay."

I shook my head. "No, sir. Those I'll interview myself. We need crewmen from second class to interview the others."

"Second? Only got six stewards there." He frowned. "Why second class?"

"Add the waiters. They wouldn't have access to the first-class deck, yes? It could well be a first-cabin crew member who killed the don."

Hawley grimaced. "One of my crew?"

"I passed the music room before lunch. It was teeming. The alarm was given just after two, so it happened between noon and two o'clock. Need to know where each passenger was during that time. Also, who was with them, to match up statements."

"We've got hundreds in first class!"

I remembered Diana reading the passenger list and said, "Four hundred and thirty-six. And their servants. And any crew with access to the music room."

I left Hawley looking as though he'd eaten something rotten and turned my mind to the problem of the locked room. The French windows at the bow gave on to an open deck. Catching sight of Chief Steward Johnson, I sent for Timothy, the deck steward who'd opened them. A coolheaded killer might escape through one, then wait nearby, to answer the chief steward's call.

"Were they locked? All of them?" I asked the handsome, round-bellied youth.

"Yes, sir. Every one." He licked his lips and swallowed.

I watched him closely. "Where were you, when you were called?"

"I've got the port section of the bow. Until four. Then I serve tea and go below."

He had not answered me, so I raised an eyebrow and waited. He said, "I heard the disturbance, sir, and rushed to the music room. In case someone had fainted. From the heat."

He seemed guileless, but I repeated, "Where were you standing, when you heard the ruckus?"

He blinked. "On deck, sir. In my section."

"Who did you serve last?"

"A young couple." He did not know their names.

"Did you see the Spanish gent enter the music room?"

"No, sir. In the afternoon I work to port and oversee the passengers on the foredeck."

I sighed. The door to the music room was amidships, toward the center. But that meant he was standing outside the bank of windows at the back of the music room.

"See anyone leave through those?" I pointed.

"No, sir."

I shook hands and thanked him. He had no alibi, but his grip was weak and fleshy, his clothing clean and unrumpled. Somewhere on the ship was a killer, perhaps cleaning the don's vomit off himself this very minute.

* * *

Sometime later I returned to our cabin and found Diana in a state. She took my hat, her face blotched, her nose reddened. The sick look in her eyes tightened a vise inside me. God, we needed to talk, but now I had not the time for it!

Leading her to the couch, I told Diana about the murder. Our argument forgotten, she listened, eyes wide, not interrupting. I'd known few women who could do that.

"Oh, Khodai! A mirror. To see himself . . . being killed?" She shuddered. Shouldn't have said so much, I thought. She rarely spoke in Gujarati, her mother tongue. But when I hesitated, her look propelled me on. Reluctantly I said, "There's another possibility. The killer . . . may have wanted him to see his executioner."

"That poor man!" She rose and swished around the room, radiating outrage. "We have to catch this maniac!"

We? I frowned, my thoughts flying in a dozen directions. I should keep Diana out of this, but the ship was more her environs than mine. She'd traveled to Europe and knew the vagaries of polite society. I glanced at my timepiece. "Let's dress, sweet. It's almost six."

As I unpacked a suit and shed my clothes to change, she went behind the screen to dress. From there she called questions, which I answered: the door was opened because Miss Rood wanted to play the piano. No, the deck steward had seen nothing untoward.

She came out in her corset and petticoat, and lowered a lemon green evening dress over her head. "The room was locked? Then how'd the killer get out?" she said, turning her back for me to button her up.

I did the needful, noting the low bodice with a silent groan. Fellows would come running like sepoys at mess call.

I replied, "Isn't that the question. Hawley needs me to find the killer before we dock. He insists we keep to the usual routine. Dinner as planned."

I put on my blue silk waistcoat and held out my tie.

Frowning, she tied it deftly. "You think something's not right. With the captain?"

"He's scared. Not sure what of, but it's got him jumpy as a hare."

Diana tapped her fingers about—for her cigarette case, perhaps. She'd given up smoking because the fumes brought back memories I'd rather forget, but occasionally I'd seen her fingers twitch as though looking for something.

When I sent her an inquiring look. She stilled, then sat and pulled on black opera gloves. "Jim, I'm not sure this is a good idea. We're on holiday, aren't we?"

I glanced at her. "Weren't you saying the killer's a maniac?"

She bit her lip. "I remember the Spanish couple, the woman all in black lace. They were with the captain when we boarded. But the old fellow, the don, he was someone important. He had a young scribe-looking person with him, dressed like an undertaker. And a dozen trunks. With guards, Jim. There could be more to this . . ."

Guards? Yes, I recalled uniforms escorting the pair with a slew of luggage.

"Find that passenger list, will you?" I rummaged about in a trunk. "Long night ahead. Where did I put our notepaper?"

I found the ream I'd stashed to write down the story of our adventure in Chicago. Long days of even sailing, I'd imagined, long afternoons when I could jot down my recollections at the World's Fair and go over it all with Diana. Man proposes; Neptune—and a bloody killer—had other ideas. Guilt prickled my skin like a rash I could not itch. Why had the Spanish gent summoned *me* right before he died?

Diana pinned on a brooch which threw sparkles across the floor and walls. "Think someone will have seen something useful?"

Hefting some paper, I opened the door for her, saying, "People have no idea what they've seen. It's those who *don't* speak up that I'm really interested in. That's why we'll take detailed statements from our willing witnesses. Let's see who was around but doesn't admit it. Flush them out!"

The don had penned his note to me before noon. Something must have alarmed him, to send for me in such an abrupt manner, but what?

CHAPTER 5

A MISSING WITNESS

At dinner, I mulled it over. Who was Don Juan? He'd spoken French when he came to my aid last night. It was no surprise he used the international language of Europe. Our ship contained Americans traveling to the Continent as well as returning Europeans. An educated Spaniard might speak French and English as well as other languages.

When I replied in English, the don seemed disappointed. It puzzled me. Had he been looking for a sign that he could trust me? I recalled his brusque retort before he left—a cantankerous man, or just one accustomed to deference? His quiet company had made no judgments, accepting me as a fellow soldier. But the gruesome way he'd been murdered was surely significant. Why was he killed before a mirror? This was no crime of impulse, but a *crime passionnel* nonetheless, vicious and intensely personal.

At dinner's end, Captain Hawley stood and cleared his throat. Someone rang a spoon twice against a glass for silence.

Beside me, Mr. Evansworth sucked in a breath. "That's bad luck. Ringing a glass on board foretells a death. Strike three times to avert it." He glanced at me as though apologizing for an outburst. "I was in the British navy." It was the first time he'd spoken an entire sentence.

Hawley gained the room's attention, and announced that a fellow passenger, Don Juan Nepomuceno, had died unexpectedly.

Waiting until gasps and whispers subsided, he went on, his Scottish accent thickening, "If you saw the Spanish gentleman today, would you please remain seated. Other guests may leave. My crew will meet you outside for a short interview. Please accord them the courtesy you would give myself."

With murmurs of surprise, passengers shuffled out to where the ship's staff would divide them into groups. Moving four hundred passengers was a task in itself. It would cause a to-do, but officers were arrayed to prevent a crush near the door. I hoped our methodical approach would yield some witnesses.

In the dining hall, Stewardess Miss Pickle and Chief Steward Johnson stood among the remaining passengers. I introduced myself to the group, instructing them to write when and where they had seen Don Juan. Gliding between the tables, Diana handed out paper and writing instruments. As though this was one of the games played on board, one by one, gentlemen in satin lapels raised their hands like schoolchildren to hand her their pages.

Glancing across the magnificent chamber at the fine folk assembled, I wondered, was the killer here, watching the proceedings with amusement? Pulling in a breath, I drew aside the three who'd found the body—Miss Rood, who'd had time to dress for dinner, Miss Pickle, tall and slender, with Nordic hair and eyebrows of white silk, and Johnson. Taking their pages, I asked. "Let's start from the beginning. How did you find Don Juan?"

Tossing a black, feathered stole over her shoulder, Miss Rood said, "I wanted to practice on the piano, but the door wouldn't open. Edna, our stewardess, was on the promenade, so I called to her. We thought the wood might be stuck and struggled with it for a bit. Five or ten minutes, perhaps?"

The women were useful witnesses. Any little observation or oddity now might lead me to the killer. "I see. Edna—Miss Pickle?" I glanced at her page. "You were above, on the promenade deck?"

Wide-eyed at the attention, she nodded. "The music room isn't locked, not usually." She'd been unable to open the door, so she'd got Johnson, who used a master key.

I turned to him. "You entered first?"

"Yes, sir. I tried to keep the ladies out, but it was too late. Edna, ah, Miss Pickle rushed to bring the chief officer. Miss Rood remained with me. Unfortunately, a number of passengers also arrived."

The grisly news had traveled quickly, bringing more gawking viewers. We established that they'd opened the door only minutes before two o'clock.

I gazed at him, puzzled. "When you entered, who was in the room?"

"Just the don—terrible state. You saw him."

"The music hall. Is there another way out?"

Johnson drew back. "N-no, sir."

"Then the killer was inside when you arrived."

His eyebrows shot up, then he shook his head. "Just the gentleman on the chair, table overturned, the planter broken, soil everywhere . . ."

"If the door was locked from the inside, how did the killer escape?"

He thrust a hand over his wide forehead. "I don't know, sir. The windows? But Timothy said they were bolted. It was choppy the first day, so we'd closed them."

Recalling the wide music room, I said, "I noticed a nook on one side. Did you search it?"

He gasped. "The serving pantry. It's open to the hall, sir. I didn't see anyone."

"But did you examine it?"

He groaned. "Not closely, no."

"So, our killer might have walked over to join the gawkers?"

"Might have." He looked unconvinced. "But you'd have seen him, sir. He'd be facing you. You came with the doctor just after we cleared the room."

I'd hurried past the crowd outside, but couldn't identify any of them. If Johnson remembered the scene accurately, it meant he hadn't been as flustered as he'd seemed at the time.

I thanked him, adding, "If you recall anything else, please let me know," then turned to the remaining witnesses. Some glowered and thrust their pages at me, eager to leave, but I bade them wait. Grumbling, they sat back down. They'd rather be at their card games, I supposed. Had they stayed from a sense of duty? Or was the murderer hiding in plain sight?

Hawley sent someone for brandy. Bottles arrived. It must have been the good stuff because thereafter my witnesses became quite vocal.

A good many passengers had seen Don Juan and Doña Josefina on the aft deck that morning. Well before luncheon, the Farley brothers saw the don's wife leave her deck chair. She'd told Edna, the stewardess, that she would dine in her room. Don Juan seemed asleep, so they did not disturb him.

I asked some more questions, then approached the captain and first officer. "Mrs. Nepomuceno isn't here . . . ?"

He gave a weary shake of his head. "The widow is distraught. Leave her till tomorrow. And O'Trey, don't see her without me." He raised his eyebrows in a meaningful way. "She's, ah, rather influential."

We dismissed the witnesses, who hurried out as though the last would be forced into kitchen duty. Once the room emptied, Diana looked up from the pages she'd been sorting.

She placed a hand on one pile. "These noticed him while walking on the upper deck . . . it joins the aft deck where the chairs are set out. I suppose the last person with him was Nurse Shay," she said, tapping a page.

"Did the don go to the sickroom?"

"N—no." She looked up at the chief officer. "Mr. Bigby, you saw him with the nurse and told Mr. Johnson. He wrote it down."

Bigby blushed. Not a slight staining of the cheeks but a full-blown pink from stem to stern. "I said I *might* have seen him. Not sure now that it *was* him. I was looking down, from the bridge, sir, before you relieved me," he explained to the captain.

I asked, "When was that?"

"'Bout half past noon. We take the noon reading together, then add it to our chart. Got to know exactly where we are, at any given time."

Despite the late hour, Nurse Dewey Shay was summoned. With her came Doctor Witherspoon in rumpled shirtsleeves and vest, who seemed discomfited to see us gathered like a tribunal.

Captain Hawley introduced me. I asked, "Miss Shay, where were you this morning?"

Witherspoon scowled and answered. "She was with me, in the aft hospital. I came, of course, when the captain sent for me, about two o'clock. *You* were there."

"Quite." Why was he so disgruntled? It made little sense for him to antagonize the man investigating a murder. I explained, "Nurse Shay was seen assisting the Spanish gentleman before that."

He snapped, "Impossible. We had many cases of seasickness, including the Evansworth children. Miss Shay was on duty until six this evening."

I turned to the nurse. "Miss, did you go anywhere else this afternoon?"

Her voice barely a whisper, Nurse Shay said she had not.

I asked her more questions, but each time the physician answered. I'd need to speak with her alone.

When they'd gone, Diana handed me a page with raised eyebrows. "Look at this. Someone's written 'Good Riddance.'"

I felt a cold touch between my shoulder blades as I turned over the sheet. "It's unsigned."

Well, well! An anonymous note. Somebody who'd seen Don Juan that morning didn't like him much. Or was it a crewman? A number of them had collected the passenger statements, or encountered the don during their duties and therefore provided an account. If written by the killer, the note was a bold move, almost an announcement, printed in tight capitals, neither violently large, nor small and secretive.

Bigby shifted from foot to foot as though eager to leave. Remembering that he'd been on duty since that morning, I sympathized as I asked him, "Just what did you see?"

His forehead knotted. "Can't be sure. Likely someone else."

"The Spanish gent was rather distinctive—all that white hair and his goatee."

Bigby nodded. "The woman, I . . . assumed it was Nurse Shay. Obviously, a mistake."

"Can you describe her?"

Bigby hemmed and hawed, then said, "I just saw a nurse—'least I thought it was, 'cause of the white cap—you know that bit of scarf they wear. He was leaning on her, seemed sozzled. It surprised me—before luncheon; bit early for that sort of thing. Deck stewardesses went back and forth all morning. As nurse-stewardess, Nurse Shay often lends a hand. Looked as though she was taking him to his cabin."

"Except he didn't get there. You're certain it wasn't a stewardess?"

He wasn't. Bigby mopped his forehead. "Wish I'd paid more attention. Only glanced down 'cause she's a sweet thing, that Dewey Shay. Doctor keeps her locked up tight."

Trouble was, he'd blushed again. It made him the fourth person who'd lied tonight. Among the others, I counted the author of the anonymous note; from the physician's behavior I took it Nurse Shay had something to hide; and the composed Miss Rood . . . what was it about her that irked me?

People lie for all sorts of reasons. Some keep matters to themselves from an abundance of caution. Others might wait until they could trust. Some were probably hiding unrelated secrets they'd rather not make public. And then there was the killer, keen to send me chasing buffaloes—or wild geese. He'd be gloating over this early success. He'd escaped detection among a shipful of people. Now I rather thought, he'd appear innocuous, or brashly confident, or head me off with a lot of nonsense. It was my job to know which was which.

Captain Hawley said good night, so Bigby dismissed the last of the crew. The cooks departed, scowling. They'd go straight to preparing breakfast without sleep tonight.

Diana had her head pillowed on her forearms. She'd wanted a nice quiet crossing. I touched her shoulder to rouse her.

As we trudged back through freshly painted corridors, past rococo mirrors and frescoes, what had been inviting in daylight now seemed closed-off and mysterious. If only I'd got Don Juan's summons earlier, I might have found a way to protect him.

Entering our velvet-draped room, I grumbled, "Got to find that missing witness, the one mistaken for the nurse."

Removing her overdress with a flourish, Diana scoffed. "Oh, tosh. Take this off and presto. A white skirt. Bigby could have seen any young woman—" She paused.

I met her gaze, realizing the hopelessness of my task. "Or any woman on board."

CHAPTER 6

AN ACCUSATION

DAY THREE: MORNING

On our way to interview Don Juan's widow, Captain Hawley pulled Bigby and me aside. He said, "Gentlemen, something you should know, but it must go no further. Don Juan was the unofficial Spanish ambassador to the United States."

I stared. Our victim was an important diplomat. Was this why it took so long to arrange an audience with his widow? Apparently meeting her involved some protocol. As we followed Hawley, my mind spun. This case might have wider implications than I'd imagined.

He sent me a meaningful look. "Six days left, O'Trey."

I hoped the don's widow might offer some indication of his state of mind. Why had he summoned me that morning? Had he feared someone aboard? And I had another concern. By compiling last night's statements, I'd learned that except for the unknown nurse, the don's widow had been the last person with him.

Hawley rapped smartly on an ornately carved stateroom door.

It was opened by a young man in a high collar and dark coat. With a narrow nose and deep-set eyes, he looked like a student from some venerated university. His dark coat buttoned to the neck had a clerical appearance.

As we stepped inside, a woman shrieked across the room. *"Delincuente!* You killed him! Murderer!"

Bigby and I exchanged a startled glance. Murderer? Whom did she mean? The captain took a shocked step back as a lady in layers of black clothing came into view.

The young man at the door beseeched, "Excellency, *por favor!*" He went on in voluble Spanish, his tone conciliatory. Yet his words did not calm the widow.

The morning sun showed her angry, contorted face. "Coward! My 'usband is sleeping and he is *murdered*! But you cannot face me yesterday? Cowards. Pah!"

Behind us, walkers on their morning constitutionals paused, all agog.

"Madam, please calm yourself." Glancing over his shoulder, Captain Hawley grunted and thrust his way past the young man. I followed him into the largest stateroom I'd ever seen.

The don's widow retreated to a long set of trellised windows that overlooked the stern. Behind her, a woodcut screen rose to the high molded ceiling. The gilded furniture was what Diana would call the Queen Anne style. Oval mirrors graced the patterned walls. Three marble statuettes. An ornate fireplace. A white satin rolled chaise. These were emperor's quarters.

The stiff young man said, "Please forgive Her Excellency, Doña Josefina Rosa Maria Lopez y Carrillo. She is, how you say, distraught. I am Armando De Cullar, señor, aide-de-camp to Don Juan Lorenzo Nepomuceno de Burriel."

Had she been overcome when Dr. Witherspoon broke the news to her? Now she heard our introductions with stiff formality.

We gave our condolences, then I asked, "Aide-de-camp? Was Don Juan a military man?"

De Cullar's onyx eyes glittered. "He is the governor of Bilbao, señor."

Over the next hour Doña Josefina said very little. She watched us from a chair at the far end of the chamber and worked her rosary, her pallor stark against the midnight veil, glaring suspicion. If we'd been in the dining saloon, I'd have counted table knives just out of caution. She peered at me too, but in my civilian clothing, I did not merit as much vitriol as the ship's officers.

De Cullar was of little use. At half past eleven Don Juan had sent him for an inkpot. He'd had trouble finding it and proceeded to search the don's numerous trunks. At a quarter past two he was with Doña Josefina when their steward told them of the tragedy.

"You looked for ink—for three hours?"

His long, expressive fingers rubbed the fabric of his coat. "It was time for the luncheon, señor. And then the siesta . . ." His cold voice rebuked me.

"Where did you take luncheon?"

"In my quarters. The señora was served here. His Excellency does not take the luncheon. He prefers a soup which is prepared for him at one o'clock."

"He dined on deck?" No member of the crew had admitted serving him. If he was anything like his madam wife, it seemed likely they stayed out of his way. Yet I remembered him smoking beside me that first night, gazing out, giving me a moment to collect myself.

De Cullar gave an expressive, Gallic shrug and began speaking, but Doña Josefina abruptly stood. Tall and regal, she snapped, *"Basta!"* flicking bony hands to shoo us from the room.

The captain repeated his deep regrets. Doña Josefina grimaced as though she smelled a cesspit. De Cullar did not shake hands as we left.

I asked Captain Hawley, "Governor of Bilbao? Why didn't he travel on a Spanish ship?"

He mopped the perspiration on his brow. "Don't know, old chap. I was told to keep the Spanish gent happy. Peace with his country depends on it. This is the worst thing that could have happened."

"Why?"

That was all it took. He glanced back to see that Bigby had fallen behind, then said, "My captaincy, man. If we can't find who's responsible, I'm finished. This will be my last ship!"

That could explain his earlier distress, I thought. "But peace with Spain?"

Bigby caught up with us and answered. "America is well out of it. But Britain's caught in the middle. Damn Spaniards. Their king is just eight years old and ruled by his mother. Bloody Basques cause trouble everywhere. In Catalonia they shoot people every few months. Except when they hang them."

His bitter tone startled me. "Isn't there an elected government?"

"Ha! The two parties take turns! *El Turno Pacifico.* But it's all the same blighters, cousins and nephews of the Bourbons. Not like Britain, 'course. No wonder the Basques are up in arms."

A country in turmoil, with a queen regent running things for an underage king. That sounded curiously like my first case, where I'd ventured into an unstable Indian princedom ruled by a dowager queen.

Leaving the companionway, we came upon a uniformed group who snapped to attention. As Hawley said a few words, the officers' faces relaxed, but their gazes did not leave his face. The ship took its cue from the captain. And something was gnawing at ours like a monkey with a whiskey canteen.

Before Hawley left us, I asked, "A moment, sir. What was the don doing in New York?"

"No idea, O'Trey. To do with the Rothschilds, I'd heard."

Bigby's eyebrows shot up. He had not known this. Rothschilds? Old money, I thought. What the devil had I stepped into the middle of? It was likely Doña Josefina also came from old money; her contempt had a fine vintage. It made me uncomfortable, as though I was sent into enemy terrain without knowing what lay ahead. I felt . . . exposed, and worse, out of my element.

No, I thought, these hallowed parties might belong to the upper echelons, but this was murder, and that I knew how to investigate. Someone would have seen something. They might not know the meaning of what they'd seen, but I'd gather those bits and lay them together, building the threads into a noose for a vicious killer.

With neither colleagues nor police to help fill in the gaps, I'd have to work quickly. First, I needed to grasp the lay of the land, see where the don was seated and how he'd got to the music room. Once Hawley departed, I asked Bigby, "Could you perhaps find me a map?"

He took me to the chart room, a fine bright space with glass windows overhead, where I studied a plan of the ship's five decks: promenade, upper and saloon decks above water, while main and lower decks lay below the waterline.

A large map covered the table at the room's center, with a lamp swinging over it. Instruments crowded the wall behind.

Noticing my interest, Bigby said, "Many officers are capable of navigating the ship at any given time. There are always two at the helm."

Gesturing, he introduced the gruff senior second officer, and a ridiculously youthful fourth officer, who rolled up a chart of the ship for me.

Eager to learn the ship's configuration, I followed Bigby down narrow stairs amidships, to a hallway where the engines reverberated underfoot. This central foyer separated first-class passengers from second class with a pair of narrow doors and a flowing fountain in the shape of a marble swan.

I tried the handle, which did not yield. "Are these always secured?"

"Of course." With a cordial goodbye, Bigby offered directions to my cabin on the saloon deck. This did not mean I could disregard the second class, I thought. There were surely numerous other entrances and egresses in a ship this size.

As I returned, Doña Josefina's vehemence struck me as curious. Why had she accused the ship's captain? I considered the curious interview: her fierce demeanor, her cold obsidian eyes, the narrow mustache quivering on young De Cullar's lip as he strove to calm her.

This murder had a strangely staged quality—a diplomat cruelly garroted in the music room; his servant searching for ink for an inordinate amount of time; the widow with her wild accusations; a mysterious nurse that may or may not have served a dozen people, but that no one could identify. So someone distracted De Cullar, then dressed as a nurse and . . . But no, De Cullar said that it was Don Juan who sent him off on that errand. So was De Cullar himself the killer, disguised as a woman? His inability to find the inkpot was a weak alibi, pathetic, really . . .

I pulled back. Hadn't Sherlock Holmes said it was a mistake to theorize before one has data? I recalled "The Adventure of the Speckled Band": "Insensibly one begins to twist facts to suit theories, instead of theories to suit facts."

Back at our cabin, I found that Diana had pinned pages from last night's inquisition to the curtains suspended over our porthole. She was standing on a bed in her stockings, hands on hips, scowling at them.

"What's the matter, sweet?"

She made a moue with her lips. "A missing bowling ball, two bottles of wine, and some cheeses."

"Hmm?" Relieved that she'd forgotten our argument, I tossed my hat on the couch, shed my coat and yawned. How did these posh fellows wear such silly togs all day? As I stretched, my hand whacked into the bulkhead. I bit off a curse and dropped onto the settee to watch Diana.

Tut-tutting, she put away my hat on a clever shelf by the door and grumbled. "I went up to the sewing room—they call it the 'boudoir'—oh what a to-do. The murder, that's all anyone can talk about. They're horrified, but . . . it's a sort of excitement, too. 'A crewman was knifed on the Kensingtons' last crossing—drunken sailors fighting over a card game. This is so much worse!'

"I asked if they'd seen anything unusual and of course, everybody had. This, dear Jim, is what the ladies consider suspicious: A ball (white in color) is missing from the bowling lane, and Mrs. Evansworth insists six cheeses wrapped in cloth were stolen. She has four children . . ."

I caught her hand to tug her close. Her eyes widened, then went soft as she sat down beside me. She touched my hair. "It's gone too long again."

Before she could find more to complain about, I kissed her. She didn't protest, and the distance between us, for the moment, seemed bridged. Would it last? Or would the cause of that reserve return to haunt her amber-flecked eyes? Worse still, what had caused it? Was it something I'd done? I gathered her close.

Later, when I'd told her about Doña Josefina's accusation and Hawley's political theories, she said, "The captain probably thinks the don was assassinated by Spanish rebels of some persuasion. He thinks he'll be blamed."

"He will be. Governments need to hold someone to account. Let's play it out. Someone wants to assassinate Don Juan. But why's he killed on board? Why not in America?"

Her shoulder moved against my chest. "He'd be well protected on land, wouldn't he? On board, he's only got that little undertaker fellow and the angry missus."

I considered that. The puny aide-de-camp might be easily overcome but a ferocious Doña Josefina could likely curdle an assassin's blood. "He was just as defenseless on the voyage to New York. Why kill him now?"

"Perhaps the assassins couldn't get aboard that ship. Or they didn't know which one he'd take. Maybe in New York they bribed someone to find out, then hired on here."

The captain wouldn't hire men without someone to vouch for them, I thought, but decided to ask whether the ship had taken on any new crew.

Diana made a humming sound that ratcheted up my pulse. Her breath was warm and thoughtful. "What'll you do next?"

I twisted around to see the clock above the door. "There's time before luncheon. I'll try to waylay Nurse Shay without Doctor Witherspoon's protection."

"Brute," she said, but there was no edge in it. In fact, she snuggled closer.

With our present tenuous bond, I'd half expected that she'd pull away, aghast that I was working a murder investigation on what was our time together. But Diana had assisted me without being asked. And God, she felt good.

And then I had it, the reason why I had to find the don's murderer and see things right. In Bombay, the murder of Diana's sisters had led me to unravel a foul plot—but I'd have been killed if it wasn't for her and Adi, her brother. Then again last year, she'd followed me to Chicago and helped uncover an anarchist group. It terrified me to have her involved . . . No, I acknowledged, that wasn't it. Truth was, I needed to show her that this, at least, I was good at. Yes, I lacked the social graces of more educated men, their manners and charm with words. But dammit, I was a detective.

CHAPTER 7

SECRETS

Doctor Witherspoon stepped into the sick bay with his wet hair clinging to his head. Had he come in a hurry or been in the Turkish baths below? He stopped abruptly, seeing me at his desk in the aft clinic which Nurse Shay said was only for women. Fortunately, at present it held no patients.

He barked at the nurse, "Dewey, you're all right?"

"Yes, Doctor," she said, standing like a schoolgirl in the headmaster's presence.

I continued writing to give him a moment, jotting down what Nurse Shay had told me. What was it between them? Was the doctor afraid she'd say more than she should? If anything, she'd been too reticent, repeating the doctor's statements word for word. "Mrs. Evansworth's children, the health forms, et cetera."

"You've been very helpful, miss," I said, with a quick smile.

I stood, as though preparing to leave, and gestured to the back. "Ah, is there a water closet here?"

"No, you'll have to go back to the staff lounge." With a relieved smile, she went to the door to point the way.

"Yesterday you were here from"—I consulted my notes—"nine in the morning until six in the evening. You'd have walked to the staff lounge to use the facilities?"

She nodded. "Ah, yes. Now I recall, I did."

I turned to the physician, who glared, his mouth in a knot. "You, as well, Doctor?"

He stepped back and raised an arm toward the door. "I'd like you to leave."

What was he hiding? I sat back down and turned to the nurse. "The staff lounge is on the port side, isn't it? Did you go round the stern? Or through the galley passageway?" Open to both sides, this ramp allowed stewards to bring up trolleys from the kitchens.

"The galley," she whispered, after a long moment.

"Who'd you see there? On duty?"

Her face crumpled. I put down my pen, for Diana was quite wrong. I was indeed a brute. Miss Shay seemed too fragile—the nurses I'd known in Cantonment hospital had been tough old birds under whose gaze burly Pathans and surly Gurkhas quietly took their medicine.

"You went over, through the promenade deck, yes?" I smiled at the nurse.

Mouth tight, Witherspoon handed her a fresh white handkerchief.

I went on. "Who'd you see there, miss?"

It was no use. She sat and sobbed into the kerchief, her shoulders shaking.

I paused in surprise, then realized what it meant. "You weren't here, were you? What about the afternoon?"

Witherspoon flinched. "Stop this instant. Sir, you are not welcome here!"

I hoped I would not need his services this voyage because I'd likely not make it off the ship alive. "Where were you yesterday morning, Doctor?"

His face turned crimson. That's when I realized the source of his ire. "You were together. In your cabin? I'm not a newsman, Doctor, no one need know."

He stiffened, observing me with the attention one gives a coiled snake. But he did not deny it. I kept my tone casual. "Just before two, you were called from this room. What time did you get here?"

I'd almost given up on an answer when he replied, "A quarter to eleven."

"Alone?"

He glowered, debating perhaps which of my members to amputate when given a chance.

"Who'd you see on the way?

"I don't recall! There were loads of people around."

"You'd look to see who you should avoid. Who was there?"

He slumped into a chair beside the nurse, who'd stopped sniffing, and muttered, "The captain. I ducked into the games room."

The tightness around his mouth warned that he'd not soon forgive my insistence. Well, Bigby had given over the bridge to the captain at about half past twelve. So Hawley's being on the promenade deck before eleven made sense.

The nurse and Witherspoon agreed they'd taken luncheon at the staff dining room at noon and returned together, after one. They named a dozen crewmen who could attest to it. Then Miss Shay glanced at the doctor and away. A furtive glance, at once afraid and yet . . . caring.

Closing my book I said, "Would you escort me to the staff lounge, Nurse?"

When the doctor made to rise, I put up an open palm. "I'm sure you are needed here, Doctor. I've got my answers, for now."

People often let their guard down when they think you're done with them. Walking back along the promenade, I made some trivial remarks, then said, "Bad business, this tragedy. Is the body to be carried to Liverpool?"

Nurse Shay darted a look up at me. "No, sir. Bad luck to carry a corpse. There's to be a funeral, I'm told." She answered easily but seemed troubled.

I asked, "Anything odd happen yesterday? Other than the, ah, death, of course?"

She shook her head. We'd almost reached the lounge when she paused, her step uncertain. When I moved toward the rail, she followed.

Brow puckered, she said, "Yesterday I got to sick bay first. The medicine cabinet door was ajar. It worried me. If something's stolen, it would be my fault, you see?"

"Is it usually locked?"

"No," she said unhappily, "because it should be accessible in an emergency. Can't be searching for a key if someone's deadly ill."

"Anything missing?"

She worried her lower lip, like Diana when brooding, then said, "Chloroform. We keep it for minor surgeries . . . broken bones and tooth extractions."

And she'd been seen with the don, who'd leaned on her, looking groggy.

"Chloroform? Why didn't you say, when I asked you?"

She mangled her perfect little lip, and blurted out, "The doctor's a good man. I don't want to get him in trouble. You won't suspect him, will you? He can't have done anything. He's a physician!"

I smiled at her innocence. "You were together all morning?"

She nodded, searching my face for the expected condemnation, then looked relieved. "He's married. But she doesn't deserve him. She's all high and mighty, looking down on him as a lowly ship's surgeon. I try to be, well, a friend."

＊＊＊

Our ship made good time and my seasickness receded. The doctor and Nurse Shay's reticence had been explained, but not Bigby's odd behavior in the dining room. Something about him irked me, like a map where something was amiss, but one could not tell what. With dozens of passengers and crew to question, he and I had come up with a plan, though it was not much of one—Bigby would question crewmen. I would continue inobtrusive inquiries with passengers. Given my reservations, including him in the investigation was ill-advised, but until I had something to confront him with, it seemed best to keep close watch on him.

"The line's reputation is at stake, so please be discreet," he'd repeated this morning, with a meaningful look.

At luncheon, the company at our table held a subdued conversation about the chance of sighting dolphins and whales. Furtive looks revealed cracks in their camaraderie. Was it you, their glances questioned as they gazed at each other. They retreated into formal politeness, their replies guarded and excessively correct, their elbows in, sitting stiffly as they consumed the chef's sumptuous, herbed salmon and creamed potatoes. Our steward served silently, his hands no less deft than before, his cheerfulness conspicuous in its absence.

Afterward, standing with Diana at the guardrail, I contemplated the ocean. The fog of previous days had dissipated, and passengers lay on their deck chairs in the sun. Even the steerage deck was crowded, people sitting or lying stretched out on the boards. Below decks must be sweltering right about now.

I ducked toward Diana and said in Hindustani, "Something's been puzzling me. Why didn't Hawley trust this investigation to his chief officer?"

An excessive precaution, perhaps, but others could hear us as they passed. Without missing a beat, Diana replied in the same language, "Mr. Bigby? Think he has a hand in it?"

"Unlikely. But he certainly knows more than he's saying."

I didn't hold that against him. He didn't know or trust me. A seasoned officer would not give up private intelligence easily. But no, it was more. Something was off in the rapport between him and the captain.

"Bigby seemed ah, cagey, almost . . . uncomfortable. Kept shifting on his feet. If he wants the crime solved, why hold back something crucial? To protect himself?" I remembered the concern in his face. "Or is he protecting someone else? Hawley seems eager for me to get to the bottom of this. So why's Bigby afraid?"

She shifted, frowning. "Jim, do you think . . . perhaps he suspects the captain?"

That startled me. "Captain Hawley? He was quite visible that day. He'd taken charge of the bridge at half past noon."

Diana tilted her head. "Over an hour before the body was found. He could have done it and walked upstairs cool as you please."

I considered the music room, the don's body still on the chair, his head slumped forward upon his chest. Not Hawley, surely? His weather-beaten face had been creased with worry. He'd seemed keen that I take on the inquiry. Was that so he could appear to make an effort without really doing so?

I said, "There was no blood, so he'd hardly need to clean up. But you could say the same of Bigby. They took the noon readings of the sun together at twenty past twelve. If he gave the bridge over to the captain ten minutes later, that's time enough to lug the don to the music room and kill him."

She stared, her brown eyes shocked. "Then neither of them have alibis for those two hours."

CHAPTER 8

A FUNERAL

The don's funeral was announced after luncheon, so we returned to dress for it. Diana put out a new black morning coat for me. I lifted a sleeve, feeling the expensive fabric. "When did we acquire this, sweet?"

She smiled, lacing on her kid boots. "Made some purchases while you were away." Her indigo skirt and bodice were paired with white hat and gloves and short velvet cape.

Through bustling corridors, we set off for the foredeck. With exhaustive inspections and five meals to prepare, the crew's routine must have been strained to accommodate the funeral, yet officers and crew came in full uniform. Bigby and Captain Hawley held their uniform caps under their arms.

Our ship coasted along steadily, casting a long bow wave that whispered over the waters. A crowd lined the deck three deep, with more assembled along the port and starboard deck.

The killer was here. I was certain of it, though I could not explain why. He was standing among us, and most passengers suspected it. The space they kept between themselves, their wary sideways glances shouted suspicion. "It has to be a madman," Mrs. Evansworth had written in her testimony. "No one else would do a barbaric thing like that!"

No—a madman would be caught. The methodical way this murder had been carried out denoted no insanity but a vicious, determined foe. Who hated Don Juan that much? Trouble was, I had no suspects—or too many. With only days to Liverpool, I could not afford to work each of them out before moving to the next. I'd have to explore them simultaneously.

Three black-clad figures sat at the bow: the heavily veiled widow, another Spanish woman and De Cullar wearing a high collar, his expression remote. Behind them, an honor guard of officers stood at attention. Was there a protocol for the death of a dignitary on board? Dressed in somber colors, passengers assembled on the forward upper deck toward midship. By the portside rail, a stretcher bore the deceased wrapped in dark canvas.

Though I'd served fifteen years with the British army in India, I'd not witnessed a burial at sea. But in my first year as a groom I'd been commandeered into grave duty with other sepoys on the retreat to Khandahar. We'd found bodies strewn over a hillside, identified them as the Bombay Grenadiers and Jacob's Rifle Regiments. We lifted and covered them, and then set to digging. They would remain in Maiwand. There was no gun salute, no assembly; the lads were too weary, eyes dull, hands blistered. Passing slowly down the trench, the company padre said a few words over each grave as a body was lowered. Records were kept, personal effects stowed carefully. Sutton wrote over six hundred letters to families in Bombay. The next month we gathered reinforcements from Kabul and forced the emir into a treaty. We knew where those bodies lay. The arid slope would be covered with yellow-green brush now. But this . . . I gazed over the rail at the vast, unmarked ocean.

Bigby made a brief introduction and offered his condolences to the bereaved. Opening a book, he read in a deep, clear voice, ". . . therefore commit his body to the deep . . ."

Among the audience would be witnesses who'd seen or spoken to the don that morning: deck stewardess Edna Pickle, the brothers Farley, Madame Evangeline Pontin, and Mr. and Mrs. Evansworth.

I did not know Madame Pontin by sight but picked out the Farley brothers among a knot of smoking-room chaps. Mr. and Mrs. Evansworth stood in front, sans brood, their faces devoid of emotion. They'd likely conscripted a stewardess to watch the young ones. Shouldn't the two older children have attended? Did the Evansworths not want me interviewing . . . what were their names? Miss Rose, I recollected, and Leo.

Miss Pickle, pale and blond, was flanked by a pair of stewardesses . . . for moral support? Why did they think she required it? Had someone mentioned the "nurse" leading the don to his death? As the only woman serving on deck that morning, she might well be suspected of involvement. The stewardesses had linked arms with her in solidarity.

Struck by the similarity of their build and hairstyles (coifed under neat hats), I realized they could pass for each other at a distance—or seen from above. Was one of *them* the mysterious nurse?

Among the passengers, a statuesque woman stood alone, observing the ceremony from under a wide plumed hat. I guessed this was Madame Evangeline Pontin, whom Diana had described at dinner as "actress, once famous." Nearby, three young women were flanked by a host of dashing fellows making remarks. The group tittered, drawing stares. A tall military man scowled at the young peacocks, dampening them to silence. Blast, I had neither suspects nor evidence. Nothing, in fact, no leads.

Well-fed men of industry watched stoically, their bowlers in hand. Was one of them suppressing a grin at his clever escape? Frustration clenched my gut. Dash it, I had few days left. Only days to unveil the culprit and not a clue where to begin.

"Made like unto his glorious body . . ." said Bigby, perspiration shining on his forehead, ". . . we commend Don Juan Nepomuceno to Almighty God, and commit his body to its resting place."

I remembered the gaunt, proud gentleman beside me the other night, a man from another era, his life cut short in ruthless fury. Four sturdy sailors raised the gurney bearing the don's canvas-wrapped body. Walking in slow unison to the rail, they raised one end of the bier. The long shape slid forward slowly at first. It dropped into the waves with a small splash.

Don Juan passed into history as an unfortunate victim on board a fine steamer; an inexplicable death, as yet unresolved. Still somber, the crowd waited until the captain escorted the widow and her entourage away before dispersing. There had been no music, no solemn hymns, no thirteen-gun salute—he'd not been British—no pomp or ceremony for a governor. And no one offered the widow condolences! Her unbending posture and layers of black veil precluded it. A sobbing wife would have received more sympathy.

Passengers moved as though uncertain they should resume their activities. Some cast wary looks as they queued at the lower stairway to the cabins. Trouble was, it wasn't over. Until we had a culprit and an explanation, the don's death would pose a question in each mind, an uncomfortable thought that would haunt each exchange: Was it you?

"I've found something," Diana murmured, her hand secure in the crook of my arm.

I glanced at her in surprise. "A lead?"

"The brothers Farley. Look them up, will you?"

"Those two? Likely wagering over cards or the ship's speed or drinking themselves silly."

"Now, now. Don't be glum, Jim, it's most unbecoming." She grinned as though she'd just eaten an enormous bowl of Bassetts ice cream.

I hid a smile. Was it the sea air or the investigation that lit her face and brought that keen edge to her gaze? "What did you find?"

"Vernon said the old man disapproved of them. Called them 'silly fops' to their faces. Remember that anonymous note?"

Silly fops? What had they done to merit that? "Vernon? I wouldn't believe it of him. Much more likely to be Algernon."

Her eyebrows twitched. "Maybe. He seems so proper but has a look . . . as though he's assessing a person and making nasty deductions."

Had one of them penned the anonymous note? If the pair disliked the don enough to write it, that might denote a previous relationship, and not a cordial one. It seemed a crowing sort of arrogance . . .

Diana went to call on Mrs. Barlow. Locking my jaw, I asked the thin chief steward for the whereabouts of the two brothers Farley. He obliged, and I tracked them down in the smoking room.

Located across the hall from the ladies' boudoir—marked with a fanciful sign WINTER GARDEN—the men's domain boasted wood paneling, dark leather seats and piles of old newspapers under a cloud of expensive smoke and the comforting smell of spirits. Still in black frock coats, both Farleys held crystalware containing amber liquid.

After some polite remarks, I said, "You sat on deck near Don Juan?"

The younger one nodded, hand curled around the glass for support.

I glanced at him. "Vernon, yes? Did you speak with him?"

"Gosh, no. Didn't look like he wanted to be disturbed."

"What d'you mean?"

He made a face, shrugging. "One knows, doesn't one? Obvious he didn't think much of us. Just in the way he looked." He turned down his mouth in a sneer.

"You knew him?"

"Goodness, no."

"You'd spoken to him before?"

I went on, probing my way through the maze of social relationships—the don was an acquaintance, yes, a nodding acquaintance, but not a bloke one sought out. Then he said, "Anyway, one couldn't get a word in, because the other fellow kept whispering to him."

"Other fellow?"

"Palmer Bly. Of the McKesson-Blys?" When I showed no recognition, he looked askance. "Owns half the hills in Vermont. Dairies, farms, railways, canal traffic. You're not from Vermont, are you?" He smiled at his own wit.

Mr. Bly had not provided a statement after dinner that first night. Had he missed the meal and the captain's announcement?

"And Mr. Bly was alone?"

The older brother, Algernon, sent Vernon a warning look, so I turned to him. "Weren't you there too?"

He huffed. "Must have slipped my mind, for goodness' sakes. We were on deck from about ten until noon, and we left for luncheon after the bell. All there is to it."

"Was Mr. Bly with someone else?"

"The deck was full, man. Lots of people about."

Fewer than a dozen had come forward. It didn't surprise me. "Did you speak with the don?"

He chuckled. "That stiff? God, no."

"Stiff? He was already dead?"

He drew back, startled. "N-no. I just meant. Stiff shirt, y'know? He looked down on the young as gadflies. Terribly supercilious."

We'd been waffling about this business for too long. Time to be more direct.

"Why were you there?"

He shrugged and patted his vest for something. "It's the promenade—smoking room wasn't serving the good stuff yet. Too early. And, well . . . why not?"

"Who did you speak with?"

I glanced at Vernon and realized I should have directed the question to him. Settling my attention upon him, I waited. Few can bear the weight of a long silence without breaking it.

Seconds later he wilted. "Mrs. Bly. She's from New York—a distant relation, actually, on my mother's side."

His brother snapped shut his cigarette case with a loud click. I kept my gaze on Vernon. "You knew she'd be sailing on the *Etruria*?"

"No! We'd just met at dinner!"

He'd protested too vehemently. "You've sailed together before?"

"We met on other crossings, yes."

"Right." I frowned, returning to the day of the crime. "Mr. and Mrs. Bly were speaking with the don. Did they sit to either side of him?"

Vernon looked appalled. "Good Lord, no! Bly was beside Don Juan. The don's wife was on his other side."

I made a note to ask Mr. Palmer Bly about his conversation with the don.

"Did you see the nurse on deck?"

Vernon looked blank, then relieved. "You mean Edna, the deck stewardess?"

Edna. He knew her name. But why did he look as though he'd been offered a reprieve? I paused, then said, "Let's start with her. Did you see her serve the Spanish couple?"

"I suppose. Didn't notice, sorry," he said, his manner unapologetic.

"Did you?" I asked the older brother.

Algernon shrugged. I wasn't getting anywhere. Idly, I asked, "Did you speak with Mrs. Bly?"

Algernon shot up, glowering. "What are you insinuating?"

I blinked. What on earth had upset him? "She's your cousin, yes?"

"And a damn fine girl," he snapped, daring me to contradict him.

Well, well, well. That's why they were on the promenade deck at ten o'clock.

"Was the nurse there that morning?"

My change of topic disconcerted him. He'd been preparing to defend his relationship with Mrs. Bly, but I wasn't concerned with shipboard romances. Now he frowned in concentration. "Edna took our orders, and Mrs. Bly had a lemonade. That's all I recall."

He hailed a friend, made his apologies to me without a glance and the pair dashed off. They'd made a quick escape to avoid further questions. Or was it because of the odd looks we'd been getting from other patrons?

I leaned back, pondering their words. The fashionable Blys had been with Don Juan but had not come forward. If the don was meant to recognize his killer in the mirror, wouldn't it be someone he knew?

Disapproving glances followed me as I left the smoking lounge. Now that I was known as a detective, had I been demoted from fellow passenger to a working-class bloke? I'd need to push my witnesses harder if the first-cabin passengers had closed me out.

Later, in our stateroom, when I mentioned this to Diana, she scoffed. "Upper classes? Whatever do you mean?"

"They joke in Latin," I grumbled. "*Nil desperandum! Ex pede Herculem*. You heard them at dinner. You understand it."

"*Nil desperandum*—do not despair—from an ode by Horace. *Ex pede Herculem* . . . thus by his foot, we can measure Hercules," she translated. "A part explains the whole."

"That's what I mean. I don't have the same background, the classics, the old Etonian education. How do I get them to trust me, to spill what they know?"

She bent over a wardrobe trunk and rummaged around, then with a satisfied look, she returned with a round mirror. "Think of one of them. Algernon, Mr. Evansworth."

What was she up to now? I brought Captain Hawley to mind, his deep-set eyes and russet beard.

"Now look." She handed me the glass.

A gloomy fellow gazed back, with neat hair and a grim, clean-shaven face, jaw framed by a snowy white collar. Upper class? Well, I certainly looked the part, I thought as I handed back the mirror. Seated beside them, I'd fit in. A competent disguise.

Diana sent me a long thoughtful look, then said, "Jim, you distrust them, so they're careful around you. That's all it is."

I considered it. Was I skeptical because of my ragged upbringing? At fifteen I'd run away from the mission orphanage to join up. As a stable boy in the British Indian army, I'd traveled on carts and slept in stables. I'd woken with a start of fear each morning, a flood of shame when I could not decipher the officers' English. So I learned to speak it.

As a sepoy I often led the morning drill, keeping my gaze down because officers watched for signs of insubordination. Smiling was "Bloody cheek!" Laughter invited the back of a hand across one's face. I'd taken blows in the orphanage without knowing the cause, as well as in the army. Only later did I learn that my name was an abomination—the joining of a good clean English moniker with my Indian last name, my mother's name. My mixed-race heritage brought astonishment, when people learned of it, and then disgust. Later, when I began boxing, men were careful around me, yet I read their distrust and kept my distance.

I'd had some luck too. After Maiwand, Major Sutton was promoted to Colonel and took an interest in me. Sturdy, blond and affable, he taught me to box. True, returning blow for blow in the ring gave me much satisfaction. There at least, I was equal. Sutton's boxing prodigy—Englishmen left me alone after that. As I rose in rank, however, sepoys got cautious around me too.

I'd had few close friends, Rashid Khan—the surly Pathan, Amit Pathak who could lift my heart with a tune, and Jeet Chowdhary, who'd once been a dockworker. They'd been plain, working-class men, as was my friend Stephen Smith, an Englishman who enjoyed whiskey and was often in debt. The British officers, the erudite editor Byram in Bombay and Diana's prosperous father, Burjor, those men I'd watched from afar. Was that why the toffs seemed so alien to me, so suspicious?

CHAPTER 9

A MISSING HAT AND A DIPLOMAT

An investigation is often built from the accounts of those nearest the victim, yet I had scant time for a systematic inquiry. I was fairly certain that the old don had been drugged with the missing chloroform. A nurse might have led him down the promenade deck toward the music room at the bow, but the only person to notice her was our chief officer. Edna, the deck stewardess, insisted she'd not left the area until noon, and that no nurse had assisted her. Wouldn't that mean the "nurse" was Edna herself?

I'd set out to interview Miss Edna Pickle the stewardess, when the debutante Miss Rood waved her kerchief to draw my attention. Surprised, I climbed to the games area where I contemplated the calm young woman in her slender gloves and white-trimmed ensemble. She'd dressed for deck activities and steady seas.

When I reached her, she reported a stolen hat.

"I had it in the morning, but at lunchtime, it was gone," said Miss Felicity Rood.

"Your missing hat."

"Yes." She glanced at the group of young people playing shuffleboard, clearly eager to return to them. "I took it off in the Winter Garden. A straw bonnet with white ribbon and roses on the side. Small roses, done in pink."

I smiled at her detailed description. She'd summoned me to convey this most essential information. A set of burly sailors passed us, touching a finger to their foreheads as they passed, which puzzled me, until I realized it was the nautical version of a salute.

It was no hardship to spend a moment in Miss Rood's company, yet I groaned. Now that I was known as the ship's detective, I was approached about all manner of frivolous matters. Fellows protested their losses to card sharks; women reported rude stewards; dowagers complained about flighty stewardesses. It did no good to tell these charmers that I was investigating only the murder of Don Juan. Captain Hawley would prefer they forgot that bit of unpleasantness. So I jotted down their concerns and sent them away, content.

I left Miss Rood, feeling as though I were drowning in minutiae. Hats, bowling balls, secret assignations. An old man had been garroted, but it must not ruin a pleasant crossing. Feeling morose, I went to find the deck stewardess who, along with Miss Rood, had found Don Juan's body. After all, who had a better opportunity to spike his drink than the one who served it?

I found Miss Pickle in the staff dining room holding court like a blond deity. Surrounded by uniformed staff, she was saying, "I don't know that anything was different. He seemed half asleep, poor dear. His wife, now—oh, she's something, always, get this, girl, get that. The lemonade's too sweet, or too warm, or too cold!"

Her glance met mine and she jumped to her feet. "Oh! Sir, I'm so sorry." She blushed, looking mortified.

"My apologies, miss," I soothed, "I realize it's your time off. Might I have a word?"

Reassured by this politeness, she was all smiles, and graciously accompanied me to the open upper deck.

I started off with a bit of small talk. She was from Lewisham, a working-class town near London, she said. She'd been with Cunard four years.

With her milk white lashes and light grey eyes she'd be a favorite on any deck. I smiled. "You started young."

"At eighteen. One must have the energy for it, at any age, 'course." This in deference to my far greater years. She was a diplomatic little thing. How old did she imagine I was?

Propping my notebook on the railing, I asked what she'd done yesterday morning.

"Just the usual. A few children to be taken to nanny, requests for lemonade, fruit juices."

"Beer?"

"Oh yes. Other drinks are served by the deck steward, but I bring the little bottles out, since they are chilled with the pineapple and apple juices. At eleven I helped Terry serve the bouillon. That's from a trolley, see?"

"Did Don Juan request anything?"

"White wine. Terry brought it, but I took it to him, with señora's lemonade."

"Which she rejected."

She gave a weak smile. "Yes. I went back to the pantry, but I had other drinks to fetch."

"What other drinks? Who else was with them?"

She frowned. "They were alone for the most part. I went over to the port side for a bit—it was sunny there, so Lily needed help with her lot. We're always short of chairs on the leeward side, my side, which is shady. But passengers get hot in the sun and are more . . . well, they need more help."

"They request more libations," I supplied, and was rewarded with a grin.

"Did anyone sit by the don and his wife?"

Her lips pressed together in concentration. "I think so, but if they didn't ask for anything, I didn't notice. Oh! The two young men, of course. The younger wanted a beer, but the older wouldn't let him. They both had pineapple juice."

"Recall their names?"

She looked blank, then said, "The older one said, 'Don't be an ass, Vernon.' Yes. I'm sure he said that, because Vernon was quite cut up about it, and I had to pretend I didn't hear and ask them to repeat the order because the wind was so loud."

A diplomat indeed! "Anyone else?"

"A woman, I think, but señora kept me going back and forth, and my shift was almost through. I'd got a blister from my new shoes, you see, so I couldn't wait for it to be done, that morning."

I smiled at the young lady and closed my book. "Just one thing more. When you left, who was still on deck?"

"The don was asleep. He'd asked for a blanket and tucked it around himself."

"Alone?"

She paused, blinking. "Yes . . ."

"But you're not certain. Was the señora there?"

She worried her lip, then said, "I don't think so?" She glanced hopefully at me. If I'd said Doña Josefina was present, she'd gladly have agreed. I waited, but it was no good. Her face fell. "I wish I'd paid more attention. I was rushing to get my shoes off."

"Did you visit the sick bay?" When she gaped at me, I added, "For your blisters?"

"Bless you, no. I have a salve in my room. I just needed to remove those shoes."

"You returned to your quarters, and then?"

"Then, to the staff dining room, where you found me today."

I jotted down her alibi, which included Chief Steward Johnson. She gave the women's first names but was more formal with the males. Proper decorum ruled among the liner's staff, it seemed. "What time was this?"

"Just past noon. The luncheon gong went, on my way to the staff dining hall."

"How long were you there?"

"Almost until two, I think. One of the bartenders was singing. He plays the banjo."

If confirmed, it put her in the clear. Yet her restless fingers plucked at her sleeve. What wasn't she saying? Was it just the awkwardness of being questioned, or was something else on her mind?

I asked, "So . . . why did Miss Rood call you to open the music room?"

"I was off duty, but she didn't realize." She smiled.

I closed my book, and she left with a girlish flounce of her skirt.

At the staff dining hall, the chef consulted a ledger. Edna had an ironclad alibi for the mealtime, but he could not recall when the music ended. Weary, I sat down at a table and considered my suspects: Edna's shift ended at noon and she resumed duty at five. Being at passengers' beck and call meant she'd been on her feet for hours. Her afternoon was her own; it did not prevent her returning on deck while off duty.

Nurse Shay and Doctor Witherspoon—they alibied each other and the missing chloroform was convenient, but why tell me? And Bigby. What the devil was it about Bigby that felt odd? Had he invented the suspicious nurse "helping" Don Juan? Why? Was it to divert suspicion? Stewardess Edna—only because she'd been on deck and could see when Don Juan was alone; and possibly the Farley brothers, because through flippancy or arrogance, they avoided questions.

That reminded me to check their story about Mr. and Mrs. Bly, so I borrowed paper and ink to dash off a short note, and dispatched it with a deck steward.

Time was short. I returned to the list in my notebook, feeling low. I was missing something. What the devil was it?

The deck shifted, tilting my chair. A steward beside me smiled, saying, "Just a bit choppy today, eh? We've got a blow coming."

Grunting a reply, I returned to our cabin and huffed to Diana about Edna and Miss Rood.

She scoffed. "Missing hat? Silly girl's left it somewhere. It'll turn up, and she'll come round to report it." She gazed steadily at me. "She's rather taken with you, you know." Her eyes glinted in amusement. "Careful, Captain Jim, her sort loves a fellow in uniform, but you'll do. Your military stride, I'm afraid. Unmistakable."

I chuckled at the irony. A vicious murder had been perpetrated but nothing stopped girls batting eyelashes at "uniforms." As I shed my coat and vest, I pondered our situation. Death did not exempt these gilded halls. Someone's sophisticated veneer hid a seething fury. My chest felt tight, and now the cabin seemed to close in around me. My head throbbing in time with the dull beat of the engines, I paced the floor as Diana brushed out and twisted her full, curly hair into a high "do," preparing to join a card game in the upper lounge.

With almost a thousand people on board, how the devil had the killer managed to escape notice? Dropping onto the sofa, I picked up my new book, Diana's recent gift, *The Adventures of Sherlock Holmes*, to help me unwind my tangled thoughts.

"It seems to me," I said a short while later, "that 'The Adventure of the Speckled Band' and 'The Red-Headed League' are really the same story. A client arrives and poses to Holmes and Watson his or her conundrum. They reconnoiter the location, where once again, Holmes deduces far more than poor Watson." I had developed an affection for the diligent chronicler whose narration so admired the famous sleuth. "The pair then arrive before the crime and wait in darkness for its execution, well in time to put paid to it. It seems quite easy, when all the pieces are laid before one!"

"Now, Jim, don't grumble," Diana said, settling against me. "Everything's easy in hindsight. In the moment, while one is standing there, it's far more confusing."

In the moment. Standing there. I stilled, remembering a burly officer outlined in the fog against the lighted bridge. Those square shoulders. That wide-legged stance.

"Diana," I said. "That morning before luncheon. Fellow arguing with the distraught woman—remember him?"

Her breath caught. She swung around to me. "Goodness—the officer on the quarterdeck. Why, it looked like Mr. Bigby!"

CHAPTER 10

MAL DE MER

The sun gleamed overhead as I got up to find the first officer, but I felt overheated and stifled in my lounge suit. I rubbed my midriff, feeling an unease brought on by the swing of the deck. Dammit, not now!

The engine vibration jarred the boards under my feet. How had I managed the three weeks from Bombay through the Suez? I frowned, remembering. I'd barely left the cabin. Either I lay in a daze of nausea, dreading I'd puke up my meal or kneeling, my head hanging over the water closet. Even when I'd eaten nothing, my stomach forgot and insisted on having a go at it.

My belly heaved. Thrusting open the door, I lurched to the water closet and emptied my stomach, clutching the ceramic as I regurgitated my breakfast. The rictus eased, leaving me as weak as a newborn foal. Wobbling to my feet I washed, relieved for the moment, though my headache boded ill for the evening.

Bollocks. I needed to question Bigby, but my cranium pulsed as though an ax was chopping industriously at the base of my skull.

"Poor dear," said Diana, passing me a cold cloth. She'd given up any hope of her card game, knowing I was a poor sailor on most days.

Sinking into a couch I pressed my throbbing temples, then let out a
grunt as the ship tilted left. My mouth watered a warning. I swallowed
hard, but it was no use. Just in time I returned to the lavatory where
my stomach conducted a violent revolt. Thankfully, Diana stayed on the
couch, calling out encouragement.

Groaning, I splashed my haggard face and dabbed it with a pink-
tasseled towel. Tossing my lunch should have dispelled my nausea, but it
was gathering again.

"Hmm." Diana regarded me, feet wide, standing at an angle of twenty
degrees. In a soothing tone she asked, "Jim, can you swim?"

"No. Can you?" I sat, screwing my eyes tight to avoid looking at the
porthole where the horizon hung at an impossible angle.

"Oh, yes. As children we swam often at the *talav* pool in Bombay.
People thought I was a boy. In Ooty we had a darling little pond in Papa's
coffee estate."

I leaned back in surprise. She was trying to distract me. Despite the
fond image of a teenage Adi and coltish young Diana, lean and bronzed
by the sun, leaping and splashing each other, it wasn't working. The floor
rocked back to center and began to creak its way up the opposite wall.
My stomach wanted to go the other way.

Hovering nearby, she said, "People float, you know. Especially in
salt—"

"You, perhaps. I'm rather heavy." I pried open an eye. The cabin was
still moving and now the engines added an odd thumping noise.

A dimple appeared in Diana's cheek. "You can float too."

She prodded my chest with a finger. "If you're clenched up like this,
you'll drop through the water. Stand stiff like a pencil"—she stood and
imitated a wooden soldier, arms tight at her sides—"and you'll go deeper.
Spread out like a jellyfish, and you'll float." She spread her arms wide,
her feet in a large V.

Curling onto the settee beside me, she went on. "When you first hit
the water, your chest clenches tight. That's good. Hold on to the air. It
makes you lighter, like a rubber balloon."

I filled my lungs, to see how long I could hold my breath. The bands around my cranium constricted.

Patting my arm, she went on. "Don't fret about it. When it starts to hurt, let it out slowly. Your body will right itself. Reach up, cup your hands and pull the water toward you."

She demonstrated, grabbing the air with each hand in turns. "When you come up, flip onto your back. You'll rock a bit and settle. Your eyes will likely sting a little. But you'll be face up, able to breathe. Don't leave your mouth open, though, because you'd dip about and get splashed."

I could envision that. Faceup, water bobbing in my ears, my mouth clear of the waves. I could stay like that, I thought. That wasn't terrible.

"Jim, come, pop your ears," she commanded, demonstrating. "It's something I learned at Boston Presbyterian. Hold your nose and build up the air inside. Like a kettle about to go off."

I grinned at her comical face and tried to replicate it. A crack sounded in my head, near the jaw. The vise holding my temples released and went off to torture someone else.

"My God, Diana," I said, hopeful for the first time this trip. "You are a marvel."

"It's nice to be reminded!" She grinned, jumping up to pluck a page pinned to the sheet on the wall. "Now back to work!"

One by one we reexamined the witness statements.

I explained, "I've been thinking about that argument we witnessed. Bigby didn't mention it when we spoke. Sound suspicious?"

Diana scoffed. "Oh, I don't know. The murder would overshadow other things."

"I'll ask him," I said, getting to my feet. The cabin rocked. I tensed, but my stomach seemed all right.

Diana grinned, putting on a scarf. "Well, well! Don't tell me it worked!"

I glanced about, trying to gauge the motion of the ship. It had steadied, for the moment. Or I had.

CHAPTER 11

A CRY

I found Chief Officer Bigby on the bridge, writing in the ship's log. Stopping at the door, I cleared my throat and waited, watching him. Why hadn't he protested when the captain handed the investigation to me, a civilian, instead of him? If I was him, I'd be furious over the slight.

"A moment, O'Trey," he said, completing his notations, then came over and shook hands with a confident, firm grip. Older than me by a few years and heavier by twenty pounds, he looked like he knew how to use his fists. He was light on his feet. One can always tell a boxer by the way he walks.

I'd need to jar that careful composure to get at the truth. At any other time, I might have liked the man, but now I could not afford to. My task had put us in opposition.

A direct question would take him by surprise. Pointing to the outer door, I said, "Day before yesterday—before dinner, you stood here and spoke with a woman. Who was she?"

When he didn't reply, I opened the glass door that led outside. He followed me to the top of the companionway and paused, dark eyes wide, but did not deny it. Instead, he stepped out and shut the door behind us. "You mean a passenger?"

"She seemed upset."

"Oh, yes. The woman was hysterical. Why'd you ask?"

Gazing out, he awaited my answer calmly. Flicking a glance at the pulse at his throat, I said, "In a murder investigation, any little matter may prove important. Her name?"

He tightened his lips. "Alice Fry. Works for Mrs. Barlow, the invalid in the wheelchair."

"What did she want?"

He drew back, eyes hooded. "She was upset, ranting. Difficult to understand her."

This blatant falsehood surprised me. Then I recalled that he had not seen Diana and me, standing below. He'd said, "Been twenty *years*!" with suppressed emotion. Yet before confronting him, I'd question the distraught woman. It might be a personal matter unrelated to the murder. This case was a conundrum, and I could not afford to ignore any peculiarity.

Changing tack, I said, "That morning, was the captain walking the upper deck before he took the bridge?"

He nodded. "He mingles with passengers when we have calm seas. Gives them confidence. Cunard encourages it."

"Where did you go after you left him?"

He gave me a look. "Back to my quarters, dead tired."

I searched his bland features. "Mr. Bigby, Edna the stewardess was at luncheon in the staff dining room. So, who did you see with the don?"

He grimaced. "I was standing above them. Could have been one of the other deck girls, I suppose."

Trouble was, there were only four female staff including Nurse Shay, and their time was tightly supervised by the stewards. They attended the children from first class, who dined separately. Old ladies like Mrs. Evansworth kept a close watch, if only to complain about them.

"Staff, or passenger?"

"Staff, I thought. Can't be sure, O'Trey. Wish I'd looked harder!"

"No one else noticed her. Where were you standing exactly? Can you show me?"

He flushed. "Now?"

"Yes."

He ran a hand through his neatly shorn hair, looking harried, his eyes darting about.

Just then a female voice spoke below us. "Hello, gentlemen!"

Miss Felicity Rood approached, sliding a red scarf off her neck to fan herself. Her face glowed with the flush of exercise—or was it something else? She smiled up at Bigby with an offhand familiar manner.

Bigby had turned stonelike. Drat. Diana could be right. Perhaps Miss Rood did have a penchant for men in uniform. I said quietly, "Croquet, Miss Rood? In this heat?"

"Shuffleboard, Mr. O'Trey. As for the heat, tosh! It's a lovely day. Like yesterday afternoon, when I saw you on the bridge, Mr. Bigby. I waved, you recall?"

"Ma'am," said Bigby.

"Hmm." My sideways glance confirmed his color was still high. He studied the ocean with close interest.

I studied the young lady, "You're certain that was yesterday, miss?"

"Of course!"

"Righto," I said, giving Bigby a nod in farewell, since Miss Rood had alibied him. Where did that leave my investigation? A strange nurse, and everyone away at luncheon when the Spanish diplomat was killed between noon and one forty when Miss Rood arrived at the music room. Fifteen minutes to struggle with the door and find the chief steward seemed reasonable. But until I understood the nature of Bigby's argument with Alice, I would not dismiss the incident.

* * *

I returned from Mrs. Barlow's feeling something was amiss. I had knocked on the door to her cabin, but no one was in. At the ladies' lounge, too, I'd had no luck. Where were the women this morning? Leaving a message for Alice with their steward, I walked back along the open promenade deck, collecting my thoughts.

Diana wasn't in. I looked around the empty cabin. Had she said where she was going? I could not recall. Next, I worked through passengers' statements, tying off alibis, crossing names off our passenger list as I progressed. Many concurred, but most had been in their cabins or did not recall who they were with.

My pen rolled away as our cabin tilted. I drew a cautious breath, assessing. Was I going another bout with the water closet?

Diana returned, her skin glowing, and told me she'd enjoyed a game of quoits with the Farleys and Miss Rood.

I'd always preferred army life over sailing, but I was damned if I'd let the sea turn me into a jellyfish. Daring the heavens to crank that screw again, I put away my things with a touch of bravado and asked, "Shall we try the upper deck?"

In answer, she picked up a stole. "Come on, then. Walking will help."

On deck, she chuckled as wisps escaped her coiffure in the breeze. Her despondency seeming long past, her arm tucked into my elbow.

Stomach knotted, I stepped carefully, conscious of Diana's easy gait. How did she develop those sea legs so quickly? On our first sailing it had taken me weeks to settle down, well past the Suez. I sighed, thinking of our sweet wedding night. She'd curled over me, her astonishing mass of hair tumbling around us. Then I'd tossed up my dinner in the chamber pot—a fine end to a promising evening! I glanced at the sea and stifled a groan at the memory of retching as my gut tried fervently to turn itself inside out. Bless her, Diana had been all gentle concern.

Treading the sparsely populated deck, the sun dipped toward the horizon as I admired the freshly painted lifeboats creaking against their pullies. Almost a day had passed since the murder. Why didn't Hawley want me to speak directly with the widow? Damn this protocol. I puzzled over it as we took our third turn, passing the shuffleboard and quoits.

I checked my old pocket watch, the only object I owned that came from my own blood. "Dinner at half past six, yes?"

Before she could answer, a cry rang out, a shriek that rooted me to the boards.

Ahead, a young couple pointed, exclaiming. Behind a lifeboat, something white fluttered beyond the railing.

A woman, leaning over the water? She seemed to totter on the outer edge. Drat! Had she got past the ship's rail?

Voices cried, "Come back, miss!" "Oh, save her!"

Dropping Diana's hand, I charged across the deck. The woman swayed forward, or was it backward? Her white dress flapped. A large hat obscured her face.

Before I could reach her, she dropped, falling through the surface with barely a splash.

"No!" I heard Diana's shocked cry. My palms hit the railing as I bellowed, "Man overboard!"

Shouts repeated up and down the deck: "Throw the Kisbee rings!"

Along the side, crew tossed out life preservers tied to ropes.

Searching the spot where she'd fallen, I clenched the rail in frustration. Like most soldiers, I'd never learned to swim. The sea held the same sort of fascination I felt for large carnivores. The growl of the ship's engines abruptly ceased; the throb and vibration ebbed, but her bulk swept on, cutting through the waves with merciless speed.

"Make way!" I called, moving back along the railing, my gaze trained to where I'd seen the woman sink. Was that the spot? The ocean undulated alongside.

An officer cornered me, cutting off my view. "You, sir. You were near. What happened?"

I peered around him, calling, "Diana, mark where she went in!" My shout was redundant. Passengers lined the rail, scouring the surface.

To the anxious officer I said, "Don't know. Barely saw her."

He asked a few more questions, but I could only wave him toward the young couple who'd alerted me.

Over the officer's shoulder I saw Diana back away, her gaze steady on the water. She stopped where the deck ended, her hip against the aft rail.

It is no mean feat to stop a steamer of seven thousand gross tons. Our information pamphlet said it consumed three hundred and twenty tons of coal daily. With a shuddering screech, our engines reversed, churning the ocean into great bubbling froth as we turned in a slow curve. How close was that propeller? Would its current drag the woman into the blades?

I could see no sign of her, neither white dress nor straw hat floated on the surface. Waves curled against the hull as we slowed.

From our present height, I estimated she'd fallen over two floors. If she hadn't broken her neck when she hit the water, the shock of cold would make her gasp. Would she come up? Her clothes would cling to her limbs, wind around her like a shroud to drag her down. Was that when she began to drown? Or would she rise, fighting the watery push and pull? The need to breathe would build and build. She'd put it off, fighting the urge until her lungs screamed. Then she'd pull in a breath, and find it wet, chilling, cold. Water flooding her nose, her throat, her lungs. Struggling to expel it, churning, flailing in desperation, she'd pull in brine. Silent combat with an icy foe. How long could she survive? I drew out my timepiece. It was ten minutes past six.

The officer demanded, "Where'd she go in?"

It was hard to tell, since the long swells rolled, and my eyes tended to follow.

Diana pointed. "Four o'clock to the ship. Hundred yards out."

She was using nautical terms from a game we often played, pointing out interesting people to each other to guess their occupation or habits. The officer glanced at Diana's profile with new awareness. He narrowed his eyes to comb the waves as our ship coasted in a wide curve. She said, "At five o'clock now, and further out."

A pair of seamen dove into the waves. A cheer broke out along the rail. "Well done, lads! *Bonne chance!*"

We watched their progress, our urgency growing with each minute that passed. Dragged along, life buoys littered the surface, ropes curving as they spooled out. Silence blanketed the unwilling vigil. When the swimmers returned and another set went out, passengers watched, their hope threaded with dread.

A querulous voice demanded, "The woman—who was she?" The bony shouldered woman in black peered down from the promenade, clutching the arm of a young man in a frock coat. I had the sense she was "someone." The effect was unusual—like staring at a portrait only to see it move, and then to realize that the picture frame was really a window.

Recognizing her, I said, "That's Don Juan's widow."

The commotion had drawn her out and now she withdrew. The company on deck moved about in a desultory manner as the ship continued its slow arc. The smoking-room lads would be all poked up, those who wagered we'd make fifteen knots or more today.

A soft wind stirred Diana's hair. When I covered her white-knuckled hand on the rail, she turned in to my embrace and laid her head against my worsted coat. I held her, feeling an ominous weight. A suicide, three days into our crossing. Who was the woman? Why had she done it?

The sun went down in a bank of cloud, and the murky sunset faded. Electric lights were lit, which cast crisscrossing shadows on the boards. Shortly after, the swimmers returned, shivering as they clambered up a Jacob's ladder hung over the side. I could no longer tell where the woman had entered the waves. Too much time had passed.

"Gentlemen!" Captain Hawley addressed the crowded deck from the promenade. "And ladies. A sad duty falls to me today. One of our company has been lost at sea." Scots accent deepening, he went on. "Alice Fry, a ladies' maid. Therefore, this evening's entertainment will not go on. The purser, Mr. Dix, will hold a service in the starboard lounge of the main deck."

Passengers trailed away, speaking in hushed voices. Alice Fry! My insides plummeted. I'd planned to ask about her altercation with Bigby.

"I'd just left Miss Fry a message. Dash it, Diana." I met her worried gaze. "What set her off?" What I didn't say was, could it be *that* which set her off? How could my innocent note cause such panic? Just days ago, I'd seen her in the lounge, harangued by her invalid mistress. Had there been any mark of deep distress?

Diana frowned. "Jim? She was wearing a nightdress . . . so how'd she get all the way up here? Wouldn't the deck steward send her back?"

I had no answer as we turned back toward the row of sailors in white coats.

Mr. Johnson stepped out, saying, "I'm sorry, sir, this area's restricted." Recognizing me, he said, "Oh, beg pardon, Mr. O'Trey."

I asked, "Was there a deck steward on duty here?"

He sighed. "Felix. Unfortunately, he'd just returned to the galley."

Dammit. Alice must have waited until no one was around, then climbed over the railing. Yet the timing rankled. Why now? Sending Diana on to the dining saloon, I examined the deck and railing with Johnson, but in the dark, there was little point.

* * *

Dinner was late. Most attended, but only the scraping of forks and knives filled the loud silence. With whispers and knotted brows, our companions cast doubtful looks at the table where Mrs. Barlow usually ate. It was conspicuously empty.

Afterward, a steward summoned me to Captain Hawley's cabin. He sat at a glossy wooden table, his open, weather-beaten face drawn, the skin around his eyes permanently crinkled. He shook my hand. "Mr. O'Trey. Good of you to come."

We spoke briefly, then he said, "Obvious case of suicide. Glad we have witnesses, though. Twists the ship in knots if there's doubt. Damn nuisance." He pressed his lips together. "You were nearby . . . when she jumped?"

A nuisance—because her death had caused a delay? I frowned. "She . . . leaned, rather than jumped. I couldn't see much. She was behind a lifeboat."

He nodded, tapping his compass. "Tragedy, of course. Unfortunate. The company doesn't like this sort of thing. Look into it, will you?"

There seemed little to do, but I said I would oblige.

"Good man," he said and poured me a glass.

I asked, "Did she leave anything in her room? A note?"

"We found nothing but have a look yourself."

Johnson and I had found none by the lifeboat. Unless weighted down, paper would blow away. Over an expensive Glenlivet single malt whiskey, Hawley asked about my investigation, the passengers I'd questioned, then said, "You'll be discreet, eh? Any suspects?"

"Not yet." In most investigations, one looked for something out of the ordinary that might point to the killer. Here, I felt completely at sea. I said, "I need a sense of the ship, the routine, the crew."

"Ask Mr. Bigby tomorrow. He's got the dogwatch—till 'bout six."

Bigby puzzled me because no one could identify that mysterious nurse. He'd dissembled over his altercation with Alice, and now she was dead. It was suspicious, to say the least. I searched Hawley's troubled face but found no clues there, so took my leave.

I returned to our room to find Diana gripped with distress. She paced around the pale blue carpet, wearing out the fleur-de-lis pattern. "I don't understand. Why now? We've just set off! I spoke to her just yesterday, Jim. What could have upset her so?"

Dropping to the settee, I tried to remember. "You said she was a mite strange while boarding?"

Diana smoothed her fingers over her forehead. "Yesterday, before the hullabaloo, she seemed watchful and . . . closed. Mrs. Barlow's just . . . grumpy. The younger girl Dora was in tears over a silly bit of sewing. But . . . why would Alice kill herself?"

I shrugged. "Couldn't face eight days of Mrs. Barlow's unrelenting demands?"

"She'd be accustomed to it, after seven years." Her eyebrows peaked. "What did the captain want?"

"I'll see Bigby again in the morning. Early." I laid my palms over the ornately carved table. "What did you talk to Alice about?"

She settled on the damask couch, tucking her feet under her. "Mrs. Barlow's riding accident, years ago. Alice had a slow way of speaking, Jim. I suspected she wasn't—quite there, until I saw her eyes. She had the saddest eyes, terribly knowing and . . . weary. How I wish I'd said something kind."

Her words took me back two years to when I first met her brother Adi in Bombay. Pale, his jaw set tight, he'd insisted that his wife, Bacha, had not committed suicide, nor their teenage sister, Pilloo. He'd been right. Adi had been stiff and reserved when we met. Only later did I realize how questions tormented his sleepless nights.

I said, "God, what Adi must have gone through. When everyone was calling it suicide."

Diana's brown eyes had a velvet softness that drew out what I was thinking. Perhaps that was how she managed to get so much information. She gave the witness her attention, and they started talking. It felt so good, they probably couldn't stop.

She said, "Adi stood his ground, didn't he? After that ridiculous trial, when the court ruled it suicide. My little Pilloo, only sixteen. And Bacha, Adi's bride, so beautiful, so poised. We knew we had to accept it, the not knowing, that we would never know what happened. But not Adi. He went against Papa, you know, to hire you."

"Mmm." I put an arm around her and she came, curling against me.

"Oh, Jim," she said. "I feel I should have done something. Alice must have been in such terrible pain. Standing right before me, and I didn't know."

"Diana," I said, "The woman quarreling with Bigby? It was Alice. Bigby said he didn't know what she was on about. He's lying to me. I just don't know why."

CHAPTER 12

DORA

DAY FOUR: MORNING

I surprised Chief Officer Edwin Bigby on the upper deck in the early morning. Rumpled uniform, bleary eyes and the heavy shadow on his chin told me he'd had the night watch.

He greeted me, assuming I was here to view where Alice had climbed over the railing to meet her end. In fact, I'd already examined it. No, I was here for him. Alice had words with him on our first day out of New York. Did that signify a previous relationship? Why would she call a senior officer a nincompoop? And why kill herself soon after the don's murder?

A thick pearly fog enveloped the steamer, so I could see little past the railing. Our ship floated in isolation, a world unto itself. Bigby led the way in silence. The deck had been scrubbed and mopped by the time we reached the lifeboats. Spools of rope were stacked neatly to left and right, while some trailed from above.

I nodded at a metal pole. "What're these called, then?"

Bigby's mouth twitched. "Bollards. To moor the ship or hold other cables."

Suspended over the deck, the row of lifeboats creaked. Most people could walk under them, though I had to duck. I reached out and touched a hull, noting the new paint gleaming in the cool morning light. Though the old injury in my knee stabbed a warning, I crouched to examine the railing where I'd last seen Alice Fry, moments before she dropped. She'd been on the outside of the ship's rail. Had she stepped off the ledge, or just let go and fallen? Two deaths, and I'd been close to the deceased on both occasions—summoned by the first, and only twenty feet away from Alice. Why did death constantly hover around me?

Ahead, our bow cut through the swells, great curls of foam hissing as they radiated out to the sides. A fine spray touched my face like the promise of redemption. I tasted salt on my lips.

I looked up at Bigby. "Up all night? What time's your shift?"

He gave a brief smile. "It varies. I had the dogwatch. Four to six."

I glanced at my timepiece—a quarter past six. "Won't keep you long, Mr. Bigby. The deck's swabbed. Who's been here, d'you know?"

He went over to the bow and returned with a pair of deckhands, a young colored man with a singsong voice and an older, Irish seaman. I asked what they'd done that morning and received a report with more nautical terms than I cared for.

"The rigging's snug, 'n the hawsers tight. Mooring lines too, 'n halyards o' the mizzen mast."

Making no pretense of understanding, I waved a hand. "Anything out of place?"

The older one said, "Jus' puke. Rough night for some."

The younger one grinned, then squinted at the lifeboat. "Some idiot left a fishing line."

"Here?" I glanced out. We were surely too far above the water? "Where is it?"

He shrugged. "Got rid of it. Tangled mess it was. Were up there. I'll show you."

He reached for a rope and hauled himself up on the railing, then clambered into a lifeboat as easily as a monkey. When I didn't follow, his head and upper body reappeared.

Peering down, he called, "It were 'ere. Looped all about the gunwale."

"Tied by a passenger? Or seaman?" A sailor would know knots.

"Hah!" He sneered and swung down, dropping to the deck without benefit of ropes. "Not one of us, for sure."

When the sailors left, I confronted Bigby. "You haven't been honest with me."

His dark eyes flashed making his face seem pale. "How so?"

"I heard you speak with Alice that afternoon. You said, 'Been twenty years!' Now she's dead, it's damned suspicious. How d'you know her?"

Gazing into the fog he rubbed the back of his neck, then said, "I'll tell you. It won't help, but here it is: Twenty years ago, a Spanish corvette caught a little paddle wheel steamer off the coast of Cuba—you know where that is?"

"No."

"South of Florida. Spanish colony. The *Virginius* was a small American ship. Spain claimed they were pirates. Impounded the ship. It caused quite a to-do."

I frowned. "What's it to do with Alice?"

He heaved a sigh, his face strained and weary. "She'd remembered the scandal. The Honorable Don Juan—he was in Santiago in 1873."

I absorbed the implication. When I'd met Don Juan on deck that night, he'd made a curious remark. "It was my duty"—at the time it had struck me as defensive, as though I'd made some accusation.

"How was he connected to the *Virginius*?"

Bigby shrugged, then nodded his farewell.

I knew well the harsh duty of a soldier. Did the don regret his orders, or was he justifying them? But how did Alice, a ladies' maid, know about this? I pondered the contradiction. If the deluded woman had heaped abuse on a ship's officer—perhaps she'd even accosted the esteemed Spaniard! Was that what alarmed the old soldier, the reason why he'd summoned me?

* * *

Mrs. Barlow would not speak with me. I knocked, repeated my request and waited. Alice had seemed fretful to Diana, but entirely in control of her faculties. Why had she killed herself?

Mrs. Barlow's young nurse slipped out of her room, wide-eyed in apology. "I'm Dora, sir. Mrs. Barlow's feeling poorly. She can't receive anyone."

"Dora?" I asked, surprised at her smooth Asian features under the large mobcap.

"It's not the name I was born with. Dor Ahn Zhu. But Mrs. Barlow says Dora is easier to remember."

I smiled, having taken some liberties with my own patronym as well. In fact, Agnihotri was my mother's name, since I didn't know my pater. She'd died when I was two years old, so I had no memory of her face, yet each time Diana opened her bottle of sandalwood perfume, I had the urge to turn, as though Mother were standing behind me. On sunny days I sometimes felt her touch on my face. Jasmine flowers stringed over temple doors brought that memory, too. But we were a long way from sandalwood forests or tropical gardens.

"Where are you from?"

"San Francisco. Mrs. Barlow owned a vineyard."

"Tell me about Mrs. Fry," I said.

Dora's face crinkled up. "Miss Fry. Alice. I cannot believe it, sir. But I should have known. I should have suspected."

"Why?"

"She'd been so strange. Ever since we boarded."

"What happened on the gangway?"

"She just stood there. Wouldn't move. We'd been asked to wait, since a Spanish somebody was to pass. It was no trouble, but Mrs. Barlow took offense. Oh, sir, I'm so worried. She's not well at all. How will we do without Alice?"

"Tell me about Alice."

"She was my friend, sir. Came from New York as a maid for the missus. She'd been a dresser in the theater, once. But . . . she scared me, sometimes."

"Scared you, how?"

"She used to speak in her sleep. She'd cry out, sometimes. It made my hair stand on end."

I pulled a quick breath. Did Diana feel that way when my dreams escaped my grip and spilled into the dark? Did it terrify her too? I recalled her pallor some mornings, the worried downturn of her lips. Had I cried out something that alarmed her?

In the distance a passing steamer hooted a salute. Ours answered, a deep mournful blast. Alice had been troubled, like me, her nights beset, like mine, with ghosts of the past. In the next few minutes, I learned that although the two women had been close, Dora knew nothing of Alice's family.

When I asked to see her room. Dora stepped to a nearby door and keyed it, saying, "Alice and I shared this one."

"Did you find any note from her?"

Dora sucked in a breath, shaking her head. I looked away from the shimmer of tears in her shocked young eyes. Giving her a moment to collect herself, I examined the sparsely furnished room. The narrow chamber housed a pair of bunks, one above the other. A basin and some trunks completed the accoutrements.

"I'm afraid," whispered Dora, her face crunched up like a toddler. "I don't want to sleep here. What if she comes back?"

Her gaze darted at me, then sought the faded patterns on the rug.

I touched her shoulder. "She's gone, child."

She gave herself a little shake. "Yes, yes. Gone."

CHAPTER 13

RELUCTANT WITNESSES

I sent a steward with another note to arrange my visit to Mr. and Mrs. Palmer Bly without much hope of a reply. Then I interviewed crewmen and stewards, checking each alibi for the two hours in question. Slow plodding work, but necessary to eliminate unpleasant surprises. Since staff duties were systematically recorded, most checked out quickly, though some took longer to verify. Diana saw I was immersed and left me to it. It was later afternoon when I set aside the pages and climbed up to the Blys' cabin on the upper deck.

The Blys were not pleased to be interrupted in their cabin. I should have waited for a response to my note, but with no evidence in hand and a shipload of possible suspects, I needed to act on every lead. Assessing me from under thick eyebrows, Palmer Bly shook hands, hearing out my introduction with an impatient nod.

Keeping an even tone, I asked, "You received my letters?"

"Ah, yes," he replied, without apology. I tried not to take umbrage at his casual manner.

He might have been the last person to see Don Juan alive. Why hadn't he spoken up? And if he owned half of Vermont, what of it? Did he imagine he was above the law? I kept a neutral manner but could see that he was not charmed. Diana would have him snapping to attention in no time. No, I thought, men measured each other differently. If a fellow held his ground, I rather admired him for it. He'd seem dependable. A changeable bloke was unreliable or shifty. Which of these was Bly?

"Ship's detective, Bertha," Bly said, over his shoulder, letting me in. Since I was investigating the "unfortunate events," he assumed I must be on staff. I did not disabuse him of this notion.

Decades younger than her husband, Mrs. Bly was statuesque in a grey and peach evening dress that likely cost a year's salary for me. The string of pearls around her neck held an ornate square pendant that would have had Diana's eyes glowing.

Her hair done up as high as a sergeant major's helmet, she gestured gracefully toward the couch, then said in a serious, formal manner. "Of course. How can I help?"

His long whiskers giving him an old-fashioned look, Bly was watchful, on his guard. I directed my questions to his wife. "On that morning, can you tell me your movements?"

Mrs. Bly turned astonished blue eyes upon me. "Am I accused of something?"

She could not be mistaken for the petite Nurse Shay, so I smiled. "No, ma'am. It would be useful if you could recount where you were, who you spoke to that morning. Helps identify where people were seated."

"Oh. All right. We breakfasted with my cousins, Vernon and Algernon, and then spent some time on deck—"

"Which deck, ma'am?"

"The upper deck was rather congested, so we walked all over. It was a little choppy, and of course Mr. Bly insisted I must stay on the leeward side. We settled on the promenade deck."

I glanced at her husband, who sat at his writing desk during this interlude and put on a pair of glasses. Had Mr. Bly sought out the don on the promenade deck? If so, Mrs. Bly was unaware of it.

I asked her, "Had you planned this visit long?"

"No, indeed! It was just a week ago Mr. Bly put away his business affairs to take me to Europe. I do love the Swiss Alps in the summer-time!"

So Mr. Bly had decided upon the *Etruria* quite recently. I turned to him. "Did you know Don Juan Nepomuceno?"

"Hmph?" I could not tell his expression through the lenses of his spectacles. He leaned back, taking his time with the simple question, then answered slowly, "We had been introduced."

His considered manner reminded me of Superintendent McIntyre of the Bombay constabulary, where I'd worked for some months. McIntyre liked to play things close to the vest as well. I asked, "What was your conversation about?"

His eyebrows shot up. "Conversation?"

I paused. "Would you answer the question, sir?" I spoke mildly enough, but his face darkened.

"Young man, there are serious matters afoot here you cannot comprehend."

His blatant cut pulled a doggedness into me. I plowed ahead, "Educate me. About these serious matters."

He folded his newspaper with an irate motion, and said to his wife, "You're ready, my dear? That *was* the dinner bell."

I'd heard no gong, but it was likely past six. "I'm afraid I must insist. Captain's orders," I said politely, then remembering Hawley's concern, I guessed, "Are you acquainted with the Rothschilds?"

Now I had his full attention. "I've met Mr. Lionel de Rothschild," he said, gauging me, face expressionless.

I waited. Hawley had inferred that Don Juan was negotiating with the famous banking family on behalf of Spain. What else did one speak to the Rothschilds about but loans?

Bly did not expand on his reply.

"He's rather well-known," I said, recalling a rumor some years ago. "Didn't he lend the British government four million pounds—for a stake in the Suez Canal Company?"

He took off his glasses and cleaned them with a snowy white kerchief.

"Ye—es. His loan made England the principal stockholder. But that's over twenty years ago." He went on to mention others of Rothschild's investments in an offhand manner as though reporting titbits from newspaper accounts. If it was a distraction, I saw no way to pierce it.

The dulcet tone of the mealtime gong sounded outside. Politeness required that I make my goodbyes, but I hesitated. Something lay just outside my reach; I searched for a lever to extract it.

He'd pronounced the Rothschilds' name with a French inflection, so I said, "They've taken a stance in France, yes?"

A quick movement told me I'd surprised him yet again.

He huffed, "Well, the liberation loans of the seventies, 'course. Saved France from becoming a minor province of Prussia." A slight smile accompanied his little joke.

A warning rang in my mind like unexpected hooves at midnight. Alice had protested loudly about something that happened twenty years ago. I wasn't sure the first officer's story could account for her vehemence. But twenty years ago, France and Prussia had been at war. As attaché to Colonel Sutton, I'd read accounts to him while he was being shaved each morning. The Rothschilds could prop up entire countries. What had we got in the middle of?

Shooting in the dark, I asked, "Were you negotiating with Don Juan?"

"Good Lord, no." His startled glance flicked over to his young wife.

Seeing her surprise, I realized I'd misstepped. He would say nothing in her presence.

"Forgive me," I said, rising to my feet. "I've kept you from dinner long enough."

His eyes gleamed like pebbles as he took his wife's elbow. She made some polite remarks, ending, "I hope we will see Mrs. O'Trey this evening?"

Smiling, I bowed in assent. Was this why Bly would not speak before his much younger wife? Her innocent parting words told me that they'd checked the passenger list where we were listed as Captain (Ret.) and Mrs. O'Trey. I'd not needed the pretense of ship's detective at all.

Before I left, I asked Mr. Bly, "Was the don alone when you left him?"

Patting his pockets as he prepared to leave, he said, "Hmm? No. His wife was with him, 'course."

"You're certain?"

He frowned. "She'd gone somewhere while we were talking. But she returned before we left."

I turned to Mrs. Bly. "Did you see her too?"

"We are quite late now," said Mrs. Bly, tugging on white gloves. "Yes. I think the Spanish lady approached as we departed." She did not meet my gaze. Perhaps I should have waited to ask her without Mr. Bly being present. However, now I had a lead. I pondered how to proceed. Another visit to Doña Josefina was in order, but Captain Hawley had been insistent that I should not speak to her alone.

I could make a pretty good guess why the Blys had evaded my earlier requests. Had some negotiations in New York failed? Perhaps Bly had joined the ship to further persuade the don. This was troubling, because when the fate of nations hung in the balance, the life of an old man might not weigh much at all.

As I picked up my hat to leave, Mr. Bly said, "Those two young rascals mentioned us, I suppose. Well, O'Trey, I'd take a close look at the older one."

"In what way?"

"Young Algernon likes a flutter. Asked me to spot him for a loan, second day out of New York! Wouldn't surprise me if he asked the Spanish gentleman as well."

Asked and been turned down and called a "silly fop," I left with the sense that I'd been neatly turned around. The brothers had set me upon Bly and now he'd cast suspicion on them. Tit for tat, or masterful misdirection?

* * *

Dinner was at half past six. Smiling affably, Captain Hawley joined our table, shaking hands all round while place settings were added. Setting his cap down by his plate, he beamed upon Diana and engaged her in a conversation about Bombay's harbor. On my other side, Bigby sent me a conspiratorial grin. Apparently, Hawley had an eye for enchanting ladies.

I shrugged a reply. Couldn't really fault him for that.

Diana was saying to the captain, ". . . and we saw little of you the first two days."

He smiled. "In the narrows, chief officer and I alternate on the bridge."

I asked, "You took turns? Why was that?"

"The fog," said Bigby. "Bane of seagoers everywhere."

Hawley said, "But we're better equipped with our greater steam power."

Bigby seemed to bite back a protest, as the captain launched into a story. "In '88, the *Umbria* plowed into the French freight steamer *Iberia*. Happened like this. She'd made the passage down the bay through the gathering fog in the narrows. After passing the lightship, the fog thickened. She rang the bell to reduce speed.

"The engines were slowed when the lookout cried, 'Steamer dead ahead!' They musta seen a looming big beast, square across the bow. Their captain ordered 'Engines reverse, full speed!' but it was too late. Momentum, sir! The *Umbria*'s prow—solid iron, yes?—plowed through the other ship. Sheared her port quarter clean off."

My God, I thought. A collision at sea was surely fatal?

Bigby joined in, "That portion floated away in full view of passengers and sank. The injured steamer, *Iberia* of the Fabre Line continued afloat in the fog. Had her bulkhead given way, she'd have foundered like a shot, carrying down all souls." The edge to his tone was not complimentary.

The table's company murmured. Diana said, "It must have made a terrible noise!"

"You'd think so, eh?" Hawley said, "Her captain's a man I'm proud to call a friend. His foghorn was blowing as the ships collided. So was the *Iberia*'s, but the shock was so slight that not a soul on the ship moved."

"Was anyone . . . ?"

"No loss of life, thank the dear Lord."

This launched a heated discussion about fast ships, whether safer or more dangerous. Younger men preferred speed, ladies denounced it.

To set the matter to rest, Hawley said, "We can do nineteen knots in a pinch, and I'm glad of it. Speed gets us out of a jam quicker.

"Going full speed, all is as still and as quiet as the grave. Ears and good lookouts are ready for the least sound. The moment you hear another ship, up helm and bring the horn, or whistle abaft your beam which is comparatively a place of safety."

Bigby tightened his lips. Was this the only source of their discord? Professional differences?

I asked. "How would the other ship know what you intend? If both make the same adjustment, would that not lead to collision?"

"The foghorn." Captain Hawley smiled, raising first his left hand, then right. "Blows once if we're turning to port. Twice, if to starboard."

As the plates were cleared, he inclined his head at Bigby, who said, "A word, Mr. O'Trey?"

Taking leave of Diana, I followed him down a series of stairways to a corridor where shelves stored copious stacks of folded linens.

"We have no laundry facilities?"

"Uses too much water. We carry what we need."

Marching through, Bigby said, "Captain Hawley runs a tight ship, Mr. O'Trey. But these events have thrown us off. The crew is anxious. Passengers asking all sorts of questions. Until the culprit is caught, we will all be ah, floundering."

I chuckled at his pun as he strode forward at a clip. The thumping of the engines grew louder. Soon we'd need to shout above the din. I called, "Where are we going?"

He gestured for me to precede him down another stair. "You need to see this."

CHAPTER 14

SAILORS' TALES AND A CLUE

We entered a gleaming pantry, where dozens of cooks moved with admirable economy in the crowded space.

Shining utensils lined the wall, smallest at the top, making the kitchen both orderly and neat. Pans of potatoes—or were they bread rolls?—stacked in ovens, dozens of fowl roasted, sauces simmered, kettles hissed. The place ran with military precision and a modicum of speech.

Bigby brought me to the head chef, bald, yet heavy with the arms and shoulders of a wrestler. His sweating, pale skin gleamed like one who's gone months without sunlight. Wiping hands on his apron, he pointed at a white fabric piled on a chair.

"Found it late yesterday. Under a food tray."

"Where's the tray?"

He conferred with a cook, then reported, "Gone to be cleaned."

"A tray from first class?"

He nodded, looking grim. When I lifted the garment, a part fell away—a napkin, streaked with dark blood. The larger piece was a white skirt, torn at the waist. I sniffed it. The smell of cooking overpowered any perfume it might have preserved.

Had Don Juan's assailant worn it to impersonate a nurse? Whose blood was it? I recalled there had been no blood at the scene. Perhaps the old don had fought back? The narrow skirt had been made for a thin woman. The tear could mean it was worn by someone heavier. I asked, "Who found it?"

A dark-skinned cook's assistant came forward, thick coal-black hair escaping from the kerchief around his head. Licking his lips, he mumbled, "Bobo, sir."

"Beg your pardon?"

He grimaced a smile. "My name is Beau Lattibeaudiere, sir. I'm called Bobo."

I asked a few questions. He shook his head at most of them. In a lilting rhythm he said he'd been alone and seen no one leave. He did not know who'd brought the tray down, or where it had been brought from.

Barely able to hear above the din of the engines, I bundled up the garments and asked, "This galley lies below the dining room?"

He confirmed it, his eyes wide and anxious as he glanced toward the head chef.

"How do you take the food upstairs?"

He motioned me to a long chute that sloped upward. "It takes the trays up. The waiters unload it there."

"There are stairs, I presume?"

It was in the opposite corner, a busy nook that led to the cooks' cramped quarters. The garbled sound of dining-room chatter permeated the air.

"What's further down?" The map I'd been given lacked this detail.

He shrugged. "Storeroom, pantry and ice hold for the meat."

A winding stairway led up to the busy dining-room pantry, where stewards hurried past bearing covered dishes. Backing away to let them pass, my hip hit a lever that started a grinding noise.

"What the devil?" I swung around to see a set of trays moving toward us in a narrow chute. I asked Bobo, "Where does that go?"

He pointed upward, his palm pink against his midnight skin. "The music room, sir."

My heart sprang into a gallop. "Is there a stairway?"

There was none, he said, since the chute served to convey dishes quickly and could be unloaded without spillage. Beckoning me to follow, he led me through a series of crooked corridors and stairs, flicking on light switches as he went. No gas here, I thought, the *Etruria* had modern electric lighting in passages.

Breathing hard, I approached the empty pantry abutting the large music room, presently cloaked in darkness. The gentle clatter of cutlery from below echoed within the empty chamber. Distant conversation and muted laughter, the faint music of strings playing a waltz. These brushed over my skin like memories of our first evening, when I'd left Diana twirling on the floor to seek the air outside. The ghosts of days gone by, I thought, remembering Don Juan's weary expression.

Bobo had lit the pantry lamps and stood expectantly to one side, so I entered and searched for the opening of the chute. A turn of the lever stopped movement in the chute. Running my fingers around the edge, I found the hatch. It was masked by a jib door to seem like part of the cabinetry. Peering inside I noted the narrow space between the trays—barely a foot. Surely no human being could fit in there?

Frustration wound through me. Our killer had most likely left the torn skirt on a tray and sent it down. He'd been standing here when he shed the telltale clothes. Had he panicked, glanced about in desperation? The mystery remained. *How had he got out?*

In the neat pantry, with row upon row of crockery tucked behind glass doors I studied the surfaces, looking for smudges. Nothing. The killer had been here but left no trace. Wouldn't he have to search about for the lever to open the jib door? It swung out smoothly.

"D'you see anything amiss?" I asked Bobo.

Reassured to be asked, he opened hatches and closets with careful attention. "All good, governor," he said.

Remembering his wary glances, I leaned against a wall. "What is it you couldn't tell me before?"

His eyes flashed white as he stiffened so I showed him my palms. "It's all right. Go ahead."

"The head cook, he don't like us talking 'bout it."

"Just between us." I painted on a relaxed expression.

To my surprise, he blurted out a torrent of words in a low voice. Stopping him with a raised hand, I said, "Slow down, friend! You're in no trouble."

Gradually his rapid speech slowed into something I could understand. "I don't believe it, now. But the island stories, they go 'round . . .'bout Sade an' Cassidy. Get their revenge one way or the other."

"Sade? That's a name? And . . . Cassidy. People on this ship?"

"Don't know what they are. Old stories from Jamaica. Some men took Cassidy, an' now Sade come take what she want."

She. I glanced at the clothing wrapped under my arm. "What's this to do with it?"

"Story is, she's white—Cassidy. The other, she's like me, from the island. Some foolish sailors took Cassidy, that's the tale. I don't believe it, sir."

A spirit would hardly leave behind a torn garment? Careful to contain my skepticism, I asked more questions. He launched into other unexplained losses and crimes. Here was an able cook on a luxury liner, yet fear rimmed his deep-set eyes.

"Why now?" I probed. "Why are these stories being told now? What's changed?"

"It's the Spanish gent. Him that was killed. Sade kills men like that, with the garrote."

"And that's the only reason, because of how he was murdered?"

He frowned, his head weaving from side to side with a motion I understood to be deep consideration. "That, and the ropes."

"What's happened to the ropes?"

His accent grew thicker. "Some gone missing, some maybe moved. The swabbers swear someone cut them. The seamen keep the rigging tight, for the sails, sir. The main and mizzen were all right but the foremast, missing some rigging! No one owned to it, and the bosun, he was fit to be tied."

We'd hit some high seas last night, I recalled. That might account for the disarray in the cables, but . . . ropes cut?

The troubled cook said, "There are more things in heaven and earth, Horatio, than are dreamt of in your philosophy."

I stared. "Shakespeare."

His teeth flashed an impish grin, "I was well educated. My mother saw to it. Said you mus' speak their language if they's to respect you. They will not believe you're smart without the white man's language, yes?"

He'd detected my mixed race, I thought, contemplating his mournful tone. Curious how people trusted those who looked in any way similar to themselves. I hoped suddenly that it was not him, this friendly young man with the smooth cheeks and high forehead, who'd killed the don. If he had, I'd take him in, but God, it would hurt.

Regardless, I decided to check what shift he'd worked on the day of the don's murder.

As we left the pantry, the last rays of sunset glimmered through the curve of windows. Bobo looked over the darkening swath of sky. His mouth twisted. "God help us, it's the green flash."

"What d'you mean?"

"Green water be unlucky. But look at that sky. We're in for a spell, sure, it's coming." A sickly tinge smeared the sky, like a wound gone bad. Was this the green flash?

He quoted, "Fair is foul, and foul is fair. Hover through the fog and filthy air."

Macbeth's three witches? He touched his cap to leave, but I stuck out a hand. "Thank you, Mr. Lattibeaudiere."

Few passengers braved the open air when I retraced by steps from the music room. Some smokers lingered over the rail, peering out at the gathering dusk. I grabbed hold of a strut to tether myself as the ship's tilt shifted. My stomach wound tight, quivering like a thoroughbred preparing to leap, I clutched the bundle of torn clothing and staggered back to our cabin, more puzzled than when I'd left.

Any strange occurrence on board might bring up sea legends and myths. Soldiers told stories of skirmishes, near misses and quick action. As a groom in the cavalry, I'd savored these tales, although begging for more meant I'd have scant time to sleep. Sailors were likely no different. What else would they talk of at night below decks but the sea, ships, monsters, mermaids and such?

But that did not explain the terror in the lean cook's eyes as he'd clutched my hand in farewell.

CHAPTER 15

DARK WANDERINGS

That evening I returned to our stateroom to find we had company. Dora, the Chinese girl who attended Mrs. Barlow, huddled on the settee beside Diana. As I entered, room key jangling, both turned, eyes wide.

"Evening," I said, and put away my hat. Drat. I needed time to consider my next move.

"Please! I cannot go back," Dora whispered, clutching Diana's sleeve. She got up, pleading as though I threatened to evict her. "I beg you, let me stay."

I flicked a glance at Diana's troubled face. Ah. When we first met in Bombay Diana had told me, "I hate breaking things!" Since then I'd learned that her philosophy encompassed a great many things and people of all ages.

"What seems to be the trouble?"

"Mrs. Barlow won't let me in. Please, sir. I'll sleep on the floor. I don't need anything."

Diana grimaced an apology as she took my coat, saying, "I went to look in on Mrs. Barlow. Because she wouldn't speak with you after . . ." Her eyebrows rose to caution me.

"Right. Dora's berth is in second class?"

Dora's childlike face twisted, fingers pressed to her lips. Voice muffled, she said, "I can't sleep there, I can't."

Diana replied, "No, there's a small room near Mrs. Barlow's—the night steward's. But she requested it for Dora and . . . for her employees." She bid the young woman to sit. "Dora, tell Captain Jim about it."

Dora made a mewing sound and applied the kerchief. Her voice wobbled as she said, "A ghost. I saw it."

Diana caught my surprise and shook her head in warning. She patted Dora's hand. "Where was this?"

"In my room. Last night."

"But Alice didn't die there," said Diana. "Will you avoid the winter garden and the dining salon, and the chairs on deck?"

Dora burrowed her head, her kerchief crushed to her mouth. Diana's voice gentled. "You've been sleeping in Mrs. Barlow's room?"

"On the couch. But she complained that I snore. I don't snore, miss, it was Alice that snored! It was no use. Mrs. Barlow sent me back, last night."

She glanced at us and took heart. "I turned in just as usual. The wind was so loud, I put my head under the covers. Then she came." Her voice dropped to a whimper. "I didn't dare peek out, but I heard her, miss. She came in softly like and moved about the room. I heard breathing."

Tempted to point out that ghosts don't need to breathe, I stopped at a sharp glance from Diana. Someone had been in the child's room? I didn't like the sound of that.

Dora pleaded. "Please, could I stay? I'll be no bother, I promise."

Diana turned to me, face troubled. "She's been like this for hours. Won't go back to Mrs. Barlow."

"She's turned in, ma'am! I daren't disturb her."

Opening the door, I beckoned to a blond bedroom steward coming down the passage with extra pillows. I explained the situation, but he dithered. "I'm sorry, sir, I can't find a spare cabin at this time. Please consult the chief steward in the morning."

When he left, repeating apologies, concern and reluctance warred in Diana's face mirroring her quandary.

Sighing, I collected my pajamas from their hook. "Right. I'll take Miss Dora's berth tonight. Tomorrow, we'll see the chief steward, yes?"

I held out my hand for her cabin key.

Dora's eyes opened like a child given an unexpected treat. Mumbling her gratitude, she handed it over. Each passenger was given a key with their cabin number engraved on a metal slide. Pulling out mine—number 114—I exchanged it for hers.

Diana brought my dressing gown, saying under her breath, "Thank you, dear."

I took it, grinning. If I was to be banished for a night I'd collect a fee, I decided, and brushed a kiss over Diana's warm cheek.

She smiled, but Dora gasped audibly and turned the color of ripe tomatoes.

Chuckling, I glanced at Dora's key and headed off to number 75.

It was smaller than our stateroom, a long, narrow chamber pressed up against Mrs. Barlow's cabin on one side and a pantry on the other. A porthole nestled over a small washbasin where a mirror might have hung. Along a wall, two bunks were stacked, the top one barely more than a shelf. I doubted it would take my weight.

A slender table with a stubby ledge kept a bowl and some toiletries from sliding onto the floor. In the scant space left near a tower of trunks, a narrow door opened into a tiny water closet.

Dropping my dressing gown and clothes over the meager bed's head-rail, I donned my pajamas and lay down on the thin mattress. The neat dimity sheets were all right, a grey checkered pattern, but the bed proved too short. However, I'd slept in far worse conditions. The *Etruria*'s modern conveniences, electricity, flushing water closets and refrigeration far surpassed army barracks or lodgings on campaign: tents and open encampments on India's North-West Frontier, hammocks in Rangoon, mosquito nets tented over tree branches.

I could not sit up without bumping against the upper berth. Pushing one of the smaller pillows, of which there were four, against the brass rail, I made do. Nor did I close the porthole drapes, for the room seemed small, its steep walls closing in on me. Turning to one side to prevent my feet striking the bottom rail, I reached and put out the lamp. Just one night, I promised myself. Tomorrow I'd find the girl accommodation and reclaim my bed.

I missed Diana immediately, her scent of tuberoses and dessert, the sense of someone near, willing to listen, the piquant excitement of her lively wit. Through the porthole, a silver moon came in and out of view, sending shadows sliding over the walls. As I pulled a cover over myself, an old memory flickered in my mind.

Two years ago, I must have traveled from Karachi to Bombay by ship though I had no memory of it—unsurprising perhaps, for I had a wound on the side of my head. After that, I had only the impression of movement, the sharp smell of munitions, gun oil and damp wood. I recalled being strapped on a pallet, carried and placed on a plank floor with someone constantly moving by my side. Someone had cushioned my head, turned me, restrained me, replaced my bandage when it slid off. Who was that? Who'd been with me, tucking my arms back onto the stretcher? Might it have been Dr. Jameson? He'd seemed to have a soft spot for me in Bombay. I recalled his trim, neat appearance, his penetrating glance that seemed to see far too much. Or was it Stephen Smith, the blond major who'd been with me during our ambush in Karachi? He'd come to see me often in hospital, my only visitor.

No, this was an older man with unkempt hair, a turban, coarse beard and deep, troubled eyes, given to muttering prayers. Could it have been my army batman Ram Sinor? I knew he's survived the skirmish. We'd been part of the vanguard, hurrying south to Karachi. Hearing shots, I'd sent him back to warn the main company lugging guns and provisions behind us.

I frowned, trying to bring that face back into focus, but it had dissolved. Only the scent of the boards, oil lamps and the damp remained, so tangible that if I turned my head, I'd be back in the belly of that transport.

Why now? Why did that moment return to me here? Strange that bits of memory should drop into my mind at such a time.

My mind returned to my present conundrum: Who'd murdered the Spanish don, and why? Someone was traipsing about on deck, dining as usual, chatting with other passengers to hide in plain sight. The methodical preparation, stealing a bottle of chloroform, learning when the old man would be alone . . . the cold-bloodedness of it twisted inside me, sharp edged because of the nagging sensation that if I'd been quicker I might have saved the don's life.

We had passed the midpoint of our crossing; only four days remained yet I had no leads. Nurse Shay had an alibi. While she could have administered chloroform, I could not see her hauling an old man down a long deck to the music room, then strangling him. Doctor Witherspoon? He'd have far easier ways to do away with the don. Alice? It seemed lazy to fob the crime off on a disturbed woman, a suicide.

Bigby puzzled me. Who had he seen with the don—a stewardess? A man, wearing a skirt and scarf? With passengers away at luncheon, why wasn't the don killed on the empty deck? Too exposed? The killer had wanted him to know something, to see . . . what? To see himself vulnerable and helpless, at the killer's mercy? Some perverted form of victory over the old man?

Or . . . to see his killer. Was it someone the don would recognize? Perhaps the murderer wanted to talk, to tell him why he was about to die. One could not speak on deck, for anyone below or in the public lounges might hear.

I was looking for a passenger or a new crewman, then—someone who'd come aboard to kill the venerable old Spaniard. Tomorrow I'd ask the boatswain about new crewmen, and Spanish sailors too, or those who's served in Spain.

I dreamed of sliding things, trunks that slipped their ropes with a clank and sacks of grain dropping heavily in the hold. After a lifetime on horseback or in trains I should have been accustomed to motion. On occasion I'd even strapped in and slept in the saddle, a dangerous practice frowned upon in the army, but necessary on occasion. But the ship's yawing motion is not a soldier's natural state.

A sack of grain rose, swinging to and fro.

It came down upon my face, pressing down on my nose, my mouth, shutting out all sound. Sheets swaddled me, holding me down. Paralyzed, a sour taste in my mouth, I froze. Panic spurted. God knows I'd had nightmares that gripped me by the throat. The man I'd fought in Karachi—my friends, broken and twisted on the ground. But this?

The weight ground my lips to my teeth. Blind and trapped, instinct drove me. I lashed out. My fist connected. Panic billowing, my knee dug upward, struck something. I kicked but the pressure over my nose and mouth let up, and above me there was only emptiness.

The door opened, light filtered into my room. I was facing the porthole. I twisted, my line of sight blocked by clothes over the bedrail. The door swung shut as the ship rocked. I pushed out of bed, shoving against the entangled sheets. My knee gave way, sending me crashing to the floor.

Swearing, I got to the door and hauled it open, squinting against the electric light in the corridor.

To left and right yawned an empty hallway. My heart banging its call to arms, I tried the nearby pantry door. It was locked. The cabin on the other side was Mrs. Barlow's. That door too held tight. Where was my assailant? The long corridor mocked me.

"Sir?" An elderly night steward stood at the far end of the hall.

I went toward him and demanded, "Did anyone pass just now? In the corridor?"

Blinking in surprise, he said, "Just you, sir. Is everything all right? I heard your door . . ."

Could *this* be my assailant? He approached me with a deep limp. No, he could not have got to the corridor's end so quickly. Had he dozed off on watch? He'd come out from his desk under the stairway nook.

Waving him back, I retreated, my confusion growing. Had I latched my door before lying down? I could not recall. Returning to Dora's chamber, I turned on the lamp and narrowly missed stepping on a pillow. Hadn't I placed the small, ornamental ones against the corners of the bunk? There they remained, though in disarray.

I snatched up the pillow at my feet, intending to replace it on my bed, and stopped, incredulous. Mine was on the bunk, holding the indentation of my head.

There was no pillow on the berth above. I was holding it in my hand.

I slumped on the bed, breathing hard.

Something malevolent had indeed entered. If Dora had been in that bed, she'd have been found dead tomorrow. But she was with Diana.

Throwing on my dressing gown I gathered up my clothes and ran barefoot to cabin 114. I passed the fair-haired steward near Diana's door, met his startled gaze and demanded. "Felix, did anyone pass here?"

"Not in the last hour, sir," he said, his forehead ridged.

"What time's your watch?"

"Twelve to four. My shift ends in a few minutes."

So it was almost four in the morning. "Right."

I pounded on Diana's door, echoing the beat of my heart. Dia-na. Ans-wer!

My breath burned. I needed to see her, to hear her.

"Who is it?" Diana's voice was crisp, a trifle angry.

I gasped my relief, blurted, "Me, sweet, open."

Her footsteps pattered over to the door. It swung wide.

"Heavens." Pale arms shining, eyes sleep drenched, Diana pushed her tousled hair back showing pillow creases on her cheek.

Stepping in, I latched the door and wrapped her in my arms, my mind a blur. If some eerie thing had neared us, it had not got her.

CHAPTER 16

A MISSING KEY

DAY FIVE: EARLY MORNING

Both girls gaped at me, but neither demurred when I said I would stay. My heart still hammered like boiling water. Shooing them back to their bunks, I lowered myself to the floor, knowing it was pointless to attempt sleep. An ominous sensation in the pit of my stomach left me breathless, like standing on one foot over a frozen river. Diana brought me a pillow and blanket without protest.

What had just happened? Someone had tried to suffocate me, of that I was certain. But where had he gone? The corridor lay empty, pantry next door locked. Might he have entered Mrs. Barlow's cabin? Her door was locked too. I could not imagine her sleeping through an invasion of her room. One thing was certain: a murderer was still on the loose.

Who was it? *What* was it? My memory warred with common sense. I'd heard of ghosts and spirits aplenty in my army days but always treated them as fairy tales. A modern man of science could not countenance such things.

Yet séances were now a frequent part of Boston life. More than one notable personage had written fervent letters in the press, claiming this clairvoyant or that was no fraud but a medium communicating with the spirit world. I'd believed none of it. Yet *there was no one* in the corridor. I puzzled over this with increasing confusion. Worse, I'd heard no footsteps, neither before nor after the strange attack. No door, closing. A chill shimmered over my skin, a warning.

I went over it repeatedly in the hours that remained, but each time faced that empty corridor with the same stunned alarm. Where had my assailant gone?

At some point, I must have dropped off. I woke feeling sore, having slept with my feet against the cabin door. Since it opened inward, this ensured that no one could get in without waking me. An excessive precaution perhaps, but one that allowed me to defend Diana and Dora even asleep. I'd locked our door, but our steward would have a master key, and the ghoulish nocturnal assault had set me on edge.

Stretching out on the carpet, I flipped onto my belly for my morning drill and discovered new aches pinching my back and swollen knee. After gritting through a few push-ups, I felt more like myself and worked my shoulder as well. Though I'd made no noise, Diana sat up, rubbing sleep from her eyes. Catching sight of me, she smiled.

Questions spilled from her eyes. When her lips parted to speak, I jerked my head toward Dora, a still, small bundle under her sheets, scarcely visible.

She nodded. We could not discuss things with Dora in the room.

Once Diana completed her toilette and put on her corset, petticoat, shirtwaist and skirt, I put up her hair—there was a lot of it, heavy and curling over my fingers. As I tucked in the last pin, she pointed her chin at the washroom, and then the cabin door. I went to dress. We'd not spoken, yet a plan had been proposed and agreed to.

Pulling on my old army boots, I said mildly, "Left my slippers last night. I'll go get them."

"All right, I'll come too," said Diana. She turned to Dora who was sitting up, blinking. "Get dressed, Dora? Then we'll see Mrs. Barlow together."

The mite agreed. It was just past six when we left. On the way, I told Diana what had occurred the previous night.

She gave a shocked gasp, listened avidly, then peppered me with a volley of questions.

Upon unlocking cabin 75, I noticed two things. It was too neat. And my slippers were not in sight. Both bunks had been made, as though I'd not slept here at all.

What the devil? I said, "Someone's been here."

Our gazes locked.

Diana nibbled on her lip. "Perhaps the steward makes the beds each morning. Ours knocks to ask what we prefer, but if no one answers, well, they have the master key."

That put the bedroom stewards at the top of my list of suspects.

I frowned. "He took my slippers?" I looked under the bed, but nothing lurked there.

Diana opened drawers and the overhead cabinet, then slid trunks aside to rummage about. Her search was quick, but thorough.

"Here!" She reached and pulled both slippers from behind the slim under-berth trunk. "Jim, if you hadn't switched places, Dora would have slept here."

I smacked the footwear together, dusting them irritably. "Why would anyone want to smother her?"

Diana cast me a worried glance. "You didn't see anyone? No cabin door closing in the corridor?"

"None."

Though I could not tell why, the texture of my sleep changed when Diana was near. I experienced fewer visitations of battles or the carnage at Karachi, or when I did, memories and imaginings intertwined so I could not recall much afterward. Ordinarily a light sleeper, last night I'd been awash with dreams, and wakened groggy and thickheaded, struggling to breathe.

Bewildered, I returned to my present conundrum. The midnight attack proved that Alice had not killed Don Juan. The killer was still on board. So where had my assailant gone?

This was the most troubling part of my account. Neither Bigby nor Hawley would want to hear it. Already rumors and suspicions rumbled through the ship with furtive looks at dinner, passengers eschewed the lounges to keep to themselves. To learn of a midnight assault could send them into a flap. Nor did I want to be the next target of our mysterious killer. Last night I'd bested, but not caught him. If it were known, my dubious credibility as an investigator and restorer of order would fizzle out like a match in a tornado. I needed passengers to trust me and share what they'd seen. Now my dash to ensure Diana's safety felt overblown, a sort of hysterics, but my dread from meeting that midnight wanderer would not abate even in daylight.

"Sir, may I help?" Summoned by our voices, a bedroom steward who seemed barely fifteen years old hurried through the corridor, beseeching us not to disturb other passengers.

Pointing at Dora's door, I said, "Would you open it?"

He pulled back, worried. "Ah . . . sir, whose cabin is this?"

Dora's key nestled in my pocket, but I did not retrieve it. "Mrs. Barlow's nurse. She stayed with my wife last night. Go ahead."

He looked doubtful and went to find his superior. Shrugging, Diana tapped on the next cabin door. "Mrs. Barlow? It's Mrs. O'Trey. Do pardon the intrusion. May I come in?"

There was no answer. Diana shrugged at me. "How would she get dressed without Dora? It's really rather sad. Can she not get to the door?"

We heard movement within, and the door opened a few inches. Mrs. Barlow grumbled, "Steward? I've been ringing for a good half hour! Where's Dora? Fetch that foolish girl."

Often run off their feet in the mornings, staff could take a while to appear. While Diana attempted to pacify Mrs. Barlow, Dora hurried toward us with chief steward Johnson and his miniature assistant in tow.

Grumbling, the invalid admitted Dora, her complaints continuing into a garbled blur even after the door closed.

I turned to Johnson, "Does each steward have a master key?"

"Yes, sir, in case passengers are locked out. It does happen." He smiled.

I gestured at his juvenile assistant. "Can he access all the rooms?"

Johnson cleared his throat. "Is something missing?"

"No, but it's important." I pointed at Dora's door. "Open it, please."

He drew a leather throng over his head and keyed the cabin door. Watching his assistant shuffle on his feet, I asked, "He has no key?"

Johnson's thin shoulders moved in a sigh. "He has . . . misplaced it. May I know why you ask?"

I pulled in a slow breath. "That missing key can open every cabin?"

"Only this row, sir. Fifty to seventy-five. There's a bedroom steward for every section."

"Does the chief officer know it was lost?"

His cheeks drooped. "It's the lad's first time, sir. Not yet accustomed to our methods. I hoped he might find it."

I shook my head. "Unlikely. Last night I traded places with Miss Dora and slept here. I was attacked in this room. Blighter got away."

Johnson's face creased in distress. Sending the young assistant to his duties with exhortations to say nothing, we headed to the bridge to ruin Captain Hawley's morning.

Her large eyes thoughtful, Diana stayed, tapping the neighboring door to offer Mrs. Barlow her assistance.

* * *

His cheeks ruddy with surprise Hawley gazed at me for a long moment, his lips parted. When he spoke, his voice was uneven. "You were attacked. At night. And someone's stolen the steward's key."

"That's about the sum of it."

Another stare. The engine's vibrations changed, a higher pitch of increasing speed. Hawley marshaled the boilers well; I'd yet to hear the hiss of steam escaping as he tamped off the engines. I moved my shoulders, feeling a throb match the urgency tight inside me.

Why *hadn't* I noticed where the assailant went? Had I been so sleep drugged that he'd traversed the entire corridor? Why hadn't I followed, to check the stairway? Or pressed the bell to summon the steward? So many things, in hindsight, I might have done.

Hawley cleared his throat, carefully enunciating despite his thick accent. "Do you have reason to believe that the killer knew *you* were in that cabin?"

I paused. "Can't be sure. The intended victim might have been Mrs. Barlow's nurse."

Hawley rubbed his forehead. "Have we got a madman aboard?"

"Madman or not, let's constrain him. Put the bedroom stewards on alert." I remembered that Don Juan had been killed in broad daylight. "And . . . place sentries at the stairways during the day."

Hawley groaned, pressing a hand to his forehead. I sympathized. Placing sentries would disrupt the ship's clockwork routine. Regaining his usual composure, he gave a crewman the necessary orders and added, "Tell the ship's carpenter. Aft quarter of the saloon deck. Twenty-five cabins. I want all the locks changed."

* * *

Later, in our cabin, Diana said, "Mrs. Barlow was furious about the noise we made this morning. She scolds Dora incessantly." She winced. "Poor girl, I don't know how she can bear it. But she seems so grateful for Mrs. Barlow's attention."

She glanced at my notebook. "Any leads from the boatswain?"

Morose, I sat and shuffled through the notes I'd made that morning. "The crew are old hands. No one joined in New York. At least a dozen sailors worked in Spain or on Spanish ships. And three cooks. Don't know how many firemen; boatswain didn't bring the engine room book."

I rubbed my forehead. "Makes no sense. Perhaps the don had a somewhat checkered career. Bigby mentioned a scandal some twenty years ago—about a ship he impounded. But if someone was furious with him over an old grudge, why would they wait years to act?"

She sat, her brow furrowed. "Then how it must have burned, all that anger, and nothing to be done. But . . . people remember, Jim. A little thing can set them off. Years ago, old Poolti, our Mali who takes care of the garden, got into a terrible row. He'd been asked to assemble some flowers for our friend, Mrs. Althusser. He refused and threw his trowel at her. She went down like a bowling pin! It had nicked her ear. Poor dear, she bled all over her dress."

"He attacked her? Why?"

"It took Papa a while to draw out his story. Seems Poolti's son had been working on a railroad, when the British overseer, the sahib, scolded him over a small infraction. The boy brooded over it. We're not clear on what happened next. Something dangerous needed to be done—cables carried down a well of some sort. There was an accident and the boy died. Poolti never forgave the sahib. Except it wasn't the overseer he blamed, but all white people. Mrs. Althusser was fortunate the trowel didn't kill her!"

"Poolti was sacked?"

"Mama's friend was all right soon enough. And Poolti had been with us for decades. Papa sent him off to our coffee estate in Ooty. It's quite rural . . . Tasked the manager to keep him away from sahibs. We told the police he'd run away."

I smiled. Already high in my esteem, Burjor, Diana's father, seemed the epitome of gentle justice. No doubt, he'd have faced Mr. Althusser's anger for protecting Poolti.

"Another odd thing," Diana continued. "Before she died, Alice was missing all day. There was an argument and she stalked out. Dora feels certain she was, ah, cursed."

"Dora was cursed?"

"No, Alice. She ranted about 'Back from the dead. They told me he was dead.' Dora couldn't understand her. Now after this murder and her suicide, well, it's troubling. Apparently, the crew think something supernatural is afoot."

This time I did not pooh-pooh the notion. *Why* hadn't I seen a shadow in Dora's room that night? The cabin was dark, the only light came from the corridor beyond. If someone had fled through that door, they should have cast a long shadow across my floor.

CHAPTER 17

VENGEFUL SPIRITS

The attack in Dora's room had left me rattled. The more I considered it, the more it troubled me. What the devil had I pushed away that night? No closer to an explanation, I wrestled with disjointed memories. I had kneed something solid which promptly vanished like smoke. The contradiction wore at me like the crack of distant shelling.

Coming up from the saloon level I blinked in the glare of daylight. The deck sounded festive, as a group of children chattered past carrying towels to visit the Turkish baths below. I'd started out for the upper deck, hoping a walk would clear my head. But I had little time to close my case. My feet turned toward where the don had met his end. So, entering the empty music hall, I scanned the orderly chairs and the scrollwork of the gilt-edged mirror. The broken pot had been replaced, although the borrowed plant was shorter than its partner. Though cleaned up, the place had a somber look like an abandoned wedding feast.

How had the killer escaped? There was only one door, but he could have slipped through the French windows that curved around the back. I tried one and found it locked. They lay in full view of the foredeck at the bow, but the chubby deck steward had been adamant that he'd seen no one.

After the turmoil last night, walking around the silent chamber felt restful. I lifted a chair, brought it to where Don Juan had been killed and sat down. The mirror ahead echoed the bank of windows behind me. Tall velvet drapes bracketed each transomed window in deep purple. From the bow deck came the distant squeals of children playing.

My insides clenched. I had not been miserable in the mission orphanage in Poona, yet the excited calls and giggles compressed painfully within me. My happiest memories were of reading to old Father Thomas who'd raised me. He'd been ancient even then in his wrinkled smile, white goatee and sky-blue gaze. My throat closed in an ache as I recalled my last glimpse of him.

I sat, absorbing the grandeur of the wide oval room. Why here? Did the location have some meaning to the killer? The mournful shadows told me nothing.

Our days had grown cooler as we sailed north. Warming my hands in my pockets, I entered the dining saloon, welcomed by a ridiculously wide array of breads, cold meats, desserts and compotes. Music wafted from the corner where the quartet played. Yet all was not well. Passengers milled about bearing laden plates without the usual geniality.

I served myself, nodding a greeting to Dora and Mrs. Barlow as they wheeled past.

At our table, Diana smiled a welcome, saying, "Jim, there you are! Now don't scoff, we're talking about the occult."

"Mm-hmm?" I said, nodding round the table as I sat. Until I solved the puzzle of that night in Dora's room, I could not discredit any tales, no matter how bizarre.

Miss Rood said, "If there's a djinn on board . . . what is it, a djinn?"

Mrs. Evansworth gave her a meaningful glance, "Vengeful spirits, my dear."

Diana's mouth tweaked ruefully. "*The Arabian Nights* are filled with djinns and ghouls. Stories about things like the Old Man of the Sea." Encouraged by the interest around the table, she explained. "Sinbad meets a crippled old man, who begs to be carried to his boat. But once he hoists him upon his shoulders, the djinn locks his legs about Sinbad's neck and forces him to do his bidding!"

Mrs. Evansworth shuddered. "I heard they can change shape, appear as anyone! Why I could be talking to one, and not know it. Then what happened, Mrs. O'Trey?"

Diana grinned. "It's a long story—after all, the narrator, Shehrezad, was spinning tales to save her life! Sinbad lures the djinn to a cave with treasure and makes off, leaving him stranded there!"

The Farley brothers chuckled in unison. I watched them, puzzled. They'd sat near the don that morning. Was it solely because of Mrs. Bly?

Vernon grinned. "How 'bout a riddle: Why don't sailors play cards?"

Ignoring the confused looks around the table, he grinned. "Because the captain's standing on the deck!"

"Ah. The deck." The company accepted this with halfhearted chuckles.

Mr. Evansworth protested to his wife, "Come, Madeline, ghosts and spirits?"

She shot him an irate look. "They're saying a djinn killed the Spanish gentleman. It's not poppycock, Mr. Evansworth, the best people believe in spiritualism! And the famous playwright Mr. George Bernard Shaw!"

Djinns? My chest tightened. She looked around, then gaining comfort in the engrossed audience, confided, "I rise early, sir, at five o'clock, while they're swabbing decks. As I took my constitutional yesterday, two seamen were talking on the promenade. They won't speak when we're around, of course"—she gave a knowing look—"but a lounge window was open. Well, they said the music room, where the Spanish gentleman was murdered—had been locked. Only a djinn could have got out!"

More rumors! I said, "Madam, I'm afraid that's the nautical equivalent of tall tales."

She glowered. "Then who killed the old gentleman? Tell me that."

I told her my investigation was yet incomplete, finished my meal and declined the cheeses, hoping fervently to avert another bout of seasickness. Gloom enveloped our table.

Vernon said, "Oh, here's a riddle! What happens when a Finnish gentleman falls overboard?"

"Oh?" I credited his effort to lift our spirits.

With a nervous laugh he proclaimed, "He'll-sink-i! Do you see? Helsinki."

Mrs. Evansworth gasped. The young ladies stared. Given Alice's suicide only days ago, it was in dashed poor taste. Algernon smacked his brother's arm.

His face flushed, Vernon dropped his gaze, yet he seemed grimly pleased. Did he want to shock the company as some little rebellion? Or was it something more? A criminal might take pleasure in drawing attention, as though to say, "Here I am, you fools, only you don't know it's me!"

I had not forgotten that anonymous note—was that also the killer flaunting his perfect cover? I was boxing with a shadow, a fiend. He'd stayed out of my reach so far, but when I got him, the game would rapidly lose its appeal. Vernon's mouth had a wry twist as he picked up his wineglass and swished the contents around in lazy circles.

Around us, plates were deftly cleared away and replaced with dessert—a tricolor sorbet. Conversations were hushed. The tempo of the music wilted as though the quartet had given up the job as a lost cause. My head ached.

The image of that empty corridor mocked me. How had my assailant left without a trace?

Rallying, the strings stuck up a tune I remembered from Diana's ball in Bombay, two years ago, when I'd hardly dared imagine she might look at me. It seemed an eon ago, a joyful time that sparkled in my memory. I glanced over to see if she remembered and found her holding her fork with a thoughtful look, watching Bigby approach each table with soothing remarks. From the number of questions he fended, he was not successful.

Dora eased Mrs. Barlow's wheelchair through the door, so it was a few minutes before the crowd dispersed.

The meal sat heavy in my gut as Diana and I circled the quiet deck. I had done well to avoid the cheese. Despite her age, Diana had the knack of offering company without requiring conversation, a restful change from the morning's agitation. Yet all that talk of ghouls had left me unsettled. I asked, "Why all this . . ." I waved a finger toward the retreating Evansworths.

Her eyebrows rose with meaning. "Edna told Mrs. Evansworth that a mysterious woman wearing black was seen in the music room."

"Doña Josefina perhaps? Or her maid?"

She shook her head. Just then I had little patience for such foolishness. Why did women indulge in these ambiguous revelations?

"What was she doing?"

I regretted my curt tone, for Diana reddened. "Eating breakfast. Edna glimpsed her through the windows."

"We've got five hundred first-class passengers. Mightn't some of the ladies wear black? Hardly mysterious."

Diana frowned. "Why dine alone . . . in the music room? Especially when people say it's haunted."

I shrugged. "Because it isn't." Every sighting of the Spanish women was likely to turn into a ghost story. "Perhaps the lady wants a quiet breakfast. She'd hardly eat with her employer. She didn't want to join the crowded buffet, so she brought a tray to the music room."

"Where the don was killed? I don't think so." Diana's footsteps slowed to a halt. "Nor would his wife eat there. And certainly not alone, Jim."

"Well, perhaps we have a stowaway!" I said flippantly but then stopped dead.

Diana's eyes widened. "Someone's got aboard? What if *he* stole the steward's key?" Her voice dipped with excitement. "Johnson said this morning we had a few empty staterooms."

Finally, something to do! I took her elbow and swung toward the stairs. "She took a breakfast tray? Let's check with the galley crew."

* * *

The head chef ran a finger down the page. "No sir, no one missing a cabin number. We check the name against the passenger list." He rattled off the names of passengers who'd had luncheon brought to their cabins.

I stopped him. "Wait. You said Mrs. Barlow? She was with Dora in the dining room."

He shrugged, "Miss Dora Zu came at half past one for Mrs. Barlow's meal. I assembled the tray myself."

Diana and I exchanged a glance of consternation. We'd just seen both women in the dining salon.

As we left the galley, I asked her, "What time did we get to luncheon?"

"You were about ten minutes late," Diana replied. "I was early, so I looked for you. The music began at noon—songs from Gilbert and Sullivan. You arrived during the second reel."

My mind spun. "She left just before us. Mrs. Barlow's wheelchair blocked the way."

"So Dora can appear in two places," said Diana calmly, "or she slipped out during the meal and came here for a tray. Why don't you ask her, and I'll speak to Mrs. Barlow."

Our approach did not succeed. Dora insisted she had eaten in the pantry with the staff, and Mrs. Barlow concurred. Another bizarre contradiction. Someone was sending me on tangents while they set about their own dastardly plans. Like a fool I'd allowed myself to be diverted into this piece of theater. The mysterious woman eating alone in the music room, the young woman pretending to be Dora, it was all a distraction. But for what? Dammit, who'd been in my room in the dark?

Standing at the bow rail her chin thrust out, Diana concluded, ". . . not another night!"

I'd been wrapped up in my thoughts and barely heard her. "My dear?"

"Dora. I won't have her with us. Let's find Johnson. He must have a key for one of the unused staterooms. I don't care if it's 'not done, ma'am.' I'm sorry for the girl, Jim but I don't want her in our cabin. She was gone all morning and returned just in time to take Mrs. Barlow to luncheon. Now this—she fetched a tray and won't admit it."

I glanced at her in surprise. "That child? You don't think *she's* involved?"

"No, I don't, but . . . why not?" Diana said, blinking. "How much strength does it take to yank the old man's tie over his head and strangle him with it? The poor geezer was coughing up a storm that very first day. Can't have been hard to stop his breath. I can't imagine Dora doing such a thing, but dear, do we really know her at all?"

I stared in disbelief. "She was with you when I was attacked. She didn't leave your room?"

Diana shook her head. "Jim, you know how deeply I sleep. She could have hurried back to bed, pretending to wake up all groggy."

I gripped the rail with both hands. "No, sweet. I asked Felix, our night steward. He said no one had passed." But I recalled that Felix had been deck steward when Alice did herself in. What the devil did it mean?

The sea glowed dark green, opaque under the surface as clouds obscured the light. Here and there dark patches glowered beneath the waves. My lips tasted of salt, and a fine mist hung about the air smelling of anticipation.

My head ached. Why had Don Juan sent for me that morning? Something had alarmed him. I needed to explore that, yet could not put my mind to it.

I tried to recall the exact sequence of events last night. I had lashed out, struck something. But there was no one in the corridor. Why could I not identify my assailant? Usually a light sleeper, I'd heard nothing that night, smelled nothing, seen nothing. A band tightened around my temples.

I said, "Why didn't I hear footsteps, Diana? There were none in the corridor afterward." I winced, dread growing like a vine about my throat. "Nor a shadow. The room was dark. If someone ran through the doorway, the corridor light should have thrown a long shadow across the floor. I was facing away. But I should have seen *something*."

She gazed up at me with those clear brown eyes. "All right, let's take another look."

CHAPTER 18

LADY DETECTIVE

Diana turned in a slow curve as she gazed around Dora's tiny cabin. Though it was afternoon, I hesitated in the doorway. A heaviness weighed on me, a warning in my gut as I entered. The miserable little room seemed too small for one, let alone two, sparsely furnished and morose: the grey checkered sheets, the empty nightstand. On the tray over the washbasin, objects crowded to one side: a bar of soap, cotton balls, a spool of thread.

Diana looked at the bed, and back at the door.

"Your clothes were here?" Draping a towel over the headrail to approximate my garments, she closed the porthole. Light streamed in from the corridor.

She said, "Show me what happened. Let's repeat the whole thing."

Feeling peaked, I lay down on the lower bunk. She approached, her hands wide, holding an imaginary pillow. She stroked my jaw, her gaze tethering me to the present, then grinned. "Do exactly as you did, and I will try to disappear, like your djinn."

Matching her smile, I said, "Right. I struck out—" and pushed her lightly, then thrust up with my knee.

My shove, combined with the motion of the ship, unbalanced her.

"Oh!" She tumbled onto her behind, staring up with comical surprise. "Wait! What happened next?"

I'd started to rise, but now I paused. "I was entangled . . . no, the door opened behind me."

She got up and pulled the door open. Her shadow stretched across the floor, then it was gone.

"I tried to look." I said, turning my head. As before, the towel obscured my view. "I got up, tangled in the sheets, and fell." I knelt gingerly on the cabin floor, then stepped to the door, expecting to see Diana outside.

The corridor was empty.

My heart thumped. "Diana!"

"Here!" Her reply came from behind me.

I slammed back into the cramped chamber, but she wasn't there.

Rocking on my heels, I called, "Where are you?"

Clothing rustled near the stacked trunks. She straightened up from the crevice behind them and pointed, "While you were on the floor, I got behind the door. No shadow!"

"My God." Breath filled me again, full and sweet. Here was an answer: no spirit but a wily foe. Relief washed over me, a release like a summer breeze. My tilting world settled into reasoned order.

I glanced at the bed, where I'd sat, chilled by the eerie attack. "He didn't leave at all. He knew where to hide . . . he's been here before."

Returning through the narrow passage, Diana brushed out her rumpled skirt.

After a moment, she said in a strained voice, "Your djinn planned ahead. If you'd stayed here, you could have been killed. There are two places someone could hide. There"—she pointed to where she'd crouched —"or in the washroom . . . if they'd waited there, they'd be armed."

The speed of these revelations left me feeling light-headed. "He'd have a weapon? How d'you know?"

"Because going in there, you'd be tugging at your waistband. Vulnerable." She paused. "And they'd need to stab you to get past."

That seemed logical, given the narrow space. When I believed the danger was over, that's when it had been closest. My skin tingled as though something had brushed it.

I glanced at her. "Why'd you say *they*, sweet? There was only one."

Diana nibbled at her lower lip. "Are you so sure it was a man?"

"Why would a woman attack *me*?" It was ludicrous.

I thrust a hand through my hair, as another troubling thought drew me like a jingle of reins in the dark. "How'd he get in without opening the door? I'd have heard it . . . or noticed some light."

Diana sat down abruptly, pressing a hand to her lips. Her voice dropped. "Jim, when you entered, they might have been here already. Perhaps when you opened the door they ducked in there. Waited for their chance . . ."

Feeling winded, as though I'd taken a knock on the noggin, I gauged the space. The room was lit when I'd entered. I'd turned out the light before I lay down. Whoever it was must have seen me.

"We know two things about this blighter," I said, squeezing between the trunks and the lavatory door. "He's quick-witted—dashed off without a sound. And he's thin."

Even sideways, I could not fit myself into the crevice. Already I had the unquiet sense of being trapped and short of air that urged me back. Stuff and nonsense. As I pushed through, something wrenched from my clothes and skittered away.

Touching my shirt front I grumbled, "Lost a button."

To my surprise, Diana bent to look for it.

"Leave it, my dear," I said at this curious sign of parsimony.

"Oh!" She pretzeled herself down, then rose with something that glinted—a small knife with a wicked blade.

It looked small on my palm, the creamy speckled hilt smooth and worn. "Ivory. Why'd he use a pillow instead of this?"

Her brown eyes shocked, Diana swallowed.

"Blood," she whispered, her mouth angry. "It would get on them too."

Dammit. I'd had a narrow escape.

"We know something about them now," she said.

I contemplated the scant inches behind the trunks. "He's . . . flexible, like you."

"And a coward," she said, a hard edge to her voice. Her eyes blazed. "Drugged the don to make him woozy. Attacked while you were asleep."

Her arms slipped around my waist. She was shaking. I held her, kissed her to reassure.

"Oh, Jim," she said, those two words carrying the weight of much unspoken.

A memory flooded me, threaded in silver. Forbidden by her father to court her, I'd gone to her home on an errand when Diana had waylaid me and pulled me into the coatroom.

Remembering, I ran my hands around the curve of her waist to pull her in.

"Bit larger than your coatroom this time," I murmured into her hair. Her choking laugh told me she understood.

Confound it, no one was safe until I found the don's murderer, someone thin and wiry who crouched in darkness, biding his time until he could strike.

* * *

When we returned to our stateroom, Dora was sitting cross-legged in the hallway by our door.

Diana darted forward to raise the drooping girl. "Whatever's the matter?"

"I can't, miss. She's awful these days. Nothing pleases her," Dora said, her face wan.

I keyed the door and opened it for the ladies. In passing, Diana sent me a look that held a cluster of messages. She pitied the poor girl, yes, but her helplessness also exasperated Diana, who believed everything could be "managed." She'd been troubled over Dora's behavior yesterday, puzzled, even suspicious. The Diana I'd met in Bombay two years ago had glowed, returning joyfully to the bosom of her loving family. She would not have doubted the child. Recent years had eroded her trusting nature.

Sitting on the couch, she soothed Dora, "Come, my dear, sit down. Let's us girls have a talk before we must dress for dinner."

The last part she directed to me, asking for some time alone, telling me to return in time to dress for the dining room. In this she maintained the captain's dictum: ship's protocol must be preserved. I was about ready to tell protocol to go soak its head.

Dora pleaded, "Can I stay, Mrs. O'Trey? I won't be no trouble."

Diana glanced up with a helpless sigh. Hadn't she been upset with Dora only an hour ago? I chuckled. If we ever had our own children, she'd be butter in their hands as well.

Then I hesitated. How long could this go on? Diana's glance held mine. She would not send the girl away in that state. But her look also held pleading. I must find Dix, the purser, and arrange a new berth. The child must be safe.

Smiling, I turned to leave, but Dora bawled, "Don't go, sir!" Dropping her face into her hands she spoke, sobbing so hard I could not understand her.

"Come now," Diana soothed, then whispered, "Jim, she thinks she's in danger."

"It's coming for me," Dora raised her head. "It will get me. I'll never reach England."

I crouched and took her tiny hand. Her wrist seemed as thin as the foot of a newborn foal. "Not so, Miss Dora. You're quite safe here. No one will trouble you."

Clutching my fingers, she would not be consoled.

Diana blinked. "Dora, what did you say about Alice, just before? She'd been anxious about something, fretting and seeing ghosts?"

Dora turned to her earnestly. "She knew. She knew it was coming."

"She was a troubled old woman, Dora. You're young! Your whole life is ahead!"

Dora looked shocked. "She weren't so old! Just ten years older than me, or maybe twelve. She taught me everything. Knitting, darning, makin' tea, an' pancakes. She was strong! But it got her anyway."

Diana sent me a surprised look. I hadn't considered Alice old, but

Diana was closer to Dora's age. Perhaps from her youthful vantage point someone aged thirty-two, like me, seemed far older.

Dora said, "She had nightmares. Making such noises that woke me. Scared to my bones I was. But we'd talk—'bout her dreams. I'd be tired, in the morning, drop things, forget things. Alice too. She wouldn't hear and Mrs. Barlow would holler, call us dunderheads."

The girl seemed calmer now. Her friendship with Alice had helped to steady her. Torn away, it left her flailing, a landlubber dropped into the deep.

Diana prompted, "Her dreams? Tell me about that."

Dora swallowed, looking down to remember. "They always start the same. She'd see a bed, freshly made, corners turned properly. It crumpled, slowly, like something was underneath. Then the visions came, awful things she's told me. Fire, and charred flesh, and mouths gaping open. Heads . . . people's heads stuck on poles, their hair drooping around them, their eyes sad."

Those were oddly specific descriptions. The hair on my arms prickled. Where had Alice seen such things?

Dora's face crumpled. "I see those dreams now. Don't want to sleep, but I see the bed, the sheet, and it starts."

"Listen to me," Diana said firmly. "Those are awful dreams. Poor Alice. But it's over. It's in the past."

Dora took a shuddering breath. We'd taken pains to ensure that she should not know I'd been attacked. I paused, recalling how I'd entered Dora's cabin, sat and turned down the lamp. The hidden assailant might have believed it was Dora who'd returned. Her fears now took on an ominous hue.

She wasn't wrong. Someone might indeed have tried to kill her.

CHAPTER 19

THE ARISTOCRAT

Diana and I settled Dora's nerves and took her to Nurse Shay, then had time to ourselves after what seemed like an eon. A flesh and blood midnight visitor, no matter what his intent, was preferable to the alternative. Buoyed with relief, I reviewed the facts of my case with Diana. We examined Bly's reticence and the Farley brothers' nonchalance, Bigby's dissembling over his argument with Alice. That brought me back to the stolen chloroform and the clothes discarded in the music room pantry.

The blood smears on the napkin—did they indicate the killer was scarred? The don might have struck them, but where? We discussed ways to look for such injuries, but the sheer number of passengers posed an insurmountable difficulty.

When we returned to the dining saloon, dinner was already being served.

Dix, the purser, a short blunt fellow, hurried over to our table and said that Dora could be housed with Mrs. Evansworth's children. Of the four, the older pair shared a cabin and the Evansworths had the youngest two in their suite. The toddlers had wept when their nanny left them in New York and would be glad of Dora's company. He would give Dora the news himself.

Diana sighed with relief and bestowed a smile upon the purser that had him fairly glowing as he skipped away.

As I glanced across the hall, I recalled Mr. Bly's snide remark about the Farleys, which had left a sour taste in my mouth. He'd pointed me back toward them like whacking a tennis ball on a court. Yet I was bound to follow all leads, so I joined Vernon regaling a group around the dessert table.

"What note do pirates sing?" he asked cheerfully.

I waited—how bad could it be? He chortled, "High C. Pirates on the high seas!"

Weak smiles, groans and doubtful looks greeted his answer. No one wanted to be reminded of pirates while crossing the Atlantic. Marveling at his knack for saying exactly the wrong thing, I pulled him aside.

"Look here, Vernon," I said, "Tell me about the Blys. You're Mrs. Bly's cousin. Why the devil did she marry him?"

He darted me a look, then pulled in his lips. "Had to, old sport. To save her pa."

"Her father? How?"

He shrugged. "Gambling debts. Up to the gills in them. Bly bailed him out on one condition." He gave me a meaningful look, his voice scornful. "She's twenty years younger. Wears her like a bit of jewelry, doesn't he?"

"She seems content," I countered.

He scoffed. "Bertha's loyal, man! Does her duty." After a moment, his lips tightened. "Has to. The blighter locked her in her room when she wouldn't comply."

"Locked her in?" I frowned. So the respectable gentleman I'd interviewed had a vile temper.

In a low voice, Vernon said, "I was just sixteen, then. Bertha's two years older. Barely seventeen when they married. I'd come to visit and heard her calling, beating at her door. 'Course I tried to open it. Locked.

"She slipped a note under and begged me to take it to her brother. He got her out that evening. Had strong words with Bly, too. Her brother's married to General Grant's daughter, you know. President Ulysses S. Grant."

Well, well. This explained Mrs. Bly's restrained demeanor. Millionaire Mr. Bly had bought himself an exquisite society wife with connections, American royalty really, and blackmailed her into accepting him. Yet this did not make him a murderer—a poor husband and a brute, perhaps, but the law would have no quarrel with him.

With only three days remaining, I needed to break the case soon. Since the Blys had seen Doña Josefina return to the don's side, I told the captain I needed to speak with her.

Captain Hawley frowned. "It's almost eight, O'Trey. She hasn't come to dinner. Can't it wait till tomorrow?"

When I said it could not, he sent Bigby with me. This was awkward, but short of naming him as a suspect, I could not refuse.

Eschewing electric lighting, Doña Josefina's stateroom was lit with tall tapers set upon gleaming candlesticks. Sitting stiffly in a wingback chair, her dark eyes gleamed opaquely. Veined hands clutched the carved arms of her chair with predatory force. The tilt of her head and shadows on her face furthered that impression.

I fancied she understood English well enough, but Armando De Cullar, the don's bookish secretary hovered nearby. He moved from the bank of windows to hover at the mantel, his restless energy in counterpoint to the widow's stillness.

Repeating my condolences, I said, "Would you explain what happened that morning? Even a small point may prove important."

Doña Josefina's eyes narrowed. After a long pause, she said, "My husband was asleep. I had the . . . migraine, so I returned here. To rest." As before, her deep voice had a pronounced European accent. She opened her hand in a gesture of approximation. "It was . . . mmm . . . a half hour past eleven."

In a slow, methodical movement, she drew a black kerchief from her sleeve and dabbed the corners of her eyes.

"Did you return?"

"I have told you. I had pain . . . here." She touched her temple. "I took the rest."

A tall Spanish woman in dark clothes entered and placed a tray at her elbow. Doña Josefina dismissed her with a flick of her hand and a brief command.

I paused. Though spoken softly, her words had a peculiar inflection. The intonation of her words was intimate, a phrase used often, accepted without question.

Doña Josefina did not drink from the steaming cup. Mourning draperies framed her face and drooped over her shoulders to her waist. Was this her usual attire or did she just happen to have mourning garments at hand? I supposed Spanish women might commonly wear formal black garb, but my knowledge of European nobility was as bad as my Latin. If her previous behavior had been erratic, now it was overly restrained. Was this her usual mien? I could not read its meaning. The difficulty of questioning foreign individuals was compounded by their unfamiliar customs.

Keeping my tone noncommittal, I said, "Some guests saw you return before luncheon."

"Tsch." She flicked her fingers as though swatting flies. It was a curt dismissal.

"Doña Josefina, what did Mr. Bly discuss with your husband?"

She bent her head to young De Cullar, who whispered deferentially, then straightened. She said, "I have no knowledge of this."

"They spoke beside you, for quite some time."

She shrugged, a slow lift of a bony shoulder indicating supreme indifference.

I persisted. "You recall them speaking?"

She nodded, a grudging admission.

"How long was Mr. Bly with your husband?" When she frowned, I prompted, "Was it a half hour? Longer?"

She waved away my question. If they spoke, what of it, she seemed to say.

"Did your husband have enemies? Someone who might want to harm him?"

That brought forth a volley of incomprehensible Spanish. I put up my palms to stem it. "English, please."

De Cullar said, "She believes there are many in Spain who are, er, jealous of Don Juan's successes, his stature, his er, status among the highest of persons, you understand? But she claims no Spaniard has done this."

"Did she recognize someone on board, perhaps, from Spain?"

This drew only a large shrug and downturned mouth.

De Cullar said, "Doña Josefina does not think so. But our enemies could have hired, ah, an assassin, señor."

This was his own convenient explanation for the tragedy, then. Dash it, I was getting nowhere. I needed to jar the lady's composure, break through that blasted wall she'd put up.

"Doña Josefina, you are religious, yes?"

Her demeanor dared me to question it.

"Perhaps you've forgiven your husband's killer?"

Killer. I said it quietly, but Bigby glanced at me with horror. Doña Josefina's harsh breath told me my barb had found its mark.

Her voice simmered with emotion. "I do not forgive him."

"Then help me bring the man to justice. Find who did this."

Her haughty demeanor melted into cold fury. "I know who has done it! You English! I will have justice! I am related to Maria de las Mercedes, the late queen. *Comprendes?* I am aunt to the king of Spain!"

An aunt of the Spanish king? Bigby and I exchanged a quick glance.

I was losing control of this conversation, so I asked, "Señora, why is your name different from that of your husband?"

My distraction worked. She turned in an annoyed movement, then raised her chin at De Cullar.

He explained, "Unlike the English, a Spanish lady does not take her husband's name after marriage. The children take both names, with the father's first. Therefore, *Her Excellency* Doña Josefina is named Lopez y Carrillo, you understand?" He stressed her title, leaning forward to underline it.

Ignoring his priggishness I nodded, then addressed his mistress in a low tone, "Madam, Don Juan spoke with Mr. Bly for some time. Was he engaged in acquiring funds, perhaps?"

She stiffened, her lips tight, then stood. "Leave us!"

We complied in sober silence. Drat. She was keeping something from me, but at present I had no means to extract it. Her suspicion complicated matters, but I had not expected much cooperation. De Cullar now, he was interesting. He'd enjoyed explaining Spanish customs to me, the ignorant investigator, his satisfaction suppressed under a formal teaching manner. His alibi—searching for ink—was laughable, yet I had no evidence against him.

Mopping his forehead as we left, Bigby groaned. "O'Trey, I fear we've done more harm than good. I've got to apprise the captain. Will you come?"

Despite the late hour, Hawley received us immediately, dismissing the two officers with him. His hair rumpled as though he'd clutched it, whiskers awry, he demanded, "Found your assailant, O'Trey?"

"No, sir."

He rubbed a weary hand over his face. "We've got to arrest someone soon. Who's your main suspect?"

"No one at present."

"Suspicious passengers? Crew?"

Doña Josefina had contradicted the Blys, but who did I believe? When I shook my head, he grunted, saying, "Right. So what do you know?"

I apprised him of Doña Josefina's exalted relations and her accusation against the ship. "Why is she adamant against Britain? Against you?"

His breath gusted out in a sigh. "Seeing an English conspiracy, no doubt." His eyes flickered to Bigby. His brogue thick, he said, "All right, here it is. The late Don Juan was a general and nobleman. Doesn't surprise me his wife is the king's bloomin' aunt. O'Trey, this murder could set off a storm."

Bigby said slowly, "The War Ministry will want answers when we dock."

Hawley nodded. "Spain . . . will descend into ruddy chaos."

"Why?" I gazed from one to the other. What the devil had I stepped into?

Hawley leaned back. "You've heard of *les Bases de Manresa*?"

More Latin? I stifled a groan. He explained. "The Catalan area is industrialized—its leaders want independence. Rest of Spain's mostly farmland, so the monarchy's not going to let the fatted goose escape. That led to a coup and a nasty civil war, till the king patched things up in 1886. The present child-king's father, Alfonso the twelfth, gave in to the rebels' demands, called the Bases de Manresa. Lord, they caused a furor. Spain's been sitting on a powder keg for years. Now, seems they need to bolster their army."

"To quell the rebels?"

"That's what the Prime Minister's said." He tilted his head. "My war office connection wasn't sure. It could be spent on their navy, instead."

"That's conjecture."

He looked put out. "Spanish Prime Minister Práxedes Sagasta y Escolar . . ." His face creased into a pained look. "This is hearsay, O'Trey. I'm told Don Juan was acting for him."

I ventured a guess, "To acquire funds in America . . . that could be used against British interests?"

"God alone knows. Now, why're you asking?" His eyes gleamed.

"Bly had a long conversation with the don that morning. The Blys, Mr. and Mrs. both, saw a Spanish woman nearby when they left. She denies it."

Disbelief curling his voice, Hawley said, "You suspect the widow?"

Holding back my instinctive denial, I paused. Though she looked frail, her hand clenched on the carved knob of her chair had been surprisingly muscular. It was theoretically possible, I thought, for a woman to kill in such a way. But her outrage, and her dismissal of Bly's claim felt genuine. It made me want to believe her.

I frowned. The Blys contradicted Doña Josefina. But what if both versions were true? "The other Spanish woman who brought the widow her tea. Who is she?"

"By Jove, the attendant!" Bigby pulled out a packet from his breast pocket and scoured it, pointing to a name. "Antonia Condes-Mistral, cabin 312, second class."

Gathering my hat, I hurried from the room. Here was one contradiction, at least, that I could address.

* * *

Doña Josefina's attendant had a main level second-class cabin. I'd just reached it when she returned from the second-class dining hall.

I asked, "You are Doña Antonia Mistral?"

She smiled. Her calm demeanor, high forehead and oval face would not have been out of place on a medieval triptych.

"Sí. I am Señora Condes-Mistral. Doña is used only for the lady."

She keyed the door and invited me in. There she perched on the bunk, offering me the only chair.

Glancing around the unadorned cabin, I said, "You are Doña Josefina's maid?"

"I dress her, advise her."

Perhaps that explained the closeness I'd noticed. I launched into my questions. "Did you see Don Juan on the morning before he died?"

Her nod was somber. "Sí. But my lady was unwell, so I helped her to her room. Cool water with lavender, on the forehead, it is very good."

"Did you return?"

She looked down. After a pause, she said, "She sent me back to see if he was awake. He was not. I stayed a few moments, then returned to her."

The Blys had mistaken her for her mistress. It resolved the puzzle but left me again with no leads.

I asked, "Was the don alone when you left? Or were there people around?"

She frowned at the carpet. "The noonday gong was ringing . . . ding, ding. Don Juan was asleep, so . . ." She shrugged.

That made her the last person to see the don alive. But why would she harm him?

I took my leave, more puzzled than ever.

Diana and I had considered the possibility of a stowaway. As I strode back over the boards I recalled newspaper accounts of such incidents aboard transatlantic journeys. They were usually folk trying to emigrate to America, often young women aided by a besotted passenger or crew member. But a stowaway assassin?

It seemed far-fetched, but stranger things were reported in the daily broadsheets. Hadn't an anarchist just murdered the French president? Political turmoil and revolution in Don Juan's home country meant anything was possible.

CHAPTER 20

THE BEATING HEART

DAY SIX: MORNING

For most of my life, I'd awoken to the call of an army trumpet, scrambling in the dark to roll my pallet, toss on clothes and gallop to the troughs to clean up. We'd enjoyed few amenities on campaign. Barracks had communal washrooms. As a captain I could corner a separate privy on occasion but once tasked with discipline, I'd rarely slept past sunrise. I'd learned early that military form mattered a great deal and splurged on a batman to keep my clothing neat.

God, I wanted land below my feet, the blessed unmoving solidness of it. I stretched, remembering Mullika, my Arabian mare who moved as though she was shod in velvet—the feel of her satiny withers under my fingers, her gentle nudge and large soulful eyes that understood every tap of my heel, that was the way to travel.

A pink blush on the horizon heralded dawn as I washed and dressed quietly so as not to disturb Diana. Sometime during the middle watch I'd made a plan.

Mustering a pair of crewmen on deck, I made my way to the lifeboats. Hailing the sailors on swabbing duty, I posted them around the suspended boats—the swabbers blinked at me, then complied.

"Fetch a ladder," I instructed a puzzled seaman. Time to flush out any stowaways.

I waited while it was brought and propped up against the first boat. I laid a hand on it to climb, but a hefty sailor preceded me, swinging up easily. The rungs bounced as he ascended. I pushed upward one step at a time, jaw clenched, suppressing a wave of telltale biliousness.

Determined to hold off until my search was done, I thrust a leg over the gunwale and peered under the tarp. Only the big sailor crouched in the dim light, his head and shoulders tenting the canvas. The lifeboat smelled of chlorine, like the Turkish baths below. It held a dozen rows, and might seat forty in a pinch, I thought.

Taking slow breaths I asked, "How many boats on this side?"

"Eight, sir."

Although spacious, it was unlikely that sixteen boats would accommodate a thousand souls. Yet that was not my purview. I peered past the seaman, rubbing my throbbing knee. A boxlike affair nestled at the stern. "What's that?"

"Provisions. Water, flares, and the like."

"Open it."

Grunting, he crabbed his way back and opened the low door. Recalling the tiny nook in Dora's cabin where my assailant had hidden, I hunkered down. "Anything missing?"

Giving me a dubious look, he took stock. "Looks all right. The bosun would know what it should be."

"Count it. Compare it with other boats."

Climbing down, I divided the lads into four groups to work from each end.

"What's the trouble?" called a deck officer from below.

Climbing down, I persuaded him to the urgency of my task and the search continued. After the better part of an hour, I had some answers. The crew returned to swabbing, and I went to tell Hawley.

"Three boats are missing rations. Water and biscuits. Rest looked intact."

His bleary eyes squeezed tight, his brogue heavy with distress. "God Almighty. An assassin on my ship. Find him, O'Trey. Everything depends on it."

But he groaned when I put my plan to him.

"A search," he said, fingers drumming the table, "will disrupt the ship's routine."

Music from the dining saloon drifted upward. "It can't wait."

"First-class passengers are not to be disturbed," said Hawley and sent for Bigby, who arrived shipshape, looking rested. Not his night for the dogwatch, then. To save time, the decks were divided up and officers dispatched to search the crew's quarters and steerage. Bigby and I began a careful search of the promenade.

It was a fine day. Buntings fluttered, flags catching the breeze as children played on the forward deck. But for the churning in my gut, it would have been charming. The wind picked up, wafting cigarette smoke from the forecastle. Beginning to port, we passed ventilators and funnels, stopping to examine each nook where someone might conceivably hide.

Over the next hour, we skirted the ladder to the bridge, the viewing port, turrets and masts to scour more cabins on the aft promenade and returned to starboard. After that level we explored the upper deck toward the aft wheelhouse along the port side. The ship's bells rang as we trudged past the games area and funnels to the silent music room whose windows curved over the foredeck. Where would a stowaway hide?

The ship's business went on around us. Shifts changed, orders were called, passengers passed with cordial smiles. I worried that as they traversed the ship, so could the stowaway. Bigby's ordinarily open face became remote as we continued through each section.

We'd borrowed Johnson's master key to open empty cabins, so our search omitted nothing. At the stern was a narrow deck, with hatches closed and bolted. "Shut after sundown," said Bigby. "Steerage passengers have access during the day."

I frowned. "It's locked?" If the *Etruria* were to sink, those in steerage would be trapped. Yet it meant our killer could not be in steerage; tall walls prevented access to the upper deck.

It had grown cooler. While Bigby took measure of the blanketed passengers lounging on deck chairs, I continued to starboard.

"Any sign?" he asked, as we met on the windward side.

I shook my head, and we headed toward the lifeboats, briefly conversing with those who braved the windy deck chairs or clustered at the rails.

Spotting the officers sent to check below decks, I hailed them from the top of the stairs. Their report was quick: nothing amiss.

I asked Bigby, "The lower deck, what do we have there?"

Bigby's eyebrows shot up. "The engine room, boilers, berths for the crew and the storage hold. Doubt a stowaway could get down there."

"Why not?"

"How would he escape notice? Only way there's the luggage lift."

"An electric lift?"

Such a space would not be much frequented. Ample space for a wiry assassin. I said, "You have keys?"

He looked doubtful. "We'll need the captain's approval, O'Trey. Holds are off-limits."

I refused to budge. "Some reason you don't want me looking there?"

He snapped, "When the *Etruria* lays in supplies we take on eleven hundred bottles of champagne, eight hundred fifty bottles of claret, six thousand bottles of ale, twenty-five hundred bottles of porter, twice as much mineral water and six hundred fifty bottles of various spirits. And thousands of pounds of produce, meat and dry goods."

"I assume the storeroom is kept locked. I need to see the ship's inner workings, the hold."

Bigby tsked. "My crew know each other. A stranger would be noticed."

I stared. "You have four hundred crewmen, yes? The sailors know each other. But would they be able to identify someone dressed as a steward? The galley staff, they might know most of the stewards, but would they know the engine room blokes?"

Swiveling on his heel, he led me through corridors to a creaking lift, an open box, suspended in a rectangular trench. "After you," he said.

Bollocks. There was no help for it, so I stepped in.

Following me in, he operated a lever. With a lurch, we began our descent like Orpheus, into the underworld.

The light dimmed. I've always disliked close spaces. As usual, I searched for an egress. My path of retreat receded as the lift rattled and groaned downward. I drew a slow breath, trying to ease the warning tightness that gripped me.

Standing beside Bigby I pondered the widow's wild accusations. Could Bigby or the captain have engineered the don's demise? Hawley had arrived quickly at the music room. If he were behind it, he'd have assigned the task to a crewman. But then he could neither meet nor shelter that man. It would put the captain in that man's grasp. The only sensible course, if indeed the captain was responsible, was to dispose of the don's killer in an accident. Who would he trust? I glanced at the first officer's implacable face. Hawley could have Bigby get rid of me too.

Deep in the ship's belly, the engines' rumble was all around. We jerked to a halt in a bright, sterile space of bare walls and corridors. A pair of sailors hopped to their feet and saluted.

Nodding to the guards, he brought out a ring of keys and opened a nearby door. Flicking switches, Bigby said, "We have electric lights in lounges, corridors and staterooms."

I pointed to a stack of trunks beside the metal door. "Whose are these?"

"Passengers sometimes request their trunks be sent up. They'll be delivered in the morning." His face was a stone wall. "As each hold is filled, we batten it down and fill the next. So only the luggage hold is accessible."

It proved more orderly than I'd imagined. Trunks were stashed in long rows, roped into place. We proceeded through to the storeroom, which lay below the galley. Here, provisions stacked upon shelves ranged to either side of a long passageway.

"Refrigerated meat is forward, connected to the meat galley," said Bigby, stalking ahead. We were alone. The hair rose on the back of my neck. The ship's guards were devoted to Bigby. They would be no help to me.

He hauled open another door and entered. As I followed a blast of cold air made me gasp. Carcasses hung along one side, cartons of butter, lard or other ingredients on the other. Shoulders bunched, Bigby watched me warily. Glancing at his shuttered expression, a warning pricked my spine. *Here,* it seemed to say. If he's to attack, it will come here. What better place to close a captive than the icebox? Later, my frozen body would be found slumped against the door.

Leading me through in silence, he pulled down switches and locked the door behind us. He knew the space well, and I not at all. It would be easy to delude me, I thought.

"Why the guards?" I asked as we reentered the electric lift.

He sent me a glance. "We're carrying the mail."

But that didn't warrant an armed guard, so I raised an eyebrow at him.

A smile flickered over his face. "We carry gold too. Loaded in secret, so only the captain and boatswain know."

"And the fellows who stowed it."

It did not surprise me that the ship carried gold bullion. Army convoys had often carried funds to purchase provisions. Bigby waited for me, his eyes inscrutable.

"Lay on, Macduff," I said, rubbing the back of my neck.

His dry chuckle sounded of relief as he stepped off the elevator and started down another corridor. My head throbbed. How could a stranger have reached this deep inside the ship? Was I wasting valuable time?

Catching up, I demanded, "Where are we going?"

He did not look at me. "You wanted to see the ship."

It grew noticeably warmer as we strode down the stairs, our feet stamping a dirge. I smelled smoke before I saw it. It hung in the corridor like a haze, stinging my eyes.

Was our ship on fire? The acrid stench sent a shudder through me. I thrust away the echo of mortars in my ears, the smell of burning, dust, rubble. Untroubled, Bigby hauled open a wide door.

A dozen firemen sat around a large hall, some playing cards. Surprised faces turned to us. Eyes bright white in bodies otherwise encrusted with soot, they rose and saluted Bigby.

Just then a command was called. A man ran to a pipe in the corner, shouting a reply into it. The command was repeated. My head throbbed, keeping time with the pounding pistons.

Two men approached a chamber at the far end, their boots ringing hollowly. When they heaved open the door, a blast of heat reached across the room. The door clanged shut behind them.

"The donkey men . . . in charge of boilers," said Bigby, raising his voice.

"Anyone else come in here?" I yelled to the heavy, red-faced foreman.

He shook his head, then told me the ship had fifty-four firemen who shoveled coal into the furnaces, spread just right to burn as hot as possible. My throat burned. My eyes smarted. I had the sense of standing inside a great living creature, its heartbeat the pounding engines. Above decks she showed a smooth exterior, but here was her heart, each cavity pulsing with flame as she churned through the ocean.

As we left the furnace room, I cried, "My God. How long do they work here?"

Bigby bellowed, "Four hours on, then four off. Got four furnaces each. Three minutes to fill each one. It's a hundred and thirty degrees inside."

Four hours? I could scarcely stand five minutes. The firemen worked twelve minutes at a time standing before a raging fire to stoke it. Twelve minutes to do the job and keep from being flayed by an inadvertent touch of the furnace door.

Ears numb and deafened, I climbed to the upper deck. Eight days, I thought, it took eight days to cross the Atlantic. Eight days of four-hour shifts, endlessly feeding fires to generate steam.

CHAPTER 21

A POTTED PLANT

My stomach growled audibly as I entered our cabin. A glance at my timepiece confirmed I'd missed breakfast and luncheon. Deep in the bowels of the ship it was difficult to keep track of time. Crew came and went according to their shifts, like gears in a giant machinery.

Determined to complete the search, Bigby had apparently forgotten mealtimes as well. My sweat-stained shirt plastered to my skin, palms scratched and stinging from the morning's salt-encrusted tarps, I hurried in to clean up.

Dressed in a pale blue skirt and pin-tucked white blouse, Diana's lips made an O, then she rang for Felix and sent him up for sandwiches.

Fighting a gnawing sense of futility, I told Diana of my search as I turned on the faucet and showered. She leaned against the door listening attentively, saying little while I dressed, then brought out her salve, her face glum.

I asked, "What's the matter, sweet?"

She frowned, applying paste to my scrapes. "I wondered where you'd got to. You will be careful, Jim?"

I assured her heartily, as I plucked yesterday's coat jacket off the peg. Diana stopped me, took it and pointed at the vest and dinner jacket with satin lapels laid upon the bed. I donned them without complaint. In matters of form, she won by a length.

She loosened my tie and reknotted it, looking out of sorts, but said only, "Dora, that dratted girl. Couldn't find her all morning. Probably nothing . . ."

Felix returned with a meal which I consumed without tasting. He could have raised the cloche upon lamb in arsenic sauce, or potatoes with a gravy of strychnine and I'd have wolfed it down without a thought, because I was peering at the calendar on the desk.

Our sixth day on board. Only two days remained before we reached England. In hindsight, the ship's search seemed more wishful thinking than incisive strategy. Grapeshot got results but seldom brought down a precise target. We'd been at sea six days. No, a stowaway on the lower decks would be noticed before now.

I said, "Dash it, Diana, I'm missing something. How could the killer exit the music room? I've got to go back there." I looked around for my hat.

Handing it to me, Diana said, "I'm coming too."

She pinned up her hair for dinner, saying, "In 'The Adventure of the Speckled Band,' it's a deadly serpent that enters the locked room, isn't it? Holmes always sees things that poor Watson can't. Let's have a contest—see whether I notice everything you do."

Diana was reading Conan Doyle? I chuckled in admiration. "Your wish is my command."

She made a comical face as we walked up the stairs. "That's what djinns say—genies, in the west. But djinns aren't fairy godmothers, making wishes come true. They always extract a very nasty price! Why are Persian stories so gloomy?"

When we entered the music room it wasn't empty. Chief Steward Johnson stood at the fore. "Turn it to the right!" he called to a pair of crewmen moving the large potted palm. It looked lopsided, so he had them turn it to present its best aspect. A perfectionist, I thought, greeting him.

He bowed, beaming at us—a common occurrence whenever Diana accompanied me—and came over. "Nothing has been removed," he assured me, "but the room must be prepared for the children's fete tomorrow night." He gestured, his long face pained. "Such a tragedy. And that it should happen here!"

"Of course," I said, walking to the pantry. Dash it, had they already cleaned up any clues that might have remained? I opened and closed cupboards, conscious of several pairs of curious eyes. In daylight, the dinner chute appeared even smaller. Far too narrow to offer a route of escape—even if some trays could be removed, there was not sufficient space for a person to squeeze inside.

Returning to the hall, I began a close examination of the floor, the position of the chairs and the long windows framed by burgundy velvet curtains. Johnson was scowling at the pair positioning the smaller shrub. "Careful now! Can't have more mud on the carpet!"

How proprietary his tone was.

A series of recollections fell into place. When the two men set down the planter, I knelt and parted the fronds. Then I examined the larger one.

There. For a moment it was all I could see. Of course.

Giddy with hope I called to a thin steward, "A moment please. Would you stand behind the curtain there? Yes, up against the window."

Startled, he glanced at Johnson, then did as I asked.

The outline of his body was visible against the afternoon light.

"Thank you," I said, then bent and peered at the doorstep. It was clean. I examined the next window, and there it was: against the bottom of the French window nearest the entrance lay a clod of soil. A partial footprint smeared across a corner of the frame.

"Interesting?" I pointed it out to Diana, keeping my tone neutral to mask my excitement.

"Oh!" She gasped. "How did you—?"

Tsking, a crewman scooped up the clod and wiped down the frame.

Diana said, "That dirt was under the curtain. How d'you know it was there?"

"Remember that narrow nook in Dora's room? My unwanted guest tucked in there nicely. I have a feeling he's used that trick before."

"But . . ." Diana's lips puckered as she tilted her head. "There aren't any nooks and crannies here."

I took in the vast chamber's classical whimsy, the painted clouds, the great bank of curving glass and told her, "I've got a theory—or part of one. When something happens, where do people look? Right now Johnson's directing staff, so everyone looks at him. When he found the don, the women were overcome, so all attention moved to them. He sent Edna for Bigby and the captain, and escorted Miss Rood out. No one was looking at the plants."

"The potted palms!"

"Right. We thought the altercation toppled one. But why? The don was nowhere near it. I think it came down when the killer tried to step into it. But now there's a mess, dirt everywhere. Where can he go? No, he has one chance. He kicks the soil about, and climbs into the second pot. This time he's careful, the planter takes his weight. Look."

I brought her to the larger shrub, pointed out the bent, crushed fronds on one side. "So he waits. When Johnson leaves, he dashes to the window nearest the door. People come in exclaiming, so he appears behind them as though he's just entered."

It was a start, but first, I'd have to test my theory.

The crew were done. It was almost time for dinner. I walked over to Johnson and described the steward I'd questioned after the don's body was discovered.

"Oh, yes! Charlie Abel. He's on duty at the bow," he said, and told a steward we wanted the lad.

Diana walked around the room, while I sat, closed my eyes and waited, trying to recall exactly what Johnson had said that first day.

Charlie, the chubby steward arrived wide-eyed, hands clasped at his waist.

I made some remarks to set him at ease, then asked, "We were talking about the day the don was killed—awful, yes—you opened the windows, to let someone out, someone who was ill?"

"Oh yes. The nanny. She was near fainting sir, from the smell. It wasn't that bad near the windows but she looked so queasy, poor lady. She was beating at the glass to be let out."

"Would you recognize her?"

He blinked. "I'm sorry, sir."

"Describe her."

"She wore a bonnet, white, I think. An apron, perhaps? And uh, was quite tall. I remember thinking that."

"Taller than you?"

He blushed. "Yes, sir."

"Why did you call her a nanny?"

He showed me his palms. "She looked older, but perhaps I am mistaken. She did not seem like a passenger in first class."

"Could it be a man dressed as a woman, bonnet, apron and all?"

He gaped at me as though I'd done a magic trick. "Gosh, I couldn't say . . . she had a kerchief to her face."

"And there were others around? In the hall?"

"Oh yes. Someone ran to get the doctor and left the door open."

When he'd left, I said, "We assumed the killer left before we entered, but it's a large hall with fourteen curtains. The culprit only had to wait behind one of them until there were others about, then feign sickness. He staggered about by a window, so Johnson gave the steward his key and the boy rushed to his—or her aid."

Diana put a hand to her forehead. "Goodness. Johnson said that first day he had the windows opened because passengers were passing out from the smell!"

The lad's description troubled me. An older woman. Should I question the servants traveling second class? It held ninety passengers. He'd assumed she was a nanny but wasn't certain she wore an apron. With children playing on the bow deck, that might be an extrapolation. It had been just past luncheon, and we'd seen stewardesses taking toddlers down for naps that first afternoon.

I knew how the killer had escaped. But I still didn't have a single viable suspect.

CHAPTER 22

A GHOST ON THE MIZZEN

On the penultimate day of our landing, tradition dictated festivity, but over dinner the ladies debated the impropriety of such gaiety in our present circumstances. After the meal the wind picked up and with it, the roll of our ship increased into something resembling the slow canted walk of a drunk sailor. I was sending up a prayer to the gods of wind and water when Diana patted my hand and hurried away to the ladies' winter garden. She'd been invited to plan tomorrow's entertainment with the ladies. Leaving Diana to it, I paused at a railing, hoping the air on deck would steady me. At this rate, by the time I found my sea legs, we'd be docked at Liverpool.

Don Juan had led an adventurous life with a checkered career. I'd held an image of him as a beleaguered aristocrat in a long cape and velvet lapels. Now I envisioned the background of this painting. Hawley had described a country in turmoil, with Catalans simmering in discontent. If the monarchy was in such dire need of funds, it must mean the rebels had a great deal of support. With two parties alternating control of government, keeping the peace was a delicate balance. Had Don Juan stood for a cruel monarchy that suppressed its populace? A despised high-ranking officer could well be the target of an angry Spanish assassin. But where was that assassin? Who?

"Sir?"

Bobo touched his cook's hat, and glanced over his shoulder.

"Mr. Lattibeaudiere," I said, putting out a hand.

Smiling widely he wiped his hands on his apron and accepted mine. "Beg pardon, sir. It's something . . . you said, if something strange happened, I should tell you?"

I did not recall using those exact words but nodded. "What is it?"

"Best you hear it from himself, sir. A friend of mine. But it's not a thing I can say. Not to do right by it, you see?"

"Who is it?"

He bit his lip and said, "Best you come, sir."

Puzzled, I followed him into a stark stairway that descended into the dank bowels of the ship. Turning in to a corridor, Bobo said, "He won't be happy I've brought you, sir. You won't mind him?"

A passing sailor followed my progress with surprise. It took no great powers of deduction to know that first-cabin passengers were not frequent visitors into these quarters.

Bobo bid me wait, then entered a room tucked near the engines. Shortly after, he returned with another crewman. Bobo gestured, calling over the din, "Mr. O'Trey. This is Karim Al Farid, I told you 'bout him."

The symmetry of the seaman's swarthy face was familiar. Indian or Middle Eastern—his curling mustache, wide jaw and round face resembled my compatriots.

He yelled at Bobo, "You told him? You trying to put me in the brig?"

The engine's beat was deafening. I mimed to say I'd come to speak with him. He shrugged as though to say, "good luck!" and turned to leave.

"Can't hear a damn thing. Let's get above deck. . . ." I needed a quiet space, but where to take them? Don't mind him, Bobo had said. Karim's outrage explained this. How could I gain his trust? I doubted we'd get either privacy or quiet below decks.

"To the boatswain's cabin," I invented.

A voice behind me hollered, "Here! What's the matter?"

I turned to confront a short, wide crewman wearing a stripe on his collar who introduced himself as the chief engineer.

Raising my voice I said, "James O'Trey, I'm a detective. I need to question these men."

He agreed reluctantly. Bobo exchanged a glance with his comrade, then led the way to the forecastle. We proceeded to the boatswain's cabin, a long, narrow space at the bow near the crew's sleeping quarters. Finding it empty, I played host with the boatswain's brandy—resolving to replenish it later.

Stretching out my legs, I offered Karim a brandy, but he declined, saying his religion would not permit it. Bobo found glasses, and taking turns, toasted our absent host.

Tamping down my impatience, I let the comfort and quiet work on my companions. Drinking with a toff would make for a nice tale, I suspected, as Bobo made the most of it and filled glasses with extreme politeness. It frayed my patience almost to shreds.

Leaning back, I said, "A strange voyage, yes? Have you had others like it?"

"I've had worse, sir. On the *Umbria*," said Bobo. "December it was. Just out of Liverpool, we'd stopped at Queenstown, taken on some passengers and headed out, full speed. A quick trip over the herring pond, that's what the cap'n wanted, but no, just two days afore Christmas, we heard a terrible howl, a crying, moaning sound. And the engines blame stopped cold. Plenty of steam, so that wasn't it. No, sir, the shaft done clean broke!"

I raised an eyebrow. "The shaft which turns the propeller?"

"Yes, sir, the screw," said Karim. His voice had a familiar Indian lilt.

"So, you're dead in the water, in the middle of the Atlantic?"

Karim nodded, picking up the story. "We were rolling and pitching in a heavy sea. But Mr. Tomlinson was chief engineer, on the *Umbria*. He drilled three keyways out of solid steel in the collars and fitted steel bolts of five inches in diameter into them. One sheared clean off, when we tested, but we made another, and it served."

"He fixed a broken shaft? An iron shaft, at sea? Good Lord."

This set them into a merry mood, whereupon I learned of Mr. Tomlinson's walrus mustache and raucous sea shanties. Patience, Agnihotri,

I told myself, and asked them what time they had off. Now vocal, they listed their shifts.

Both were on duty the afternoon of the don's murder.

Was Karim ready to tell his tale? To get him talking, I lopped over an easy ball. "Ever speak with him, the Spanish gent who died?"

Both shook their heads, faces blank. They had never laid eyes on him. Bobo said, "Our shift don't allow much time, sir. I'm in de galley, or down sleeping in me hammock."

Karim nodded. He had the night watch until midnight. As a sailor, he had swabbing duties. I asked him, "Ever notice the Spanish couple on deck?"

"No, sir. Swabbing is in the dogwatch, before five. Rare to see a passenger, 'cept those from the smoking room," he said, teeth gleaming white, head weaving as he imitated a drunken walk.

"This has been a most peculiar voyage," I said, tossing down the rest of my snifter.

"Sir," said Karim. "I . . . I saw something. But you will not believe me." The muscles of his face working, he shook his head in slow despair.

"Told anyone else about it?"

"No, sir. I will tell you now, but if anyone asks, I will deny it. Yet it must be told, in case . . ." He trailed off.

Heavens. This was his testimony in the event of his own untimely demise. Seamen were known to be superstitious. Yet I did not scoff. Only yesterday I could not stop thinking about that invisible midnight wanderer. I said, "What was it?"

"Up in the crow's nest two days ago, it was dark, past midnight. Well, sometime before sunset, I saw a vulture."

Vultures this far from land? Bobo did not refute this, gazing at his friend with worry.

"A gull, perhaps? An albatross?" I'd read Coleridge's "Rime" but had not cared for the ancient mariner's mournful tale to the reluctant wedding guest.

His head shaking slowly from side to side, Karim Al Farid recognized neither bird nor poem.

"A vulture, this big." He spread his hands three feet apart. "On the lower yardarm of the mizzen, it was all black, huddled there. I could not believe it, but I watched it for a long time. I was not asleep, nor dreaming. The ship's bells rang four. I had to check the water for ice floes. When I looked back, the bird was gone."

I searched his dour face. The fellow did not drink, nor did he seem to want the notoriety such a tale would bring. A dream born of exhaustion, perhaps?

He shrugged. "I wanted to be an engineer. But ten years ago, the bosun asked if I was afeared of heights and I said no. I should have lied!"

"Tell me about this . . . vulture," I said. "You're certain it was a bird?"

He shook his head. A tremor ran over my skin.

"A man then. Crouched on the yardarm. A sailor?"

"Not wearing black. No sailor would." He scowled. "I have heard of the rukh, a mythical bird of Persia which comes to sailors. I pray it was a rukh, for they have no malice. Some say they aid travelers in need."

He paused and seemed reluctant to continue. Bobo's mouth drooped.

I told Al Farid, "Say it, what you fear. Get it off your chest."

He jerked. "Why did you say that, *off your chest*? This is what the creature is said to do, the one I fear. It is called the nasnas, a half man, with half a head and half his limbs. If he touches a person, one's flesh falls away. Pah!" he snorted. "Old tales. Stories to frighten children!"

He straightened, thrust out his chin, but his eyes retained a dull wariness.

Was that our stowaway, up on the rigging? If so, the don's killer was likely an experienced mariner. And that explained how he'd known of the chute leading from the pantry and used it to dispose of the telltale clothing.

Karim looked sick to the gills now that his tale had been voiced. Old tales indeed.

I sent him a half smile. "But they linger, yes? And return in the twilight before sleep. It's our job to know what's real, friend. You saw something. But not a rukh or nasnas, no, there was something there, which can be explained. For now, do not tell anyone else. But if you see the bird again, give the alarm right away."

* * *

Although I did not know what to make of Karim Al Farid's strange story, I checked their alibis with the stout purser. Mr. Dix confirmed both were on duty when the don was killed.

Relieved, I returned to the upper deck, thinking about the clump of soil I'd found, tangible evidence at last. Could it have dropped there in the days after the Spaniard's death? Unlikely. Johnson would not have left the spilled soil to be ground into the carpet by staff or passengers. No, it meant the killer had stood there, behind the curtain. He was able to mingle with curious passengers who'd entered before me and been shooed away by Johnson. No crewman, then, but someone masquerading as one of us. The sooner we had him in the brig the better I'd sleep.

"O'Trey!" Bigby called, from the companionway above. "Captain wants you."

I headed up the ladder and shook hands. He'd cleaned up too, but our search had taken most of the day, so he'd go straight on to duty without sleep tonight. He waved away my apology with a laugh.

As we entered the bridge, Captain Hawley glanced at Bigby.

The first officer shook his head. I absorbed their brief communication, realizing I'd been quite wrong. There was no discord between them. That confirmatory glance held the mark of long acquaintance. If Hawley had planned the don's murder, there was no one he was more likely to trust the deadly task to than his burly chief officer. Trouble was, he'd never squeeze behind the potted palm and escape notice. No, the don's killer was thin and nimble—and Bigby was about as agile as a rhinoceros.

Hawley turned to me. "The lower decks are reported clear. What now, Mr. O'Trey? We've got little time."

"Well, I've got the answer to *one* riddle," I said, and told him about my midnight assailant's hiding spot.

He perked up, exhaling. "Bloody hell."

Showing him the ivory dagger, I said, "We found this in the crevice."

He took it, examined the little blade and hummed. "So you think—" His hair awry, deep worry settled in the creases around his mouth. He lifted his chin, waiting for my reply.

"Two separate incidents in as many days—chances are against it. We have an assassin on board. Can't imagine why he'd attack Miss Dora . . ." I paused. Had she seen something but did not know its significance?

Hawley's face shrank, lines deepening around his eyes. Dropping his chin to his chest he absorbed my conclusion. In fact, I was less certain than I'd sounded. The don's murderer laid in wait for me, but how could he know I'd change places with Dora? I shifted my weight against the sway of the ship. Perhaps he'd impersonated her before. Using the missing master key, he could enter her cabin and steal clothes for his disguise.

"Anything else?"

"We know how he left the music room," I said, and briefed him on my discovery of the muddy footprint.

"Captain, sir," said a lad at the door.

Hawley looked up. "What is it?"

"I'm Felix, sir, saloon deck. Message for Mr. O'Trey. From Mrs. O'Trey."

Diana had sent a crewman after me? A warning clarion blared in my mind.

"Yes?"

"A passenger . . . your wife says she cannot be found."

My pulse jumped. A bitter taste tinged my mouth. "The young girl, Dora?"

"No, sir. It's Mrs. Barlow. She's not in her cabin. Nor in the other lounges."

CHAPTER 23

A MISSING PASSENGER

DAY SIX: NIGHT

Eager to make up lost time, Hawley had the *Etruria* doing eighteen knots. Now orders were hollered down to the engine room to drop our speed. With a shocking sound, steam screamed through the funnels as it was let off. Like trying to stop a cannon rolling downhill, I thought as I scrambled toward the saloon deck. If Mrs. Barlow had gone overboard, there was little chance we'd find her in the pitch-dark.

Chief Steward Johnson stood outside my cabin door, his grimace telegraphing helpless distress. He said, "She was frantic, sir. We feared an accident."

Exactly who he meant became apparent when he opened the door. Inside, Dora cringed, her face buried in her hands while Diana tried to calm the trembling girl.

Diana said, "She brought Mrs. Barlow her nightly cup of milk, Jim. That's the last anyone's seen her."

I crouched beside them. "Miss Dora, when did you take it to her?"

Her voice muffled, she said, "At ten. When I came back, she wasn't there! Nor her wheelchair."

Diana told me, "We looked in the winter garden and music room, then tried all the lounges on both decks."

Dora cried, "It's the curse. I shouldn't have told her. It's all my fault!"

Pity etched on her lips, Diana rubbed the child's shoulders. "What did you say?"

Dora whispered, "Told her about Alice. I think about it all day. Oh, miss, why'd she do it? And now . . . I've got no one . . ." Dora's voice broke.

I asked, "Can Mrs. Barlow move her own wheelchair? Without aid?"

Dora's face crumpled like a child's. "No, sir." Despite the widow's harsh treatment, she seemed devoted to her mistress.

Leaving them, I strode up the stairway. An officious voice rapped out commands on deck—Bigby among a circle of officers.

"Last seen in her cabin before dinner," I told him. "Dora took her a tray."

"Hope we find her playing cards with friends," he said fervently, then pointed to the quarterdeck. "We're setting up lights."

He marshaled the crew, dividing them into groups. All day we'd looked for a stowaway. A missing passenger was far worse. Tall lamps lit up the deck like noontime, as searchlights crept slowly over the waves.

Standing above us at the helm, Hawley's ruddy weathered face reminded me of my old commander, Colonel Sutton, looking over the bloody hillside at Maiwand.

Most passengers knew Mrs. Barlow; skirts and evening jackets flapping, they gathered around the deck. One by one, officers returned from parts of the ship with glum faces. Now the sea had all our attention.

Watching the lifeboats go out, my frustration billowed. In the ring, I knew what was coming. One couldn't dodge them all—the blows that knock you back, the sting as they landed. God, they'd take my mind, in those moments. I'd try to stay on my feet, do some damage. I'd worn out better fighters by just holding my ground. But this case bewildered me. I couldn't tell where the next blow would come—or who it would strike. I suppressed a groan. I was boxing a shadow. A ghost who targeted the weak.

"This ship is leaking *passengers!*" Vernon said with characteristic tact.

Gasps and angry looks impaled him at once. Looking pale, he ducked his head.

A mast creaked above us, its rigging taut. In fair weather, the unfurled sails were a welcome change from the hammer of engines; sailors would crawl up the masts as deftly as a band of monkeys. Now in darkness, the rigging creaked as though it brought ill tidings.

In "The Red-Headed League," Holmes claimed, "The more bizarre a thing is the less mysterious it proves to be." But our voyage had started out with a murder, progressed to a suicide, and now advanced to an abduction. What in blazes did it mean?

Time passed. A sickly green moon crept up and shimmered on the dark water, an iridescent glow. The air carried a crisp tang like after a downpour. A wave washed the deck, sending up spray like spittle. Standing beside me, Diana had the presence of mind to turn, but droplets dripped down her forehead. I offered my kerchief. It was quietly accepted.

Beside us, Bigby said, "Two hours and no sign. God Almighty."

Except for the sounds of wind, water and rigging, the ship seemed to hold its breath. My mind turned over a different question: if she *had* gone overboard, where was the wheelchair?

Hawley signaled his chief officer, "Call the time."

Taking out his timepiece, Bigby announced, "It is twelve thirty on the nineteenth of August, eighteen ninety-four. Mrs. Augustine Barlow is presumed dead, lost at sea."

Diana flinched, which drew the captain's attention. She ducked her head and laid a hand on my arm like one who's just remembered something.

Hawley stepped toward her and asked, "Mrs. O'Trey? Are you all right?"

Diana nodded.

He turned to his officers. "Send the lads down and return to your duties."

"Oh no!" Diana pressed her lips together, shaking her head, her grip tight on my arm.

Hawley said, "Madam, is something amiss?"

"It's just . . . a very old way to find something. An odd method. Perhaps . . ." She glanced at me and came to a decision. "It might work to find a person, Mr. Hawley."

"What is it?"

Her voice gathering strength, she said, "Some years ago, my family lost some important papers. My mother and I conducted the, ah, procedure. It indicated that they remained in our residence. Some weeks later Jim found them at home as the method predicted. This way of searching, it's ancient . . ."

It was the first I'd heard of this curious ability. Since Diana had studied abroad, I could well understand why she felt uncomfortable with the old ways, but here she was, suggesting it to Hawley!

Taken aback, he glanced at me for confirmation.

Though unprepared for this turn of events, I knew something of what she spoke. When I'd investigated the deaths of her sister and sister-in-law, a missing letter had been the central piece of the puzzle. I'd found it under the overhang of her roof.

I said, "Pilloo's letter, you knew it was in the house? No one said."

She tilted her head. "Adi asked us not to. Didn't want to bias your case. But Mama's method worked. We knew it hadn't left the house."

Hawley looked from Diana to me, and said slowly, "We've searched the ship, but if you are certain, we shall do it again."

It was a bold statement, given the grim exhaustion on his officers' faces.

Diana put out a hand. "This won't require everybody. Only the four of us: Mr. Bigby and yourself, Jim and me. Can we find a quiet space?"

Hawley shrugged. "Why the hell not? Come on."

Diana glanced at me, her eyebrows raised. Yes, I agreed, he's desperate. Calling the crew to resume duties, Hawley led us toward the captain's lounge. Behind us searchlights were doused, one by one, leaving an acrid, abandoned smell on deck.

At the base of the stairs Diana said, "I need to fetch something. Won't be a minute," and slipped away.

The senior officers' lounge was well-furnished in leather and bookcases. Hawley poured us glasses of brandy in silence. The loss of a passenger had drained the color from his face. Tendrils of guilt wove into my mind as well. If only I'd found the don's killer. Had Mrs. Barlow suffered an accident, or had he struck again?

A brass barometer dominated one wall. Hawley joined me beside it. "A change of density and pressure tells of coming storms. Ah—we'll have one soon."

A storm. My throat tightened. I had to solve this damned case before the weather laid me low again. When Hawley went to brief the officer at the helm, I pointed to a complicated bit of engineering and asked Bigby, "What's this?"

"The sextant, through which we determine our exact position. The sun sends in a report at noon. Know this one?" He nodded at an adjacent machine. Though complicated with additional whorls and numbers, it looked like an ordinary timepiece.

"A clock?"

"Chronometer, showing New York time. We fix the time on our ship from the sun's position at noon. That one has Liverpool time and shows, by comparison, the easting or westing we've made." Navigating ships was a difficult business, I thought. No wonder senior officers were treated like kings.

The door opened and Diana entered carrying something wrapped in white cloth. Sitting at a table she laid the parcel down with care. Bigby stood and greeted her, looking mystified.

When Hawley returned, she said, "Shall we begin?"

She bit her lip, looking very young, and admitted, "I've never done it for a person, but the method is the same." She turned to Hawley. "First, I say a silent prayer—takes only a few minutes. Then we prepare the book and ask questions. Do you have an iron key?"

"Any key?" When she nodded, he took one from a drawer, looking curious, yet indulgent.

Diana went to a window, her head covered with a cloth like a nun. She reached at her waist and unwound the lambswool twine she wore there, the kusti, a sacred thread she'd worn ever since her initiation into the Zoroastrian faith. As she whispered quietly, Hawley and Bigby glanced at me, eyebrows raised.

"Best we don't speak," I murmured, remembering her need for quiet at morning prayer. Silence descended, now scented with anticipation and mystery. What the devil was Diana up to?

Mouth slack, Bigby's eyelids drooped. Hawley and I exchanged a rueful glance.

Returning, Diana placed her yellow twine on the table and unwrapped the cloth bundle, revealing a worn, brown book. "Right. Let's begin."

Bigby blinked awake, as she held out a hand. "The key?"

Hawley handed it over. Placing it between the pages, she wrapped the sacred thread around it, keeping the head of the key protruding from the pages. After securing the ends of the twine, she turned to us, smiling at our mystified expressions.

"Now I'll ask a series of question to each of you. First Jim, then Mr. Bigby, and then the captain. But I don't know the ship very well, so you can help me by saying what is situated after what. We'll start at the top, on the promenade deck, and work our way down, all right?"

Still puzzled, we agreed.

"What's the foremost point, near the bow?"

"The foredeck and capstan, you mean?"

"Right." She had me sit across from her and place my forefinger under one edge of the key, her own at the other.

When she released the book, it swayed, balanced delicately between our fingertips.

"Lord of wisdom, guide us to find Mrs. Barlow," she intoned, repeating the chant three times. The book swung gently.

Diana said, "Where is Mrs. Barlow? Is she in the sea?"

Nothing happened. I glanced up. Who was expected to answer?

"Keep your mind empty," Diana said. "Do nothing."

That was easy, I thought. But it proved difficult as her questions continued.

"Is she on the foredeck?" She waited, then repeated the question.

She glanced at Bigby. "What comes after that?"

"Ah, foc'scle, navigation room, then funnels . . ."

"And viewing deck," supplied the Captain, leaning forward, intrigued.

Eyes closed, Diana continued the questions through the upper deck and progressed down the port side, the captain naming parts of the ship.

The ship's gentle rocking did not trouble me. A clock dinged. A half hour had passed. If she was going to repeat the entire sequence with Hawley, now watching with close attention, and Bigby—presently fast asleep—it would be dawn before we were done.

And then it happened. "Is she near the lifeboats?" Diana asked.

Lifeboats. I had not checked inside the lifeboats. The key turned, the book dropped to the table.

"I'm sorry," I said, "I was distracted." But Diana was beaming at me.

"She's near the lifeboats," she told Hawley, the certainty in her voice astonishing both of us. "Check the lifeboats."

Bigby woke with a start, saying, "What's happened?"

I explained as we hurried from the bridge. Hawley gestured to a pair of sailors to join us. We did not have far to go, down a narrow iron stair to the upper deck and along the starboard side. The lifeboats there seemed in good order, so we returned and crossed to port.

There, under the second lifeboat was a shadow, jammed between winch housing and deck rails. A wheelchair. Slumped in it sat Mrs. Barlow, her bonnet askew, chin resting on her chest.

Was she dead? I crouched beside her. "Mrs. Barlow? Are you all right?"

Her wrist was warm. Someone moved the chair, dislodging it. With a gasp she woke, startled eyes blinking. "Eh?" She gave a choked sound and caught at me, gripping my sleeve.

Hawley's accent deepened as he said, "You're safe, ma'am. Are you hurt? Do you know where you are?"

Her head wobbled in a disoriented manner. Bigby snapped out an order to summon the doctor.

Diana's whisper came from behind me. "Oh, Khodaiji, thank you."

She'd done it. Incredibly, her peculiar method had worked!

CHAPTER 24

SUSPICIONS AND SECRETS

DAY SEVEN: MORNING

Doctor Witherspoon came in his pajamas. No, she would not be taken to the infirmary. Mrs. Barlow had suffered a shock. She should be examined in the comfort of her stateroom.

The last of the crew departed to their duties or to a well-earned rest as Witherspoon and Nurse Shay wheeled the disoriented Mrs. Barlow away. Bigby, Diana and I followed them through the galley ramp to the saloon level to Mrs. Barlow's chamber, where they left us outside.

The floorboards juddered underfoot as the engines growled to life. I flung out a hand to the nearest wall to steady myself. We'd lost time. Hawley would have us skimming along to make it up. The boiler room lads would be shoveling hard, the furnace glowing as they fed it. My old timepiece said it was past one in the morning.

Bigby waited with us, leaning against the wall. My arm around Diana as she swayed with fatigue, I was preparing to leave when Witherspoon returned, cautioning us to silence. "She's deeply shaken. However, she's suffered no injury."

Bigby said, "I don't understand. Why didn't she call out?"

"Drugged," said the doctor, his brow ridged. "It's a mercy she didn't fall overboard. In her state, she'd have had no chance."

Drugged. And a bottle missing, I recalled. I asked, "Chloroform?"

He nodded.

"Who put her there? Did she say?"

Witherspoon's face closed like a book slammed shut. "That's a matter for the captain."

Diana gasped. "Then she did!"

"I'll see the captain tomorrow at eight," Witherspoon said. "Good night."

* * *

To keep ahead of the coming mid-Atlantic storm the *Etruria* was sailing at a good lick, her vibration sending untethered objects rattling about. Glasses knocked against the table-rail, pens rolled off the sideboard and frames thumped against the wall. Diana moved around the room with the quiet efficiency of a surgeon.

Shedding clothes I laid down, but despite bone weariness, my mind spun like a dervish.

The hours before daylight differ from sunset in some essential quality, different even from the later glow of sunrise. High on the north Indian slopes, with Nanga Parbat—the naked mountain above me, I'd found them a time of truth. At daybreak one could cover oneself in conversation, don one's occupation and make plans for the day. But earlier, when only stars glimmer above, one's mind is bare. The truth comes softly in such moments.

On one such morning, alone in a hospital ward, watching the sky brighten behind palm trees, I'd faced the truth about my military prospects. Both my mixed race and my injuries meant I had no future with the British Indian army. I could have begged a job in provisions or ordnance, but I had no excitement for it. The prospect of such a lifetime was an anvil pressing down on me. A moment of truth, painful yet precious.

Since sleep turned me away, I puzzled through the recent events. Diana's mysterious "method," her reluctance which had increased both its credibility and the implication of an occult hand at work. How had that key turned of its own accord? Diana had no reason to jostle it. If it had not happened under my fingers, I would not have believed it.

"All right, Jim?" Diana said, turning up a lamp. "You've been so restless. Can't you sleep?" She reached for a bottle of lotion and smoothed it over her face.

I asked, "How'd you do it? The trick with the book and key?"

"There's no trick, Jim," Diana said, her eyes crinkled. "I don't know how it works. I was a child the first time I saw it done. In Simla, when I lost my pup I was so upset—sometimes they're carried off by wolves. Mama and my grana did the ceremony. They sat quietly, asking questions in the stillness. When Grana said, 'Is he near the laundry?' the key turned. We found my poor puppy, whimpering at the bottom of the chute." She bent to put away her lotion.

"Looked like some sort of magic."

She huffed out a laugh. "I've never been comfortable with things like that. And one shouldn't ask too much from . . . luck, don't you think? It's as though . . . oh, this will sound foolish . . . as though there might be a—a price to it. That's nonsense, but you see why, don't you?"

"Hmm." Diana's reluctant admission astonished me. Accustomed to her practical manner, I'd not seen this part of her. Was she really fearful that our own good fortune would not last?

Instead, I said, "Can't believe we missed seeing Mrs. Barlow. All that time, sitting in a lifeboat's shadow."

She came and perched on my bunk, frowning. "Jim, what if you *didn't* miss her? What if she was put there after you searched?"

"After? Scores of passengers about," I scoffed. "She'd have been seen."

"Would she? I was watching the hullabaloo. Hawley sent passengers back to their rooms. After searching each deck, you moved to the next. No one went back, that I could see."

I tried to picture it but the evening was a jumble. Diana turned down the light and lay down by me. I slid an arm over her, glad of her presence, her mind, her shape.

This whole investigation was bizarre. I'd struggled with convoluted cases before, traveled the breadth of India to solve her family's case. It had seemed impossibly obscure, but when I'd been attacked in the street, I knew I was close, that my foe feared being uncovered. At each step I had the sense of a competent enemy, a careful planner.

The Spanish don's murder had no such hallmark. At first methodical, the killer's actions now seemed ill-thought and poorly executed. The assault on me, abducting Mrs. Barlow—bold, rash moves. Could it really be the work of one person?

"Jim?" Diana whispered. Moonlight from the porthole filtered across her face.

"Yes?" The ship's engines revved to a higher note of warning.

"I think something's happened to Adi. I wrote to him two months ago, but he didn't reply."

"Tsch. You know Adi. Probably busy with a new venture, sweet. I'm sure he's all right," I replied, keeping my voice placid. "It's late now. Go to sleep."

Diana would be furious later, but I could not betray Adi's confidence. Feeling like a cad, I returned her soft "good night."

Secrets were part of my job. Yet keeping them from Diana felt like a betrayal.

* * *

Before eight the next morning, we climbed the narrow stairs to the bridge, where the doctor made a brief report. Diana had insisted upon coming, since it had to do with Mrs. Barlow.

Sitting at his table in a crisp navy blue uniform, Hawley's eyes bulged. "Her maid. The girl Dora? You're certain?"

Witherspoon said, "Mrs. Barlow had just finished the milk when her maid wheeled her out. She could not turn and see who it was that took her on deck. Assumed it was Dora, sulking."

"But Dora was distraught!" Diana protested. "She's the one who alerted me."

Hawley's mouth twisted as though he'd tasted something sour. "Is the girl deranged?"

Diana pleaded, "There must be another explanation."

The captain leaned back. "Mrs. O'Trey, I'm sorry. Even if Mrs. Barlow is unharmed, such an accusation . . ." He spread a hand toward me.

"Was her door latched?"

The doctor said, "Apparently not. The girl carries things in and out, so it's kept unlocked."

Diana said. "Mr. Hawley, there's some mischief afoot. Earlier the head chef mistook another woman for Dora."

I nodded. "It is just possible: Mrs. Barlow was in her room—the door opens behind her. Perhaps a cloth or napkin is tucked around her neck. She hears, 'Time to get some air,' and she's wheeled out of the room."

Diana protested, "But she'd be furious. Holler bloody murder."

"Under the effects of chloroform?"

The doctor interrupted, "The touch of a napkin would not be enough. She'd have to breathe in the anesthetic several times. Most do not understand the effects of these vapors. Too little would give her a head-ache, fatigue, dizziness. Too much and her breathing is suppressed. She would die."

I puzzled over that. Wouldn't such knowledge of sedation require medical training? Diana had worked in a hospital briefly. Perhaps the killer also?

Getting slowly to his feet, Hawley said, "Who's behind this, O'Trey? You must have a theory." His ruddy complexion had faded to a grey cast.

Why had Mrs. Barlow been abducted? This did not seem the work of a political assassin. Unless that was what the killer intended? Hawley's question brought to mind a snippet from my time at the Dupree agency, a dark possibility.

Diana covered a yawn. She'd done well last night and once again sur-prised me. Persuading the ship's officers had taken courage, and persistence.

"You've done enough, Diana. Why not rest today?" I suggested, not wanting her to hear my suspicions.

When she'd departed, I said, "Our crossing takes eight days. On day two the Spanish don was killed. Mr. Bigby saw someone in a white skirt leading the don to the music room. The killer discarded it in the galley chute—a torn white skirt and scarf. A bottle of chloroform was taken from the sick bay—likely used on both the don and Mrs. Barlow. This implies some knowledge of medicine, but his nurse is in the clear. She's got an alibi for both relevant times. The physician for the first, and patients for the evening Mrs. Barlow was taken.

"And the person who attacked me is thin, nimble and quick-witted."

Hawley rubbed his eyes and puffed out his lips. "Is this a man or a woman?"

I got up and moved my aching shoulders. Could my assailant really be a woman, as Diana suggested? Wouldn't a woman *feel* different? "A man masquerading as a woman, perhaps. I cannot imagine a woman taking such risks."

"Don Juan and Mrs. Barlow are aged. Wouldn't take much," he reminded me.

"But Dora and I aren't—you think he preys upon the weak?"

Fear spurted in my belly. Diana's narrow five-foot frame might strike some as fragile, though I knew otherwise. "He killed an old man, abducted Mrs. Barlow. Could have finished her off—"

Hawley demanded, "Why didn't he kill her? Why take her and leave her there? You think we surprised him? He had to hide, get away? Your wife was quick to sound an alarm."

I squinted, trying to see my way through the maze. What was different about the two abductions? "Don Juan was taken by daylight, Mrs. Barlow in the evening, and quickly missed. I wonder . . . was it too dark for his purpose?"

What else? What did not happen in the second instance? An ugly thought snaked through my mind. "She may have been unconscious. Sedated, Mrs. Barlow didn't serve. He wanted her awake . . . to see him?"

It would take a determined foe only seconds to strangle the old lady. What killer needed his victim awake? It made little sense.

"But why?" Hawley said, picking up and tapping his pipe.

I heaved a breath. "Papers reported a series of murders in London some years ago. Vicious killings."

His face grew somber as a funeral. "Young women . . . butchered. Streetwalkers, I recall."

I replied, "When I joined the Dupree agency, we studied these killings. Happened six years ago but they were never solved. Dupree said that if we ever came up against something like that, they'd look like separate events; we should consider connections between them. God help us if we've got a homicidal fiend aboard."

"He did not kill Mrs. Barlow," the captain reminded me.

"No," I agreed. "The papers dubbed the maniac Jack the Ripper. There's an ugly bit of evidence that wasn't revealed to the press. However, police departments were told so they'd be on the lookout. In case he came to another city."

His skin took on a sallow cast. "What was it?"

"Someone mailed a box to the Whitechapel constabulary, a box containing half a human kidney. That seems unrelated, doesn't it? Until you make the connection. Some of the victims were missing, ah—organs."

He looked as though he'd gagged.

"But Mrs. Barlow was only moved, not strangled," I said. "It could be unrelated. A joke that went awry. The culprit may not have intended to harm her at all."

"You think it's a prank?"

"Maybe. Who'd play a practical joke after a murder? An ill-timed gag?" Vernon Farley knew of Don Juan's death, but not that I'd been attacked. Was this a bit of tomfoolery gone too far?

"We need an answer before we dock." Hawley said, rising from his chair with a groan. "The local constabulary will take charge. You'll need to go over every step, each deduction. You've attended inquests?"

I felt grim as I took my leave. My conduct of this investigation would soon be under scrutiny. I did not relish the prospect of explaining my monumental lack of progress.

* * *

Too much had happened too quickly. Hawley's admonition ringing in my ears, I sat down and listed the peculiar events each day of our voyage. I'd soon need to justify my line of inquiry, list the steps I'd taken and already they were a blur.

When Diana returned from the washroom, I thumbed my pile of notes. "It's impossible. There are too many passengers unaccounted. Did they see nothing? Or not care to come forward?"

Diana sat down beside me. "Jim, you were ill the night before the murder. It's likely others were too, and they may not have recovered. Might have stayed in bed."

I huffed. "A ship this size, with an army of witnesses. And not one solid lead." I caught her hand and held it against my lips, breathing in her creamy smooth scent.

She smiled. "Well, Mrs. Evansworth's little army is eager for their fancy-dress contest. It's a fete, tonight. Dora and I are helping sew the children's costumes. The stewardesses will help too, if they can ever get away from their duties."

"Right." I grinned and released her. Then an idea filtered into my mind. "That's a good way to lie low for the remainder of the voyage. If you're seasick, folks leave you alone."

"Ask Johnson. He knows who's on which deck. And perhaps he'll even loan you an army!"

As usual she was right. Johnson sent off a note to his stewards who in no time reported which passengers were laid up seasick the day of the don's murder.

Handing me the lists, he said, "It's a common practice, sir. We mark the cabin bell with a ribbon if they're ill. A sort of priority, if you will, to attend them promptly."

His genial smile told me he knew I'd had a ribbon myself that first night.

"Could someone from steerage get up here?" I tapped the map, indicating the upper deck by the music room.

"Dear me, no, sir." Johnson replied at once. "The gates are always locked."

"What of second class? Can they access this area?"

"Well"—his mouth twisted to left and right—"the musicians can. There are some servants and the like, who attend their employers like the Spanish nobleman. They have a stairway at the end of your deck. But the lounges, sir, those are only for first-cabin guests."

No, I thought, I was going about this all wrong.

Finding a deck chair in the open air, I considered my patchwork investigation. At the top of my list was Mr. Bly. I didn't know what business he had with the don, and it troubled me. The Farley brothers might have tried to interest the don in a card game, though it was unlikely they'd try to borrow on so slight an acquaintance. The nurse and Witherspoon dreaded the scandal of exposure, but I had no evidence against them. Captain Hawley feared that he'd be blamed. Bigby had flushed scarlet that first evening. What the devil was he hiding? But he could not be my midnight assailant—just as big as I was, he'd never fit behind the trunks.

Why had the killer wheeled Mrs. Barlow away? Someone had to have seen her, I thought.

Hailing Edna, who was serving from her trolley of tea things, I drew her aside. Yes, she said, she was on deck last evening, on duty.

"Did you happen to see Mrs. Barlow last evening?"

She smiled without guile. "Yes, her girl brought her up as usual. I couldn't believe she went missing! Is she all right?"

I reassured her, then asked, "Who else was on deck late evening?"

The list was surprisingly short—Mrs. Evansworth and Madame Pontin, a soprano. The don's murder had alarmed travelers, and most stayed indoors.

I found Madame Pontin in her stateroom reading an old newspaper, her hair done up in intricate whorls. When I introduced myself, she invited me to join her at tea and asked, "So you like opera?"

I smiled. "My wife does—partial to a fellow called Verdi. Italian, I think."

I'd found that my marital status reassured some ladies and thankfully dissuaded the attentions of others. Madame Pontin was among the latter group.

She glowed. "*La Traviata!* Ah, such melody! Such pathos! I was a magnificent Violetta, you know. The New York papers were very complimentary. The new one, now, *Falstaff.* It is all the rage in Europe, but I don't know . . ." Her nose wrinkled up like a child refusing to eat peas.

Having surpassed the limits of my knowledge of opera, I directed her attention to the day of the don's murder and asked, "Where were you then, Madame?"

"Ah?" Her creased face lit up in a smile that told me she would be beautiful even at the age of a hundred. "Am I a suspect?" she asked hopefully.

When I grinned, her face drooped in disappointment. "An old woman needs some excitement, young man."

She had been in the library the afternoon of the don's death.

"The lady in the wheelchair, did you see her yesterday?"

"Indeed, I did," she said at once. "Her nurse wheeled her past me at about six o'clock. I was astonished to hear she was missing! Thank heaven she was found."

My excitement rose. A witness, at last! "The woman pushing the wheelchair, what did she look like."

"The nurse? It was that girl who works for her. Who else would it be?"

"Did you see her face?"

Taken aback, she replied, "N-no, I've seen them often together, going the same path. We don't speak, of course. We haven't been introduced."

When I found Mrs. Evansworth, she concurred as well. She sniffed, saying, "I called a greeting after them, but they did not hear."

"You're certain that was Mrs. Barlow's nurse?"

Her eyebrows rose. "Are you questioning my eyesight? Of course, it was she! Standoffish little miss. Wouldn't say 'hello' back, after all I've done for her, allowing her to berth with my little ones. Why, the arrogance of that little miss!"

CHAPTER 25

ON THE KNIFE'S EDGE

DAY SEVEN: NOON

After spending the better part of the morning quizzing witnesses, I returned to our cabin. An ache ground at the back of my skull as I slumped on the settee. Without a word, Diana offered me a glass.

I sipped. "Water? Could use something stronger."

"Another headache?"

I quirked an eyebrow at her. "In some times and places, they'd call you a witch, my dear."

"I just know that look." She chuckled, unpacking my best suit—white tie, blue vest, pipes, long tails and all. At my look of surprise, she said, "For later. Children's fete tonight."

Since I'd left early, I took a shower bath, grumbling through the door about the difficulties of this investigation.

I completed dressing, as Diana pinned on her hat, saying, "Well, Mrs. Evansworth was extremely cross about these 'tragedies' as she calls them. If it ruins the fete, she will be furious!" She chuckled. "She rather admires you, dear, called you an upstanding man. Imagine that. Mrs. Evansworth, who doesn't like anybody!"

I grinned, tying my shoelaces. "A fine judge of character!"

Diana glanced up, her brown eyes puzzled. "Jim, I tried to speak with Mrs. Barlow, but she will only admit Edna, the stewardess. And she's dismissed Dora from service!"

"Ah."

She puffed a weary sigh. "She didn't remember being on deck last night. What with the doctor's questions and so many people asking after her, well, it's all been too much."

"Probably just as well if she stays in," I said, running a hand over my hair. "Safer that way."

"Tsch." Diana handed me a comb and glowered like a schoolmarm until I used it.

When I told her of the two ladies claiming to have seen Dora wheeling Mrs. Barlow, she threw up her hands. "That's impossible! The poor girl is so terrified, she won't let go of me. Takes me an hour to persuade her I must leave to go to bed! Dash that supercilious Mrs. Evansworth, this will upset Dora even more."

"It wasn't just her, Diana," I said, frowning at my reflection. "Madame Pontin saw them cross the deck. That was hours before Dora sent us searching for Mrs. Barlow. Have you noticed anything, well, not right about her? The captain . . . he asked if perhaps she was unhinged!"

Diana scoffed. "Who wouldn't be? Her friend kills herself, leaving her alone to care for a cantankerous woman. She's superstitious and fearful, with good reason, it seems! If you hadn't taken her place, I don't know what might have happened to her—and then her employer's drugged and carted away! It's enough to make anyone dotty! Jim, she's awful fragile as it is. Please don't upset her."

I'd have liked to comply, but we had a killer on the loose. I pulled in a breath, trying to view Dora objectively. Diana thought she had nothing to do with it, but she matched Bigby's description of the mysterious nurse to a T.

Instead, I said, "Diana, there's something I'd like you to do for me . . ."

She listened closely, then hurried away.

* * *

I joined the officers on the quarterdeck for the noon sighting, where Captain Hawley was barking rapid-fire orders.

He signaled me to wait, then continued addressing the group. "Our docking must be perfect. We're a day late, but let's have everything ship-shape. Every bottle accounted for, everything in order, yes?"

A day late! I had another day! I felt a jab of quick relief. I hung back, noting his vehemence as he reprimanded a youth for an apparently minor infraction.

Gesturing at the sextant, the captain snapped, "The sun's lower limb, sir! The lower limb is always added! If you'd taken the upper limb, you'd subtract!"

The young officer blushed crimson.

Dismissing the somber group, Hawley waved me up to his stateroom. There, he tossed the British Admiralty *Nautical Almanac* on his desk. "Since 1767, O'Trey, that's how long we've known to calculate our latitude from sightings of the sun! And still young pups get it wrong." He poured himself a stiff drink and gulped it down, then remembered to offer me one.

I declined, troubled to see his agitation.

Eyes bloodshot, he said, "The murder, Mr. O'Trey, I've got to know who did it. I need proof! We're late but we've got coal enough to make Liverpool. God help me if we don't have an answer!"

He seemed unsettled, even desperate as he poured another drink.

"Why, sir?" I probed.

Hawley thrust a hand through his hair. "I hoped it would not come to this, but it's best you know, Mr. O'Trey. This will cause an international incident!"

I gawped at him.

He took a swallow and went on. "You recall that French president Mr. Sadi Carnot was assassinated in Lyon? An anarchist, Sante Caserio, climbed onto the president's carriage and plunged a blade into him. He died that night."

I asked. "How does this concern us?" At the World's Fair the previous year, Diana and I had confronted a cohort of international anarchists in Chicago. But that was a different story. I sympathized with the demands of workingmen, but assassination? It alienated the public and set back the cause of labor.

Hawley said, "Caserio asked for no mercy and got none. Guillotined before we sailed. Now hear me."

He placed both palms on the table. "The government suspected he was part of a larger plot. More world leaders would be assassinated. That's why I was charged with Don Juan's safety."

I drew a long breath. "His death on an English ship looks bad."

"It smacks of collusion! Spain will demand we turn over the assassin, O'Trey, but it's an English court for him. I need you to find the killer!" Head thrust forward, he leaned on his forearms.

"And if we cannot find proof? What then? Bring in Scotland Yard?"

He drew a hand over his face. "It's worse, O'Trey. Spain is unstable. Archduchess Maria Christina, the regent, she's Austrian. See the trouble?"

I didn't. "You fear that the don's death might be a pretext for . . . what?"

His face had taken on a grey tinge. "Spain is on a knife's edge. If they cannot raise funds to fight rebels, there'd be another coup. Nothing unites so well as a quarrel with Britain. We must offer up the killer as proof of British justice."

I leaned back, absorbing his argument. Was this why he'd asked me, an American, to investigate? Diana and I had arrived at the new Ellis Island station in the fall of 1892. Over the course of a long afternoon, we'd been processed as immigrants and granted naturalization. We'd rejoiced to become newfound Americans—getting accustomed to the idea, though, was another matter. If I delivered the culprit, it offered the credibility of a disinterested party. If I was unable to, he could point to my incompetence. Yet his bleak manner suggested no such machinations.

He gazed at his drink. "Been at sea since I was sixteen, O'Trey. This will end my career in disgrace."

A ship's captain bore the ultimate responsibility for his floating city. Don Juan had been killed on Hawley's watch. He sipped his whiskey, gazing over the water. "The authorities need a scapegoat, Mr. O'Trey. If you cannot find the killer, I'm it. No one will believe an assassin could operate on my ship without assistance."

Transatlantic travel had mired me in international politics, but I felt sorely unprepared. He needed answers, but so far, I had none. With the sinking feeling that I was letting the side down, I took his leave.

In the dining saloon I helped myself to the cold buffet and sat down, conscious of doubtful glances. Word of Mrs. Barlow's strange abduction and reappearance had spread. It took an inordinate effort to appear untroubled as I joined Diana at our table.

Talk of the evening's fete occupied my companions. I ate without tasting the meal, for I received a host of visitors, each eager to share some rumor or suspicion.

Why did we spend so much time at meals, I wondered? Perhaps because for passengers, there was little else to do. With the usual entertainment abandoned, most kept aloof and eyed one another with caution.

Weary and heavy-headed, my spirits sank as I dabbed my face in the overheated hall. Sherlock Holmes would have got much further in three days and likely found crucial clues that pointed irrefutably to the killer. I had little evidence, only a slew of possible suspects who likely possessed enough influence and connections to hop off the ship in Liverpool and swagger away.

As I mopped my forehead, Diana said, "What's that kerchief, Jim?"

I handed it to her and stirred my pudding, blinking to clear my head.

Diana gazed at the kerchief. "This isn't yours! Where'd you find it?"

I closed my eyes. Was every single thing to be mysterious today, even a damn handkerchief? "It was in my pocket, sweet, whose else would it be?"

"That's odd," she said, sniffing. She frowned at it, then tucked the kerchief into her capacious little bag.

My headache had returned like Hamlet's vengeful ghost, full of ire and portent and I was no closer to the truth. Keep going, I thought. That's all I could do. But what was my next step? What cages could I rattle, what trees could I shake?

The *Etruria* bobbed slowly, each dip the breath of a great beast making steadily for home.

CHAPTER 26

DAMNING EVIDENCE

I used the gymnasium that afternoon, pounding my frustration into the punching bag until droplets streamed down my temples. It hurt, but it filled the hole inside me that had been crowded with confusion. Releasing that felt good.

"This killer is—unnatural," I told Diana, unlacing my army boots to clean up for the evening's grand fete. "It's just—awkward, the clues, like that torn skirt, the muddy footprint. Soon we'll dock, but I'm no closer to an answer. The peculiar features of a case often explain it—"

"Holmes, no doubt?" Diana put a fresh shirt from our trunk on the bed.

I gave her a half smile. "We've got a host of peculiar features. Everything about this case is peculiar."

Diana brushed her hair and began to wind her complicated coiffure. She said, "The don's gruesome death . . . isn't it telling? The killer . . . what do we know about him?"

"Three things," I counted on my fingers. "Got some medical knowledge, he's thin, and quick on his feet." Was that all I knew?

"A thin djinn?" Diana grinned.

I chuckled, glad of the levity. "Thin-jin he is. He killed the don on the second day of our sailing. How did he manage it? Barely time to prepare."

She tilted her head like a bird. "Prepare?"

I yanked off a boot and considered that. "I'd first steal the clothes and chloroform—"

"And Felix's master key," Diana inserted.

"Yes, then locate a quiet spot and find out how to snatch the don."

That part had been well planned. Or the killer was incredibly lucky. He'd found the Spaniard alone and taken advantage of it. But how had he known the music room would be empty? I frowned. A simple way to ensure that would be to simply lock it. So how did he have the key? This line of thinking might lead me back to a steward, I thought, recalling Johnson's flustered countenance as I undressed.

Perhaps after the murder, the killer was less prepared. He'd attacked me helter-skelter and the pointless abduction of Mrs. Barlow seemed like impulse . . . like a magician trying desperately to draw our attention elsewhere. So what was he hiding? Shaking my head, I went to shave for the evening.

Through the door, Diana said, "Oh. I checked what you asked." Tucking in a pin, she patted her hair. "Nurse Shay did have some clothes in the infirmary. For when children throw up on her. When I asked, she looked in a cupboard. They were gone."

Excitement rose in me. "A white skirt? White scarf?"

"Yes. A shirtwaist and shoes."

"Shoes!" I stared at Diana. Nurse Shay was a small woman. "Could *you* fit in her shoes?"

Diana pulled in her lips. "Probably. *Ex pede Herculem*, right? From the part we can deduce the whole. She's about my height."

I ran the straight razor over my jaw with the ease of long practice. "The skirt was torn. But . . . why would he take her shoes?"

Diana gave me an exasperated look. "Perhaps, because he's a she? Doesn't mean the shoes will fit, but perhaps they will be planted somewhere to implicate Nurse Shay!"

"A female killer?" Applying pink tooth powder to my brush, I set to with gusto, scrubbing to rid myself of the sour taste of this dratted business.

"Jim, look at the facts! Thin-jin impersonated the nurse, drugged Don Juan with chloroform, then helped him to the music room. He'd go with a woman."

I rinsed and mopped my face. "Then she turned him to face the mirror and garroted him? The rest I give you, it's possible. But that form of murder, my dear? A woman might poison, or push someone over a cliff perhaps, but to wind his cravat over his throat, then pull and pull, tightening it . . . he'd choke, gasp, flail around, so close. Agonizing. Could she keep it up, watching him die?"

I shook my head. "A thin, vicious man, perhaps, but a woman? Say you're right—let's play it out. She does it, achieves her goal. Where does she hide?"

Diana put on her corset and tightened it. "In plain sight. She'd return to her cabin, if she travels alone. If not, she'd explain away her absence. Now, if she's a stowaway, well! She can't impersonate a stewardess, they're well known and there are only four. Sailors and crew are crowded below decks. So she'd pretend to be a passenger. There are a dozen women who wear black—particularly older ladies. Crew daren't question us, and the guards change every eight hours. I doubt they can tell us apart. Most passengers don't know each other, nor visit the same part of the ship each day. She could just lie on a different chair right in front of everyone."

I buttoned on trousers and set the stiff collar to the new shirt. "Where would she eat? Passengers know who's at their tables."

"She'd get a tray, sometimes. Didn't she impersonate Dora? Perhaps that was her in the music room. And what about the second-class dining hall?"

The other mess hall. "They're fairly class-conscious there too. People are assigned to specific tables. Even if she got meals sent to her on deck, where would she sleep? She'd surely stand out if she looked . . . ah, unkempt."

I wore my blue brocade waistcoat and cutaway dress coat with satin lapels. "If she stole Felix's missing key—another neat piece of planning—she'd sleep in one of the empty staterooms. But the carpenter's changed the locks. So if she's found a nook for her nights, why not stay there?"

"She must come and go for food," Diana reasoned, fixing my white bow tie. "That's not easy. You've posted guards and the spare cabins are locked. What does that leave? The lounges?"

I considered the ship, deck by deck. "The gymnasium, Turkish baths and sauna are locked at night. The watch patrols the deck—they startled some young couples near the lifeboats," I said ruefully, then paused. "Something we haven't considered, Diana. What if it's not one person, but two?"

"Two! Heavens. That could be any of the couples on board."

Inserting my only pair of cuff links, I paused. The image of a large black bird returned, a bird hunched upon the boom, peering down at us. I swore under my breath, then told Diana about the sailor's fright.

She shivered, lashes wide in surprise. "They're seeing witches on the sails, now!"

"On the yardarm. It's the boom across the mast that holds up the mainsail."

She huffed. "And the bird disappeared, of course. Jim, they're afraid. Stuff and nonsense. Think how fearful Thin-jin must be!" She gathered up a swath of turquoise fabric and put her arms through the sleeves.

I said, "All right. Say she's scared. Patrols, guards, she can't go about. How'd she wheel Mrs. Barlow off under everyone's noses?"

Buttoning her bodice, Diana frowned. "Jim, the question that troubles me is—why? To give the impression of a spirit at work? A vengeful spirit," she said, framed meditatively in the mirror like the portrait of a sixteenth-century princess.

"Vengeful?"

She shrugged. "Oh, I don't know. When you described it . . . the mirror, poor man gasping, choking, probably tearing at his neck . . ." She shuddered.

"So why doesn't she lie low? Why attack me, and then Mrs. Barlow?"

"She's diverting attention. Got the captain suspecting sailors now,"

Diana said, admiration threading her tone, then her brow wrinkled. "But Mrs. Barlow, that's taking an awful risk. If she'd come 'round, she'd have hollered. Perhaps Thin-jin meant to kill her, but couldn't bring herself to do it?"

"Compassion." I flicked back my tails to sit, the word bitter in my mouth. "You think she felt sorry for Mrs. Barlow."

"Thank heavens she did. Everyone's in a tizzy—"

"Wait." I dragged in a breath. "Is that why? To terrify passengers? He—or she—creates a ghost to unnerve the crew, abduction and danger for the passengers."

Diana said, blinking, "It fits."

I was glad. A malicious foe was easier to consider than a compassionate one.

"But," said Diana, squeezing up her eyes like a child learning arithmetic, "it's too . . . ambitious. Could one person do all that?" She looked skeptical. "Taking Mrs. Barlow in the wheelchair. Anyone might have stopped her, Dora might have seen her! And if she wanted to terrify passengers, why not complete the job and strangle Mrs. Barlow? She'd have the decks all to herself, if she did that!"

Our eyes met. I read the answer in hers. "Terrified passengers wouldn't leave their staterooms. She wouldn't be able to hide among them. No, my dear, this isn't credible. It's too, ah, circuitous. The simplest explanation is often best. The killer took the shoes to cast blame on someone else. He wanted to kill Mrs. Barlow, but was interrupted."

Diana took out a velvet box and put on earrings. "Everything else seems well planned. She must be getting desperate."

I envisioned a thin, distraught woman, starving in her bolt-hole, desperate to escape the watch, a tragic creature, face obscured in mist. Uneasy at the direction of these thoughts, I swiped a washcloth over my patent leather shoes. It had to be a man, didn't it? Could I collar a frightened, desperate woman? Could I send her to the gallows?

Then Diana dropped to the settee and buried her face in her hands.

* * *

Twisting her fingers together Diana said, "Jim, I've found something. You won't like it. I feel awful about it myself." Her voice throbbed with reluctance.

"What's happened?"

She bit her lip, then took a small glass object from a drawer and offered it to me.

The dark bottle looked like something one would find in a hospital. A sniff of the sharp smelling stuff made me gasp—sweet, almost citrus, but overpowered with a chemical scent. Mrs. Barlow. When I'd bent toward her . . .

"I know this stuff. Smelled it on Mrs. Barlow. What is it?"

Her brown eyes were deep pools of worry. "Chloroform."

My God. I held it up. "Where'd you find it?"

She cringed. "After we spoke, I thought, where is Dora anyway? She wasn't with the children or the reclusive Mrs. Barlow, so I went to her old cabin. Oh, it makes no sense, I know. It couldn't be her. I had Felix open it up and looked about. In her trunk, by her tooth powder and scissors, was that bottle."

My legs felt weak. I slumped onto the couch. "You suspected *Dora*?"

"No!" She shook her head like an insistent child. "I wanted to . . . I don't know, prove her innocence!"

"Why?"

"Dora and I sewed with the ladies, Jim, we made those costumes together! She's unpredictable. Says she'll be somewhere but then when I arrive, she isn't . . . it couldn't possibly be *her*, doing all this. So I went to Dora's room—well, she's small, Jim, she could fit in that tiny space."

I leaned back on the settee. "Little Dora?"

"The kerchief," she whispered. "That handkerchief in your pocket. It's not yours, Jim, that's not my embroidery."

She brought it out, wrapped in a piece of paper. "The stitches are long and uneven, twisting to the right." She winced. "Dora sews her stitches like that. It's evidence, Jim," she said gently. "Smell it."

One sniff was sufficient. "Bloody hell. I mopped my face with that all day!"

She groaned. "No wonder you had a headache! You were poisoning yourself with chloroform."

Chloroform found in Dora's room—and on a kerchief in my pocket. But Dora? Bollocks.

I pulled out my pocket watch. "I've got to tell Hawley. You know that."

She covered her face with her hands. "No, Jim. She wouldn't strangle an old man . . . or stifle you in your sleep." She looked up. "How could she put the kerchief into your coat? Tell me that. You've hardly been near her!"

When had I last seen Dora? I licked my dry lips, trying to remember. "We met her yesterday, before dinner. I put an arm around her, remember? She clung, wouldn't let us go. You found the bottle in her cabin. She's been lying to us."

"I can't believe it, Jim. I'm so fond of that child."

Child? She was only a few years younger than Diana herself. I recalled Hawley's question: was Dora not right in the head? We should have been jubilant to have found the killer. Instead, my heart pounded a slow dirge.

Diana's shoulders drooped. "Do we have to tell the captain?"

I nodded. "I'm sorry, sweet."

CHAPTER 27

TRAGEDY

It's not true, sir!" wept Dora. "I'd never leave Mrs. Barlow out on the deck!"

Diana sent me a pleading glance. When we brought the chloroform bottle to the captain's attention, he'd immediately sent Bigby to fetch Dora. He'd also summoned Doctor Witherspoon to his lounge.

Distraught over her employer, Dora did not appear to understand that she could be accused of all of it, the murder of the Spanish don, the abduction of Mrs. Barlow and the midnight attempt to suffocate me.

Why did she remind me of Chutki, the child I had long ago befriended on the road to Simla? Holmes had warned, "The emotional qualities are antagonistic to clear reasoning." Should I distrust that painful twist in my gut, that ache at Dora's babbled protests? She'd been shocked, overcome. Could it really be a pretense?

She rushed on, "Ask Miss Rood! She called me to do her hair, sir. I was with her that evening. Then I went to ask Mrs. Barlow if she was done with her tray. She warn't there!"

Diana whispered, "Jim, this is all wrong."

To head off more pleas, I handed the doctor the bottle. "Can you identify this, sir?"

He raised it to the light, then gingerly unstoppered and held it to his nose. One sniff sufficed. "Chloroform," he said to Hawley.

The captain turned to Diana. "Mrs. O'Trey. Where did you find this bottle?"

We'd just told him, but he wanted Dora to hear it. Diana's voice trembled as she described her search of Dora's old quarters.

"Were you instructed to do so?" Hawley asked.

Diana glanced at me. "No."

I laid the incriminating bottle before Dora, "Have you seen this before?"

"No, sir."

I raised my eyebrows at Diana, and asked, "Whose is it, then?"

Dora said, "Why would I need medicine? Mrs. Barlow brought her own, sir."

Diana took an audible breath. "That bottle, Dora, it was missing from the doctor's sick bay. How was it in your room?"

Dora's face crumpled in protest. "But, miss, I don't go there no more. Took my things to the new cabin. Couldn't stay there no more . . . not after Alice," she sobbed. "It's no good, sir. It's the curse. I'll never reach England."

When Diana put an arm around her thin shoulders, she clung, shaking. Tears dripped from her nose. The evidence damned her, yet she could not be further from my image of the killer. Her distress seemed directed inward. No, I thought, the killer was someone filled with rage, who'd made Dora a convenient scapegoat.

That reminded me of her earlier fright. I told Hawley, "She heard someone in her room at night. Wouldn't sleep there, after that." Turning to Dora I asked, "When the person entered, did you hear the door open?"

She struggled to grasp the question. "No, sir. I must have been asleep."

"Something woke you?"

In the long pause, we heard commands called from the nearby bridge, repeated and answered over the ship. "Hoist the main and topsail!" We were putting out the sails to avail of strong tailwinds.

"I heard a sound," Dora said, blinking. "It was like metal. But soft."

A chill ran over my skin. I recalled hearing that *thunk* too. A metal lid. A trunk. Someone had closed a trunk in Dora's room.

Blast. I'd brought Hawley a suspect, and now must do my damnedest to exonerate her.

"Thank you, Dora." I turned to the captain. "With your permission, I'll question Felicity Rood about Miss Dora's alibi."

"All right, but for God's sake, keep it private," said Hawley. "And Mrs. O'Trey can chaperone. In the meantime, Miss Dora will remain in her cabin."

He assigned a crewman to guard Dora's door and dismissed us, saying, "God willing, we dock tomorrow night. But there's a storm coming. O'Trey, if we do not resolve this business, our late arrival will be the least of our worries."

Bigby escorted Dora away, while Diana and I visited Miss Felicity Rood's cabin.

Begging pardon for interrupting her preparation for the fete, I asked her when she'd last seen Dora.

Without hesitation she replied, "She was helping me with a new do for my hair. It's quite the thing in Paris. But the girl heard the clock chime and ran off to attend to Mrs. Barlow."

She arched her eyebrows, her eyes flickering back from Diana to me. "Her employer was found unharmed, wasn't she? What's this about, Mr. Detective?"

Thanking her, we left without explanation. Any whiff of Dora's arrest would spread like fire in a haystack.

Diana looked pensive as we left. She'd been quiet ever since we showed Dora the bottle that implicated her. I winced, recalling Dora's shock, her bewilderment. Diana would not soon forgive the blow we had dealt that girl.

Out under the open sky, I went to the railing, where I drew deeply of the salt air, already threaded with evening cool.

I said, "We're forgetting something, Diana. Dora was seen by too many people that day, wheeling her employer down the deck."

"Yes. Too many," said Diana darkly. "Jim, she's being framed! Now I wish I'd kept her with us. But . . . it seemed so awkward, having her in our cabin. Jim, I don't know. Mrs. Barlow's enough to send anyone into a rage. Alice and Dora couldn't oppose her, of course, they'd just have to bear her harangues."

I understood both her ambivalence and her urge to defend little Dora. "She'll get off, sweet. There's no motive. Why would she murder Don Juan? Dora didn't occupy that cabin after the don's death, so the chloroform could have been left there by our midnight visitor." Then I remembered. "But the locks were changed! Does that mean it was already there?" I pounded the rail as my frustration bubbled over. Someone was playing with me, like casting stones to distract a pup. And why implicate Dora?

Diana caught her lip between her teeth. "Jim, I know this may sound as though I just want to find another suspect, but hear me out. You spoke to the boatswain. Now didn't he say no one joined us in New York? Then why did the head steward, Mr. Johnson, say Felix was a *new* assistant steward?"

I leaned on my forearms and considered it. "He might have served in a different capacity. Worth checking that." I glanced at Diana, taking in her pallor. "Miss Rood corroborates Dora's version of events, my dear. But I suspect Dora isn't telling us all she knows. Did she know the don from before? Or his wife? Something seems out of place."

Soon we would dock in Liverpool. My lack of progress chafed like the burn of a broken saddle, but our impending arrival excited the other passengers. Soon we joined the voluble throng entering the dining saloon.

Diana had been right to put out my good suit. Everywhere men in white-tie attire—snowy white shirt and vest under black suits, satin lapels gleaming, held glasses of champagne. The room overflowed with ladies in evening dresses of satin or tulle. Around the crowded dance floor fluted white lights hovered over sideboards glistening with silver.

The fete would be held before dinner, so children were served first. Bright-eyed, red-cheeked boys in suspenders grinned in their grown-up costumes. Stewardesses bustled the children forward, little girls in smocks over white dresses, crisp and freshly scented, eyes aglow with excitement.

"Whose idea was the fete?" I asked Vernon, who was picking idly at his cuffs.

"The ladies. After the, ah, difficulties these last days, they announced it yesterday. I asked, why is it only for children? They laughed, Mr. O'Trey, and said I was too old. What's that got to do with it, I want to know? On European liners, adults dress up too. It's a great lark."

Hawley had suspended the usual games and musical events, so Vernon's churlishness might be excused, I thought. The children were led off to don costumes, leaving adults to the buffet.

We ate, the halibut served quickly after the consommé. I chose the sirloin with pomme croquette without much thought, while Diana had the spring lamb with mint sauce. Pilaf of chicken, roast beef, ox tongue, Cumberland ham, vegetables of all colors, then Windsor pudding, gooseberry tarts and petit madeleines came with desserts I could not name. As though to make up for the dismal crossing, our chefs had done Cunard proud this evening.

My coffee was dark and aromatic. Diana sipped her tea quietly, observing the company. As the quartet struck up a joyful number in preparation for the children's arrival, Nurse Shay invited Mrs. Evansworth and Diana to join the judging committee, so I left them to it and returned to the upper deck.

Déjà vu, that's what the French called the eerie sense that one has lived through a moment in the past. As I walked to the deck chairs, twilight touched the railing where I'd thrown up the first night. I'd met Don Juan here, though he had not given me his name. He'd been kind, and I had the feeling he was not often so. Just twelve hours later, he'd been murdered. All along the killer had moved quickly, and I'd struggled to catch up. I needed a plan. What would he—or she, if Diana was right—do next?

Vernon hailed me. "Mr. O'Trey," he said, flapping his hands, "You recall that young woman Miss Ahn, Dora Ahn? Have you seen her today?"

"Why?" I demanded, puzzled at his flustered manner.

His mouth opened and closed as he stammered a reply. At last he admitted that Dora and he met daily in a nook between the funnels. He'd waited two hours this afternoon. She had not come to the fete—did I know where she was?

"There you are!" Diana called, fanning herself as she approached. "The pumpkin won the costume contest, if you must know. There's dancing now. But the music room's so crowded, I thought I'd join you here." She glanced at Vernon. "Whatever's the matter, Mr. Farley?"

* * *

Behind me, Vernon gasped, "God, no! Is she alive?"

Diana and I gaped into Dora's room.

Out of pity, we'd sworn Vernon to secrecy and told him of Dora's arrest. When he begged to see her, I'd refused, but his manner was so earnest, so bereft that I conceded, hoping a short visit might yield some new intelligence. But had we come too late again?

In the cool light of an electric lamp, blotches of red spattered the sheet like unholy petals. Dora curled on her side in a fetal position. I stepped in, trying to fathom what had occurred.

Her ear pressed to Dora's chest, Diana bawled, "She's alive!" She held the sleeping girl's shoulder. "Dora? Dora, wake up!"

Vernon made a choking noise, then gasped, "I'll get the doctor!" Turning, he ran as though chased by the hounds of hell.

Over and over Dora had said, "I'll never reach London. It's coming for me. I can feel it." At the time, I'd believed her despondency was caused by Alice's suicide. But vivid bloodstains now soaked her grey coverlet. Someone had attacked her. How the devil had she known?

Other than bloody bedclothes, the room seemed untouched. Turning to the shocked guard in the corridor, I demanded, "Who's been here?"

Eyes bulging, he insisted, "No one, sir! I've been outside since she was locked in."

I felt paralyzed, locked in a quandary. Could I carry Dora to the infirmary? If we moved her, it might worsen her injuries. We should wait for Witherspoon, but God, I wanted to do something!

"Don't weep for me, miss," Dora said in a faraway voice.

Her dreamlike state came from loss of blood, I thought, bundling a scarf and handing it to Diana. "Can you stem the bleeding?"

Diana tried to ease the counterpane away from Dora, but she whimpered and clutched the bedclothes. As Diana tugged at the sheets, something clattered to the floor. She reached for it, then recoiled, staring. A pair of scissors lay near her knees.

"Oh, Dora! What did you do?" she said helplessly, searching the girl's crumpled form.

What did she mean? Had the friendless girl tried to kill herself? Jaw clenched, I sent the guard to inform the captain.

Diana leaned over her. "Oh, Dora, why didn't you tell me? Why didn't you say?"

"I . . . couldn't," Dora whispered. "So sorry, miss. I . . . so ashamed."

Her voice was a fragile thread. "I tried to hide it but . . . Mrs. Barlow knew, somehow. She kept such a close watch, frowning at what I ate, remarking when I was poorly. She guessed it. Then she said we must take this trip, there'd be doctors in England who could help me! I couldn't believe it, she being so grumpy and all. But she said we'd go, and she'd take care o' me. That's why . . ." she sniffed, then began to sob. "When she wouldn't speak to me no more, I didn't know what to do!"

She gasped, each breath shaking her frame and I realized what she'd done.

"Keep her talking," I said. Where was Witherspoon?

Diana said, "Where's the father, Dora?"

"*Who's* the father?" I wanted to demand, my outrage barely contained. Mastering it, I held my peace.

Nestled in Diana's arms, Dora whimpered, "I don't know, miss! Mrs. Barlow was feeling poorly one evening, so Alice sent me for a powder. I cut through the cemetery, to get there quicker, and someone grabbed me, miss. Threw me down, and sat on my back! When I came to, I was all topsy-turvy. It hurt so bad. Could hardly walk."

Fury choked me. Some foul beast had beaten the girl down and taken his pleasure of her while she was insensible. I wanted to punch someone. Alone and terrified, she'd borne the consequences, knowing that if she had the child, no decent household would employ her. How had I not guessed that something was amiss with the girl? Absorbed by my case, I'd dismissed her frantic pleas for help as hysteria.

Dora wheezed, pulling in shallow breaths. When she spoke, her voice flickered like a candle against a window. "I was so sick, afterward, I feared . . . My ma had had a babe, so I knew, but hardly dared to look at Alice, she stared at me so strange. I knew she'd not take kindly to it."

Diana flinched. "Oh, Dora, why not see a doctor?"

"There's no women doctors, miss, not in High Point, California, any-how. The doctors, they'd ask questions . . . I couldn't. Just couldn't." She whimpered, her breath unsteady.

Diana smoothed the hair back from Dora's forehead, then shot a frantic question at me.

I checked the corridor. No sign of Witherspoon.

Diana curved her arm around the girl. "Why did you do this, Dora?"

Dora struggled to speak. "Who'd want a wife like me? But I had a chance, miss! With Vernon. Only, his brother would never understand. I've no place in that world, but Vernon . . . he might have had me, if it warn't for the . . ."

I flinched. Did Vernon really intend to marry her? He'd been meet-ing the girl in secret. Dora had to know she was below his station, but perhaps she'd still dared to hope. Her arrest had squashed that dream. All along Dora feared harm from some occult power. But the danger came from herself. No, I thought, she'd been driven to it by a world that would not aid her. She'd trusted us—Diana and me, but we'd been no help either.

CHAPTER 28

THE ROOT OF ALL EVIL

Did we cause that?" Diana whispered, as Nurse Shay, her face tight, bundled us out of Dora's room. Within, Witherspoon's muffled voice questioned Dora in a solemn tone.

Did we cause it? Guilt sawed at my insides, but I'd avoided giving voice to it. Not so Diana. She confronted it with a clear-eyed gaze.

I asked, "You think someone planted that bottle. How could they know you'd find it?"

She looked up, unflinching. "Don't know, Jim, but I did. They may have loaded the weapon, but I fired it."

"Dora's . . . actions could be seen as a confession." I said, without conviction. "If she killed the don."

Diana rounded on me. "Then why didn't she talk about it just now, rant, express regret? She had nothing to do with him, or abducting Mrs. Barlow. She's just . . . convenient."

I weighed this. "Mrs. Barlow calls her a dunderhead in public. She's untethered, panicking after Alice's death. A convenient dupe? The killer impersonates her, plants the chloroform on that kerchief and leads you to the bottle."

The clatter of footsteps sounded as the Farley brothers came down the corridor still in evening attire.

"Is she all right?" Vernon demanded. Behind him, Algernon scowled. I caught Diana's arm, squeezing it gently to prevent her answering.

Vernon gaped at me, the whites of his eyes showing. "I told the doctor, then went to get Algy. Where are they?" he demanded, his voice jerking with emotion.

What better time to get at the truth? I pulled my pocketbook from my waistcoat and took out the anonymous note. "Did you write this?"

He gave it no more than a cursory glance. "Tsch. What's that matter? Where's Dora?"

I answered with a long look. He hadn't needed to read the note. "You know what's written."

In a weak voice Vernon said, "It was a joke, man!" He sent his brother a pleading glance.

Algernon's lip curled in a sneer.

Vernon said, "But we were together on deck. Go on, Algy, tell him."

Instead, Algernon addressed me. "May I see that?" When I handed him the note, he read it carefully. "Bad form, old chap," he told Vernon. "Shouldn't have done it."

He was smooth from his neatly oiled hair down to his shiny patent leather shoes. It rankled, an urge building in me to shake him. "You know about this?" I rapped out. "You said you left for luncheon together the morning of the don's death. D'you stand by it?"

Algernon waved the anonymous note. "This is . . . almost an admission, yes?"

Vernon's mouth fell open. "Algy."

His brother pulled out a bundle of papers from his vest and unfolded them. "Why don't you sign, Vern, then we can put this all to bed."

Vernon stared as though he'd never seen his brother before. "But . . . told you, Algy. I don't understand the dashed thing!"

"Now, now," Algernon soothed, unscrewing the top of a fountain pen. "I've always managed things, haven't I? Let's be done with it"—he turned to me—"sorry, sport, won't take a moment."

Vernon's eyes squeezed in desperation as he reached for the pen.

Diana snatched it from his hand, demanding, "What is that document?" Her tone sent a tingle of warning over me. Algernon was pressuring his brother into something, but it was so matter-of-fact, that I had not understood.

"Don't sign anything you can't read." Diana's voice was icy as she glared at Algernon. "And *never* under pressure."

Algernon looked astonished as though the furniture had slapped his face.

I took the note from his fingers and flicked a hand toward Vernon. "You put him up to this, and now you want him to sign. Something to do with your gambling debts?"

Algernon's face froze. Refolding his document lengthwise, he tucked it into his jacket and walked away.

Vernon blinked at me. "Debts?"

I said gently, "He's short, Vernon. Asked Bly to spot him a loan a week ago."

Diana said, "Don't sign anything. He'll take whatever you've got and gamble it too." Her face softened. "Dora's alive. The doctor and nurse are still with her. You can wait with us, if you like."

We did not speak much after that. An hour later, Witherspoon came out in his shirtsleeves. When he saw us gathered outside Dora's room, his eyebrows shot up.

Glancing from one to the other, he settled on Diana and said, "She's lost blood. And the child . . ." He shook his head. "But we got her sewn up and she's sleeping. Nurse Shay will stay with her."

Face pale, Vernon shook his hand, mumbled some words of gratitude and left, walking unsteadily. The boy seemed to be reeling from shock. Perhaps it was time he grew up, I thought. One could not dislike the chap. While no sparkling wit, his outlandish humor brightened an otherwise dismal crossing.

I said. "At one time, I'd considered whether he might be the killer."

Diana turned astonished eyes upon me. "*Vernon!*"

I shrugged. "Playacting the fool, it's a good disguise. That's his sort of outrageous humor."

Squeezing her eyes, she shook her head. "The anonymous letter, you're attacked, Mrs. Barlow abducted—all diversions to keep us from the real culprit."

Our gaze locked as I said, "To keep me from one simple question. The don knew he was in danger. How could his wife and servants not have noticed?"

It was past ten o'clock, but I did not care. Turning, I marched toward the Spaniards' stateroom.

"Jim!"

I slowed, seeing Diana at my heels.

"I'm coming!" Her tone brooked no refusal.

This time I did not follow protocol and seek Hawley's permission but pounded on the door to Don Juan's stateroom.

The young secretary admitted us, bowing to Diana as I made introductions. Doña Josefina was indeed in, and would see us. Wearing a black velvet robe, her face stark and devoid of color, she set aside a small book.

I introduced Diana. "My wife, Diana Agnihotri." I paused, realizing I'd given her my Indian name, before it was misheard on our first sea voyage and broken in two, resulting in James Agney O'Trey.

"Mr. and Mrs. Agnihotri. You are Italiano?" demanded Doña Josefina. She'd garbled my name so that it sounded like "Angiotti."

Diana shook her head. "We lived in India, but . . . we're now naturalized American citizens."

Doña Josefina drew back, black eyes flashing. "*Norte Americano!* But you are to find my husband's killer. Have you found him? Yes?"

"Not yet."

She looked from Diana to me. "You do not look American."

Diana smiled. "Everyone in America is from somewhere else—except a few they call American Indians. In fact, *I* am an Indian, from India!"

Seeing the woman respond to Diana's charm, I said, "I need your help, señora. Did your husband argue with anyone recently? Someone he dismissed perhaps?"

She raised her shoulders in an expressive shrug. If he did, he had not told her.

"Does he keep an appointment diary, perhaps?"

She gestured. "Armando, *por favor.*"

De Cullar brought out an embossed book. The don's engagements were listed in Spanish, so I asked him to translate the last dozen entries. These were dinner engagements and the like. Bly was listed twice. Lionel R was listed three times. Lionel de Rothschild?

I included De Cullar as I asked, "Was anything on his mind? Did something go wrong, perhaps?"

Doña Josefina's eyes widened. A torrent of Spanish dropped from her lips like pebbles. She rang furiously for the steward, and when he came, demanded to see the captain.

"What the devil?" I glanced at Diana. "What did I say?"

Her attendant Señora Antonia came in and hurried over to the Spanish widow.

Still dressed in formal uniforms from the festivities, Captain Hawley and Bigby entered, looking astonished to see me. Before I could explain, Doña Josefina said, "My husband's trunk. I want it brought here. *Inmediatamente!*"

He gaped, then asked, "What is this about?"

"*Por favor!*" cried Doña Josefina, beseeching me with open palms. "The precious gems. I must have them now."

Hawley looked puzzled, then discomfited. "Madam, I realize you are concerned for your property. I assure you, it is quite safe. Your husband made the arrangements before he boarded. It has been stowed most securely."

"No. No!" Her head moved in pendulous negation. "It is a million pounds! I want to see it. Bring it here."

A *million* pounds? That was five million dollars!

Hawley asked, "Señora, why not leave it be until we are safely in Liverpool?"

A blast of Spanish blew past me like a volley of bullets. Apparently, señora was an insufficient term of address for a Spanish noblewoman. I waited, letting the storm blow itself out.

"Captain," Diana said in her clear voice. "If she wants her trunk, can't it be brought up?"

Hawley stepped back and apprised Diana and me, "You understand what I tell you must be kept in confidence?"

Accepting our agreement, he said, "The late Don Juan brought a quantity of gemstones with him, as the lady says, worth a million pounds. The trunk is quite safe. She's got her wind up, but if we bring it here, it would no longer be secure."

"Set the matter to rest," I said. "Satisfy the lady and then send it back?"

"It's highly irregular," said Hawley, his eyebrows knotted. Taking stock of the fervent expectation on the three Spaniards' faces, he relented. "All right."

Sending Bigby to do the needful, he sat down to wait on a brocaded chair with legs that looked dipped in gold. Doña Josefina settled on a tufted couch. The secretary, De Cullar, and Señora Antonia retreated to the bank of windows overlooking the stern.

Music wafted from the dining saloon below. I glanced at my pocket watch and caught Diana's questioning look. Surely it could not take more than half an hour to extract a trunk from the strong room? Although heavy, they had only to drag it to the electric lift.

Approaching footsteps stomped to the door. Bigby and two broad sailors entered and set down an embossed metal trunk. I crouched to check the complicated seal. It was unbroken. I squinted at it, puzzled. Where had I noticed something like that? It had been quite recent.

Bigby traced the wax seal with his fingertips and nodded to the captain. When we withdrew, Doña Josefina drew out a key and handed it to De Cullar.

What did a million pounds in gemstones look like? We encircled the trunk.

Kneeling with great ceremony, De Cullar broke the seal and inserted the key. I breathed in relief as the lock dropped smoothly away.

He lifted the heavy lid and slowly set it back, then gaped at the contents.

I frowned, puzzled. Was this the right trunk? It seemed stuffed with old books.

"*No!*" Doña Josefina shrieked.

Leaning over the trunk she tore off the volumes, tossing them aside in wild disarray. Her face twisted, a torrent poured from her lips, each syllable sharp as a blade. The Spanish gems? I glanced at the captain, my mind numb. Hawley glared at the chest with stiff outrage.

I happened to glance at Señora Antonia just then. A fleeting glint passed over her eyes, gone so quickly I could not be sure I'd seen it. She pressed her fingers to her mouth, face creased in dismay.

Doña Josefina snarled, tearing at the papers, spitting curses such that the previous volley paled in comparison. Her English bitterly accented, she accused the captain roundly of negligence, of conspiracy and deceit and finally, highway robbery. "It belongs to my country! You steal from the king of Spain, from my homeland!"

Hawley attempted to placate her, "Madam, let me get to the bottom of this."

She did not hear him. Tossing the last book at his feet she howled, "Thieves! For this, there will be war!"

Hawley's jaw dropped. Recovering his grim manner, he conferred with Bigby.

Doña Josefina stalked about, vindicated in her distrust, hands flying out in exhortation. She seemed less vitriolic now, more bereft. But that flash of emotion, Señora Antonia's grim flicker—what did it mean? Was this the final act of a well-planned drama? The Spaniard is killed and his treasure stolen. His faithful wife denounces the ship and all its crew!

I crouched to examine the iron chest. The hinges seemed sturdy enough and unbroken. A label marked number eleven dangled from the handle. I picked up a book and examined the Spanish notations in long handwritten columns—a ledger of expenses, perhaps.

Abruptly, Doña Josefina neared and caught my sleeve. Her eyes glittering black as onyx, she hissed, "That terrible Mr. Bly. He sees us at dinner, and somehow he is with us, at our table! We are on deck, and there he is, again! We try to rest, enjoy the sun, but he is asking, 'A moment of your time, Don Juan!' What does he want? He speaks to my husband, long, long time! It is him. He is the thief!"

Promising to question Mr. Bly, I suggested that given the late hour, Diana should return to our stateroom. Still unsure of what emotion I'd seen in Señora Antonia's expression, I did not apprise her of it. Truth be told, I could not be certain.

Hawley turned at the door. "I'm going to the hold, O'Trey. Coming?"

Bigby and I followed him to the electric lift, and then down various companionways. I glanced at the first officer's stoic face. He hadn't brought me here during our tour.

Glowering like a routed field marshal, Hawley ordered a crewman to open the heavy doors.

The strong room was a large metal box about ten feet wide. An electric light shone on walls devoid of ornamentation. It was lined with shelves on two sides, a container without air or escape. My chest tight, I stepped in. One could suffocate inside this windowless jail.

Only three trunks lay inside: the first marked with the British crown, the second with a large French seal. Both were padlocked. The third was marked ROYAL MAIL in white letters.

Hawley gestured bitterly. "Nothing else. No sign of the don's chest."

"This room was locked?"

"Yes. Under guard every second."

I glanced around the cramped space. "The don's seal was unbroken."

Bigby said heavily, "I poured the wax myself. We sealed it in the shipping agent's office, just before boarding, O'Trey."

Shoulders hunched in the small space, the boatswain swore that he and Bigby had carried the trunk straight to the strong room moments before departure. It had been under lock and key ever since.

I asked, "Has the hold been searched?"

Hawley's voice held a low, defeated sound as he said, "There are four holds, O'Trey. Ten thousand square feet. We'll examine everything, every barrel of flour, every haunch of beef."

His voice hoarse, Hawley removed Bigby and the boatswain from duties, giving orders to secure them in their quarters. They had been tasked to stow the don's treasure. Its loss put them squarely in the captain's sights.

We spent the next hour quizzing the guards about who'd been in and out of the hold.

Past midnight, as I climbed back above deck, I pitied the captain's plight. The boatswain and chief officer were as innocent as Dora. No, here was the motive I'd been looking for, something larger, more momentous and far-reaching than the death of the Spanish general.

Money—the root of all evil. The theft of the Spanish chest changed everything. Spain's government tottered on the brink, fending off rebels to either side. Don Juan had been his country's secret envoy, sent to shore up its coffers. Now the fate of his nation hung by a thread. My mind reeled as I returned to our cabin. Was the don's murder the distraction to mask another deadly game?

CHAPTER 29

THE PERFECT COUPLE

DAY EIGHT: MORNING

Diana had requested breakfast in our cabin, so I thumped down before it, freshly shaved, hair still wet. Dash it, we had only a day's sailing left.

"They say we'll dock tomorrow." I leaned back, closing my eyes as I faced the possibility that I might not entangle this case in time. Dupree had a drawer of cases that had bested him. He'd called it his "humble box," and invited each new recruit to crack them. I'd been the only one who'd had, although by a stroke of luck rather than any skill I possessed.

But this would be my first failure. I supposed it had to happen sometime—no one could win every bout, but dash it all, the prospect of giving evidence against Bigby, or worse, Dora, wrenched my insides.

I mumbled, "A murder and a suicide, occult sightings and stolen treasure. All on one ship."

Diana set down her cup. "That's only two crimes. Another is Mrs. Barlow's abduction, and . . ." She paused, but did not mention my midnight skirmish, saying instead, "Jim, I wonder, is this keeping you so busy you cannot find a moment to think?"

"Go on, what aren't we seeing?"

She assembled a plate, heaping it high. "We think rather differently, you and I."

Taken aback, I said, "Don't you want this killer caught?"

Sending me a fond look, she held out the dish. "'Course I do. But what of the other passengers? Mightn't some of them know the Spanish couple? You look for evidence, don't you? Facts, tangible things."

"And lies," I added, taking the plate. "Contradictions in what people say and do. Gaps in their accounts. Lies of omission."

"People . . . you mean witnesses, or suspects?"

"They're all suspects," I replied, cutting into a slice of ham. "People hide things, secrets they'll reveal only when compelled."

"That's what I mean," she said. "You work methodically. For me, the answer often comes in a glimpse, almost a daydream at the oddest time. So, what'll you do about the theft?"

I ate, thinking. "I'd like to have the answer in a blinding flash, my dear. But one cannot count on it. No, investigation is about building a picture. Who was the victim, and what was he killed for? That will lead us to the gems, and the culprit. Guards swear no one's been in the hold but the usual stewards. So where are the gems? That's a lot of gemstones to carry about in one's pockets."

Finishing the meal, I rubbed my eyes. Sleep had been elusive last night, as I went over and over the peculiar events. Dora and Bigby were both under suspicion of murder and theft, but I did not believe they had anything to do with it. I'd collected bits and pieces of evidence, recorded the odd glances and blushes of witnesses. But what did it amount to? The question sat in my belly like an undigested meal.

Diana handed me a napkin. She'd been to the infirmary early that morning.

Dabbing, I said, "Thank you, sweet. Dora all right?"

She put down the bun she'd been nibbling. "I'm worried, Jim. She's lost so much blood."

A chill touched my skin. Unbidden, I remembered Chutki, the girl long ago, who had called me brother. Stoic little Chutki, walking on bloodied feet. Why did Dora remind me of her?

Diana was right, though. The answer might come in a moment of clarity. Bly's name was in the don's appointment book, and Doña Josefina had twice said she suspected him. Time I saw the New York man of business again. He'd tried hard to persuade Don Juan about something. Perhaps he'd been unsuccessful. Had he stolen what he wanted and killed the don to hide it?

* * *

I took Hawley's leave to bring two hefty crewmen to the Blys' stateroom. Mrs. Bly was away, so we searched their belongings while her husband watched from the settee with a dry smile. They had six trunks, two under the berths and four traveling wardrobes. Besides clothes, papers, letters of credit and books, we found only delicate Eastern ceramics.

"Handle those with care, please. They're gifts," said Bly.

He carried a generous quantity of guineas. I counted out eleven hundred pounds.

Unconcerned, Bly said, "For travel expenses."

That was a lot of expenses. I returned it, considering my line of approach. Dismissing my escort, I sat and asked whether he knew of Don Juan's treasure.

His mouth opened in astonishment. "Gold? Bullion? Gemstones?" Glancing at his trunks, his eyes widened. "My God . . . that's why! They're missing?"

He had not known of it. "Can you keep that in confidence?"

He agreed, goggle-eyed. "You thought it was *here*? Dash it, O'Trey!"

"What was your business with him?"

He spread his hands, mouth grim. Tomorrow we'd reach England. Determined to shake him, I said, "Talk! Or you'll be arrested at the dock. For the murder of Don Juan."

He drew back. "If I could steal a chest of diamonds, why would I need to kill him?"

"Diamonds?"

"How would I know—gemstones are more portable. I assumed they were South African diamonds." He gazed at me. "Or Indian gemstones."

"What did you talk with him about?"

He placed his hands on the lacquered table. "Let's just say, I was, ah, negotiating for another party."

"To sell him something?"

He grimaced, then composed himself. "That's all I'll say, O'Trey."

"You'll talk to the magistrate, then."

He shook his head, his eyes gentle. "The American ambassador to Britain is a friend. I expect he will extend the usual courtesy."

What in blazes was he on about? "Courtesy?" I said, my voice sharper than I intended.

"Immunity from prosecution by a foreign government."

"An Italian assassinated the French president, Mr. Bly. He got no immunity. Governments tend not to protect murderers."

"God's sake, man. That fellow was an anarchist.'

"He was guillotined before we left New York. Britain favors hanging."

Bly opened and closed his mouth, looking put out.

"Where are the gems?" I asked, watching closely.

His eyebrows peaked. "How would I know? But . . . look here, O'Trey, the Spaniards aren't telling you everything. I've been trying to recall it, you see. The Spanish woman did return. She stood on the stairs between the promenade and upper decks.

"When the luncheon tom-tom went, Mrs. Bly and I took our leave. The don gave me a courteous reply and we departed. Then my wife said she wasn't sure if she'd left her stole behind. We turned to look for it. The Spanish woman was standing behind Don Juan."

* * *

Doña Josefina kept me waiting an hour before she appeared, heavily veiled as before, with attendants to either side. Her manner told me she'd set up fortifications complete with ramparts and moat. I needed to break through those defenses. Given her imperious manner, it seemed about as likely as a snowfall in Bombay. Bly's words gave my interview an added urgency. If she had indeed returned to her husband after the Blys departed, that made her the last person to be with Don Juan. It also made her a suspect.

It wouldn't be the first time a theft was faked for the insurance monies. No one would suspect she was behind it. And she'd had the key to the trunk. But murdering her own husband?

Yet I needed to tread carefully. My experience interrogating women was sparse. I wished abruptly that I'd brought Diana. She'd have turned the interrogation into a social call, extracting intelligence with her dark eyes and sympathetic smile.

"Madam." I bowed toward Doña Josefina. "May we speak alone?"

A flick of her hand sent De Cullar and Señora Antonia silently from the stateroom. She took a high-backed chair and pointed me at its partner. Now for the tricky bit.

Unscrewing my fountain pen, I kept my voice even. "The veil, Madam. I do not know to whom I'm speaking."

She sniffed, then put up the black lace to reveal a lined, angular face with a high forehead like a portrait of a suffering saint. Picturing her with the old *general* who'd smoked beside me, they seemed a noble pairing. But Hawley had mentioned trouble in the Basque and Catalonian areas. I started there.

"Your husband was governor of the city of Bilbao. Ah, is it near the Basque region? Or Catalonia?"

She was as still as a steeple at sunrise. "Bilbao is the main city of the Basque."

Was Don Juan trying to quell the Basque rebels? My palms tingled. "Did you perhaps recognize someone on board?"

"From Bilbao? No."

"Elsewhere in Spain, then?"

She only shook her head. But she wasn't the only Spaniard aboard. I asked, "What of De Cullar? How did he become your husband's aide-de-camp?"

She leaned back. "He was the child of my own *niñera*, my nursemaid. She begged a position for his advancement. Don Juan's aide was taken ill so he accepted Armando."

"How long has he been with you?"

"He came last year."

That meant De Cullar was a fairly new addition to the household. "And Señora Antonia?"

"She has been with me for many years."

"Why is that?"

A groove deepened between her brows. "*Sí?*"

I found it difficult to interpret her emotions, complicated as they were by Spanish mannerisms. She understood English well enough, I thought. Her pretense might serve to buy her time to answer, or was it meant to soften me toward her?

"How did she come to be your attendant?"

The rings on her fingers glinted as she lifted a crystal carafe and poured some wine.

"She was employed at my father's house. Forty years ago, before I was married. She came to me as part of my *dote* . . . mmm, the English do not have this. Like a marriage portion."

So Antonia was a longtime retainer. She resembled Doña Josefina in many ways. In their black garb and fancy lacework, one could hardly tell them apart.

I rubbed my temple in frustration. I needed a sense of the don's personality. He'd been a thin man, white-haired with a drooping mustache. "What was he like? His nature."

"He was a strict man, Mr. O'Trey. He could not bear the company of fools."

"A stern man? Were there children?"

"We were not blessed with a child."

"Señora, you understand I must ask these questions?" I said with regret.

Her lip curled. "I am addressed as Excellency." Her demeanor dared me to continue my impertinence.

I needed to crack that icy mask. "Pardon my question, Madam. Could there be a child—a by-blow, perhaps?"

"A love child?" She laughed, a high, painful sound like something breaking, and picked up a glass decanter. "No."

She sounded quite certain. Did she simply not want to admit the possibility? Or was there another reason? I marked it with a large question mark in my notebook.

"Tell me about your husband," I said. "How did he become a soldier?"

The clock struck ten mournful dings as Doña Josefina gave a fine impression of a stone Madonna. "He was sent to military school at the age of twelve."

I prompted, "A career soldier. Was his father also . . . ?"

"He was Field Marshal Antonio Burriel Montemayor. Commander of the Spanish army."

"A military family."

Her black eyes glittered. "He was a cousin to Don Alfonso Francisco de Asís Fernando Pío Juan María de la Concepción Gregorio Pelayo, *the king of Spain*."

I stopped writing. "If the king had no heir, was your husband in the line of succession?"

She painted a smile on her mouth. "Now you understand."

My God, the case had larger implications than even Hawley realized. If the child-king died, Don Juan could have had the Spanish throne. Was *this* the reason he was killed?

Over the next few minutes, I learned that Don Juan had been in the Carlist War, the Spanish civil war. His widow said, "Without him, Spain would have no king! Even as a young man in 1856, the rebels in Zaragoza could not best him." He'd been promoted to commander of the corps that same year and led a Spanish expedition to the Philippines in 1862.

Gathering steam, she went on in glowing tones, "In Cuba the rebels killed many Spaniards. Filthy mulattos. A strong leader was needed. My husband was sent as military commander of Matanzas."

The don had been a dashing, if ruthless soldier, defending Spanish interests wherever needed. He might have collected a host of enemies along the way, but which of them had murdered him?

"Madam, did you send Señora Antonia back to Don Juan that day?"

"*Basta!*" She slammed down the crystal decanter, upsetting the tiny glass she'd filled and stalked from the room.

Good grief. Lunging, I caught the rocking decanter before it toppled to the ground and set it back on the mahogany table. The port spilled over its surface looked rather like a pool of blood.

* * *

Señora Antonia, the attendant, received me soberly in a voluminous black dress, but without her usual veil. If she was a political assassin, no one would suspect her, with a long pale face that might have belonged in the mission orphanage where I'd spent my childhood.

I was looking for a rebel supporter, a Catalan. I found instead the quiet abbess of a well-endowed see, who assured me, "They are much respected, the Excellencies. *El gobernador—perdón, señor,* the governor." She went on to praise her employers at some length.

I said abruptly, "You were the last person to see Don Juan alive. What time was that?"

I'd fired that volley in the dark. To my surprise it struck true.

Her eyes widened. "I brought soup . . . at noontime, señor."

Soup? It was the first I'd heard of this. I paused, watching her closely. Was that . . . fear? Surely everyone on board knew that the don was killed before two o'clock? Perhaps not. The doctor and nurse were unlikely to broadcast it. The stewards had been sternly instructed not to speak of it. I'd noticed that the Spanish group did not fraternize with other passengers and generally kept to themselves. My pause shook her nunlike calm.

"Where did you obtain the soup?"

"Someone . . . brought it. A steward."

"To Don Juan's stateroom? Or the promenade?"

Another long pause. Too long. If she'd accepted the soup and carried it to her employer, it should be an easy matter to explain. But the deck steward had denied bringing the don a meal. I had specifically asked what he served Don Juan. He'd replied "A Chardonnay. But it wasn't good enough." Was Señora Antonia a rebel sympathizer capable of garroting her employer? It seemed about as likely as seeing her clamber up the main mast to the crow's nest.

She'd been with Doña Josefina for decades. Was she simply obeying her mistress? "You did not approach Don Juan while he was asleep, did you?"

She looked stricken.

"You were told to say that. By whom?"

She quailed, looking down. I had my answer.

"Your mistress. Why did she order it?"

She tilted her head backward in a helpless gesture.

In the silence, a clock ticked away—*tick, tick, tick*—marking her complicity. She pleaded, "She is a God-fearing woman, a good woman. *Religiosa, señor.* The master . . ." She pulled in her lips.

"He wasn't?"

"*Es soldado.*" She shook her head sorrowfully.

I'd been a soldier too. Was that what civilians thought of us? Feeling grim, I left her and retraced my steps.

Doña Josefina had ordered her servant to lie to me. At last, I had something to work with. Neither woman had brought soup, for there was no tray or bowl by the don's chair. The Blys had seen a woman wearing black when they left. Why had Doña Josefina returned? Why had she gone to her cabin in the first place?

To retrieve a bottle of chloroform, perhaps? I marched back to the promenade, planning my line of attack.

CHAPTER 30

AN UNHAPPY SHIP

For the moment, I had the deck to myself since passengers were at breakfast. Upwind lay the game room, the shuffleboard markings under the covered deck, the curve of the funnels. Beyond that would be the glass bulge of the music room, where Don Juan was killed.

Doña Josefina had said he was a hero of the Spanish Civil War which, I understood, had occurred just before India's Sepoy Mutiny in 1857. Just four years later, the United States were no longer united, but locked in their own civil war. I recalled that Don Juan had governed on the Spanish island of Cuba. Didn't Cubans have a right to their own land? Didn't Indians? I remembered Adi's flashing eyes as he espoused Home Rule for India. The midcentury had posed crucial questions for many peoples. Last year in Chicago, Diana and I had learned that Americans hadn't healed their schism either.

An image came to mind, a turbaned man, grimacing, teeth bared. I touched my side where his blade had struck. Ever since I'd regained pieces of my memory, I saw his enraged glare, dark eyes accusing. Did I have a choice then? The tribesmen had surrounded Major Smith . . . the leader had come at me, furious, knife glinting in this hand. I'd taken the blow, felt the cold blade slice into me and locked my hands around his throat. He'd flailed, clawing at my hands, his nails digging trenches into my skin. I'd known only that I had to finish it, that Smith and the others were dying, their shrieks and cries raking me. When I reached them, only five of my company remained. Although I'd left India, I was the same weary soldier who'd killed with his bare hands, feeling human sinews strain under my fingers, seen the light leave my foe's eyes. Would I ever recall it without my heart battering like a caged beast?

The red dust of Karachi tasted bitter in my mouth as I turned away from old memories. "It's in the past, Jim, let it go," Diana had said, but it would not let go of *me*.

Four years had passed, and I was a married man now, a man of means even, if Diana's copper mine could produce more than a pittance. Our friends Collin and Tito were running it, with the help of Mrs. Box. We'd not seen them since they departed for Detroit County, Michigan, but now and again we exchanged letters with twelve-year-old Tito, who'd learned to write. I missed that rascal. He'd clung in the doorway as their train began to move, his eyes squeezed together, trying not to cry. They were our family too—distant but fondly remembered.

Antonia's testimony sat in my gut like a swallow of lead. I turned to Don Juan's quarters, considering his reserved Spanish household which had all the cozy warmth of a Boston blizzard. Had they conspired to kill him?

Hammering on the door, I demanded to see Doña Josefina again.

De Cullar opened it, his pen still in his hand, apparently in the midst of taking a letter. "*Sí, señor?*"

I said curtly, "Leave." Hawley would be furious when the widow blasted her cannons at us but now I could not be troubled with protocol. I needed the truth.

Once he'd gone, I held Doña Josefina's gaze and said, "Madam, your husband knew his killer. He was sedated with chloroform—made weak—so that he could be overcome. Then he was turned to the mirror and strangled."

She glared, her lips bloodless, fingers clenched on a faceted glass paperweight.

"There are three people aboard who your husband would recognize instantly. His servants, and you."

Her eyes dark like the bores of revolvers, her mouth twisted. She spat, "You know nothing!"

"Would your servants go against you? I think not. So whatever was done, it was with your blessing."

I half expected her to hurl the crystal at me, but her mask held. One last tap, then.

"Was he a good husband? I've questioned Señora Antonia, so please, the truth." The implication that I knew something unseemly lay between us like a snake.

She hissed, "How dare you. My husband is dead six days—"

"I see no tears," I said flatly. "Someone hated your husband, Madam. Who was it? De Cullar?"

Her nostrils flared. "Armando adored my husband. He revered him!"

"Did Señora Antonia?"

She flinched, a quick tightening of the eyes.

"She's devoted to you, is she not? What did she see?"

Doña Josefina looked away. "She is loyal."

"Loyal, yes. But something changed, didn't it?" I was grasping for something out of reach. "You were very certain there could be no child. Why?"

She stiffened, her shoulders high.

I guessed, "Was he—"

She cut in. "He could not father a child. An injury, when he was young. It did not matter."

"I think it mattered very much. It changed him, didn't it?" When she made no reply, I switched tacks. "I've been asking one question. Why now? Your group traveled to New York, to"—I consulted my notes—"Philadelphia, and now back to Liverpool. Why was Don Juan killed now? What changed?"

She scarcely seemed to breathe.

Taking a chance, I said, "Here's what I think. Don Juan did something cruel. He'd been harsh before, but now it was too much. You could no longer bear it. Your loyal servant would help. You sent Antonia to the sick bay on the first day, when you were seasick, didn't you? I think she noticed the bottle of chloroform in the cabinet and told you. You see the don sleeping, what better chance will you get? You tell the stewardess you are leaving, giving yourself an alibi. Your attendant douses a cloth with chloroform, holds it over the don's nose and mouth. A short struggle. The sedative works. He's pliant, it's easy to lead him to the music room."

Her eyes glittered, her mouth hard.

I went on. "But the anger burns. He must know what the punishment is for! He's dragged to the mirror and choked. Struggling, at last he sees the killer's face. And knows there is no escape."

It was a vile picture, but a necessary cruelty. She staggered up, the back of her hand to her mouth. "Why do you say this? Begone!"

"You left him there, on deck. You knew the plan. Your servants do not act against your will."

"No!" She flung out a hand, grasping the back of her chair, her voice cracking. "I did not order it. He was a hard man—chosen by my father. I did not want his death!"

When she buried her face in her hands, it was like seeing a statue crumble. I steeled myself. "Why did you send Señora Antonia back to him?"

Shoulders trembling, Doña Josefina did not seem to hear. She raised her head inch by inch, midnight eyes dry and creased, awareness growing in them, and dread.

"You didn't know she went back?"

Her face settled into a grimace. I had little skill reading women's expressions. Their distress usually impelled me to sympathy. Doña Josefina's restraint seemed honed over decades. Her silence now bore a terrible weight. Was this from learning of her attendant's guilt, or was it something else, something akin to . . . remorse?

I stared. "Or . . . it wasn't her at all. One woman in black dress and veil looks much like another. Perhaps . . . it was you."

She stood. Looking down at me, she whispered, her voice cracked. "Find my treasure. It belongs to my country."

Without proof against the don's widow, there was little more I could do. Could she have killed her husband? It seemed improbable. I could see her setting her attendant to it, even De Cullar. But to strangle him, staring him in the eye as he died? That spoke of a seething, long-nurtured fury. Could a man's wife kill him like that?

Standing at the railing I went over our conversation again. That moment when she'd looked up, understanding dawning in her strained face . . . and she had not once defended herself. Long moments later when I stepped down from the promenade, the seaman Bobo was tying down a rope.

He looped the cord around a bollard and saluted me with a broad smile. How good it was to see it! I rolled his fine French name on my tongue like a rare vintage. "What's the mood on board, Mr. Lattibeaudiere?"

Growing serious, he said, "Not good, sir. Mr. Bigby is a fine officer. Folks say he's locked up. Saying he killed the Spanish gent. And the green flash say a storm's coming."

Despite his ominous words, his lilting voice danced into my ears, familiar and comforting. "The crew is unhappy?"

"Some say the ship is cursed. Crew told not to talk about it. But in the islands we say, it's Shay and Cassidy. Be Cassidy dead, and Shay's all distraught." He shook his head in a tumble of braids. "I don't believe it. But 'something wicked this way comes.'"

I smiled at him. "*Macbeth* again? Be easy, Bobo. We'll get to Liverpool."

He lowered his head toward me. "We'll have another death, sir. They go in threes. The woman as jumped, the Spanish gent, and one more."

CHAPTER 31

A SLIP OF THE TONGUE

The Spanish women contradicted each other, but which one did I believe? No soup was served, of that I was certain. The galley recorded each tray delivered with rigorous exactitude. Antonia's claim only cast suspicion on her mistress. But that realization in Doña Josefina's anguished eyes, it was like she'd just become aware of betrayal.

She was right though. I had to find the gemstones. That meant I had to keep digging.

I'd twice interrogated Mr. Bly, but he had evaded me. Nor would the old coot reveal anything, unless I confronted him with evidence. The canny man of business was a sophisticated poker player. He'd pointed me at Doña Josefina, and she at him—an impasse. I had too many damned clues, but not one viable lead.

What had Bly been trying to convince Don Juan to do? He didn't know about the gems, so what did he want to sell? The fate of countries hung on such arrangements. Had the don refused, leading to his murder?

I could not imagine portly Mr. Bly donning the nurse's garb, but then, he didn't need to. Diana had reminded me that any woman in a white skirt might be taken for Nurse Shay, so I left in search of Mrs. Bly.

An operative's job required deceiving the innocent and guilty alike. Lately I'd begun to question this. Yet anyone might possess that crucial missing link, the clue that could break the case. I paused. Could a devious killer wear the face of an angel? Holmes had said, "It is of the first importance not to let your judgment be biased by personal qualities."

My frustration high, I pounded the boards toward the winter garden lounge, a favorite spot of the ladies this time of the day. "Mrs. Bly, a moment?"

She looked up from her sewing, surprised at my appearance in the female domain. This was deliberate. She'd have to answer questions from the other ladies and be remarked upon.

I did not smile. Pressure can take many guises. I hoped it might pry loose some useful intelligence.

Dressed in embroidered peach velvet, Mrs. Bly was younger than her husband by perhaps two decades. A second marriage for him? Her slender, youthful neck bore a string of rice pearls. More dangled from her ears. Her boots were made of the same fabric as her dress. Bly was a wealthy man and wanted his wife to show it. I tried not to dislike him for it.

Leading her to a pair of deck chairs, I sat. After some preliminary remarks about the weather, I said, "It is imperative you tell me the truth, you understand?"

Eyes wide, she nodded.

Watching closely, I asked, "How do you know the Spanish couple, Mrs. Bly?"

She shook her head. "I don't know anything about my husband's business matters."

"So, it was a business association?"

"I . . ." she floundered. "I don't know anything about his . . . I don't know."

That was the trouble with memorizing a given line. Under duress one could well mangle it. Her face scrunched up like a rumpled child, so I bowed and removed myself. She'd been prepared with a well-rehearsed line. Bly must have something to hide, but what? I could not see him strangling the elderly don, so nearly his own age and of such a respectable position. No, a *crime passionnel* did not fit. If he was in it, there must be an accomplice with a simmering vendetta. What sort of fiend were we up against?

As I stood at the rail, the sun dipped behind a bank of clouds. I'd long since given up wearing a hat on deck. As the wind ruffled the hair above my ear, which not even Diana's pomade could persuade to lie flat, I had the sensation of being watched. Feeling a chill, I glanced over my shoulder at the empty deck and promenade above.

An investigator's role is contradictory. One must develop some rapport with suspects to draw out the evidence. But on board I was firmly established as detective, so witnesses were reticent. Details that might possibly implicate them were carefully obscured. It was my job to wheedle them out. How could I delve deeper into the Blys' lives?

I headed back to the windward side. Clouds filled the horizon. There a near gale swept the boards and kept the reefed sails snapping. The deck tilted farther as I turned toward the smoking room.

Card games were under way as I entered. Drinks were being served. Some were reading the week-old papers. Catching Vernon's gaze, I jerked my head toward the door. His eyes widened. He glanced around, then joined me as I stepped outside. He'd seemed awfully fond of Mrs. Bly, until he met Dora.

"Is she all right?" he demanded, all trace of the jokester gone.

"Dora?"

He shot me a look. I said, "Diana's been with her. Said she'd lost much blood."

He swallowed. Well, well! I watched him with rising curiosity and said, "Too bad about Mrs. Bly."

"What about her?" His eyes flickered and dropped.

Turning the screw, I said, "Vernon, she's in trouble. I fear a lady of her delicate constitution will not do well in prison."

He gripped my arm. "Here, O'Trey. What d'you mean?"

"She's not being honest with me."

A look of panic flashed in his eyes.

"They were the last to speak with Don Juan, you see? Makes them key suspects. Some business dealings gone sour, I expect. A falling-out over something. It's too bad she'll be implicated." I added, "Failure to report a crime . . ." I tut-tutted, keeping my face somber.

He stepped close, his voice urgent. "I'll tell you something. Don't know what it's about but it's to help her, see? Day the don died, she came to luncheon all chipper. So I needled her—just a lark really, she doesn't mind—I said, 'Bly's leaving you a rich widow, eh? How long do we have to wait?' I was only teasing, 'course.

"I'd picked a poor time for it because she scolded me something fierce. Said 'I'll have you know Mr. Bly's succeeded again. The Spanish gent, he said yes! Another business triumph. So don't you mock my husband.' I didn't ask what it was about, 'cause she blushed, all upset, like she'd spoken out of turn. That's what I wanted to tell you. Bly and the don had come to some agreement, so there was no falling-out. That's all I know."

* * *

Armed with Vernon's titbit, I pondered, how should I confront Palmer Bly? Get him off guard with conversation? The man knew his history, so seeking his advice might loosen his tongue. Encouraged, he could let slip some private self-congratulation, a look, a word would be enough, but I had no time for a prolonged interview.

The gong sounded—what was the time? I'd lost track of meals. My stomach rumbled as I stepped down to the dining saloon.

Despite the high winds and tilting deck, the tables were surprisingly crowded. Perhaps the silence of the engines and their incessant vibration had cheered passengers. But no, the mood inside was dark as a monsoon day in Bombay. I had always enjoyed the annual downpours, thunder crashing overhead, sheets of rain pelting down. On my sure-footed mount I'd often volunteered to deliver dispatches when others looked askance. But my fellow passengers on the *Etruria* sat quietly, barely glancing at one another. Not even the quartet's jolly tune could coax passengers to gaiety today.

Dressed in a blue day dress, Diana was already seated, so I dropped into my chair.

Nodding at my greeting, she said, "Felix knocked on each cabin, asking people to attend luncheon. The captain's going to make an announcement." She shook her head doubtfully. "We were supposed to reach Liverpool tonight."

"And Dora?"

She pulled in her lips. "Edna and I take care of her. Jim, there's something else. Edna told me that on the first day out of New York, Dora asked her for rat poison. She said she was afraid of rats and wanted some to put out on the floor, but Edna didn't like the sound of it. She refused." She met my startled look. "She worried that Dora wanted to poison someone."

"The don."

"Or herself. Because of the baby."

This also explained why the blond stewardess had been conflicted when we spoke. She'd worried about the request but feared accusing a passenger.

The doors parted. A procession of cooks entered, setting soups and meats on the buffet: root vegetables roasted around whole ducks, filets of sole and mustard sauce, baked haddock over mashed potatoes, and on and on.

Apparently reconciled, brothers Vernon and Algernon gave us careful nods of greeting. Behind me, a high cultured voice enquired. "Oh, Mr. O'Trey! We're having a dance tonight! Shall I hold a place for you on my dance card?"

I smiled at Madame Pontin, bedecked in red dress and feathered boa, then bowed and introduced Diana. The ladies exchanged greetings. It should all have been charming and gracious. But passengers hurried to fill their plates, barely glancing at the arrangements of garnished liver pâté.

During dinner I observed the Blys. Scarfing down his meal, Vernon also glanced frequently at his cousin Mrs. Bly. I had sworn him to secrecy but had little hope he could restrain himself for even a day. If I did not act on his intelligence soon, I'd lose the element of surprise.

The officers arrived after dessert, when, tired of awaiting the impending announcement, most passengers settled into conversations. Ringing his glass with a spoon, Hawley gave the impression of a grave father freshly spruced up to make a toast at his daughter's wedding. He announced to the passengers what I already knew: we were delayed by a day but, being well provisioned—which brought out smiles and chuckles—it would be no hardship. He offered his regrets without much disappointment.

Then, clearing his throat, he said, "You are aware of the tragic death of a Spanish gentleman. Therefore, there will be an inquest. We will not disembark immediately, but all passengers should prepare to answer the authorities' questions. I'm sure you will agree this is necessary." He sat down, while most were still grasping his meaning.

"Does that mean we can't get to port?" called one gent. People craned around to look at him.

Hawley put up a hand. "It is only until the matter is resolved. That is all. Thank you." Since more questions were being called out, he bent to confer with Chief Steward Johnson, waved a farewell and left the hall.

He should have smiled. It might have reassured everyone. Instead, a barrage of questions pummeled me from all sides. My calm replies pacified some, while others expressed their frustration.

Fending questions, I said, "It is indeed slow work, sir. One cannot make arrests without conclusive evidence. No, ma'am, there is no malicious spirit at work. If there were, I assure you the ship's officers would have them in hand in no time." I smiled to take the sting from my remark.

As I led Diana out, she murmured, "Oh, well done."

Her eyes crinkled in a sidelong glance that drove the breath from me. I wondered, recalling her previous dark malaise. I'd been so preoccupied with the case I'd quite forgotten about it.

* * *

Diana went to the infirmary to see Dora, so I returned to the upper deck alone.

Through the window of the smoking room, I caught sight of Palmer Bly. Why did I hesitate to confront him? Was it his age, respectability, or competent manner? No, his public persona was a sham. A man who locked his wife up did not deserve my respect. Yet Mrs. Bly had defended him to Vernon. That did not sound like an unhappy marriage.

Setting aside my qualms, I approached the card table. "Mr. Bly, a private word? Could use your help," I said, since my arrival had interrupted his game.

He took leave of the others and accompanied me back to his stateroom, saying, "That was prettily done, O'Trey."

Surprised that he'd remarked on my tactful approach, I dropped into a chair. He offered a whiskey, which I declined. He poured, decanter rattling against the glass to tap out a high note. Mr. Bly was not as calm as he appeared.

He glanced at me, then stoppered the decanter and went to the porthole. His stateroom on the promenade deck offered a fine view of the open sea, where waves kicked their heels in expectation of a fine to-do.

Time to pay the piper. I drew a breath of anticipation. A storm was coming, and not just on the ocean. I said, "You've lied to me. You knew the Spanish gentleman and had negotiated an agreement with him."

He stood stock-still against the overcast sky, then turned, a smile tweaking his lips.

"My wife, hmm? Well, can't be helped. She's young."

He seemed untroubled by my revelation. I said, "It wasn't your wife. Why did you lie?"

Repeating that word underscored the seriousness of our discourse. Politeness would not carry the same weight. This was not unlike a boxing match, our words scoring the blows. Again, mine did not land.

"Not her? Who, then?"

I raised my eyebrows. "Why, sir?"

He sat opposite me, and leaned back, assessing me. "Would you swear an oath that none of this will be repeated? Has nothing to do with the old fellow's death, but you'll want the whole story. You'll have it, if you give me your word."

He wanted me to withhold his intelligence from the captain? I held his gaze. "Can't oblige you there. This is an official investigation."

"Right." He dropped his glance and thought, then leaned forward. "If you find that this matter is, er, not related, you agree not to discuss it? With anyone. It is in the national interest."

National interest? I scoffed. "You work for the United States government? Can you prove it?"

He chuckled, took out a cigarette case and offered it. I declined, so he set one into a long black holder and lit it. Leaning back, he drew on it, then contemplated the smoke. "Well, do you agree?"

I frowned. "All right. If it is indeed unrelated, it will remain between us."

Tapping his ash lightly into his empty glass, he said, "I serve on the board of a banking institution—which one doesn't matter. From time to time, matters of, shall we say, a delicate nature are placed before me. This was such a matter. But for you to understand it, I shall have to explain what occurred twenty years ago. Now, you're rather young. Have you heard of the *Virginius* Affair?"

The American ship that Bigby had mentioned? What the devil?

Bly pulled on his cigarette. "Cuba lies off the southern coast of our country. Yes, I'm aware that you and Mrs. O'Trey are naturalized Americans. In fact, I was advised to seek your aid, should things go awry." He smiled at my astonishment but his grip on the cigarette looked unsteady, dropping ash on the carpet as he continued.

"Native Cubans have mixed with Spaniards so much that there are now three groups: Spanish colonists, locals who are colored, and well, mulattos, those of mixed heritage. For many years the latter two have banded together to seek independence from Spain. A civil war, a war of independence, you understand? While the United States cannot overtly support such an effort, we have, on occasion, aided the revolutionaries with arms and provisions. To promote democracy in other nations, Mr.

O'Trey. The Monroe Doctrine warns European nations of extending in-fluence in the Western Hemisphere."

I said, "And it's awkward, having Spain on our doorstep."

He glanced up, then nodded. "That, as well. Now the *Virginius* was a small, high-speed side-wheel steamer. In 1873, she loaded arms and munitions in Jamaica but was caught by the Spanish warship *Tornado*. She was treated as a pirate ship, boarded and brought to Santiago harbor, in Cuba."

He puffed his cigarette and tapped its ash, a tremor shaking his hand. Bigby had mentioned some of this. Where did it lead? The pause felt ominous.

He went on, "Among the crew were British and American sailors. At the time, the United States possessed few warships, certainly none that could take on a Spanish armada. Telegraphs went back and forth, Britain dispatched a sloop—HMS *Niobe*. But it was too late. A Span-ish military tribunal condemned the crew and executed fifty-three souls."

"Executed them!"

He looked me in the eye. "The affair caused an uproar. We were close to war with Spain over it. Secretary of State Hamilton Fish negotiated the return of the remaining sailors and mercenaries."

I flinched. Mercenaries! Our county had sent soldiers to fight Spain in Cuba.

"Right after that, Mr. O'Trey, President Grant had five warships built. A reluctant Congress approved them. Steamships, armored ironsides. We would not be caught off guard again."

He dropped his cigarette into the glass, signaling the end of his tale. "Don Juan owns property in Santiago which forms a natural harbor. I was trying to buy it for America."

A harbor on a Spanish island. I sucked in a breath. "If the don agreed, America would own property in Cuba."

He smiled, a calm knowing in his eyes. "A private transaction, per-fectly legal. My bank would own the property, docking light yachts and pleasure craft. But yes, we'd have a foothold there. I had a handshake agreement with Don Juan, but so far, his wife does not recognize it."

So that was why he'd repeatedly sought an audience with her.

He tut-tutted in regret, running a shaking hand over his hair. "So, you see, I'd no love for the blighter, but politics makes strange bedfellows. Regardless, I had no reason to murder the old boy."

"Don Juan was in Cuba, at the time of the *Virginius*?" Bigby had implied that.

His gaze sharpened, then dropped. "He was."

"And took part in the slaughter of the sailors."

He nodded, his manner reserved. I considered his words, then stood and offered my hand. He took it, examined my face, then appeared satisfied. I left with cordial goodbyes and a conviction that it would have been impossible for Palmer Bly to overpower Don Juan: his shaking hands denoted neither anxiety nor deceit.

The man was ill. His palsied grip trembled on the cigarette holder and could barely grip his whiskey glass. He wasn't the killer.

If we shook hands earlier in the journey I'd have saved a great deal of time. Treading the boards back from the aft deck, Bly's story troubled me. I found it hard to reconcile his account with that of the stalwart old soldier I'd met that first night, who insisted, "I did my duty." A shiver trembled over my skin, remembering the tight cast of his face as he repeated the phrase.

My knee protested each step down to the saloon level as I contemplated Bly's task. If Don Juan had agreed to sell his Cuban harbor, surely Spain would strive to prevent it? Had *that* precipitated his murder? But who could have learned about the agreement? They'd have to know what it meant for Spain, and understand the ramifications. The don had been closemouthed, even to his own wife. He'd be unlikely to tell another passenger.

The ladies Doña Josefina and Señora Antonia did not seem likely candidates to carry out a political assassination. Armando De Cullar, now—lithe, inquisitive, determined, and privy to all his employer's papers—he was quite a different matter.

CHAPTER 32

THE COMING STORM

I gazed down at my stack of statements and the scrawls in my notebook. What was I missing? My interviews of Doña Josefina and her attendant Señora Antonia had uncovered a contradiction. Either of them might be lying, for I could conceive no more motive for one than the other. Both might have been subject to the don's harsh tongue and burned from it, but what might drive them to kill? And why just then? And why would either one harm Mrs. Barlow?

An envelope fell out of my book—Don Juan's note. I gazed at the words: ATTEND ME INMEDIATAMENTE. J. NEPOMUCENO. Sloping letters formed in a firm hand. Written in black ink.

Damn. Armando De Cullar. He'd searched for ink for three hours.

On the way down to see De Cullar, I spotted the purser's office by the grand staircase and veered to it. I knocked and found the stocky bespectacled Mr. Dix making up his records, ledgers open on his desk, pen and inkpot at the ready.

I broached my query. "Mr. Dix, which steward was assigned to the don on the first day of our sailing? I need to see him right away."

"Well, Mr. O'Trey," he drawled, leaning back, "that's more than one man. There's the bedroom steward, the deck steward, the saloon steward who attended their table, and also the bath steward, not to mention the 'boots' and the smoking-room steward. Each of them would serve the don as part of his duties."

"I doubt the don visited the smoking room," I said, "and the waiters might have little bearing. Could you jot down the rest?"

He pulled up a ledger and ran his fingers down the page, making notations on scrap. I received this list, offered heartfelt appreciation, and obtained directions to the "glory hole" where the stewards slept.

As I took my leave, he said, "Mr. O'Trey, the lads work from five thirty in the morning until eleven at night. Why not see these two first"—he tapped the names at the bottom—"and then try Dugas and Poupart? They'll have the evening shift, so they'll be up soon."

The deck steward was in his recess at the end of the line of cabins. A beanpole of a bloke with longish hair and the alert look of a greyhound, he hung his head as he admitted the don had been abducted under his watch. He'd gone down for a spot of lunch in the first-cabin pantry. "The deck was bare, sir. It seemed all right to go."

"Was Don Juan asleep when you left?"

"I saw no one. Wish I had, sir. Wish to God I had!"

"What time was that?"

"Past one, sir." His crestfallen demeanor and beetlike color revealed his distress. So the don had already been taken by one o'clock. He'd been tortured in the music room between then and twenty to two.

I asked a few more questions and then sent him to summon Glatz, the "boots" who cleaned footwear for passengers in the promenade cabins.

Puffing, Glatz appeared behind the lithe deck steward and snatched his hat off his head. The short fellow had not much to say, for he spoke little English.

By pantomiming the question, "Did you serve the Spanish don?"—Spanish denoted by mimicking drooping mustaches—I learned that a pair of shoes had been lined up outside the door, which he returned, duly shone, at six the next morning. He'd seen no one from the don's cabin.

It was already four in the evening, and a cool wind sang down the boards. Unable to wait for a more convenient time, I went to find the deck and bath stewards. This meant descending a narrow Jacob's ladder to their sleeping quarters.

Grasping the bent pipes that formed its head, I peered downward and caught my breath. Though well-lit, the rungs descended forty feet like a deep well. If anyone were to climb down behind me, it would bar my return. My chest compressed, as I fought the overwhelming urge to turn back. But no, we'd soon be dockside. I could not delay.

During my army years, I'd frequented trenches and dugouts built with earth or piled stone, some so narrow one had to slither sideways. Some instinct in me avoided close spaces, and when forced into them, gave constant alarm. Give me a fast horse and an open field. Give me hillsides, mountains, even ravines, before a deep airless well going down into the deep heart of a ship.

I turned and asked the shoeshine bloke, "Is this the only way in?"

He nodded vigorously, so, groaning inwardly, I descended rung by rung, my knee protesting and pinching at every step.

At bottom, the wide corridor gave onto a room containing about twenty bunks. Metal pipes framed each berth to retain the occupants in poor weather. There was no other furniture, no windows, of course, yet lit with electric lights, it looked restful and well ventilated.

A few bunks were occupied, the others neatly made with grey checkered linen. I presumed the stewards took turns sleeping, so the room was always occupied. Below the beds lay rows of wooden boxes.

"Sir?" a young man sat up, his hair tousled, blinking at me.

I apologized for waking him and asked, "Which one's Mr. Poupart?"

He pointed out a lump a few bunks away.

"Thank you. And you are?"

"Rene Dugas," he said, twirling the r with a French twist.

Dugas? I glanced down at my page and smiled to see him listed. "Well, since I've woken you, why don't we have a chat? I'm O'Trey, investigating the recent deaths. What time's your duty?"

He consulted a pocket watch. "In 'bout an hour, *monsieur. Pardon*, if you please."

Sliding out a box from below his bunk, he offered it as a seat, and went to visit the lavatory. He returned in his uniform, hair neatly combed. I asked how much he made in his position.

He replied with an eager smile. "*Oui, monsieur!* The pay, it is fifteen pounds a month, but the tips, they are very nice. I 'ave many cabins, the passengers, most of them tip ten shillings—ah . . . two dollars and a half. Five pounds in tips, more if it is a good sailing, *n'est-ce pas?*"

When I agreed, he hurried to say, "Of course, I pay for my uniforms and the laundry bills. Each trip I must tip fifty cents to the 'boots'—he keeps our hole clean. Fifty cents to the shore steward—he serves the meals at port, and fifty cents to have my box taken away from the ship and brought back."

I commiserated, then said, "Have you worked long on the *Etruria?*"

"Three years, *monsieur*. We are sailing every month, one week to America, one week to return. While the ship she is being cleaned and painted, we have a week of shore leave."

He looked at ease, so I broached my questions. "Did you serve the Spanish gentleman, Don Juan?"

He crossed himself. "Yes, sir. I was his bath steward."

"What can you tell me about him?"

The youth shrugged, "He liked the water mild—lukewarm, yes? Said it was too hot. I fixed it. A leetle adjustment, *non?*"

I probed, asking questions about Doña Josefina, but he had not spoken with her or her attendants. Finally, I asked, "Did anything out of the ordinary occur?"

"Well," he said, "just . . . a little, er, argument. But it was the next morning, *oui?*"

The day the don was murdered. A jolt went through me. "Go on."

"I was arranging the bathwater, sir. The gentleman, he shouted at the young man, his *secrétaire*. Something could not be found, *oui?* So he was angry. He threw a book . . ."

THE SPANISH DIPLOMAT'S SECRET

I said mildly, "A book. At De Cullar?"

"*Oui, monsieur.* It hit him on his head, almos' knocked him down. I came out from the washroom just then. They all looked at me, then the don told him something, and he left."

They *all* looked at him. "Doña Josefina was there? The wife and her attendant also?"

He nodded. Damn it, not one of them had mentioned this.

I asked more questions, then thanked him and woke the bedroom steward, Mr. Poupart, who sat up, curious and smiling. Yes, he said, he had been on duty during the night, but neither the don nor his wife had needed anything.

Then he said, "The next morning, sir, they had me move the trunks around. It was early, so most of the other passengers had not yet rung for me."

"What did they want with the trunks?"

He shrugged. "The gentleman was looking for something. Sent his man up and down, over and over."

"Up and down where?"

"To his cabin in second class."

Well, well. Something was missing the morning of the don's death. My spirits lifted. Here was something useful, something that meant more. Here's what had disturbed the don so much he'd summoned a passenger he'd just met the night before, summoned him because he'd been a soldier.

Thanking both stewards, I returned to the upper deck where tea was being served from a trolley. There was no sign of Diana, so I stretched out on a steamer chair and accepted a cup.

Sipping the hot brew, I tried to fit the bits together, turning pieces of the puzzle this way and that to see how they might connect. The Spanish treasure was missing from a trunk in the hold. And the don had required the bedroom steward to position his trunks, perhaps to scour them, sending De Cullar repeatedly to his own cabin.

I had the sense of climbing a rise, crawling on my elbows to spy on the enemy. Each movement brought me closer, yet I could not envision the enemy camp. I'd almost reached the ridge, I thought, my pulse a drumbeat of anticipation. I was close.

I handed back my teacup with a sense of irony. A murderer was loose on this ship, and I was drinking tea.

"Jim!" cried Diana, waving at me as she sashayed up in a long velvet skirt of dark blue. "Hurry, or you'll be late for dinner. It's a grand event in the music room, the final dinner. There's even a dance!"

Reluctant to return to civic duties, I climbed to my feet. I needed time to think but was being called to attend festivities. Bollocks. But Diana's eyes shone with excitement, and I gave in. Remembering the state of my wardrobe, I ran a hand through my hair. "I've no more clothes, sweet. My evening jacket's in the hold."

She smiled. "I had our trunk sent up. One can, you know. I sent down a trunk of clothes we'd worn, and brought up fresh ones. Aren't you glad we had those new suits made?"

Trunks sent down.

Something clicked in my mind, an image of a gold crest embossed upon a chest. A chest stacked near the lift, ready to be sent up the next morning.

Diana peered into my face, her hand on my arm. "Jim? Are you all right?"

Hope billowed like the waterspout of a pregnant whale. I grinned. "Go on to dinner. Don't wait for me."

Most of my shipmates would be at the grand event. I strode back to the purser's office, thumped on the door and burst in on him as he was donning his uniform coat.

"Mr. O'Trey?" Dix's gaze sharpened. "What have you found?"

"Passengers' trunks. You keep a record of who wanted them up?"

He extracted a book from his shelf, turned pages and offered it to me.

I checked the date and ran a finger down the page: Evansworth, Farley, Peters, Jobin, Detwiler, Langlois, Garant, Pontin, Bly, Gormier, Mistral . . . and there it was. I went down the list again, just to be certain.

"Will you come with me?" I said, smiling. "Let's visit Mr. De Cullar's cabin. I'm afraid you'll miss the fine dinner."

Buoyed by my enthusiasm he asked no more questions, but rapped on a nearby door and gave instructions to the second steward, then hurried after me. The engines growled into life as we descended the staircase to the main deck that lay below the waterline.

Reaching the second cabin hallway, we rapped on De Cullar's door. No one answered.

"Second class has its own dining hall. This way," he said, turning toward the corridor.

"I'd rather we didn't alert him," I said. "Can you open this door?"

He stiffened, his small eyes puzzled in his cherubic face. "That is most irregular."

The bit between my teeth and raring to go, I grinned. "If I'm right, the captain will be most grateful. If I'm not, we'll disturb nothing."

Head tilted, he considered me for a long moment, then extracted a crowded ring of keys. Inserting one, he tried the door, then another.

The lock clicked, and the door swung open. I followed him in and closed it behind us. At one end of the narrow space was a mirror over a sink. A bunk, barely thirty inches, lay along the side. Two trunks peeked from under the bed, which I ignored.

The third, by the desk, was a fine mahogany affair, embossed with the Spanish crest.

It was locked and sealed in wax. My pulse pounding, I fingered the tag, and read, "Number ten. I believe this belongs to Don Juan. Perhaps Doña Josefina can identify it."

Dix gaped at me. "Does this mean—"

Before he finished, the door opened. De Cullar stood in the doorway, mouth agape, then with a cry, he bolted.

"Stop!" I hollered.

I needn't have. Passengers had entered the corridor, obstructing De Cullar's escape. One of them was Señora Antonia. Her shocked gaze met mine.

"Armando!" A stream of words flowed from her as she caught at his sleeve. The ruckus brought a steward and another crew member, who looked to the purser for orders.

"Mr. De Cullar"—I motioned to his cabin—"in here, please."

He came quietly, followed by Señora Antonia, whose triangular face had grown bloodless. She whispered to him, stopping only when I turned to confront her.

Her mouth pinched in worry, she stepped aside.

Allowing De Cullar to precede me, I held up the don's note. De Cullar's eyes widened as he saw the crest.

"No ink, hmm? Don Juan had no trouble finding it." I motioned to the chest. "Open it, please."

His usually immaculate collar in disarray, he shrank back. "They are just papers. Personal letters of my master, señor. I cannot . . ."

"Perhaps Doña Josefina would like to do it."

"A moment, sir!" Dix thrust De Cullar against the wall and went through his pockets.

Señora Antonia began another flurry of Spanish. Antonia Mistral. Dix's book listed her as the one who'd summoned the trunk to De Cullar's cabin. Would she have the key, then? I sighed, how would we search the lady? Perhaps Nurse Shay or Diana could do it?

Moments later, the purser drew a leather cord from around De Cullar's neck and held it up. On it dangled an ornate key.

He slapped it into my hand, so I crouched, broke the wax and inserted it. The lock fell open with a smooth click, hanging lopsidedly against the burnished wood.

The sound of our breathing filled the dense air. Forcing my breath to slow down, I set aside the lock and hoisted the lid. Someone gasped. Dix was frozen in anticipation. Señora Antonia uttered a wail, covering her face.

The chest looked empty, until one noticed the blue velvet pouches that lined the base. I gingerly lifted one out. It was surprisingly heavy. Below it lay another layer, meticulously aligned, each embossed with a white crest.

I should have been jubilant. Instead, my chest ached, heavy with regret. Damn the boy. Why had he done it?

Teasing apart the cord, I spilled some of the contents into my palm.

Diamonds. Each as large as a fingernail, flashing fire as my hand shook. My mouth went dry as I carefully tipped them back into the pouch. Returning it to the chest, I said to Antonia, "Madam, you had the trunk sent here. Did you also switch the tags?"

De Cullar raised his chin. "No. I did that."

I'd found the missing gems, yet something was amiss. De Cullar's manner spelled a somber pride that I did not understand. Standing tall, he met my gaze without flinching.

"You do realize," I said, "you'll be arrested for theft as well as the murder of Don Juan?"

"No!" Señora Antonia caught my arm. "He could not do it! He was with me!"

I stared at her, feeling dizzy. Had I understood her right?

"With you? When he was asked to fetch an inkpot? You were . . . together?" Astonishment and dismay colored my tone, for Señora Antonia was surely far older than the youth?

"*Parada!*" De Cullar snapped, his voice as sharp as a rapier. "How dare you. She is my mother!"

CHAPTER 33

ST. ELMO'S FIRE

Our silent procession returned to the upper deck, led by the buoyant purser. He'd recruited a gorilla-like crewman who clamped De Cullar's elbow like a troublesome child. Señora Antonia followed, steadfastly refusing to leave her son. A pair of sailors hefted the chest between them, while I brought up the rear.

The deck was empty as we turned at the grand staircase where the fountain gleamed in the twilight. A melody floated from the music room where the captain's dinner festivities were under way. Lights ablaze, it glowed like a lantern on the waves. With the thump of the engine as counterpoint, the strange, elemental symphony surrounded us, the pistons slam-banging, the dynamos grinding, and above it all the violins' plaintive song.

Something sparked above me. I gasped, bumping into a sailor. He set down his end of the chest with a thump.

On the foremast, a flicker streaked across the sail. Another sparked high above.

Was this lightning? If so, it was of a sort I'd never seen. It glowed green for a second, then disappeared, returning in a bright, jagged dance.

A great flash illuminated the funnels, then a burst sizzled over the main mast, curling around the crow's nest. The smokestacks lit up as though by the crack of mortars, yet there was no sound.

Feet rooted to the deck, I gazed up, swamped by the scent of fresh earth. What the devil? We were far from farmland. The air moved restlessly. The engine's whump, the hiss of waves reminding me of our speed, and the dancing lights, like stars poured over our sails—I would never forget this moment.

I forced out a question. "What is it?"

"St. Elmo's fire," said a seaman, voice hushed in reverence. "Brings good luck."

Good luck, perhaps, and bad weather, I thought, for the wind now snatched at my clothes and the others had their caps in hand. A storm was coming, but I'd solved the case, hadn't I?

So why did it feel so wrong? My stomach roiled in rebellion.

Señora Antonia gazed at the light dancing from mast to mast, now high above, now streaming to the bow, sharp and jagged as lightning. Hands clasped, her lips moved in prayer. She'd tried to give her son an alibi, but that was a hopeless cause.

How could De Cullar have hoped to hide the theft? It seemed a foregone conclusion that he'd killed the don to prevent its discovery. No mother's alibi could refute that. Yet he gazed up at the green flickers in wonder, enchanted, without a thought to escape. And where could he go, aboard a ship on the wide ocean? I felt a pang for the young man with his neat manner and serious pride. Why had he killed his master and stolen the Spanish gems?

Sending Dix and the convoy up to the bridge with the don's chest, I strode to the music hall to tell Captain Hawley. I did not yet understand it all, but the evidence against De Cullar was irrefutable.

A dance was under way, viewed by a cheerful audience. I glanced over the stylish crowd, but Diana was not on the floor, nor could I find her among those watching. Feathered hats swayed to the Viennese waltz. Most passengers were here—but not all of them. I saw no wheelchair; Mrs. Barlow had not come. Was Diana with her?

Soon I'd need to give the captain an accounting. But for the moment, I leaned against the wall and considered the facts of the case, convoluted as they were.

Mr. and Mrs. Bly had seen a Spanish woman with the don. However, Chief Officer Bigby claimed he'd seen someone wearing white like Nurse Shay. These two narratives could have occurred one after the other.

So who *was* the Spanish woman? Doña Josefina, now, I could see her plotting endlessly to achieve her ends. She'd not quibble at blaming a lifelong retainer, but murder? The two women had vastly different temperaments, and my theory fit neither one.

Antonia said she did not go to the don as bid by her mistress. If I believed her, then the Spanish woman on deck was Doña Josefina. The widow might have returned and departed before the mysterious nurse drugged the don, but why would she deny it? She'd seemed astonished at her attendant's testimony. So she had not, in fact, asked her attendant to return to the sleeping don. Why had Antonia said so? I sighed as the answer became apparent.

Señora Antonia was De Cullar's mother. To protect her son, wouldn't she cast suspicion on someone else, even her own mistress? I frowned. Devout, sweet-tempered Antonia did not seem capable of it, but what did I know of a mother's attachment? Mine had died when I was only two, leaving me in a mission orphanage.

Evidence—I needed material evidence, and the white skirt presently deposited in a paper bag in my cabin pointed to the accuracy of Bigby's story. Someone had worn white, had helped the sedated don to the music room to murder him, then discarded the clothing on a tray to make an escape.

Was it De Cullar, dressed as a woman? His mother, dressed in black as usual, might have scouted the area and conveyed that the don was asleep. Had she pressed the chloroform to his face? Again, that did not match what I knew of Señora Antonia. That first move was the most dangerous. The don might have awoken and fought back. I doubted Señora Antonia would be able to overcome the lean, rangy strength of a tough old soldier. No, it would have to be De Cullar.

Diana believed the person who attacked me was a woman, but I wasn't sure. The pressure on my nose and mouth had been strong, the body I'd kicked had been solid. It had to be the same man who'd killed the don.

Could there be two killers aboard, one of whom had abducted Mrs. Barlow? It seemed far-fetched . . . but what if they were working together? Señora Antonia and her son, both slight, both determined to keep the don from selling the harbor to Bly? Or to keep the jewels for themselves? Mrs. Barlow could have been abducted to throw me off their scent. Yet the violence, the fury of the don's murder did not support this. The killer hated Don Juan with a passion.

I turned to the problem of the switched trunks. The strong room guards swore that no one had entered. That meant the trunks must have been exchanged before we sailed. In the shipping agent's office Captain Hawley witnessed Bigby and Dix, as purser, seal the chest of gems. It meant De Cullar or his mother had swapped the labels after that, but before we sailed. If so, how had De Cullar got the key?

I remembered that the bedroom steward had spoken of a fracas that morning in the don's stateroom. Was that when the keys were swapped? It would account for the note Don Juan had sent me.

If Doña Josefina hadn't made a fuss, the theft of the gems would not have been noticed until later. Everything pointed to young De Cullar as the killer.

The gala was winding down. Catching Hawley's attention, I gestured toward the door. A few minutes later he joined me with Bigby, tall and imposing in his officer's uniform. Ah. He'd been allowed to attend the festivities in order to reassure passengers.

Shaking hands, I led them out, saying, "Something you should see."

Hawley said, "You missed the dinner, O'Trey. Still on the job, eh? Good man!"

Stopping on the deck below the bridge, I said, "Mr. Bigby, where were you standing when you saw the don and the nurse that afternoon?"

Startled, Bigby turned. Behind him, Hawley's face grew serious.

Raising his arm, Bigby pointed to the railing above. "About there."

"Thank you," I said, stepping up the ladder.

As instructed, Dix had taken the chest to the chart room adjacent to the captain's lounge. Hawley gasped, rejoicing to see its contents. He shook my hand vigorously, then had the gems secured. His relief and joy caused an odd sensation within me. He believed the solution was at hand, the gems recovered, the culprit apprehended. So why did I feel as though I'd lost my grip on the reins, with my horse running amuck under me?

Hawley finished quizzing Dix and grinned at me, his entire demeanor bolder and younger. Summoning De Cullar and Antonia, he said, "Mr. De Cullar, please explain how the gemstones came to be in your stateroom."

The young man exchanged a glance with his mother. She said, "Señor, it was I who had the chest brought to his chamber."

Hawley gazed at her. "Did you know what it contained?"

When she cringed and nodded, he threw me a startled look.

I explained, "The trunks were likely switched before we left New York."

Hawley protested. "Mr. O'Trey, I saw the chest of gems in the shipping agent's office. It was closed and sealed right before me. It was locked, and wax poured into the keyhole. Don Juan took the key into his own hands!"

"Certainly. But another chest was already sealed. De Cullar attached the tags, then Mr. Bigby and the purser escorted the trunks to the hold. The manifest states that the chest marked eleven must be secured, so that's the one that went into the strong room. The others were stowed as usual. It's likely the other trunk containing the don's books was fitted with the same sort of lock. It would be easy to mistake them for each other."

"But then . . . how did he get the key?"

Feeling grim I said, "The bath steward witnessed a commotion that morning. The don was furious because he could not find something—the key to that most important trunk. Doña Josefina can corroborate this. But the key was found, or so the don believed, and the storm passed. In fact, he was given the wrong key."

De Cullar watched me, his eyes dark with emotion, his narrow jaw framed by the pointed ends of his collar. He whispered, "Yes, it is as you say, the tags, the key. Don Juan sent me to retrieve his pens and ink, but after his anger that morning, my mother was frightened. We met in her stateroom. I was not on deck. Please. I didn't kill him."

"You took the gems. How'd you hope to get away with it?"

His face wilted. "I planned to parcel out the gems into many boxes and leave the chest behind. My master did not concern himself with luggage. By the time it was discovered, we would reach Bilbao. It would be an incident *diplomático,* no more. The Basque patriots need the funds, señor, to maintain the revolution, for the republic! The people need it!"

His earnest eyes glowed through the round lens, giving him the look of a seminarian or novitiate. Good Lord, I thought, he believed he was a patriot, a revolutionary.

Hawley snorted. "You don't know ship's protocol, Mr. De Cullar. Owners inspect and sign for property upon arrival in Liverpool. The loss would be noticed right away. My shipping company would be held responsible, sir!"

His voice dropped as he told the Spanish pair, "This ship is British property, so you will be tried by a British court, you understand? For now, you will remain in your rooms, under guard."

"You!" De Cullar stared at Bigby, his eyes dark. "You passed us, that morning. You told Don Juan—'Butcher! Keep your hands off mine.' I heard it, señor! My master said nothing, but his face . . . it went white, señor. He was so angry."

Face bleached of color, he cried. "*Dios!* It was you. You killed him!"

Chaos ensued. Bigby shouted something, grabbing De Cullar's collar. The youth yelled, straining backward. Señora Antonia shrieked.

I struggled to get between them and hauled Bigby off the boy. Breathing hard, his face twisting, he yelled, "Damned Spaniard! Trying to put it on me! Don't believe him!"

With admirable composure, Scots accent thick, Hawley said, "Mr. Bigby, I'd like an explanation. What happened with Don Juan?"

Bigby's cheeks reddened. Dabbing his forehead with a kerchief, he said, "Old history, sir. It's of no account—"

A loud hoot interrupted him, long, high, yet resonant. With it came the hammer of running feet.

"Bosun's sounded the alarm, sir! Storm ahead!" cried a sailor at the door.

"Are the sails in?"

"Making fast, sir!"

"Batten the hatches, Merrick!" Hawley bellowed, speeding to the bridge. Following close behind, Bigby shouting a warning. "Stay clear, O'Trey. We're in for a blow."

De Cullar's agonized gaze met mine. What was in his mind I could not tell. Desperation, fear of the hangman? In one lithe movement he dashed between the startled sailor and his mother, and clattered down the corridor.

"Stop!" I yelled, giving chase, but the nimble youth was too quick. The outer door swung open and he flashed through.

The deck tilted under me, moving like a live thing as I handed my way toward the heavy door. I thrust against it, adding my weight before it yielded, then a gust came that almost lifted me off my feet. If this was the leeward side, what havoc would it wreak on the windward one?

CHAPTER 34

NEPTUNE'S FIST

A giant wave crashed over the outer companionway. Spray drenched my face. Uncertain, I tried to peer upward. De Cullar would not have gone that way. I peered to fore and aft. Nothing. Damnation!

The wind snatched at my hair as I staggered along the deck toward the grand staircase. Sailors bent over the bollards winding ropes, their clothes ballooning from the gale. The deck was bare, chairs gathered and stowed, no mean feat given their numbers. With calls and shouts, a team was drawing shutters over the glass music room. Behind me, crewmen strove to make fast doors and hatches to the lower quarters.

Reaching the stairs, I turned in to the storm, squinting against the blast. Where was the boy? Our ship banked to starboard, as though shying away from the tempest's rage.

"Hurricane, sir!" cried a seaman rushing past. "Get below!"

I searched the deck while waves the size of houses smashed over the rail. Something cracked above me. The angry wind yanked free a sail which snapped and cracked like a whip overhead. Then came a wrenching, rending sound, as some crosswise boom broke loose and swung, a massive deadly pendulum.

The deck canted at my feet. I clung to the stair rail, my boots trying for purchase against the angled floor. I had a moment of clarity: God help, if the stair rail gave way. I should leave, go below decks. But the boy?

Peering upward through a break in the rain, I glimpsed a man's form, dark coat plastered to his body. De Cullar.

He was trapped. Why the devil had he chosen to go up, instead of down to safety? The swinging boom crossed before him in its deadly arc. Something ripped and the ladder he clung to sagged. The treacherous sail snapped closer to the boy.

The next pass of the boom would toss him off the rungs like a fly. I ran toward the ladder, yelling, "Armando! Let go!"

As he peered downward, his grimace changed. Had he heard me call his name? I groaned as the boom swung back, dropping lower. The deck tilted under me as I hollered, my cry snatched away by the gale. "Armando!"

De Cullar released his grip. He fell, his body slack. I took his weight as it slammed down, throwing me backward. The deck shifted, rolling us like twigs. God, how near was the edge? A wave crashed on the deck, blinding me. Water everywhere, lifting me. Would it sweep us into the sea? I could not swim. Hot panic stabbed my chest.

The boom fell with a deafening roar. It bounced, not five feet from us, a shred of sail still spitting at the wind like an angry serpent.

Above us billowed a bulging cloud of purple, so vast it blocked out the sky. Lightning flickered inside it, as though glowing eyes blinked awake. This was why for centuries, sailors feared the capricious sea. It could grow violent with a moment's notice, its rage strangely personal as though the fiendish thing could see into my soul.

We were at the peak of the ship's tilt. Soon it would drop toward the open sea. No better time, I thought.

Gasping, I got to my knees and grabbed De Cullar's shoulder. He sagged. Clenching my fists in his clothing, I dragged him toward the stairs. His limp body caught on something, so I hoisted him up, cursing as I staggered against a coil of rope.

The stairway lay ahead, though I could hardly see in the driving rain.

I did not trust that damn boom. It moved, enmeshed in rigging that curled like pythons around us.

Was De Cullar conscious? His weight slack against me, my feet sliding on the boards, we made some headway. Then a pair of sailors emerged from the downpour to haul us into shelter.

"Go down, sir!" one yelled in my face and took De Cullar's arm.

Incapable of speech, I gave a nod, my arms aching as I supported the Spanish lad. His foot kicked my knee. He was conscious, so I set him down.

He promptly slipped and fell against the wall. A sailor gripped his arm and shouted, "I'm to secure him, sir! Captain's orders!"

Grabbing De Cullar's shoulder, I cried. "Armando! Don't give up!"

He'd lost his spectacles. Hair plastered to his head, looking like a wet pup, he met my gaze, his breath trembling. Some communication passed between us. No matter what he'd done, I had come after him. I could not tell what it meant to him, but he went peaceably with the sailor.

Shivering, I glanced around the wind-torn canted deck. Where was Diana? I headed down to our stateroom, at times walking at an angle of sixty degrees. When the ship shuddered and swung the other way, I fell to my knees, palms splayed against the walls. But Captain Hawley had the helm—it comforted me to know that.

Stewards slid past me with pleas to return to my cabin. Breathless, I could only nod.

Reaching our cabin on jellied feet, I hammered on our door. Diana yanked it open with the cry, "Thank heaven!" and hurled herself to embrace me. "Where were you? You're sopping wet!"

She did not wait for my answer but dragged me in and thrust a towel at me. I fell into the couch and closed my eyes, trying to remember how to breathe.

I heard her voice, but not what she said, for there I lay, my stomach clenched like a fist, my mouth flooded with telltale saliva. Our trunks were tied down against the wall, and she'd covered the porthole, so the only light came from an electrical fitting in the wall. Yet I could not rest, for my belly spasmed in warning. I tasted bile. Bollocks!

I had not eaten, yet my body gave up all it could. Well after it emptied, my stomach spasmed as I retched. Then, exhausted beyond thought, I dropped to the floor, feeling the engines throb desperately to bear us away. The storm's din had retreated to a booming overhead, while from below came the pounding of pistons, crank throws and counterweights, the boilers going full steam.

My head hanging over the porcelain, I remembered that sailor's tale of losing the main shaft mid-Atlantic, metal tearing with a grinding shriek. His ship had been helpless, engines working, boilers full of steam, all useless with a broken propeller. Here we were, all twenty thousand tons, tilting, rocking, quaking while Neptune's blows hammered down from every side. How small we were against nature's punch.

Groaning, I hauled myself up to stagger from the lavatory. Only then did I see we were not alone. Dora sat on Diana's bed, all eyes, bedclothes pulled around her throat.

Unbuttoning my shirt, Diana peeled off the sodden thing and got me to my berth. There she anchored me with my leather belt, one end curled over the rail, the other knotted to the bunk frame. As she bent, pulling on the strap, I gasped, "What if I have to . . ."

"I'll get you a bucket," she said, mouth grim. She brought it, stepping easily across the room like a ballerina.

Gripping the metal thing, I huddled, fighting the instinct to sit up against the ship's outrageous jerks and swings.

Pressing a hand to my chest, Diana said, "God, you're clenched tight. Let go, Jim, it's all right! Breathe, my love!"

Thus bid, I tried to obey, but it wasn't easy. My body had a will of its own, demanding still, dry land, rebelling against this whirling place. It eased as I held her gaze and grew accustomed to the swings of the cabin, things rattling in drawers, the pounding of my heart. She held steady, smiling, though everything moved behind her. It was what I needed, one constant thing, one thing that did not shift with every mood and turn of the stars.

Long moments later, I closed my eyes as the Ferris wheel in my head came to a halt. Perhaps I slept.

My eyes opened to a quieter chamber. Had the storm subsided? I searched the room, trying to gauge its motion. It still tilted, but slower and to a less extreme degree. The low, rhythmic pounding of the pumps continued. On the couch, Diana looked up from a book.

My North Pole came over and released the strap over me. After enquiring over my health she said, "Since you're better, shall I tell you what I've done? Oh Jim, it was very strange. I don't mind saying, it gave me quite a turn."

"What happened?"

When I made to rise, she pushed me back. "It's all right. I don't understand it, but that doesn't matter." She glanced over her shoulder, then said, "Though she's been so ill, Dora was worried about Mrs. Barlow. She would be all alone, you see."

Reassured that the trouble was no greater, I nodded at Dora. "That was kind."

Diana went on, "So I went to Mrs. Barlow. But, Jim, she spoke through the door and didn't know me at all! I assured her that we had spoken before, that I only wished her well, but she began to fret and curse. She was quite vile! I fear . . ." She winced, glancing back at Dora. "Jim, I think she is not quite sane!"

"God help us!" Dora covered her face. "What'll I do now? I shoulda listened to Alice!"

"Jim, can't we help Dora," Diana said. "We could find her a position, couldn't we? My aunt lives in London, perhaps she might help?"

I smiled. Diana hated to break things. In Chicago, she'd gathered a train of followers, young and old. If I wasn't careful, she'd adopt every waif that crossed her path. Then I laughed, remembering the band of little urchins I'd left behind in Punjab.

"Let's see what happens once we dock," I cautioned. "Miss Dora, never fear. You're not alone."

Diana's smile came out like blessed rain in a drought. I soaked it in, glad of our bond, my pulse beating to know it still held strong. I'd find Dora employment, if that's what it took to keep Diana's smile.

Holding her belly, Dora set her feet on the floor and tried to rise. Diana hurried to prevent it, saying, "You must stay in bed! The doctor insisted!"

Dora's next words astonished me. "Mr. O'Trey, sir, I haven't been honest with you."

Diana stiffened, her eyes wide in consternation.

Dora blurted, "It's Alice. She was smart, she was, but miss . . . I said she would weep, and that's true, but . . . she had money, once, you see? Her father was a sea captain. When he died, Alice told me things got awful bad. She had a hard life then, no money for food. I told you she knew things, but I didn't tell you everything. She took work in a circus! She used to fly on the trapeze! That's why I was afraid o' her."

Diana blinked. "Afraid of the . . . trapeze?"

Sniffing, she said, "She'd be angry for no reason, muttering in the night. Once, when Mrs. Barlow hollered at us, Alice said it would be nice if she died. Said we'd come into a bit then, wouldn't we? She was quite calm about it, like we were talking about the weather. She'd be a mean ghost, miss, she wouldn't rest. It's her that's made trouble for us. She brought the storm. She was strange, and talked, cried out while sleeping. But she was kind to me, miss. She called me 'little bird.'" Dora clutched the bedcover and pressed it to her face.

"Come now, rest." Diana covered the girl with the duvet.

Why did Dora think she hadn't been honest about Alice? She had both admired and feared her troubled friend. But no ghost had killed the old don, or pressed a pillow over my face.

"I had to do it," Dora said, so softly I could scarcely hear. "I wanted it to end, just to go to sleep and not wake, see. But it doesn't end, does it?"

She choked and sobbed. Diana whispered a reply, but I could not hear it.

Hours later, the storm abated. When I sat up and looked around in the dim light of the porthole, Diana and Dora were huddled in the next bunk. They looked like weary toddlers as they slept.

CHAPTER 35

AN UNEXPECTED DEFENSE

DAY NINE: MORNING

I woke at dawn and dressed in the murky glow, reluctant to wake the sleeping girls. Diana's curls tumbled in a dark waterfall over the side of her berth. Dora made barely a bump in the rumpled bedclothes.

The storm had passed, yet my body ached as though I'd gone too many rounds with a heavyweight. A band of scrubbers was working on the main mast, their calls repeated up and down. This ensured the message was understood, a clever way to avoid misunderstandings.

Stifling a groan, I gripped my notebook and made my way up to the officers' lounge, recalling De Cullar's accusation. He'd overheard Bigby argue with Don Juan the morning before he was murdered. I hoped to quiz Bigby before Hawley confronted him.

In the officers' lounge, a beardless young third officer looked at me curiously, then introduced me to his senior, the second officer.

"Second?" I did not recognize him.

He smiled. "I'm the alternate second, sir. There are three second officers—we take turns on the bridge, as do the third and fourth officers.

So, there's always a second officer on duty as well as a junior man, a third or a fourth officer."

"Is Mr. Bigby on the bridge now?"

"No, sir. We've just come off the dogwatch. He'll be out cold till midday." With a grimace, he said, "Don't mind me saying, sir, you look like you could do with a rest yourself. We'll make dock today. The captain's summoned the officers at thirteen hundred hours, and, well, he's keen on a smart appearance."

I rubbed my scruffy jaw, contemplating his bright, unblemished cheeks. Hawley wanted us at one in the afternoon. That gave me only the morning to complete my investigation. As it now stood, De Cullar would likely go to the gallows. God, I needed to think.

I thanked the young chap and poured myself a large cup of coffee, then settled into a round corner chair with a freshly baked roll. It went down well with the smooth, bitter coffee, while the armchair's cushioned contours hugged my aching frame.

In most other cases, I'd examined a set of suspects. Questioning their alibis, uncovering motives, this was my trade. Under the wear of repeated questioning, most cases narrowed to a few unlucky suspects, and then to one. This unusual case had not followed that pattern.

To start, I had only Bigby's word that there'd ever been a nurse helping Don Juan to the music room. The torn skirt and scarf might well have been placed there later, to substantiate his report. If Bigby had murdered the old man, he'd covered his tracks well.

Though established as American aristocracy, the Blys appeared to have motive—valuable Cuban property. However, the don's death destroyed Bly's hard-won agreement . . . and his infirmity meant that he could not have done the deed himself. But had he paid someone else to do it? If so, he'd be pressing Doña Josefina for the sale of that harbor. But he wasn't.

I paused. What if Mrs. Bly had lied to Vernon . . . a little social pride, a small white lie. What if Bly, a practiced diplomat, had deceived me? Had he been unable to convince the don? With him out of the way, Bly could pressure Doña Josefina to sign away the harbor. Frowning, I rubbed my forehead. No, other than her initial complaints, she'd had no more to do with Bly.

This brought me to Señora Antonia and De Cullar, mother and son, who'd admitted to stealing the don's gems. I had the sense of watching a play, actors proudly proclaiming their parts, while in the wings something stirred—an invisible intellect sending men and women out on time, moving sets, acts starting and ending to his design.

Who had choreographed this brutal murder? I scowled at my empty cup.

To clear my head I walked along the upper deck, passing funnels, game areas, and the ship's offices. A glance through the window of the boarded-up infirmary showed stacks of chairs. The fallen boom was being hoisted and the watch swabbed away at last night's debris.

Near the stern deck, I passed the stairway to the promenade. Don Juan had come down and sought chairs here, on the leeward side. His own stateroom overlooked it. The nurse must have been a common presence, going to and from the sick bay.

I peered across the empty deck. Something was wrong. I glanced toward the stern, then back upwind toward the bow. Soon the breakfast gong would sound and passengers would descend to the saloon level. But here, as I stood on the stern deck, something was missing. Something I should see, and yet I could not tell what it was.

Anyone on the promenade deck above could have seen Don Juan dozing in the chair. I went to where the Spanish couple had lounged that fateful day. To my right would be Mr. and Mrs. Bly, eager to make a deal with him, speaking, persuading, though the don feigned indifference. Further along, the Farley brothers had vied for Mrs. Bly's favor.

To my left, Doña Josefina would be huddled under a blanket. The sea had been choppy that first day, sending me to my knees in our cabin. I recalled Nurse Shay's words—Doña Josefina had been seasick as well and had visited the sick bay to request something for it.

I paused. Why had she not sent Señora Antonia?

Perhaps because she was not nearby. Between noon and two, De Cullar had been dispatched for an inkpot, or so he said. More likely he'd made himself scarce, sulking from the morning's argument. Señora Antonia had been in furtive conversation with him, pleading perhaps, that he reconsider his rash act. She had not yet sent for the swapped-out trunk. Perhaps he was begging her to do so.

From the deck above a voice warbled, "Señor Agnihotri, is it true? My gems are found?"

Doña Josefina clutched her scarf at her throat. Her hair knot had slipped to one side. Deep lines scored her cheeks. She said, "The steward says my servants cannot come. You have arrested them?"

The wan tone struck true. Alone perhaps for the first time in her life, the aristocratic woman wavered, looking frail.

The breakfast bugle sounded as I climbed the staircase to her. The upper deck would soon be crowded, but the promenade was quiet.

Greeting the widow, I said, "Your gems are secure, Excellency. I'm afraid Señora Antonia and Señor De Cullar have been—detained. We have some questions for them."

When she did not reply, I said, "That was the call for breakfast. Will you not go?"

She flicked a hand to show it was of no consequence.

"Perhaps you would like a stewardess to attend you?"

Inviting me to sit, she lowered herself into a chair and pinned me with her dark gaze. "Why did you arrest Armando?"

Armando, not Señor De Cullar. I drew a slow breath. "The trunk containing your husband's gemstones. It was found in Mr. De Cullar's cabin."

She flinched, then whispered, "But . . . Antonia?"

Did she know? I waited until her mouth turned impatient, her kohled eyes piercing. "She is his mother."

She blinked, but otherwise made no motion.

"You already knew that. Did your husband know?"

She looked as though she had not heard, then shook her head. "She was my handmaiden from my childhood home. When she was with child . . . ah, *Dios!* Unmarried, and disgraced, her *familia* would cast her off. I feared she would . . . come to harm.

"I was to visit a convent in San Vicente de Abando, so I took her with me. We stayed the summer, and then the fall. The nuns found a *jauntxo*—a minor nobleman to foster the child. For many years we visited him. Armando was gentle from the start, always questions, reading books, more questions."

Her face contorted. "That teacher, Arana . . . Sabino Arana . . . writing vile pamphlets, always arguments about independence! Armando was fascinated . . . joined his political party—Partido Nacionalista Vasco.

"But he was a fool. Teaching a young boy about *limpieza de sangre*, pure blood of Spanish heritage! Armando became angry, accused Antonia of such foul things . . . she was losing him, losing her child. So I persuaded Don Juan to admit him to the military school. A new career for him, an advancement, a chance for great prospects! But the foolish boy would not go. We were *agitado*. However, by the grace of God, when he met my husband, it changed. He admired Don Juan as a *general*. He would obey no one else."

She turned to me with the searching look of an eagle. "Don Juan was good to him. God gave us no children but sent Armando, a blessing for our later years. Now you say he stole our gems? Ah . . . ah! It is well my husband is no more. It would have torn his heart!"

I made no reply. Armando would likely be tried for the don's murder. Instead, I asked. "Excellency, why would De Cullar commit such a crime?"

"Tsch!" She flicked away the question like shooing a mosquito. "It is that teacher, Sabino Arana. He cares little for the monarch's line. A young fool! My husband should have arrested him long ago. He poisoned Armando against the monarch."

Her tale showed more compassion than I expected. Yet her earlier remarks had praised Don Juan for crushing a revolt. He'd not been a pleasant man, yet to be garroted by one's own protégé seemed a hard lot. De Cullar did not seem to have cause for such intense rage, such violence against the man who had taken him under his wing. I could see him as a political rebel, seeking to impress his firebrand teacher, but a brutal killer?

"The stones are mine," Doña Josefina said, her manner curt, as though she regretted the openness of our discussion. "Bring the chest to me."

I assured her that it would be returned to her in Liverpool and took my leave. But would it? It hardly seemed in the interests of Great Britain, which would likely conduct a protracted legal wrangle to keep the fortune from a longtime rival.

Feeling dissatisfied, I walked back toward the bow. Had I run down every lead? Recalling De Cullar's strange accusation and frantic flight, I wondered, where was Bigby when the don was killed? He said he'd returned to his quarters. Miss Felicity Rood's casual aside had provided him an alibi. Now I questioned it.

A half hour before breakfast, I rapped on Miss Rood's door to announce myself. Behind me, the storm spent, a soft blue sea and open sky boded well for our arrival in Liverpool. The engines beat steadily. I'd forgotten my hat again. A breeze lifted my hair and smoothed it down.

I heard the swish of movement within and rapped again, saying. "Miss Rood, it's James O'Trey. May we speak?"

I expected to be told it was too early, and I must return at a civilized hour. Instead, she opened the door, eyebrows peaked.

She pulled back. "I thought you were Mr. Farley. I'm afraid this isn't a good time, Mr. O'Trey. I'm just leaving. I have an appointment."

She wore no hat. I gazed at her steadily. "It won't take long. Will you step out?"

Moments later, I led her, looking miffed, to the railing. It was still quiet on deck this morning. Watching her slap her gloves about, I said, "You saw Mr. Bigby the morning of the don's death, d'you remember?"

She pulled on a white glove and buttoned it. "That was ages ago. I can hardly recall."

"Then you may not have seen him? Very well, miss." I took a step back as though to leave.

She burst out. "'Course I did! I told you I did."

"Right." I smiled briefly. "Where were you standing?"

Her thin eyebrows arched. "You cannot expect me to remember that."

"Where was he?"

She shrugged, putting on the second glove with a series of tugs. "On the bridge."

"You saw him through the glass window? Quite sure it was him?"

She fiddled with her pocket watch, her brow ridged. "Perhaps he was outside. Yes, I'm sure he was."

"On the staircase? Going up or down?"

"I don't know. No . . . at the railing, outside the bridge," she said, her voice flat and certain.

"You remember this, why?"

She half turned. "Well, I waved to him."

"Did he wave back?" It seemed unlikely. Bigby would not wave at young ladies while on duty. The younger blokes would smirk too much.

Her voice dropped. "N-no, but he smiled."

She'd been near enough to see his smile? "What time was this?"

"Can't be certain," she said, then snapped. "That's all I recall. Oh! I'm terribly late now."

I gave her a stern look. "Now, miss. This is a serious matter. Was it before breakfast?"

She moved about like an impatient child. "No. I'd looked for him at breakfast that day. He wasn't in the dining room."

"So what time did you see him?"

She dithered, shrugging, hands turning in pantomime. Not once had she met my gaze.

I closed my notebook. "You didn't see him, did you? You're worried that what you say may contradict the other officers on the bridge."

She looked up, eyes large and worried, dropping her pretense. "Oh, Lord. What did they say?"

I sent her a half smile. "Why'd you give him an alibi?"

"For goodness' sake, he couldn't have done it!"

"Why?"

She pulled in her lips, then tossed her head, saying, "Oh, all right. I met him in April when I traveled to New York on this ship. A splendid crossing, so calm, so bright. Edwin . . . Mr. Bigby, he was very attentive. You will say it's silly, a shipboard romance, why it's almost de rigueur on a crossing these days! But . . . he wasn't like the others. He truly meant it." She glanced at the open sea. "I would have accepted him, Mr. O'Trey, if it wasn't for my parents . . . well, too late now."

"It's an offense to give false evidence, Miss Rood." I closed my book, feeling pity for her, and sick for Bigby.

She had lied about seeing him on the bridge.

CHAPTER 36

CONFRONTATION

As I left Miss Rood, a squabble of gulls called overhead in a noisy convoy. A long coast showed grey along the horizon. Eager to make up time, Hawley had eschewed the usual halt at Queenstown, Ireland. The boards hummed under my feet, while our bow wave sizzled away to both sides. I could smell the upcoming breakfast sizzling in the galley.

Bigby. I swallowed past the dry ache in my throat. A brisk wind snapped as I gazed across the empty deck. With a sense of astonishment, I knew what was missing.

Blast. It was right before me, but I had not seen.

My old army boots hammering the boards, I hurried down the stern hatch where the officers had their quarters and rapped on the chief officer's door. Dogwatch or not, I needed a word.

Moments later, Bigby yanked it open, bleary-eyed and rumpled in his pajamas, blinking at me in confusion. Expressing my apologies, I asked for a moment of his time.

"What for?" he demanded, looking put out. "I got off at six, so I'm not due till one. Can't it wait?"

When I insisted it could not, he stamped off to his washroom. Unasked, I sat and looked over his collection of books. Classical tracts stood against nautical history and astronomy, *Tales of the Punjab* by Flora Annie Steel and *The Memoirs of Sherlock Holmes*! I was flipping its pages, eager to purchase my own copy on land, when he returned.

"Conan Doyle," I said. "Marvelous fellow. Did you read *A Study in Scarlet*?"

He had not.

"*The Sign of the Four*? Dashed fine story."

He rubbed his eyes. "You woke me to discuss books?"

The leather binding was smooth, even slippery under my fingers. After what I had to say, there'd be little chance of borrowing it off him.

I sighed, for I liked Bigby. Yet did I really know him? Perhaps most people could be roused to vicious murder if pushed hard enough.

"Day of the murder, Edwin. You lied about your whereabouts. You didn't see the nurse and the don from the bridge."

His frame turned rigid. "What d'you mean?"

"You said you saw a nurse helping the don toward sick bay."

"I did," he said, his voice rising. "If it wasn't Nurse Shay, then someone else."

"Toward the sick bay? Or near the music room, toward the bow?" From the bridge, the sick bay was one direction, the music room opposite.

He dithered. "Can't tell exactly where on deck they were walking. I was looking down, toward the stern."

But just now, as I stood on the promenade, I'd realized that the sick bay could not be seen from the bridge.

"You were at the bridge," I said, watching him closely. I felt like a cad as he stepped into my trap.

When he nodded, I heaved a sigh. "You can't have been, Edwin. The funnels bulge there, they're in the way. And the deck's enclosed for the most part, so . . . where were you?"

The question uppermost in my mind was, did the nurse really exist?

He dropped into a chair with a groan. "Dash it, O'Trey. Does it matter?"

"'Fraid so. Where were you between noon and two that afternoon?"

He frowned at his feet. "I was on duty till almost one o'clock. After that, Felicity . . . Miss Rood said she saw me. I was on my way here when Johnson sent a boy running up for the captain. He told me about the ruckus."

It was curious how he'd worded that—*said* she saw me. "Miss Rood? What time was that?"

His color rose. "Don't know exactly. Between one and two, most likely."

"What did you talk about?"

"Ah . . ." He shrugged, lips pulled down. "Probably passed the time of day."

I gave him a look. "Miss Rood was mistaken. She could not stand by her alibi."

He blinked. "She withdrew it?"

I nodded. "So where were you, Edwin? You see, I'm inclined to think there was no nurse with Don Juan that afternoon. You were the only one who mentioned her."

He reared back, affronted. "You think . . . Christ. 'Course she was there."

"Near him? With him?"

"He was leaning on her!"

"Did they see you?"

He pressed his lips together. "Shouldn't have said anything. God-damn it."

"Shouldn't have said, Edwin? You saw the killer! Unless . . ." I shook my head. "Unless you killed him yourself."

"No!" He shot to his feet. "Damn it, O'Trey!" He cast a wary glance at me. His shoulders slumped. "De Cullar told you . . . all right. I had words with the don at breakfast. After my shift I went toward his stateroom to explain myself, to apologize. Knocked, but no one an-swered. Looked down and saw him on the upper deck. Leaning on a woman."

I had noticed, just an hour ago that the promenade deck overlooked the stern upper deck and any passengers lounging on the steamer chairs below. "The don and the nurse. You saw them near the chairs?"

"Yes. Since he wasn't alone, I headed back. He'd likely forgot about our argument. Hadn't complained yet, or captain would've said something."

"The altercation at breakfast. What was that about?"

"Privilege makes some people cruel, O'Trey. Old bastard struck a bellboy that morning. The boy was slow fetching something. Left a mark on the lad's cheek!"

"And that's why you confronted him? Or something else?"

He groaned. "Damn it, O'Trey. I lost my head, all right? And then the old blighter's killed! How do you think that looks?"

* * *

The ship's breakfast buglers had been hard at work while I quizzed Bigby. His last question still echoed in my mind. "Must you tell Hawley? About my altercation with the don?"

I'd promised I would keep it to myself as long as I rightly could. He'd have to be happy with that, for my mind was swamped with doubt. Bigby had no alibi for the time of the don's murder, while De Cullar did. It was not a strong alibi, for the court might well determine that the bonds of motherhood would have her swear to anything.

But could I let De Cullar face the rope? Bigby had had words with the don, defending a bellboy. Combined with his history of animosity toward the don, would this convict him? I did not think an English jury would find it plausible. But what then? Already relations between the two countries were strained. If no clear verdict emerged, what would Spain do?

I expected to find our cabin empty, and Diana gone to breakfast. Instead, she was poring over witness statements, her brow ridged.

"It's like a picture puzzle," she said, waving a hand at my desk. "You've collected all these pieces. To build the picture, we need to find a corner. Just a little piece to start us off."

"I might just have it." I told her Bigby's story.

Her eyes widened. A slow gasp escaped her lips. "So it's just possible that . . ."

"He could have done it—in a fit of rage. He told the don, 'You butcher. Keep your hands off my crew.' Perhaps he even mentioned the *Virginius*. The don was offended, saw it as a slight, ship's crew sneering at him. Proud old geezer, in another time he might have drawn swords over it.

"So after his shift ended, Bigby went back to smooth things over. Head off the old blighter, so he wouldn't make a complaint. Bigby says that's when he saw the nurse leading the don away, so he went down to his cabin. It looks bad. By his own account, he was the last person to see Don Juan alive."

"Except for the unknown nurse."

"If she exists."

Diana's voice wrapped around my insides like a snug bandage. My headache eased as I stretched out on the couch, watching the sunlight dance over her coifed hair.

"We'll dock at Liverpool soon. I've run out of time."

My insides felt entangled with doubt. I still could not, with any degree of certainty, identify the murderer. Neither Bigby, tall and well built, with a tendency to blush when he was lying, nor De Cullar, small, determined and scholarly, seemed *right*.

In stories, Holmes usually caught the would-be criminal in the act. How could I force the killer's hand? Perhaps I could convince him that he was in danger of imminent discovery, and make him show himself. I needed to set a trap.

I considered it for some time, trying to work out the details. Diana sewed quietly.

Then I said, "We've no time left, sweetheart. I've got to draw out the killer. If we let it be known that we could identify him, would that not attract him?"

Eyes darkening, Diana said, "Or indeed her. But, Jim, she's ruthless. You'd be putting someone in awful danger. Who'd you have in mind?"

I put on my coat, feeling grim. "The fellow most likely to hang if we don't find the murderer," I said, and headed to the captain's quarters. Yet I was not as sanguine as I'd led Diana to believe. Baiting a trap with De Cullar was a bad risk, yet he had to be shown to lure in the killer.

In the captain's stateroom, Hawley heard me out without interruption, then picked up a decanter and poured himself a whiskey. He drank and set down the glass with extreme care. Only then did he address me. "Will it work?"

"I'd not have suggested it otherwise."

"Will De Cullar agree?" His stare questioned my willingness to risk the youth.

"Think so. I won't force him." Up until now, no one could fault our movements. But if De Cullar was killed, it lay squarely at our door. Hawley and I would be held to account. I met his gaze evenly. We had a murderer on board and would lose him if we did not act.

Hawley rubbed a hand over his eyes, and ran a hand over his mustache. He'd aged a decade over the course of our voyage.

"All right, O'Trey. I'll give orders to dock tomorrow instead of tonight. Hope you know what you're doing."

Before I left, I asked one last question. "Mr. Bigby had served on the HMS *Niobe*. Did you know?"

He nodded, jowls sagging like a sad bulldog. Summoning Johnson, he sent stewards around to announce a further delay.

* * *

As we'd planned, at luncheon, Hawley came over to our table and shook my hand with ceremony. Playing his part, he said, "Well done, O'Trey!" He stuffed a trembling hand into his uniform pocket.

We had not included Bigby in our plan. Now he said, "So you've got the culprit?"

I smiled briefly. "Soon. We have a witness."

The rest of the afternoon was spent making arrangements.

That evening, De Cullar was brought from the brig to an anteroom near the forecastle, ostensibly to be handed over to the authorities in the morning. Numerous passengers and crewmen had seen us, so I had no doubt word would travel the ship.

"Try to rest," I said, as De Cullar entered the small chamber. "Do exactly as I said. Your life depends on it."

Dressed in his usual clerical garb, the young man's eyes were dark in his pale face. "Am I to have no weapon?"

"A weapon will not help you," I said and stuck out my hand. "I'll be nearby."

He gripped it tightly and said, "Catch him. I did not want the old man dead."

CHAPTER 37

BAIT

Night closed slowly over the steamer. A muscular seaman sat guard in the lamplight and rolled his cigarette as I watched from behind machinery at the bow. As instructed, the guard walked across the deck, smoking, then slouched on a chair by the forecastle. Soon he'd begin to snore. Through a few judicious remarks we'd made it known that De Cullar had seen the don's murderer and would testify in the morning. Would the killer approach?

How bright the stars were! They spread over the heavens in a tapestry of light. On the horizon Liverpool was a thin row of streetlamps that clustered together, then petered out to each side.

Crouching on the boards by the bow was not unlike riding an elephant. The deck rose slowly, then dropped like a mastodon taking a stride, hitting the waterline to send up a shower of spray. Recalling my first night on board when I'd doubled over the railing, I watched the shadows sway. A man could creep up between the ship's machinery and cables but to access the door beside me, he must cross the open deck.

Grunting, the guard sat up, scratching his back and went toward the privy at the head. I'd asked him to leave every hour or so to tempt the killer. Could Diana be right? A woman assassin? My nerves felt twisted into a knot. Perhaps no one would come, I thought.

Was it midnight? I shifted a little to ease the stiffness in my knee but did not extract my timepiece. It was useless in the dark. My back ached but I dare not stretch as I peered downwind to port and starboard.

Something moved. A large figure left the gloom and cast a wide shadow as he loped toward the bow. He approached with the easy gait of one accustomed to the sea. A sailor at the end of his shift? Pulse drumming in my ears, I waited. Was he going to the head? Instead, he turned toward the forecastle. Glancing over his shoulder, he tried De Cullar's door.

In a trice I swung up and caught his arm.

Before I could say, "Got you," the fellow knocked me back with a blow that numbed my jaw. Christ!

I sidestepped the next and landed one at his midriff. It jarred me to the teeth. He only grunted. Where was the night watch? I'd insisted they continue as on any ordinary day, so they were likely scrubbing the quarterdeck with holystones.

Then I had no time to think or call out, for my assailant let fly and it was all I could do to block or snap away his blows.

When the moon came out, I saw my chance. I struck with the heel of my palm, driving his head back. "Ah!" he cried, "Not on *my* ship!" and lunged.

I knew that full-throated voice. As he slammed me against the door, I gasped. "Bigby!"

He stopped dead, breathing hard. "O'Trey? The devil you doing here?"

I heaved, panting. "Waiting for the killer."

"What?" His mouth fell open. "I thought . . ."

I slumped. "That you'd caught him. Dammit. Why'd you come?"

He groaned, then flung out a hand. "Heard you'd moved the Spanish bloke. You didn't set a guard?"

"'Course we did." I glanced around the silent boards. It was too quiet. Alarm bells clanged in my mind. The guard had been gone too long.

Shoving past Bigby, I ran. My knee spiked pain with each step.

Coming around to starboard, I spotted a shape slumped by the privy. The guard's skin was warm, and—thank the wide heavens—he breathed.

He groaned, touching a palm to his head as he elbowed himself up and leaned against a reel of rope. As always after a fight, my throat closed and I could barely speak. Crouching, I gasped, "What happened?"

"Dunno." He grimaced at his wet fingertips.

Bigby cursed, then whirled and dashed off. What the devil? A second later, realization dawned. He wasn't running away because he was the killer, but toward where we had secured De Cullar.

He reached the anteroom and kicked in the door before I caught up.

The small room held only a table, chair and a single bed. A supine form was bundled in a blanket. A small white object protruded from the center of it.

An ivory-handled knife, like the one I'd found in Dora's room.

Sweat dripping from his face, Bigby cursed under his breath, a long, whispered stream of desperation as he reached for the covers. I rocked back on my heels, trying to catch my breath.

In fiction, Holmes sometimes risked his client and trapped the killer. That's what should have happened. I'd used the boy as bait, but while we'd been watching the door, the deadly blow had come through the window.

From near Bigby's feet came a voice. "Is it safe now?"

Bigby staggered back with a muffled cry, as I helped De Cullar out from under the bed.

"You did your part well," I said, pointing to the knife embedded in the pillows.

His bony shoulder quaked under my fingers. "Did you get him?"

"He got away."

I went to the window and looked out of the porthole at a sheer drop. How . . . ? An idea floated into my mind, a ridiculous image of a trapeze artist in purple britches, hanging upside down as we'd seen at a Coney Island fair.

CHAPTER 38

DO YOU BELIEVE ME?

DAY TEN: MORNING

Before breakfast, feeling sheepish at having risked De Cullar to bait my trap, I went to see him. As I approached, the sailor standing guard shot up, then saluted. I nodded to him and knocked. After a pause, De Cullar opened the door and shuffled back to let me pass.

Noticing his scruffy beard and limp hair, his crumpled, collarless shirt, I said, "Did you get any sleep?"

He gave a mirthless smile that held as much enthusiasm as if I'd offered to pull one of his teeth. We made desultory conversation, then I showed him the wicked little blade. "Ever seen it before?"

He peered at it as though it might bite, then shook his head.

Meeting my gaze, he said, "Mr. Bigby said I cannot leave the ship. He will take me to the captain today. I am to be arrested?"

No point shying away from it. With no other suspect in hand, Hawley would turn him over to the police. I nodded. "Bigby didn't tell you when?"

De Cullar shrugged. "The time given was an hour ago. Six in the morning, he said."

Before passengers woke, yes, best to finish the ugly business early. I put the dagger away in a pencil case I'd borrowed from Diana and picked up my hat. "Dress well. Your mother may attend, and Doña Josefina."

He stiffened, then his chin rose. "Will you be there?"

Since I would likely have to present the evidence against him I could hardly avoid the interview, but I only said, "I will. It's not over, Armando."

His glance held surprise and pleading. Then he nodded. "I will dress."

I went in search of Bigby pondering my arguments. Two white-handled knives nestled in that box. Was it enough to beg a reprieve for De Cullar?

Since the dogwatch ended an hour ago, I rapped on Bigby's cabin and waited. Repeated knocking produced no result. No sailor sleeps that deeply, so expecting that he'd overstayed his watch, I climbed back toward the helm and asked for him.

"Mr. Bigby?" The second officer said blankly, "Haven't seen him for hours."

The bloke's cold tone surprised me. "You had the dogwatch with him?"

"I took over from Carruthers, the alternate second at six. Mr. Bigby wasn't present."

No, I had not imagined his irate tone. His lips compressed as he returned to his notations. Criticism of a senior officer was not uncommon, I supposed, yet Bigby was a conscientious bloke. "Wouldn't he hand over the bridge to the next watch?" I asked.

The young officer softened. "He usually does. Mr. Bigby's a good officer."

After an exhausting night, Bigby and I had returned De Cullar to his cabin at two in the morning. "Did the alternate say where Mr. Bigby went?"

The youth shook his head. I understood that Bigby's partner on the watch had covered for him. Yet this absence was unlike him. Did Miss Felicity have something to do with it?

The day had dawned bright and fair so I left by the outer companionway, closing the glass door behind me. Only two steps down I stopped. My breath caught.

A dark form lay slumped on the clear platform below. Bigby.

Separated from the upper deck by a wall, he lay on the glass roof of the dining saloon below. I rapped on the bridge door and hollered at the young officer, then clambered back down the ladder. Swinging over the railing, I hung over the glass, wondering whether it would take my weight.

Bigby did not move.

Biting back a curse, I dropped down beside him. Not another death. Not Bigby!

A strong pulse beat in his warm neck. As I pulled back and exhaled my relief, he grunted and turned over. Moments later he grimaced and blinked at me.

"You fell," I said keeping my voice calm. "How'd you feel?"

"Christ." He licked his lips and touched the back of his head. Above us, sharp voices reverberated. Footsteps clanged on the companionway.

Bigby sat up, groaning. "What time is it?"

I told him and helped him to his feet. We staggered over the barrier to the upper deck and gave a pair of elderly gents on their morning constitutional a nasty shock as we clambered down beside them, disheveled and somewhat unkempt. They gasped their disapproval, but before I could explain, a young steward arrived at a run and summoned us to the captain.

In his cabin, Hawley stopped pacing and swung around. "Drinking on the job, Edwin?"

Setting his jowly face inches from Bigby's bruised jaw, he sniffed.

Bigby said, "Not a drop, sir!" and glanced at me.

I agreed. "Didn't smell any liquor."

Mollified, Hawley demanded, "What happened?"

The rumpled first officer touched the back of his head with a frown. "I went outside. Thought I saw something . . ." He sucked in a breath, then shook his head. "Must have slipped. That's all I remember." He shifted his shoulders like a bear waking from its slumber.

Hawley said, "See Witherspoon. That's an order. Dismissed."

Bigby staggered, so I grabbed his arm and escorted him down to the sick bay. There the physician peered into Bigby's eyes and dabbed his skinned elbow with an orange-red tincture.

I watched the proceedings in confusion. Why had Bigby gasped? Was that a start of recognition? He'd recovered quickly, but it told me there was more. What didn't he want the captain to hear?

Eventually Witherspoon instructed, "Rest, lay off the liquor and have plenty of soup," and sent us off.

Bigby stepped heavily as we walked to his cabin. Then he tried to say goodbye at his door. I wasn't having it. I told him so and stepped inside.

Turning from me, he slumped on a chair and rubbed his face.

"What's the matter, Edwin?"

Ignoring the mumbled reply, I filled him a glass of water from the faucet. He waved it away, peeled off his uniform jacket and toed off his shoes.

Seeing him groan, I said, "Guess I landed a couple of taps last night. Want something to put on them? Witherspoon will be happy to see you again."

Ignoring my weak attempt at humor, he grunted and ran his fingers through his hair. "I'll be all right."

"What happened? You didn't tell Hawley the whole story."

He shook his head and cursed, but I pressed him again. His blood-shot eyes looked wild and shocked. Something had unsettled him, and he wasn't a man to scare easily.

"Why'd you leave the bridge?"

"I didn't!" He shook his head in apology.

I waited, letting the silence work on him. Something had troubled him in Hawley's cabin, it was now gnawing at his insides. His stunned pale face scarcely resembled the steady officer I'd known this past week. Guilt could do that, I thought.

In a hoarse voice he asked, "Did you tell Hawley about last night? 'Bout, ah, exchanging blows? I mistook you for the blighter we're looking for! Did you tell him?"

"No need to." His rough breathing and muddled words drew an echo from me. "Dash it, Bigby. What the devil's going on?"

"You'll think I'm crazy."

"Try me."

"You can't tell Hawley, hear me? I'll lose my job, my career! I'll be finished."

That shook me. Was he going to confess to murder? I hesitated. "If it's about Don Juan," I said carefully, "You know I have to tell him."

He paused. "It's not . . . not directly. But I'm going mad thinking of it. Makes no sense, O'Trey. None. I can hardly believe . . ."

"Spit it out."

He snatched up the glass and downed the drink of water like it was a welcome beer. Setting it down sharply, he said. "All right. I saw a ghost"—he waved a hand to one side—"standing square in front of me."

I stared. "Outside the bridge?" The burly first officer was the last person I expected to see a specter.

"Yes. Saw her clear. Carruthers had gone to the head, so I was alone."

Her. "You left the bridge unmanned?" Even I knew he could be dismissed for that.

At my incredulous tone he dropped his elbows to the table and clutched his head.

To make amends, I said, "You knew Carruthers would be back. So you . . . stepped outside? In the dark. You followed the gh—the thing you saw? God, Edwin, that was brave." I gawked at him, then asked, "What was it?"

When he only shook his head, I joked, "Ghost of Nelson? The headless horseman? It's all right. It was a foul night."

He groaned and looked up, his face lined. "Alice. Alice Fry. The suicide."

Our gazes locked. "Bollocks," I said. We had the makings of a whole new legend, I thought. A dead diplomat and a suicide ghost haunting the bridge.

"Yes," he said, his face intent. "She stood there in her black dress, clear as day, glaring at me. Thought I was losing my mind. I rubbed my eyes and looked again. She was gone. Bloody rotten trick, I thought, someone's playing a dirty trick on me, so I went out to catch 'em. They wouldn't be expecting that!" He gave a sharp bark of laughter that had no humor in it.

"There was nothing there, Jim. I looked along the companionway and over the roof of the bridge. We've equipment there for rain and measuring the stars. No one there."

Would I have the courage to do that? I pulled in a slow breath. "How'd you fall?"

With tentative fingers he touched his rumpled hair where Witherspoon had wound a bandage. "No idea. Next thing you were patting me like a pup."

I gave him a half smile, but my heart wasn't in it.

He choked, "I know what I saw."

I thought about that night I'd spent in Dora's room and almost suffocated. "I believe you. But there's an explanation, Edwin. You saw something all right, but it was no ghost. Besides, the culprit might have knocked you out."

His head snapped around. Such hope in his open face! I recounted my strange episode in Dora's room, and Diana's re-creation of it, ending, "So there was actually someone there. My knee hit him, I felt that. Then he hid. This bloke's strange, Edwin. Thin as a rail and mighty compact. Someone that could fit into"—I glanced around—"that trunk, perhaps."

He glowered at the luggage, then went and yanked open the lid. Slamming it closed he dropped onto his bed and stretched out.

The cabin tilted gently so I snatched up the sliding decanter and set it back inside its metal cordon. Objects in Bigby's desk rattled as they rolled. My stomach tightened as I felt a familiar sinking in my chest. Great bellowing cannons, not now! I could not be sick now!

I breathed hard, pressing a hand to my middle, then dashed for Bigby's washroom.

Returning, I wiped my hands with my kerchief, trying to breathe slowly, as Diana had taught. "Seasick, hmm?" said Bigby cheerfully. "You need to lie down. That helps. And looking at the horizon. Something steady, see?"

I dabbed my face. "Let's say you did see someone. Why would they dress up as Alice?" I asked him. "Why would that trouble you?"

He paused, a curious look on his face. "Other than that she's dead?"

The ship began another roll. I caught the edge of the table and plowed on. "Why not Don Juan? He's dead too. Why Alice? What's she to you? She called you a nincompoop, that day."

Bigby watched me for a long moment, then said, "All right. She shouted it on the bridge. Called him the 'Butcher of Santiago.' Brought it all back, like it was yesterday."

"Butcher? What did she mean?" She'd terrified Dora with her rantings. Why had it disturbed Bigby?

He sighed and sat, swinging his feet off the bed. "She said 'Remember the *Virginius*.' 'Course I did. I never forgot! I'd been on the HMS *Niobe* for Christ's sake! I saw the aftermath—the bodies! We carried them Stateside, didn't we?"

The ship's engines sped up, a mad orchestra of kettledrums. My head began to pound in unison.

I said, "Slow down, old boy. The *Virginius*? Twenty years ago?" Bly had mentioned that ship was caught by Spain and tried for piracy. "Americans were executed."

Bigby's nostrils flared, his chest swelling. "And Englishmen. Military tribunal, what rot! Don Juan Nepomuceno rushed through the verdicts, executed the captain and a dozen others the next morning! Over two dozen were shot and beheaded!"

I felt adrift. "Don Juan gave the order? Our Don Juan?"

"He commanded the garrison! I tell you, O'Trey, there can be no civilized dealings with such animals. We threatened to fire on Santiago. Seventy guns, the *Niobe* had. We'd have done it! The American consul ran back and forth begging for time, while that beggar slaughtered sailors left and right. Fifty-three killed, O'Trey! In the two days while we were approaching. Captain Fry . . . and his son were shot too."

Was Don Juan a surly autocrat intoxicated with the might of Spanish rule? He'd executed Cubans, American and British citizens, ordered the deaths of fifty-three men. I pulled in a slow breath. "You were on the rescue ship. You brought survivors home."

"They'd been starved, tortured—smelled like animals, shaking, weeping. They'd expected a simple run down to Cuba, bringing food and supplies to the rebels. The Spanish claimed they'd tossed guns and munitions overboard before being boarded. The Cubans, poor blighters, were cut down without quarter, O'Trey. No reasoning with sanctimonious Spanish overlords. And Nepomuceno the worst of them."

"Was there no inquiry afterward? No trial?"

"How could there be? He was recalled to Spain. Connected to the royals, you know. His father had commanded the army. The American ambassador protested. Useless. They promoted the don to governor, for God's sake!"

He looked at me with red-rimmed eyes. "He was a butcher, O'Trey, but I didn't kill him. I swear it."

Nauseated and unsteady, I staggered back up the stairs. I had always believed that a civilized society, a just society, must enforce the law. That's what kept us from chaos, our bulwark against barbarism. I'd viewed Don Juan as a tough old soldier. The massacre of the *Virginius's* crew shook me.

God, I wanted stable land now. The very deck below me seemed to swell with questions. With each hollow footstep, Bigby's story thudded in my mind. Did it justify the don's murder? But if anyone with a grudge felt justified to kill, why, no one was safe. It took little to anger a man. A woman might feel slighted or belittled. Did that warrant retaliation?

You're a fine one to consider this, Agnihotri, I grumbled as I staggered toward our stateroom. I'd taken part in innumerable military actions in North India. After the carnage in Maiwand, my company had been ordered to attack. Few could repel a coordinated onslaught from a professional army. In weeks we'd beaten the emir into signing a treaty.

I'd been proud to stand for the British Indian army. Now I recalled the glowering faces of tribesmen as we rode past, read their sullen impotence. Was I upholding the law, then? I'd been so certain before. The ache under my temple pulsed.

CHAPTER 39

AN EXPERIMENT

When I told her what had happened, Diana gasped. "Khodaiji! Big-by's alive? Thank goodness."

I frowned. "He's not the sort to invent ghouls. I think someone lured him out. Dressed like Alice Fry and scared the stuffing out of him. What I can't fathom is why."

She tilted her head. "Because he knows about the don's past? Or to terrify him?"

"No . . . what did the phantom—Thin-jin—gain by this? Why draw Bigby outside, then . . ." I was thinking of someone throwing a knife at the lump on the bed, the lump that should have been De Cullar. While hanging on outside the ship. Tossing a blade through a porthole, while Bigby and I traded punches. Then, a short while later, Bigby falls from a ladder. Once his altercation with Don Juan was known, he'd be a sus-pect. Or was he another convenient scapegoat? What did Mrs. Barlow's abduction have to do with this? I could not imagine they were unrelated incidents.

Diana stilled, then turned her wide brown eyes on me. "You think someone tried to kill him!"

"Because he saw the nurse with the don? Does the killer think Bigby can identify him?"

We would dock today. Something flickered at the back of my mind. In a recent story Holmes had chided Watson, "You have seen, yet you have not observed." I recalled the evening of Alice's suicide and my heartbeat sped up. I considered the deck, the shadows of the lifeboats.

"Diana . . . the afternoon Alice died, what did you see?"

She pouted. "What you saw, I suppose."

I gave her a half smile. "Humor me."

She went to the porthole, dark eyes solemn. "We were on deck. You'd been seasick, and we hoped walking would help."

I nodded. She went on, "A woman was there, near the lifeboat, and then she dropped. You ran toward her, I recall."

"Slowly, sweet. At first, what did you notice, exactly?"

"Her dress. It was white. Her hat was . . . straw, I think."

"Did you see her face, her hair?"

Diana bit her lip, then said, "Wouldn't expect to. Her hat . . ."

"The hat. Wouldn't it float, a straw hat?"

Diana gazed at me as though I were speaking Greek. "It . . . should have. I went to the railing right away, to search. Oh, how I searched. Nothing."

"No hat on the water. Let's go back. You saw a dress, a hat. What else?"

She squeezed her eyes, then shook her head. "But, Jim, you were closer. What did *you* see?"

I leaned on my elbows and clasped my hands, remembering. A high wind, a flutter near the ship's railing . . .

"Something moved by the lifeboat, near the rail, something white, flapping. It . . . rose, expanding, leaned forward, and dropped, all at once. She didn't jump but collapsed into the water with barely a splash."

"I've seen divers enter a pool very neatly with pointed feet," Diana offered.

"She didn't cry out. Not a whisper. Did you hear anything?"

Diana bit her lip. "I don't know. The couple in front yelled for help. You shouted, 'Man overboard!'"

"Hmm." I leaned back, closed my eyes and re-created the scene in my mind. It was a cloudy evening early in our voyage, and my first turn on deck. Diana was telling me about the game room as we passed. Had I seen a hat? Perhaps yes. Had the woman held it down against the breeze? She must have.

I said, "Why would someone wear a hat to jump overboard?"

And why hadn't it stayed floating on the surface? The events of the past days tangled and swirled in my mind. Miss Felicity Rood had lost a hat. And there'd been a fuss about a missing sewing basket.

I sat up, an idea trickling into my mind. Could it really be . . . ?

My heartbeat lurched into a gallop.

"Sweetheart, may I have your straw hat, the old one? And . . . a night-shirt? I'll buy you another in Liverpool," I promised.

Diana handed them over, and watched, puzzled worry creeping across her face as I assembled the objects for my experiment and emp-tied the apples from the basket on the table.

Her eyes filled with questions when I rang for Felix and sent him to fetch a bowling ball and thirty feet of fishing line. She stared, but to her credit, she said nothing.

Waiting for his return, I busied myself with ink, pen and paper. This would take some careful doing. When he returned with the objects, I thanked him and handed him a note for the captain.

Diana waited until he'd left, then burst out, "What is it? What are you planning?"

I grinned and sent her on to breakfast. "I'll send Felix for a tray. Come to the portside lifeboats after your meal, all right? Hawley and Bigby will come."

Though puzzled, thankfully she left. I needed some time alone to connect the pieces of my puzzle.

I'd believed that the person who'd stolen the gems had killed the don to conceal the theft. Now I knew *two* plans were afoot at the same time. One had brutally ended the don's life, the other a theft, carefully planned and coordinated, so that the trunks were switched by one party, and summoned by another. If discovered, De Cullar might try to excuse the swap as a clerical mistake. However, if the Spaniards got away with it, HMS *Etruria* and the Cunard Company would be held responsible. A diplomatic incident combined with the financial liability of this theft might bring down Cunard entirely, but the funds that Don Juan had acquired for Spain would be secreted over to Basque rebels. When the Rothschilds sued for the interest on their loan, Spain would most certainly refuse, and the matter would be argued in court for years.

But then someone killed the don.

When Doña Josefina had demanded to see the gemstones, the theft was uncovered early, while its perpetrators were still on board. The killer's precipitous act uncovered the theft. It left the original question: why was the don killed? I had a theory. Now I needed to test it.

By ten that morning, Hawley and his officers assembled on the upper deck where Diana and I had strolled that first breezy evening. Engines humming, our ship plowed toward land, a narrow bow wave sizzling alongside.

I saw gulls swirling, like kites at Ramadan, their cries not unlike children squealing as the wind taught their colored paper toys to soar and dive. Liverpool was near. Crouching behind a reel of cables, I kept out of sight. It had taken me a while to set up my experiment and I was eager to set it in motion.

On deck, Hawley spread his hands, turning to Diana. "Well?" The wind caught the rest of his words, but I fancied he said, "Where is the detective?"

She demurred, gesturing toward the nearest lifeboat. It swung about five feet off the deck, suspended by pulleys.

While they were eating breakfast, I'd tied my creation to one end of the fishing line, while hanging the other over the lifeboat as a pulley, tethered to my wrist. Now, by quickly gathering in the line, I hoisted the concoction: a bowling ball nestled inside Diana's basket. It was disguised with Diana's hat and nightshirt.

I cursed softly as the line cut into my palms. It was heavier than I'd expected, so I wound it over my cuffs instead. As I yanked on the line, the white clothing expanded, rising like a flag being hoisted. The night-shirt drooped at first, then a happy breeze sent it gently flapping. Was this what Diana and I had seen?

A cry broke out. The group rushed forward, thumping their way toward me. I reached up and snipped the line.

Dress, hat and basket dropped forward and sank into the waves.

Tucking away Diana's scissors, I stepped from behind the cables, just as Hawley cried, "Not again!"

"It's all right!" I shouted to stave off the dreaded call of "man over-board."

"It was a dummy," I said, pointing to show Hawley how I'd suspended the collection over the lifeboat rail. "Suspended by a fishing line. See?"

Hawley looked confounded. Diana clapped. Bigby closed his mouth.

Did they understand what they'd seen? "No one went overboard," I explained. "Alice isn't dead. She faked it, d'you see? That's how she did it!"

And Alice hated Don Juan with a passion.

Was that how it happened? When Alice saw Don Juan boarding, had it set off her long-held hatred? She'd ranted to Dora, given up her duties, even barged up to the bridge to spill her rage at the chief officer. Why? I would not know until I found her.

"But how . . . ?" cried Bigby.

I felt exhilarated. "Easy! I looped the line over the lifeboat, so," I said and stepped onto the railing, steadying myself with a palm against the painted hull.

It moved. The ship rolled toward me. The lifeboat swung out, pushing me back. I flung out a hand, but I was high up, with nothing to grasp. My right knee buckled, and I went over the ship's rail.

I gasped at the rush of air, the shocked faces.

Incredulous, I fell backward!

I crashed into the sea, my shoulders taking most of the impact. Stunned, I clenched, trying to shake my head, as though to expel the invading water, but it was everywhere. Cold. Icy. A giant frigid fist that crushed me, so cold that it burned. I could not think. Colors, bubbles, motion swamped me. I was spinning.

"People float," Diana had said. "Especially in salt water."

I wasn't floating. My coat billowed out as I sank.

Had I dragged in a breath before hitting the water? I could not remember.

"Spread out like a jellyfish, and you'll float," Diana had said. I tried to pantomime one, reaching out my arms and widening my legs, feeling the water snatch at my skin. Fighting terror, I turned, disoriented by the motion.

"If you're clenched up, you'll drop through the water," she'd warned, so I forced myself slack.

I blinked, cringing against the sting of salt, straining to see, but all around was murky green. The water darkened around me. I was still falling. Had I slowed? Dimly lit, strange shapes hung in the distance.

"Hold your breath. It makes you lighter, like a rubber balloon," I recalled her words, vaguely fighting the urge to exhale. I needed this air, so I kept it locked. The light was above me. I *would* float.

I'd reckoned without my heavy army boots. They sank, pulling me upright in a slow, gentle motion. I kicked out, twisting to regain my horizonal position, which sent me spurting forward.

Hope gushed through me. I reached out, hands cupped pulling downward desperately. My lungs burned, threatening to spill air. Alternating arm strokes, I pushed upward. How far had I dropped? Those damn shoes. I kicked, trying to get them off, but I'd laced them too tight.

Why had I stepped on the railing? It had not seemed risky; sailors climbed up and down like monkeys. The ship was already distant. How long before they sent out swimmers? Would they find me in this vast ocean? How could they?

My chest screamed. "Just a little," it begged, "lose a little air, let it out." The pressure, God, the pressure.

My arms worked of their own accord now, my mind spinning, shapes floating past—seaweed or fish? I scarcely cared. I'd have only a few more lucid moments, I thought, fighting the overwhelming urge to exhale. How long could a man hold his breath? How many minutes had it been?

Damn it! I could not leave Diana. She'd given up everything she knew for me.

Whatever happened, I must get back to her. In the reaches of my memory this was a familiar refrain. I had done this before, trying, walking, fighting to return to Diana.

"You'll float," she'd said, so I kept hauling handfuls of water toward me, kicking in a vain effort to rid myself of my boots. But Diana was lighter, as was Adi, her brother. My body was dense; I aided whatever buoyancy it might possess with frantic effort.

This might be all I had left, a few seconds more, until my lungs let go. I wouldn't let the water in, I decided. I'd hold my lungs empty, giving myself a few moments more. Would someone on board spot me? Would it be enough?

Arms reaching in rhythm as fast as I could, my lungs on fire, I fought the water, mindless now, fixing my gaze on the light above, as cold hammered my very being.

I recalled an officer saying, "A ship cannot stop quickly. We can reverse engines but that takes a while." As he said this, the blighter had actually smiled!

My chest screamed like it might explode. Just a little, I thought, just let out a little air, like releasing an overfilled football. But when I exhaled, a large bubble expanded and disappeared. I sank.

Panic-struck I propelled my arms, pulling water toward me as I tried to rise to the surface. Too far away. It was a losing battle.

Something was behind me. A fish? A shark? Purple hues mixed with greens. Something caught my shirt.

Was I hallucinating? Why did I take such risks? When I'd galloped into the Pathankot mountains, I'd known I might not return. Now I could not recall why I'd gone, only that Diana had been furious.

Not much time left. Then something touched my back. A hand. It caught my waistband and pulled.

I turned, blinking in the murk. Saw a white blur. An arm arced past my face. A mermaid floated beside me, swimming upward. Her white garment brushed my skin, her hair a dark cloud.

This was drowning, I thought, and gave up the air in my shrieking chest.

CHAPTER 40

LIGHT AND DARKNESS

They hauled me up into the light, choking and coughing. Brine stung my eyes, my throat was on fire. My body spasmed, fighting it knew not what. My blurred vision brought fragments of images. Light, searing my eyes, my brain. The gunwale of a boat. Some rope. Feet, arms, someone's chin. Words dropped around me like spent cartridges, their sounds popping without meaning.

Acrid bile in my mouth. Salt scraped my throat, as I hauled air into my depleted lungs.

My throat raw, I rasped, "What happened?"

Gagging, I convulsed and found myself on my side lying partially in water. My eyes smarted. I blinked, swiping weakly at them. Rough wooden boards scraped my cheek, my palms, as I struggled to rise. A rocking motion sent me back to the sopping, shallow bottom. Wheezing, I glimpsed open sky. Where *was* I? The ship's funnel came into view, but it was soon blocked by the burly shoulder of a sailor.

He grinned at me from a suntanned face. "Stay down, eh?"

Wet fingers touched my arm. Diana. How did I know it was her? Her grip tightened with some meaning I did not grasp. She crouched behind me. What in blazes had happened?

"Almost there," she whispered near my ear.

Her cold, thin arm was around me, but my limbs were heavy and waterlogged, trapped by sodden clothes. I ached like I'd gone through a meat grinder. Leaning over me, she came into view, soaked through, a blanket over her shoulders. Hair bedraggled, her skin seemed stretched tight over the bones of her pale face.

"You look awful," she said, eyes enormous, teeth chattering.

Pot calling the kettle . . . I winced a grin, swallowed and tried to speak, to ask what had happened, but each breath burned. My lips stung as though I'd been whacked with an oar. Our boat swung wildly, sloshing the bilgewater back at me. What the devil?

"It's all right," the skeletal version of Diana said, voice wobbling. "We're all right."

"Grab the Kisbee ring!" someone ordered the big man sitting nearby.

A white canvas object dropped against my chest. Distant shouts were exchanged. A pulley creaked above. I was on a lifeboat, being winched slowly upward. The steamer's hull rose alongside, portholes passing from my sight. The white funnel returned into view, larger now. We settled onto the steamer's deck with a thump.

It was some time before I learned to breathe again. Had I been attacked? No, I'd figured it out. I remembered hoisting the nightshirt like a sail until it caught a breeze and flapped. The group on deck had spotted it and cried out. I'd cut the line dropping the dummy into the sea to show how Alice had faked her suicide . . . and then? An image of desperation swamped me, murky green water rushing past. Somehow, I'd fallen. Bollocks. I had almost drowned. Eyelashes sticky, I blinked against the bright sky.

Diana smiled, her lips blue from cold.

I tried to say "I'm all right," but only managed to cough.

Feeling as limp as a potato pancake, I was lifted into a canvas sling and lowered to the deck. I heard exclamations and applause, but my eyelids were heavy, my mind sludge.

Squinting against the light, I saw Bigby climb down bearing something. It was Diana, swaddled in a blanket like an infant. My stretcher rocked. I closed my eyes.

Next, I was lying in our cabin. The chamber seemed dark and airless. I groaned and sat up in bed, gasping.

Dr. Witherspoon's voice said, "Lie back, Mr. O'Trey, you've had a narrow escape."

Light glinting off his spectacles, he touched my shoulder. "You've got some bruises, but as far as I can tell, nothing's broken. You're a very lucky man, Mr. O'Trey."

I croaked, "How . . ." and didn't know what I meant to ask.

Just then Diana returned from the lavatory, leaning on someone— was it Dora? No, Nurse Shay.

"Easy, now," said Witherspoon, his voice gentle. "She's all right. Plucky girl went in after you, did you know? Threw her hat in right away— literally, tossed it on the water." He chuckled. "Good thing too—it served as a fine marker. I'll have to remember that next time someone goes overboard." He seemed delighted at the prospect.

Was she all right? "Diana?"

"I'm here," she said, her tone slow with sleep.

"Let her rest now," said Witherspoon, with a warning look at the nurse. He turned to me. "Your wife hauled off her shoes and skirts and dove in. She was so quick, it left officers stunned. Two people to search for! Miss Dora assured us that Mrs. O'Trey could swim like a fish, so the captain ordered us hard about and had the lifeboat lowered. Still, we had a few nasty moments."

He smiled, tucking his glasses away. "How she found you we'll never know, but she'd got an arm around a Kisbee ring, and kept your head over it."

Diana. She'd dived in. I recalled seeing green shapes as the surface receded. The mermaid . . . She'd found me.

I closed my eyes as my heart slowed its wild thumping. A solicitous voice spoke, the sound blurred as though I were still underwater. Words could not press through my numbed brain. A blanket of sleep dropped over me.

* * *

Sometime later I woke with a pain that yanked me up. I doubled over, trying to compress the cramp in my belly.

"All right?" asked Diana. She sat on the bed in her blue kaftan. Her fingers found mine, reassuring, assessing.

I sent her a smile that was half gratitude, half apology. Her grip complained for a while, then relaxed. Our cabin seemed darker. Was it evening? I croaked out a question. "When do we reach . . ."

Coming into view like an emaciated genie, Witherspoon offered me water, saying, "We are in Liverpool. But the ship's being searched for a stowaway, so we're asked to remain indoors." He was so bloody cheerful, I felt exhausted as I strained to grip the glass.

He'd stayed with us? Surprise and gratitude flashed through me as the sweet coolness trickled down my throat. Perhaps for a physician, the well and the sick were two different classes of being, one to be glowered at, the other cheered up. I almost preferred the former.

Diana said, "They're looking for Alice Fry. Your experiment proved she was still on board."

Alice Fry. Bigby had said that name. Before I could fathom the meaning of it, a knock sounded on the door.

Captain Hawley entered, instantly shrinking our stateroom.

Taking off his hat, he asked about our health, then told me, "You gave us a scare, O'Trey. But your wife here's a wonder. A fine swimmer, ma'am!"

"She is," I said, smiling through cracked lips, then asked, "You've found Alice?"

He shook his head. "Not yet. We'll dock soon, O'Trey. The pilot's taking us into port, but no one's to be let off until we find her."

Stepping close, he thrust out a hand. "I didn't think you'd crack this, O'Trey. I was wrong. Thank you, from the bottom of my heart!"

Shortly after, the doctor and he departed. A horrendous burp eased the pressure in my belly.

"More water?" Diana brought it, her hair wound in a braid over her shoulder. I drank again from the proffered glass, feeling myself return to an even keel.

Settling back, I searched Diana's quiet face. Why *had* she been so distant? What had I done, all those weeks ago to lose her affection?

"Better?" She touched my hair.

"Diana, will you tell me now?"

She bent nearer. "Tell you what, Jim?"

"What I did? Why you. . . ." I plowed ahead. "Why something changed between us."

Her brows furrowed as she pulled back.

Damn. Why had I asked? But the need to know would not abate. I grabbed her hand before she could close me off. "Something was different when I got back to Boston. What was it?"

She looked away. Desperation clawed at me. Was I making it worse? "It's just that . . . I hoped we'd got past it. But I've got to know, sweet, so I don't do it again."

There. I could do no better. Now I must wait, but each second brought remorse. Fool. Shouldn't have said anything. Why had I reminded her?

She looked up, face drawn. "You couldn't help this, Jim."

So it was something ordinary, something that was a part of me. "It's the job? Takes me away too much?"

I spoke before thinking, and some part of me hollered a warning. Could I cease investigating, stop taking on cases? But I'd waited so long to know, I barreled ahead. "Do you want me to quit Dupree?"

Startled, she met my gaze. "You'd do that?"

It was part of me, like boxing. But I hadn't boxed for money in years. So, this too, I could change. "I'd find something. Can't promise it won't be dangerous. But I could do something else."

Pulling in her lips, she rearranged the bedclothes. "I'd never ask that, Jim. I know you. You like it, working a case, figuring it out. Applying Mr. Holmes's principles . . ."

That took my breath away. I searched her sad face.

"Then what is it, sweet?" I whispered so she wouldn't know the words were shouting inside me.

"It . . . happened. It just happened."

THE SPANISH DIPLOMAT'S SECRET

She cringed, sorrow brimming in her eyes and—oh, God—*guilt?* Fingers knitted, her mouth twisted in remorse. Just happened? I clenched the bed as though I was falling. *She'd* done something? My pulse jolted into a gallop. I'd been away a great deal those last months. She ducked her head and would not meet my gaze. I felt like I'd taken a blow to the face.

Oh, God, no. "Who is he?"

I hadn't intended that rough tone, but it tore out of me.

She flinched. Her eyes went wide, then she turned on me, growing fierce. "He? How dare you! You think I'd—what? Met someone? Gone off to have a love affair?"

"God's sake, Diana." I swallowed in relief as I tried to breathe again. "I'm a fool. You can't know how I've worried about this, being away."

No, I read from her outrage, there was no going back from my misstep. What the devil had I done? We'd just recovered from whatever blunder I'd committed! Why in God's name hadn't I left well enough alone?

Then her mouth softened as she covered my hand. Instantly the world righted. She'd let it go. I hadn't known a woman could overlook a cut like that.

She whispered, "Jim, I've said nothing because I don't know how to say it."

"Do you still—" I grimaced, willing her to understand.

"Love you? Oh, Jim."

Say it, I demanded without words, trying to keep my fingers from trembling.

She smiled, a painful twist of those delicate lips. "Always."

Always. Hearing that word, I pulled in a breath and grinned, despite the bite of my cracked lips. I felt invincible. She knew. She'd once asked me, would I have her without a penny of her father's wealth, if she left with just the clothes on her back? I'd laughed and replied, "Always."

Now she gave it back to me. We were all right. Whatever it was, this blasted thing that divided us, it would not break us.

"Sweetheart, I swear, if it's something I can change, I will."

Tears pooled in her eyes.

"Diana!"

She did not meet my gaze. "It was the day after you left, Jim."

A sharp pain skewered me. Someone had hurt her? Why had I left her unprotected and alone?

She snapped, "Stop, Jim. Just let me tell you."

I smothered my fear, feeling vicious. I didn't have to wait long, as her tale tumbled out.

"That night, my belly hurt. Here." She pressed a hand below her waist. "A sharp pain. So bad I couldn't sit, couldn't walk. I lay down, praying it would pass."

She'd been ill! She'd been so pale when I got home, listless, without energy. I should have suspected it.

"Pia woke me. I'd been bleeding, Jim. So much blood. Soaking through my skirt. Pia knocked and knocked but I didn't hear. Must have been asleep."

Asleep . . . or unconscious, I thought, each heartbeat tolling a warning.

She went on. "She'd got the landlady to open our door. Thank heaven, I hadn't set the bar across the door. They helped me clean up."

Neither woman had mentioned anything. "Did you call a doctor?"

Diana shook her head. "We knew what had happened. It was already over. I'd been with child, Jim. I lost the baby."

I searched her sweet, pointed face. She seemed older and quieter than the spunky girl I'd met two years ago. My skin felt tight, my insides twisting to think of her, weeping, bleeding, in our apartment. She'd borne it alone. How could I comfort her? I almost feared to move lest I do the wrong thing.

My throat pinched as I rasped, "I should have been there."

She looked up. "You're not angry?"

Astonished, I said, "How could I be?"

"Our baby, Jim. I know how you wanted him. Or her. I never saw the child. There was only blood. Pia said it was too early, that it happens. But I know it was my fault. No, don't shake your head. I must have caused it! Don't know how—but I must have! What if . . ." Her face creased in a grimace as her voice quailed. "What if I can't have children?"

Her ragged tone told me she was thinking too, of Dora's pain, of that infant who would never enter the world. Diana's wounded heart would have loved that child, but she had said nothing to Dora, who was scarcely more than a child herself, for that truth was too cruel.

I gripped her fingers. "We don't know that. It doesn't mean that."

It wasn't enough. How to reassure her? "If it's not to be, we'll be aunt and uncle to the Welks children. To young Tito." She looked hopeful, so I went on. "There are orphans who'd need us. We could adopt."

Her valiant little smile arrowed through me as she nestled close. Lying back with her head secure on my shoulder, I pulled in grateful breaths. We had now, we had this. Now that her reticence was explained, I struggled with remorse. She'd suffered a shock and a loss. But more than that, she'd blamed herself, feared I'd fault her for it.

Knowing that sliced me to ribbons.

She whispered, "Jim, I want . . . I need meaning in my life."

My gut tightened. "We're together. Isn't that enough?"

"Please dear. I couldn't explain, if it hurt you."

I could not see her face. "What is it? Are you . . . unhappy?" Unhappy with me, I wanted to ask, but the words locked in my chest.

"I knew you'd see it like that. I am happy with our life, Jim! But . . . you only want to protect me!"

"Is that so wrong?" I got the words out, but Diana sat up, searching my face, then touched my shoulder. Somehow that made it worse.

"I need to feel useful, Jim. When you . . . pamper me, I feel . . . useless. It's as though I'm betraying my old self. Papa had such hopes for me, Mama always said I'd make something of myself. I can't just be at home. A gilded cage is still a cage!"

I gaped at her. "You . . . want a job?"

Diana—an exhausted shopgirl, a timid typist? I pushed away the images conjured in my mind. "You could help the Lins run the bakery. They struggle with the accounts, yes?"

She bit her lip. "I do that on weekends, Jim. But . . . I need to do something more."

"You like to read," I said, frowning.

She wilted. "Reading . . . prepares one for the world, to speak with different people. It's like I'm training for something, but never actually doing it."

I touched her hair. Perhaps it was time to tell her why we were going to Britain.

"Let's talk about it when we get home, all right? Adi's in England, sweet. That's why I booked this crossing. I knew you'd be happier if you could see him."

Once we met, I'd find out what fix Adi was in. I needn't trouble her yet with that.

She propped herself on an elbow. "So you have no case in England . . . ?"

"Oh, there is a case," I assured her. "An old client of Dupree's wrote, seeking help. He needed an operative to go there. I'd written to Adi, so I snatched at the chance and said I'd do it."

CHAPTER 41

THE HUNT

With only hours left before docking, and seeing nothing else I could do on the case, Diana and I went to dinner. Despite our two-day delay, the dining saloon was crowded for this last meal aboard.

Our arrival caused a stir. Passengers greeted me, saying they were glad to see us. While news of our recovery—and Diana's disrobing on deck to dive after me—had likely made the rounds, clearly few expected to see us at dinner. Surprised at the warm reception, I returned nods of acknowledgment as I escorted Diana to our table. Chief Steward Johnson insisted on tucking her chair in himself.

"Jim!" Bigby said and shook hands, his grip tight with heartfelt emotion, then asked Diana, "You're all right, Mrs. O'Trey?"

While Diana dimpled at him, I asked, "Any luck with the search?"

He sighed. "We've looked stem to stern, second cabins and steerage, and all the public areas, but captain doesn't want first-cabin passengers disturbed."

I nodded. "That's the problem, isn't it? All along, Alice's evaded discovery by masquerading as one."

His voice dropped. "She has to have an accomplice. Someone hiding her in first." Then he cleared his throat and said, "Want to thank you,

O'Trey. You've been good about this. I should have, ah, been more forth-coming."

I sent him a half smile in reply. As promised, I had not mentioned our conversation to the captain.

Tilting my head toward Hawley's table, I told Bigby, "He knew 'bout you and the *Niobe* all along. That's why he kept you out of the investi-gation and gave it to me. Not because he couldn't trust you, but to pro-tect you at the inquest. With your history, no court would believe you weren't involved."

Bigby's sharp intake of breath told me I'd hit home. His gaze followed Hawley across the room with something akin to devotion. A moment later we were summoned, so Bigby and I headed toward the group of officers around the captain.

* * *

When I returned, the soup bowls were being whisked away, and replaced with small dishes of sorbet.

Diana smiled, then raised her eyebrows. I sat and answered her in-quiring look, "We'll soon take on a revenue cutter. A squad of customs officers will take declarations about our trunks. They'll check passports too." I nodded at our tablemates, who seemed somber. "What were you discussing?"

Diana said, "Just the oddities of this crossing. There've been so many! Thank heaven, Dora's recovering."

Algernon sniffed. He toyed with the sorbet, his disapproval apparent at fifty paces. Vernon tossed his head, saying, "She's a fine girl. A great girl!"

Mrs. Evansworth shook her head. "Shipboard associations are all very well, but they rarely continue on land," she said in the tone of one who means well. "And never, with the staff or others *not* of one's own class."

Momentarily hard of hearing, Vernon ignored this and said to Di-ana, "An eventful crossing, Mrs. O'Trey, everything that could have gone wrong has done so! Except for catching fire and sinking, 'course!"

Gasps. Shocked silence. Vernon's eyes widened as he recognized his faux pas. We were still on board. His rash remark verged on tempting fate. I chuckled in sympathy.

His face crimson, he said, "Mr. O'Trey, how does a shark greet a fish?"

"Not again," someone murmured.

I smiled. "Sadly, I'm not acquainted with any sharks at present. How?"

"Pleased to eat you!" He grinned. "Where is the ocean the deepest? Come on—anyone?"

"Well, the Pacific is deepest, I believe," said Mr. Evansworth, attempting a civil answer.

Vernon chortled, "No, sir! The ocean is deepest . . . at the bottom!"

"Mister Farley!" cried Mrs. Evansworth. "Such language! In mixed company! It cannot be tolerated." She took him to task sternly, but he only laughed, blushing, yet unrepentant.

Mrs. Evansworth simmered, her hat feathers quivering. Lacking another target, she rounded on me. "Mr. O'Trey, since you're on holiday, may we assume you've caught the murderer?"

Her loud inquiry turned heads at adjacent tables, so I pitched my voice to the back of the room, saying calmly, "We hope to, ma'am. Can we count on your cooperation?"

Now people were looking at her! Cooperation? What did that mean? Was she implicated? I hid a smile as Diana and I said our farewells around the table. Our journey at an end, some exchanged calling cards, others shook hands expressing relief.

The sun dipped toward the horizon as Diana and I took a final turn around the deck. A weight lodged in my chest, I prepared for the coming interview with police and Scotland Yard.

I said, "This won't end until we find Alice. She must have a bolt-hole somewhere."

She said, "She could just dive overboard and swim to shore."

"Not likely." I gestured toward the sailors posted at discreet intervals, ostensibly preparing the ropes and cables for docking.

She sighed. "Does Captain Hawley intend to search cabins? Difficult to do without rousing animosity. Everyone's packed and eager for land!"

"I don't envy him." I shrugged, then sent her an inquiring glance. "Seems Vernon's transferred his affections from Mrs. Bly?"

Her gaze somber, Diana said, "I hope he means to do right by Dora. He has his own money, you know. Their father passed away and both brothers got their share. This is their first venture, as independent bachelors of means. Algernon's a prig, of course. Hope Vernon gets away from him."

I grinned, amused at her disdain. How the tables had turned!

Outlined against the dying sun, the ship's exhausted staff and crew stood in a group, shoulders bunched. Hawley seemed on edge, struggling to keep up appearances though his nerves looked stretched tight. Where was the killer? That question had to be uppermost in the passengers' minds as well. My gut wound tight in desperation.

"We've got to find Alice, sweet. But . . . she's a woman. I don't know how she'd think, what she'd do. Let me ask you, then. Where would you hide?"

Diana's eyebrows shot up. "*Me?* She could fly the trapeze, remember?" She mulled it over, then said, "Didn't you say someone was seen clinging to the sails?"

I glanced upward, remembering the sailor's terror. "The ghost on the mizzen?"

Had Alice perched on one of the booms tied crosswise to the masts? What a brilliant way to observe the deck! My back against the rail, I glanced up at the scallops of gathered sails and rigging. An empty chaos of ropes and ladders creaked above.

"'Course, I wouldn't hide there," said Diana. "Much too exposed."

"Where, then? The night she tried to smother me, Alice must have crouched for hours in Dora's cabin." The memory of it made my skin prickle. "Can't figure why she did it. Did she mean to kill Dora?"

Diana stopped walking and turned to me. "The bottle of chloroform. It was in that room. Do you recall a smell that night?"

I drew a breath, remembering the press of cloth upon my mouth and nose, the sickly sweet air of a sickroom. "I do. The same odor that was on that kerchief. Blast. She meant to sedate me."

"Or Dora. Remember, that was Dora's room. When you fought back it must have given her a frightful shock. Perhaps she only meant to send Dora to sleep more deeply. She calls Dora 'little bird' so she'd hardly want to kill her."

I frowned at that generous interpretation. "Don't know about that." I rubbed my forehead. "If you're right, why was Alice there anyway?"

Diana shrugged. "She needed her trunks. She couldn't wear the same clothes each day and hope to pass unnoticed. She'd have to bathe and dress, and find a place to sleep . . . once Dora was frightened away, that would be much easier. Perhaps that's all she wanted to do, scare Dora away."

"I think she lured Bigby into the dark and knocked him out. He fell. Could have broken his neck."

"Because he could identify her?" She nibbled on her lower lip, looking glum. "If we catch Alice, what will happen to her?"

"She'll face trial. That's out of our hands."

"Trial." Diana stopped to stare at the distant sliver of land now visible on the horizon. "And then? Murderers are . . . executed. She'll be hanged." She shuddered, a hand to her neck.

My jaw clenched tight. Just days ago, right and wrong had seemed so plain. Thinking of Alice, crouched in that tiny space between trunks, climbing the rigging, impersonating Dora to get a plate of food—something shifted in my mind. God, she'd had a time of it. Yet she had garroted a man and struck Bigby off the ladder in cold blood. What drove such a woman?

The deck tilted under my feet although the sea was calm.

"Justice, Diana. What sort of world would it be if anyone could murder, and get away with it? To plan it, stalk their prey and then throttle them viciously, turning them to see that final indignity! She does not deserve your pity. She's far beyond that."

"But, Jim"—Diana shook her head—"Don Juan . . . what if he deserved it?"

"Does it matter what sort of chap he was? Should we condone the killing of someone we don't like?"

Diana's frown was troubled. "What if we're wrong, Jim?"

I had no answer for her. The lights of Liverpool were near now, stretching along the coast in a glowing serpent. A sputtering engine drew our attention as the revenue cutter arrived. The boat bobbed alongside, dwarfed by our hull. Sailors at our ship's railing tossed down a Jacob's ladder.

Customs men began climbing to where officers waited to receive them.

We had arrived in England. Desperation building like steam in a boiler, I said, "We've got to find Alice. A Spanish diplomat killed on an English ship? Peace between two countries depends upon it."

Diana said, "All right. If it were me, I'd stay in a cabin and pretend to be seasick. No one would disturb me then."

A uniformed crewman called, "Please return to your stateroom, sir!" He directed us with an outstretched arm. "We'll be dockside in an hour!"

I puzzled over Bigby's earlier words. "Staterooms are all accounted for, unless an accomplice is hiding her." I frowned. "Won't work, even then. She'd have to come out to disembark. Customs men go through every stateroom. She'd need a passport."

The groups would be gathered now, dividing the cabins between them.

Following the flow of walkers, Diana and I continued down the port side and curved around the music room, now abandoned after the extravaganzas. Passengers beside us avoided the bank of windows, averting their eyes. It had become Don Juan's memorial.

Diana gasped, her eyes dark as she clutched my sleeve. "That's how Alice's going to escape. She's killed someone else."

"What?" I stopped dead in my tracks. "Killed whom?"

"She needs a passport, one that doesn't say Alice Fry. So, she takes one. But its owner would sound the alarm. Once she does, the stolen passport is of no use."

I swallowed. "You think she murdered a woman to impersonate her? Would have to be someone traveling alone, a recluse, else we'd have heard."

I remembered Madame Pontin, the tall opera singer who'd flirted with me although old enough to be my mother. I had to get to Hawley. No, I needed Dix, the purser. He'd know which women were traveling alone. Goddamn it! A killer who'd garroted an old man could certainly overpower another woman. We were dealing with a fiend in female form.

"Alice plans ahead," Diana murmured, then drew an audible breath. "Jim, Now I've got a plan. But you must help me."

"How?"

"First, we speak with the captain. Then, I'll ask you to . . . well, wait in a particular spot. And you'll need a uniform."

She went on to whisper instructions, while I listened in consternation.

A shiver ran over my skin. "No, my dear. This won't do. Find another way."

"For goodness' sake, Jim, there's no time! I can help!"

My throat dry, it was hard to speak. "You nearly died in Chicago."

She caught my arm. "But you'll be near; it will be in full view of everyone." Seeing me shaking my head, she cried, "Why won't you let me do it?"

"God's sake, Diana, I'm a detective! I'm supposed to find the culprit."

"But must you do it all yourself? Didn't your famous Holmes have people to help?"

CHAPTER 42

THAT WHICH CONSUMES

For Diana's plan to work, I needed a porter's uniform. As sunset painted the funnels pink and burnished the ship's decks, we hurried from the bridge to find Johnson. He was in the main galley, instructing his youngest troops.

We explained briefly. Looking mystified, he led us to the linen storage and pulled out uniforms, saying, "I keep these in case of accidents . . . with the soup."

I found one that might fit my waist, took it to his office and wore it. Diana had proposed a risky maneuver, but without another way to dislodge the hidden woman, I'd give it a go. That was the trouble, I thought, it was a woman. Some part of me could not reconcile the hideous nature of the crime with my conception of the female sex.

Johnson's eyebrows rose as I strode back and shoved a uniform hat on my head.

"The trousers are too short, sir. If we have a moment . . ."

We had not. Diana tugged me toward the door, saying, "No time. Everyone's lining up. Thank you, Mr. Johnson!"

We sped to the upper level, where electric lamps were being lit. Just as when we first boarded, staff in starched uniforms lined the perimeter with all the spit and polish of a cantonment receiving a new commander.

I'd persuaded Hawley, saying, "Go on as usual, but let only one group of passengers off at a time, a continuous stream."

"God knows we need answers, Mr. O'Trey."

"Keep passengers away while we confront her."

Eyebrows clumped over deep-set eyes, he reluctantly agreed to Diana's plan. Announcements were made throughout the ship, stewards hurrying door to door to instruct passengers to remain in their staterooms.

Diana and I arrived on deck to find ship's officers at the fountain stairway, controlling the stream of passengers. Couples had begun to run the gauntlet of stewards, handing out tips, then proceeded down the plank to the dock.

The port smelled of rotting seafood overlaid with acrid notes of soot from a thousand chimneys. A pungent stench of horse manure came from the pier, where carriages lined up to whisk away new arrivals.

Diana's plan required us to break with tradition. Instead of disembarking the passengers from the topmost level, we'd begun with the aft quarter of the lower deck, cabins fifty to seventy-five, working through to the saloon level.

Shaking the captain's hand, passengers proceeded, crew following with their trunks. Mr. and Mrs. August Evansworth of cabin fifty departed with their brood. The three elegant young ladies and a series of couples followed. I spotted the Farley brothers at the end of the line.

Wide-eyed and forlorn, Dora stood to one side, her skirts flapping in the breeze. She looked to and fro, uncertain when to debark.

"Wait! I'm coming with you," cried Vernon and hurried toward her. He called to this brother, "I'll meet you at the agent's office!"

Algernon rolled his eyes as he tipped the waiting stewards, then shook hands with the captain and tramped down the gangplank.

Veiled as usual, Mrs. Barlow waited in line, a steward pushing her wheelchair.

"Oh, heaven's sake," said Diana loudly. "I'm next. I can do it." She took charge of the wheelchair from the surprised steward, saying, "Come now, Mrs. Barlow. What a dreadful trip this has been for you."

She wheeled Mrs. Barlow toward the captain, who greeted both ladies, then stepped back. Diana continued toward the gangway, saying,
"I'm sure you cannot wait to be off this ship, Mrs. Barlow. Indeed, I feel
just the same."

She sped up, then appeared to trip and bump against the chair, sending it barreling forward. My pulse loud in my ears, I crouched by a stack
of ropes. Dressed in a steward's whites, I'd followed a group and stepped
out of sight.

Now I watched the wheelchair speed toward the gangway. Only a
pair of ropes framed that plank. If Diana was wrong, we risked injuring
or drowning an invalid. I tensed, fighting the urge to intervene. "Wait,"
Diana had insisted. "Wait until the very last second. Trust me, she will
move."

She did.

With a shriek, Mrs. Barlow flung herself out of the chair. I popped up
and clamped hold of her arm. The chair hit a corner of the railing and
stopped.

It was no frail member I'd grabbed. She tried to wrench it away with
surprising strength. Warned by Diana, I wasn't having any of it. A hand
clawed at my face so I grabbed her wrist.

Diana yanked off Mrs. Barlow's veil, saying, "Alice Fry, I presume?"

A pair of angry blue eyes glared at me. Grimacing, Alice tried to
twist away. Hauling against my grip, she yelled, "What's the meaning of
this outrage?"

Behind me, passengers exploded into exclamations. Seeing the captain and two crewmen approach, Alice slumped, docile as they took
charge and bound her wrists. For the first time I saw her face clearly. A
livid scratch across her cheek was scabbing over.

So Don Juan had fought back. Now the pieces fell into place. Days
ago, I'd asked to speak with her over the altercation with Bigby. Her face
would give her away so she'd probably read my message, panicked, and
staged her disappearance.

Hawley said in a grave voice. "Miss Fry, you are under arrest for the
murder of Don Juan."

Hairpiece askew, she stiffened, leaner and taller than her plump employer. "I didn't kill a man," she snarled. "I killed a demon."

Her face contorted. Despite her bound wrists, seamen backed away. "He was Juan Nepomuceno de Burriel." She glanced around at the dark coats and uniforms, all male, save for Diana. "Why should you know that name? I've lived that day over and over for twenty years. Who remembers the *Virginius* now?"

Bigby came forward "Mrs. Fry? You're the wife of Captain Fry? But—"

"His daughter. I was there, Mr. Bigby," she spat, "I dressed as a cabin boy to save myself from the Spanish pigs."

Bigby gasped. "You were on the *Virginius*?"

She gave a mirthless smile. "You came on the *Niobe,* to rescue us. I recognized you. Twenty years ago, you were a lanky boy—we sat in the crow's nest. You gave me a gumdrop."

Bigby's eyes widened. "Alvin? You were Alvin?"

Her mirthless chuckle scraped over my skin.

"When the *Tornado* boarded us, we expected to be ransomed. Papa said so. But they took us to Cuba. You know the rest?"

Bigby said, "The officers, crewmen, and the captain were taken from their prison before dawn. And . . . shot."

"Papa was a just man, a fair, reasonable man. My brother Peter was eighteen. He was killed too. And then?" she cried. "D'you remember?"

He grimaced "I've never forgotten. They were beheaded."

A sob escaped Alice's lips. Her mouth twisted, as she said, "Those brutes paraded their heads around the city on spikes! Papa's mouth was open, he looked . . . surprised. His blond hair was orange with blood. I see it every day. Every morning, every night. I swore if I ever got near that butcher—the Butcher of Santiago—I'd strangle him with my own hands. I'd do it again if I could!"

Her words scorched me. If my family were brutally killed, defiled in such a way, what would I do? I shuddered. The need for revenge had consumed Alice. Her resolve had an edge of steel, a wild recklessness. The law meant nothing, because nothing she valued was left to lose. I'd not known a woman could feel such fury.

Diana met my gaze, my emotion echoed in her eyes. She felt it too, that blaze, that burning need to right a wrong. Denied for decades, the need for justice would fester like a wound that could not heal, scabbed over but flaming hot inside. Alice had cauterized her wound with murder.

"He should have been brought to justice," I said, feeling somber.

"How?" she spat. "Uncle to the king of Spain? Who'd hold him to account?"

Bigby cleared his throat and admitted, "Don Juan was made a governor."

"Governor? He lived like a king. While my mother, a captain's widow, worked as a charwoman. With no money, she begged from friends. We were always hungry. I didn't ask how mother earned our bread, returning in the wee hours, rocking herself, moaning. I was fifteen. I'd soon be earning that way too."

Bigby said to Hawley, "Sir, a petition was taken up for Fry's widow. Congress awarded her five thousand dollars."

"Too late!" Alice sneered. "She was already in a pauper's grave. Her brother took the cash and threw me out. When a circus came, I went with it, even had a turn with the famous Harry Houdini! But a lone woman's fair game in them cities, and no one pays for what they can take. I scrubbed floors in a hotel, ate the leavings on dirty plates. Worked my way up to lady's maid.

"Then one day, I'm on the same ship as that butcher."

Swiping away tears, Diana snapped, "You're no saint. You killed Mrs. Barlow to take her place!"

Alice laughed, her body shaking with silent mirth. The company gaped, horror etched in their faces. Was she quite mad?

She exhaled, looking out over the water. "I wouldn't kill her. She's enough pain in her life." She shrugged. "She made it easy. Brought a dozen sleeping draughts! Bottles of laudanum! Aw, she's all right. Nice n' snug in her washroom."

Diana exhaled. Hawley snapped out orders to retrieve Mrs. Barlow and alert local authorities. Our ordeal was at an end, I thought, but Alice's trial was just beginning.

"Alice? *Alice?*" cried Dora's voice.

Alice held my gaze, then turned, her face settling into tired lines.

Dora approached, her steps fairly dancing, and tried to embrace her. "Alice! I thought you were dead!"

"I was, little bird. *I am.*"

She shoved Dora backward into me.

Dammit! The girl had just left the sickroom. I caught her before she struck the boards. What came next took me by surprise.

Alice caught the ship's rail with both hands and launched herself sideways over it.

"No!" Diana cried.

Setting Dora on her feet, I searched the murky surface below. Waves sloshed against the ship's hull as it bobbed by the dock.

"Man overboard!" Shouts went up and down the deck, echoing our fright days before. But this was no sleight of hand. No head bobbed to the surface; no arm waved for aid. Searchlights were lit, peering down into the deep harbor.

I remembered icy water in my nose, my mouth, the gush against my skin, the light growing murky. Her clothes would drag her down, her lungs begging for air, her hands fighting the bonds . . .

The search continued while somber groups of passengers were let off. No announcement was ever made, but word spread down the lines of seagoers: the killer had been found.

In turn, Doña Josefina approached, alone. She asked Hawley, "That was her? A woman?"

The captain bowed, repeated his regrets and escorted her down the gangway himself. Spanish officials received her at the foot. Shortly after, Señora Antonia and De Cullar were handed over to the authorities.

During a break in his duties I asked Hawley, "What of the gemstones?"

He raised his eyebrows. "That's a matter for the Foreign Office, O'Trey.

They'll likely need assurances before they're handed over. There's talk of holding the lot at the Bank of England."

Mrs. Barlow was carried out on a litter, attended by Witherspoon and Nurse Shay. They'd take her to a convalescent home, Witherspoon said. Our fine young ladies departed, followed by their chaperones in old-fashioned crinolines. Dandies from the smoking room stalked onto the pier; a couple who'd met on board went down together; the troupe of European musicians carried their instruments. Stocky gentlemen in frock coats stomped down the plank to return to their businesses, children ran toward the carriages, squealing to be let off the ship at last.

In a feathered boa, Madame Pontin—actress, once famous—held Diana's hands in farewell, then turned to me. "Must we say goodbye, Mr. O'Trey? Will we meet again? I'm to perform in Bath on the nineteenth. Perhaps you will bring Mrs. O'Trey?"

I said we'd consider it, took her hand carefully and bid her safe travels. Group by group, passengers disembarked through the aft passage, while from the foredeck the search for Alice continued with Kisbee rings and boats circling our vessel.

We found no trace of her that night. Rage had consumed her for most of her troubled life. I hoped she was at peace, at last. I glanced toward the pier, then paused, gazing back at the *Etruria* . . . Alice had always been so prepared. Might she have secreted a blade somewhere on her person to free herself? Perhaps I just needed to believe it was possible. One life should not have to carry so much pain.

I sighed and walked toward the Scotland Yard officers climbing the gangway.

CHAPTER 43

WHO JUDGES THE KING?

In the early morning hours, eleven days after our departure from New York Harbor, the Scotland Yard detective released me from their questions. Released from the shipping office, Diana and I trudged away from the *Etruria*. The ship was still being unloaded, longshoremen going to and fro on the pier as winches retrieved sacks from the deep holds within.

With Diana beside me, I carried our valise across the pier, still feeling the ship's roll under my feet. Felix, our sleepy young steward, rolled the rest of our trunks on a trolley.

A single carriage stood at the dock. I strode toward it, thinking to wake the coachman, but a trim, neatly dressed man stepped out. He gave a shout like a schoolboy and ran up.

Adi. He could have been Diana's twin. Once my employer, he was the closest thing to a brother I'd ever have. He'd been waiting hours for us to disembark. Diana's cry rang out, bouncing off the flagstones. "Adi! Why didn't you send word you're here?"

He embraced us, arms tight around my waist, then enveloped Diana. Grinning, I roused the coachman as the siblings reunited. What Adi said I could not tell, but Diana replied in rapid Gujarati. I knew better than to interrupt their fond exchange.

His hair rumpled, uniform topsy-turvy, Felix brought up our luggage and helped stow it behind the large brougham.

Saying farewell, I palmed him some cash and climbed up beside Diana and Adi. They sat across me, arm in arm, speaking in the bursts that pass for language among siblings, half phrases and looks, grins and shakes of the head, laughing to see each other after nearly two years.

By the time we reached the hotel where Adi had taken our rooms, Diana had recounted some of our eventful trip. He pummeled her with questions while I got our room keys.

"Tomorrow, sir. It can wait." I laughed, taking Diana's elbow.

Thus reminded that he'd once been my employer, he punched my arm, chuckling.

Of course, it took Diana and him another hour to say their good nights in the hotel corridor, while I unpacked some things and prepared for bed.

* * *

I dreamed of soft footsteps dragging across a floor. An old man slowly carried a bowl. The quiet of care. The thump as a wooden door or *almirah* was shut, or was it a wire mesh icebox? No, that was at Framji Mansion, not here, in this dim, rocking world deep inside an army transport. Someone gently raised my head, spooning salty gruel between my lips.

A rusty voice asked. "Will he live?"

"Inshallah," came the low answer. If God wills.

I caught a glimpse of deep-set eyes under a turban, white eyebrows, a grey-threaded beard. Ram Sinor? No, he was younger than this man. Then it came to me. Asif, my army batman. He'd tended me—how long? I'd been taken to hospital . . . had I ever paid his back wages? The image faded, its loss leaving me pained. Another unpaid debt. I often remembered the pain in my past, but kindness had to creep through windows of sleep like a thief.

I tarried over a late breakfast, savoring the marmalade on crusty toast as I watched the bustling street. The pungent smells of Liverpool assailed me, fish and coal fires in the sunlight. Newsboys' calls, vendors, carriages rumbling, horses, bicycles banging an assault on my ears. Despite its groans and creaks, the *Etruria* had been a serene haven.

Dressed in a neat blue jacket and grey skirt, Diana poured a fresh cup of tea.

"Mmm." She savored the Darjeeling as the steam climbed over her sun-kissed cheeks. Dash it, even her hair was perfect this morning.

I opened a newspaper, but all I could see was Alice, leaping over the rail. Her agonized face, the knowing in her eyes. She had not wanted to die.

Diana asked softly, "Does it still trouble you?"

I looked up, startled.

"Her death," Diana whispered, "Doesn't seem right to call Alice a murderer, though God knows she was."

Somewhere in the hotel a piano was playing. I drew a breath, holding her gaze. "That last confrontation . . . going over it, I knew she was up to something, sweet. She had that look about her. But . . . it's not unlike a skirmish. Afterward I question each movement. What did I see? When? It happened so fast, it's hard to untangle . . . like Karachi."

If only I could let it go, just forget, walk into tomorrow as though it had never happened.

"The Pathans you fought." Her dark eyes searched me from under delicately furrowed brows. "Why does it haunt you? Because they died?"

"Because I killed them," I corrected. "They were somebody's son, someone's husband or father."

"But you had no choice!"

I considered that last skirmish in the red streets of Karachi, where most of my company was killed. Fragments still missing, odd pictures, out of order, like a kaleidoscope, my sequence of memory shattered by the bullet that scored me above my ear. "There's always a choice. A difficult one, yes, but . . . I did choose. I was so tired, I could barely stand. Had the blighter in my grasp. If I let go, I knew I'd not prevail."

That disturbed her. "You don't blame yourself?"

I exhaled, leaning on my forearms. "No. He knew the risks. If you intend to kill, then you know the price."

She grimaced. "He who lives by the sword—"

"As I do."

She flinched. "No, Jim, not like you. You try so hard to prevent harm, to seek justice."

"Those are two different things," I reminded her. "But you're right. In the moment, I dare not dwell on anything. They attack, I repel. That's all I see. If I spared a thought for their wives or children, I'd be dead. But . . . now I wonder. Could I have done anything else?"

Diana had a way of bringing the truth before me, unvarnished, so that I could no longer hide from it. She watched the clock's pendulum swing back and forth. The soft clicks of time filled our cabin, measuring my reply, judging me. I did not fare well in the assessment. Justice had seemed so clear before. Now, I was not so sure.

Her gaze was soft. "Is there an answer?"

I drew a heavy breath. "I have not found one. Alice—how those memories must have seared, day after day. It would drive one mad. The lack of justice is . . . a wound. From the moment she knew Don Juan was on board, she chose her path. One crime led to another, the second following, regardless of the decades between."

Diana frowned. "You still think she was a victim?"

My throat tightened as I considered it. "Perhaps. I used to believe that those who break the law, those who harm are essentially selfish, placing themselves above others, forcing their will upon others. But . . . Alice first impersonated Dora to escape detection. After that night in Dora's room, the locks were changed. When we placed guards at the stairs, she must have climbed the rigging, and clung to the sails. But that couldn't last. She'd have been desperate—I could pity that, sweetheart."

Diana frowned. "She attacked you while you slept!"

I considered that. "That puzzled me. I think she intended to take her employer's place. But Dora would know she wasn't Mrs. Barlow."

I looked back at that ghastly night. "I think she hesitated, standing over me with a pillow. Remember she called Dora 'little bird'? An awful choice. When she realized it wasn't Dora, she needed another plan. So she wheeled Mrs. Barlow out to the railing to drown her. But again, she couldn't do it and left her there. Later, she got into Mrs. Barlow's room, drugged her meal or drink and took her place. That's why she wouldn't let anyone in."

"No, dear," Diana said. "She put that kerchief soaked in chloroform in your pocket. You bent over the woman in the wheelchair, didn't you? She could have done it then."

I puzzled over that. "You think that was Alice in the wheelchair?"

Diana nodded. "When Doctor Witherspoon treated her, she was established as Mrs. Barlow. They're not so far apart in age! After that, she stayed in her cabin, admitting only Nurse Shay, who didn't know her before." Her drowning, I thought. Could she have got away?

I met Diana's gaze and knew she was thinking of my fall overboard. I could still feel the all-encompassing ocean, the sour taste of fear, the whoosh of air and sky. "Thank you, sweet. It's a habit you've developed, saving my life."

Her hand covered mine, but she did not smile. It was too soon. Some day we could look back on it without terror. We headed down to find Adi in silence.

While unostentatious, the Windermere Hotel's wood bannisters smelled of beeswax, and lavender, with damask couches spread around a maroon carpet. Palmer Bly spotted me and waved us over. We shook hands. The women kissed cheeks fondly, like old friends now that we'd survived the cruise together. He offered me a cigar, and accepted in good grace when I declined. The smell of smoke still brought unwanted memories.

He tapped out his cigar, then said, "Trouble's brewing, O'Trey. Just a matter of time, you know. Cubans shot every day."

I glanced up. "Matter of time before . . . ?"

"War, Mr. O'Trey, before we go to war. With Spain in our own backyard, and her armada . . . We can't have it, you know. After the *Virginius* episode we built five ironsides, repaired others. This time, we won't be unprepared."

"We'd go to war over a foreign island?"

"It's a larger question, O'Trey. When *you* catch the culprit, you turn him over to the law. But who stands in judgment upon a king? What court can we appeal to when Spain rewards a tyrant? Who holds a country to account?"

Who indeed? Was this how history was shaped, the little events that sent thousands marching into battle? If the clouds of war gathered overhead, what did it mean for Diana and me, for our friends in Boston?

As we said goodbye, Mr. Bly gripped my hand. "It's coming, O'Trey. We'll need men like you. You did well in this nasty business. Come see me in New York, eh?"

Dapper in his pin-striped lounge suit, Adi found us soon after this, embraced his sister and dropped to the couch beside her. Their animated conversation, glowing eyes, their smiles and accord melted my insides. Most all I cared for in the world was seated on that couch.

"Adi, you haven't said why you came to England," Diana teased. "Was it just to see us?"

With a glance at me Adi said, "There's time for that, hey?"

I knew Adi's thoughtfulness, his lawyerly assessment of risk. His glib reply did not ring true. But Diana was present, and above all, he would not worry her. There was more to the story.

Oh dear, I thought. Here we go again.

* * *

That night Diana asked, "Is there justice for women, Jim? Seems the law doesn't treat us fairly, does it?"

I considered that. I'd been so certain, before. If one just upheld the law, all was right and good. But after the events of this week, that no longer rang true. The law seemed to be incomplete, uneven. It valued some, served some over others.

"It is beyond the reach of many," I admitted, thinking of Dora.

Diana returned to her embroidering, her needle making slow, sad strokes.

On the street below, a lamplighter called, "All's well." The clock downstairs gonged a somber nine bells.

Diana set aside her sewing and said, "Jim, when your job here is done, do you think we could move to Philadelphia? For just two years, dearest? There's a school for women physicians. I remember an Indian woman got a degree in medicine from that school. Her name was Anandi Joshi. I . . . I don't know if they'd take me, but I'd like to try."

Philadelphia? What would her education cost? My head spun.

Diana's soft face mourned Dora's terrible quandary: too young to be a mother, bereft and doubting the world, and the shame that drove her to a terrible recourse.

When we first met, Diana had said, "I hate to break things!" While in England she'd visited Florence Nightingale's school for nursing. Last year in Boston she'd apprenticed as a nurse in a hospital. She glanced over with a smile, her cheek dimpled.

Right. I'd find the funds.

"Might take us a while, but Philadelphia it is, sweet."

EPILOGUE

To our surprise, Vernon housed Dora in our hotel and hired a companion to teach her the intricacies of English manners. He said he intended to take her to his aunt, in time.

We invited Adi to dinner at the hotel to meet our friends. He'd been rather morose, and Diana thought it would cheer him up. I knew otherwise, but other than the cable saying "Need your help," he had not confided in me.

Raising a glass, Vernon said, "One more! Why are pirates called pirates?"

Diana laughed. "Why?"

Algernon sniffed, then looked away. Vernon smiled. "Anyone? No? Because they *arrrrrr!*"

Diana dimpled. Dora smiled.

Vernon met my glance, a dusky hue on his cheek. I chuckled and raised my glass to him, wishing him good luck.

ACKNOWLEDGMENTS AND AUTHOR'S NOTES

A locked room mystery aboard a ship had been on my mind for some time. In this kind of mystery, there is no apparent way the murderer could escape the chamber where the murder took place. In addition, what if that locked room was on a ship full of passengers and crew? In the 1890s, the golden age of sea travel was just beginning, with Cunard's RMS *Umbria* and RMS *Etruria* being two of the largest, most modern ships of the time. This story is also a "closed set" mystery in that the murderer cannot leave the ship and must continue on it until it reaches Liverpool. Both aspects intrigued me.

The solution occurred to me when I attended a session on cognitive and inattentional blindness held by Dr. Mahzarin Banaji, Harvard University professor of psychology. Along with an audience of more than eight hundred, I was asked to watch a basketball video with the objective of counting the number of passes. To my astonishment, when the video was replayed, I, along with the entire audience, had completely missed seeing a woman with an umbrella who walked through the basketball court! Our focus makes us blind: we see only what is relevant. As I re-read chapter 3, I realized the solution was already there. It had always been right in front of me, but I had not seen it.

Many events I've mentioned are historically accurate. During the don's funeral, Captain Jim recalls finding the bodies of the Bombay Grenadiers and 66th (Berkshire) Infantry Regiment on the hills near Kandahar. Years ago, I had visited Bombay's exquisite Afghan church (built 1858) in Colaba, Mumbai, which commemorates the casualties in the first and second Anglo-Afghan wars, 1838–42 and 1878–80. Those British-Indian regiments were comprised of soldiers from Bombay and Bengal. The 1873 *Virginius* affair was a precursor to the Spanish-American War over Cuba. Despite condemnation in the press and numerous diplomatic protestations, Juan Nepomuceno Burriel, the Spanish garrison commander who had executed fifty-three men, did not face a military trial, but was promoted to governor of Bilbao in 1875. Later, Spain agreed to pay the families of the American victims $80,000. In the 1870s, Congress did award $5,000 to the widow of Captain Fry, who was destitute. Juan Burriel was recorded to have died on December 23, 1877, before he could be tried. Given his familial connections, I wondered whether this was a convenient smokescreen. What if, by some strange chance, he was recognized decades later by one of the few survivors of the *Virginius*? And there my story began. One must remember that the United States was no military power then. This 1873 incident was an embarrassment, since the US had no suitable warships at the time. The HMS *Niobe* was dispatched all the way from Great Britain to extract the survivors. The slaughter propelled the construction of five US armored warships, which later helped win the 1898 Spanish-American War.

A writer's job is to raise an unflinching mirror to the reader. While writing this novel, the landmark ruling Roe v. Wade was struck down by the US Supreme Court. As a result, Dora's character took shape embodying the tragic desperation of a young woman bearing the brunt of the effects of rape as well as society's callousness. When I first emigrated to the US in 1991, I watched in horror the televised trial of William Kennedy Smith, who was acquitted of rape charges. The trial was brutal for his accuser, as her character was torn apart on national TV. No wonder victims hesitate to report sexual assault.

Has the plight of women really improved in the last hundred years? A century ago, the words "legs" and "bottom" were offensive and scandalous, so to be pregnant out of wedlock would get a girl fired from work or discarded by her family. Such girls sometimes joined the multitudes of "nightwalkers," called sex workers in today's enlightened language. But last year a Florida court prevented a pregnant, parentless sixteen-year-old from getting an abortion because she was not mature enough to make the decision. Apparently, giving birth and raising a child requires less maturity. Dora is distraught and utterly abandoned when her only support, Mrs. Barlow, seems to reject her, which leads to her suicide attempt. Whether the reader will condemn her depends upon their own capacity for empathy.

As always, I owe a debt of thanks to my agent, Jill Grosjean, for her partnership in the drafting of this novel. I sent her three chapters each week during the first half of 2022, which we followed with a two-hour debrief that energized and propelled me on. Jill's thoughtful suggestions and enthusiasm were a perfect sounding board to write about historical and present-day gaps in justice and the wounds left by its absence.

I'm much indebted to Jay Langley, whose exhortations and ideas enlivened this manuscript, and whose editing added clarity and brightness, including the idea for the present opening! Jane Ricketts, the fabulous reference librarian at Hunterdon County Library, offered delightful books and resources on the Spanish-American War and on steamship travel. Thank you. To my online critique and writing colleagues, JR Bale, Elissa Matthews, and Amy Reade, thank you for enriching this writer's life. I am grateful to the team at Macmillan's Minotaur Books, who continue to shepherd this series with professionalism and competent advice. To the librarians and book clubs who have enjoyed and recommended this series, thank you. Don Leavitt from Nautiques .net found the deck plan image inside the book. The Steamship Historical Society of America and Gjenvick-Gjønvik Archives (ggarchives.com) offered an endless treasure trove of images, articles, and oral history narratives from the times. To my family, who understands that sometimes an author occupies another world, who stepped up and filled in for me, for your forbearance and constant support, I love you.

And thank you to all the readers who have enjoyed Captain Jim and Diana's adventures. Many wrote to me to share their excitement and profound thoughts. Some offered wonderful sources for future research. Thank you for being a part of this adventure.